THE MOB: SHIO CUPPACIO

LISA AUSTIN

QUICK VENT

I started on Shio back in the spring. He was initially supposed to be only sixty-five thousand words with five or six books. My editor and I made a plan: I would write him, she'd edit, and I'd drop all six books a month apart. Then it dawned on me, Shio was so much more than a short book. I picked the book up, put it down, scrapped it, and picked it up again. I questioned myself so many times during the creation process. In the end, I trusted my pen and grew to love who Shio is. Just as I had to trust myself, I ask that you do the same. Take your time reading this book. Even when you're done, sit with it and read it again. Everything that you love about a Lisa Austin book is within these pages, but on a much more elevated level. I typed all of this to say, **let me cook**. Shio is one of none. Don't compare him to no other niggas you've read, even if I am the author of them. Thangg ya!

EDITOR'S NOTE

I've dedicated thirty-four days to Shio Cuppacio, totaling more than 250 hours of content editing. This book is wordy, gradual, and realistic—both simple and complex.

Since Lisa chose me as her editor a little under two years ago, my goal has always been to strengthen her manuscripts without losing the essence that makes them hers. Shio challenged us both, but I couldn't be prouder of the outcome.

In the words of Lil' Wayne, *"Let the beat build..."*

Allow yourself to learn the characters before expecting the usual action—but trust, the action will come. After all, this is only part one of Shio's story.

Enjoy the novel—all 154,000 words. Part Two is already brewing...

-Neke from NekeReads Editing Service

SYNOPSIS

"The Don doesn't do favors."

Shio Cuppacio was sure of that. And with the Cuppacio family's merger with the Rinaldi Mob in Jagoda Bay nearly complete, all eyes are on him because it's his turn to fulfill the mob's one requirement of finding a wife.

Unlike his cousins, Ezio, Metavello, and Renello, Shio is quiet, logical, and deeply devoted to God.

The thinker and doer in his family, Shio is not a man of noise or ego. Restraint and discipline have kept his nose clean since childhood, and now, as a grown man, Shio considers himself a master of self-control. But when a favor for Don Demise pulls Shio into a situation he never saw coming, Shio's daily checklists and future plans are challenged.

Faith, control, and loyalty collide headfirst with temptation, purpose, and fate. Everyone thinks they already know what he'll do and how his story will unfold, but Shio has never been one to move to the beat of anyone's drum but his own.

Caught between what's right and what *feels* right, Shio learns that even the most disciplined man can lose balance when overwhelmed with questions and no way to answer them. Discovering that not every divine lesson comes from Heaven, Shio must decide if some lessons are worth the risk, even if they come with trouble for not just him, but everyone.

ORDER OF THE MOB

If you're new here, heyyy! Thank you for giving me a chance! Welcome to the Rinaldi Mob. In order to get the full reading experience, you'll need to start from the beginning. The reading order is listed below. Enjoy!

THE MOB

Silo Cuppacio

PROLOGUE

Shio Cuppacio

T*hree years prior*

ONE... two... three... four... five... six.

One... two... three... four... five... six.

I'd been counting the blades on the fan for the past few hours. No matter how many times I repeated the numbers, the number of blades whirring around didn't change. It was six—had been six since the first time I'd lain in this bed and would be six until the light fixture was replaced. Instead of counting sheep, my back was sunken into the mattress, left arm folded behind my head, while I counted the blades. Not missing a beat, I tracked the spinning fan creating the air that circulated the room, but those weren't the only numbers running through my head. There was a long list of shit that had been weighing on me. My body was screaming rest, but my mind was telling me I could do that shit when I was dead.

Even though the AC unit was probably in the sixties and the fan above was working overtime, I felt warm. To the untrained eye, a fan on maximum speed was a big blur, the blades vanishing in motion. But, given my focus, they were perfectly visible to me. I was able to see not only the blades, but also the chipped paneling, the black specks on the light cover from the grape soda that exploded months ago, and the slight warping of the fan's frame. It could have been from the roof that needed replacing or the wear and tear on the ceiling. Either way, the room felt warm, and it had nothing to do with the body lying next to me.

When work needed to be done, I couldn't relax. For years, all we Cuppacios did was get things done. Child labor laws didn't exist in our world when we were growing up. Every day brought a lesson to learn, a task to finish, and a punishment to accept. Even as a child, no matter how fast or disorganized life got, I could always focus. Knowing how to concentrate at an early age led to my rate of maturity speeding up. I was overly aware at all times, so while living became a distraction for most, I was the one who used it as an opportunity to marinate in my worries and hop the fuck out before the flavors soiled me completely. I'd taken this trait with me into adulthood, and although it had saved me from a lot of bullshit, it didn't reduce the childhood trauma that existed.

We'd been free from the terror of our fathers for years; however, the damage had already been done. While everyone else in the family walked around content, I was always thinking about how we could do and be better. Selling this dope—depending on what we could get our hands on, whether it be weed, pills, or crack—was cool, but it wasn't enough.

Until it was.

A bunch of kids, not knowing much but the fucked-up ways their father taught them, being pushed into the world was a recipe for disaster. We had no real direction, no solid plan, and barely any fucking money when we became the sole providers for our family. We started searching for plugs, but nothing ever really stuck. So, we used what we could get our hands on and tried our best to make it work. Things started looking better when we landed a solid plug. But like all good things, it was too fucking good to be true.

After all the shit we went through as children, we deserved more. There was a time when the Cuppacios were on the map. Our fathers had been the most feared mafia in the United States, and money was plentiful. Did they do right by the money? No. Did they steal all of their underage wives? Yes. Did they treat their children like slaves instead of heirs? Fuck yes. But we came from a dynasty. Getting the scraps from the bottom of the barrel was fine for my cousins, but not for me. So, sleep was rare and far between. I was always plotting, planning, and setting up plays for the future that I knew was on the way. I didn't know exactly what it was, but it was coming, and I had an ass of cleaning up to do.

My mother used to drill into my head, even when she was going through her own hell back then, that you couldn't cook in a dirty kitchen. It took me becoming an adult to realize that Mama wasn't talking about dishes.

"Ummm."

Groans coming from the left side of me broke my trance, shifting my orbs. The comforter that had been covering my bottom half pulled away, exposing my navy Ralph Lauren pajama pants. The TV across from the bed powered on, and the last thing that I'd been watching began to play. Now that there was light in the room, the curvy silhouette of the opposite sex could be made out. Even though she was now wrapped in the cover like a burrito, her figure couldn't be hidden.

"What I'm about to preach is going to tick some of you off in here." Clothed in a tan suit with chocolate pinstripes, dark brown gators, and a plain-faced Rolex, Pastor Washington stood.

Whenever I missed the word, I made sure to watch the service on the church's YouTube channel and sent my offering via CashApp to my mother. Whether the money made it to the church's account or not was between her and the Lord, but I did my part.

The pastor paused for dramatic effect, used the white towel resting on the transparent lectern to wipe his face, and took a sip of water. To his left, I could see a Jessica Simpson heel fastened around a foot that I knew belonged to my mother —The First Lady. She sat on the pulpit behind her husband at every sermon. He wouldn't have it any other way.

Bending his six-foot frame so that he was level with the microphone attached to the lectern, he continued, "There are two verses I want to touch on. Y'all still with me?"

Yeah, Pastor!

We with you!

"All right. Y'all saying that until I say what the Lord has called me to preach this Sunday morning." He paused again, scanning the crowd.

The camera panned to the audience. Women, in their Sunday best, fanned themselves with the paper fans that had been passed out by the ushers and held the church's logo. Niggas I've served on more than one occasion sat in the back or posted up on the back walls, garnering nasty looks from the ushers. They wanted to get the word, but the importance of keeping their heads on a swivel outweighed the protection of the Lord. Chicago niggas didn't give a fuck. They'd bust up a funeral if that meant laying down an opp.

"Keep your eyes free from the love of money..."

My body stiffened as he repeated the nine words.

"Hold up... y'all didn't hear me. I said keep your eyes FREE from the love of money, and be content with what you have because... *God* has said, 'Never will I leave you; never will I forsake you.' That's Hebrew verse thirteen, chapter five. Can I get an amen?"

Amen

Amen

Amen, Pastor

"I ain't done yet." He smirked. "Just hold on! Y'all about to be mad at me."

The camera switched to my mother, who was fanning while nodding, dressed to the nines, face not giving any indication that she'd once lived a life that was half heartache and half love. As if she knew I was watching, she grinned a little harder.

"Timothy six, ten. For the love of money is the root of all kinds of evil. Some people, eager for money, have wandered from the faith and pierced themselves with many sorrows." He slammed the bible shut, removed the mic, and tucked his hand in his pants pocket as he glided across the pulpit. "See, a lot of y'all want more. More money. More cars. More clothes. More jewelry. A bigger home. But God said, be CONTENT! Be content with what you have! See, you don't need more! What you need is to be happy with what you have! For in the end, we can't take none of this with us." He spread his arms wide to represent the "this".

"Sometimes, receiving more comes with more problems that we aren't prepared for. You are exactly where you are meant to be—"

"Why is the TV so loud?" the feminine voice interrupted as

the sermon was paused, freezing Pastor Washington, whose arms were still outstretched.

A gentle hand on my chest made me turn my face away from the TV to the pink, short, manicured nails on the bark-colored hand. Shea butter drifted up my nose as she moved the covers aside and swung her leg over my torso. My hands went to her meaty thighs as she sat on my sore abdomen.

I'd been working out recently, focusing on changing my eating habits and how I spent my time. The workouts were tough, but I knew that in time, I'd be used to it and where I wanted to be physically. There was a plethora of shit I wanted to do, and the angst of it all weighed down on me heavier than the curvy body resting on my frame.

"You rolled over on the remote, Bahati."

Rolling her neck to ease away the stiffness that sleep had created, her braids cascaded down the left side of her body. They were bra-length long with the ends curled. Being an East African Kenyan, Bahati had all of the exotic features of an African girl. Her skin was like black marble: dark, smooth, and shiny. Her lips were nearly double that of a typical woman's, but they looked good on her round face. No matter what time of day it was, her skin always looked glossy, like she'd not only bathed but slept in oils and butters.

She purred. "I'd much rather listen to music. Alexa, play 'Charm' by Rema."

Even though she'd been living in the United States since her father hauled them over at the tender age of seven, you'd think she had never left the motherland. Her voice held a deep tenor to it that tended to rise up a few octaves when she was excited and lowered when she was aroused, like now. Her hips began to gyrate as Rema's lyrics sounded off loudly, as if she didn't have neighbors and it wasn't nearly three in the morning.

"Bahati."

My hands traveled from her thick thighs to her round hips. Her ass was so big that even though her pussy, which was covered in black lace, was grinding on my stomach, her ass was still directly on the base of my dick. She'd wanted to get fucked last night, but I was too spaced out for that shit. Not only had I popped a pill, but I'd had a few sips of lean. Add that in with the way my mind had been racing, I knew I was no more good. Still, she showered, oiled down in her favorite homemade shea butter that she had religiously shipped from home, and dressed in a matching lace bra and panty set.

Bahati was any niggas type. Not only was she dark as night, but her waist-to-ass ratio should be studied. With how thin her stomach was, she had to have some ribs or something taken out. I'd seen her mother, though, and came to the conclusion that her shit was very much genetic. She wasn't rich, even though she often had the attitude of a snobby daddy's girl. With what I hit her off with and the overtime she worked at the pharmacy, she was able to live decently. Above average, actually. I'd never seen her not put together. Her hair was always braided, her skin was always glowing, and her pussy was always wet.

With her hands flat on my chest, she lowered her body so that she was face to face with me, her hips not missing a beat. *"Come here, wetin dey worry you?"* Bahati sang while she slow winded.

I could smell the spices from the Jollof rice, peas, and king fish she had eaten before bed on her breath. My plate was still in the microwave and would remain in that motherfucker.

"Bring body make I worry you? I know you senior me. I get money pass your Papa."

Bahati did shit like this, and like the song, charmed the fucking socks off a nigga. It was hard to think sometimes

7

around her thick ass. That's why I did most of it when she was sleeping. She was a walking fucking dream. But no matter how sick her body was or how wet her pussy got, she just wasn't my one. She was simply a piece on my board.

I'd met her at the library. I was looking for a tutor to teach me another language and ran right into her. I hadn't been interested in learning Swahili, but thought, *Why the hell not?* Two years later, I was fluent and had secured not only some good pussy, but a connection too. Bahati's father was a pharmacist, and she was a pharmacy tech while being in school to follow in her papa's footsteps. He was determined to milk the USA for everything it offered. As long as the price was right, he dealt us, making sure to keep his baby girl's hands clean. I wasn't mad at it. Shit was never designed for men with skin that wasn't pale. That trip to the library was one of the main reasons my cousins and I managed to keep some money in our pockets. We had our weed connect, but the shit we got from the pharmacy was the real reason we were eating.

Running her tongue across her pillowy lips, our noses grazed. Just as she was about to pop her ass again, I grabbed her neck. The pressure I applied wasn't enough to hurt her, and with the way her pussy was heating up on my dick, I knew she liked it.

I knew a lot of shit about Bahati. I damn near lived at her fucking apartment and sometimes went to sleep in her pussy. I knew she loved a nigga, even though she'd never voiced it. East African girls were stubborn in that way. I knew she liked that rough shit, even though sometimes, she complained and ran from it. I knew she thought she had me wrapped around her pretty little fingers since she was one of the reasons we ate. She thought she had a nigga on lock, and even though she had the dick the most, that didn't mean I or it belonged to her. I'd been clear with Bahati that one day, our arrangement would end.

She would always laugh that shit off. Wasn't shit funny, though.

I didn't like no motherfucker feeling like they had the power to feed or starve me. That's how I felt when it came to Bahati.

"Run that back," I instructed with a firm squeeze.

"What, bebe?" She grinded.

Instead of answering, I squeezed her neck.

"*I know you senior me. I get money pass your Papa,*" she sang.

"Yeah... that. I get money pass your Papa."

Her body rose a few degrees. "Yeah, bebe."

"I'm not getting more money than your pops—"

"Bebe, it's just a song—"

Squeezing, I halted her sentence. Letting her neck go, she sat up straight and kept on dancing.

Rema's lyrics were as exotic and exhilarating as Bahati was. If I didn't know any better, I would think that he wrote the song just for her.

Still not missing a beat, her hips swayed hypnotically to the beat. Any other nigga would have been entranced. But Shio Cuppacio wasn't any other nigga. I was a fucking king, even if I was living slightly above that of a guard, because I damn sure wasn't a peasant. The throne was mine for the taking, and unfortunately for Bahati, I wouldn't be sweeping up the princess in order to be crowned. Nah, I was straight snatching that shit, even if the current king's head had to come with it.

Running my hand down the middle of her perky breasts, I let my fingers glide down to her taut waist and didn't stop until I got to her lace panties. Scoping them to the side with my index finger, her glistening box stared back at me, leaving a sticky mess all over my abdomen as she danced.

I'd never run inside of Bahati raw, even though I knew she was clean as a whistle. The last person who had my dick

9

without a barrier had been too old to be fucking me and had been the one who introduced me to the world of sex. Tonight, though, she'd get what she'd been begging for.

Tugging harder, I ripped her panties right from her bottom, making her gasp in surprise. "Those were Victoria's Secret, bebe."

I'd more than likely bought the motherfuckers. The way I saw it, she'd worn them for me, so that meant I could do whatever the fuck I wanted to them.

Lifting her by the waist like she didn't weigh a hundred and seventy pounds, I lined my dick up with her pussy, and dropped her down on my throbbing dick.

"Ohhhh! Bebe... you know meeehhh," she half-sang and half-remixed the fucking song as I filled her up.

Keeping my expression neutral, even though she was squeezing the fuck out of my dick, I let my head hit the pillow as she did the same thing on my dick as she did on my stomach.

"So, so biiiiig, bebe."

The song repeated while she twisted her lower half. With the way Bahati was working the dick, she could have asked for anything, and a nigga would have gone broke giving it to her, except I wasn't just any nigga. If I hadn't learned anything in the last few months, I'd learned discipline. It was the only way I was going to be able to get where the fuck I was trying to go. I couldn't just think for me, I had to think for the fucking team.

She was so fucking wet, so fucking tight, and her sing-song voice, along with the sweet smells of her arousal, was enough to send a nigga into overdrive. While the dancing was cute, I needed to fuck.

Hooking my arm around her waist, I lifted us from the bed, her legs locking behind my back, and then pinned her down. I stepped completely out of my pajama pants and grabbed her ankles. Her eyes were more slanted than they normally were—another thing that she did when she knew she was about to get her fucking back broken.

I pushed her legs so far back that her ankles now were next to her ears. Hearing one of her bones pop in the process, I gauged her face for any indication of pain. Shifting my eyes, I looked down at her pussy dripping and her booty hole winking at me. She looked good enough to eat, but none of that would be going on. As bad as I'd wanted to taste it over the years, I refrained. She wasn't endgame—I'd always known that—so I held back. Now that I know what I know, I'm glad I haven't let her burn my fucking head. She was a piece on the chessboard, and I controlled the center.

"Bebe." She brought me back. I'd zoned the fuck out.

"Keep them legs back, Bahati," I demanded.

Placing my hand back around her neck, I sank into her wetness, pussy sucking me in like wet sand. Her eyes rolled to the back of her head as her pussy flowed like a fucking river. With her mug contorted, she was making the ugliest faces even though she'd been blessed in the physical department by the Most High. Trying to concentrate on the feel of her pussy so that my near flaccid dick could stay hard, I was almost losing the battle. I wasn't one of those young niggas that couldn't get his dick up. I knew most of the niggas from around the way were too drugged out to fuck, but that wasn't me. Did I do drugs? Yes, every fucking day, but that didn't affect my performance. The only time I couldn't fuck was when I was processing, and if I was processing, that meant a motherfucker had fucked up.

Bahati chewed on her bottom lip as the Afrobeat's blared from the speakers. Twisting my torso, I hit her with a curve that had her back arching and nearly lifting off the bed. With my arm around her neck, I kept her pinned in place as I gave her mediocre dick, but with the way she was whooping and hollering, you would have thought I'd been putting down my best moves.

Closing her eyes, her nails began to glide up my arm that had been holding her down. The tingling trail that it left behind felt good—too good. Touches from a woman that I liked had always been a turn-on of mine. I didn't need a woman to dress in lingerie or prance around naked, even though it was very much appreciated. Simple touches like scratching my scalp, grabbing my hand, or wrapping her arms around me did it every time.

My dick hardened, and Bahati's moans intensified.

Bahati. Pretty, black-ass Bahati had been a good arrangement. Great pussy, independent, own spot for a nigga to crash, a great cook, even though some of her native dishes were a bit much at times, I'd enjoyed her. She was a freak in the sheets and a means for a nigga to make some money. I'd told myself I wasn't going to get comfortable, but each time her papa came through with that pack, I spent more and more time in her bed. No matter how much of my dick she stomached, I had been upfront and honest. I wouldn't be her African Prince. For one, I was Black and Italian, and a king couldn't be *prince'd*.

Pushing the lust to the back of my mind, I focused on what I'd come over here for. It wasn't fish and peas. It wasn't even pussy. It was to scratch one of the things off my list that grew longer and longer the more I thought. One less thing, though, meant I could breathe a little easier and blink a little slower. There wouldn't be no sleeping going on any time soon, but I'd do a long-ass nod off after today.

A stinging feeling shot up my arm as Bahati's nails dug into my skin. Using my free hand, I slapped her arms away, and at the same time, her eyes popped open. They were no longer sleek with passion; they were bulging with fear, and the pressure from her chin digging into my hand did nothing to remove my hands from around her neck.

I didn't let up.

I kept on squeezing.

I kept on fucking.

"Bahati, baby. You know how important taking care of my family is to me. So why would you gamble with your life over some shit you knew wasn't committal from the jump?"

Sliding my dick out, I thrust back in, and even though her airway was restricted, her pussy was the wettest it had ever been. My dick was now at its full length, and I'd have to say, this was the best sex I'd ever had. Speeding my pumps up, I was beating her pussy at the same tempo as the sporadic music playing.

"For the last few months... your papa has been giving us the run around... with our supply, Bahati."

She tried gasping for air, reaching for my hands, but I didn't need my fucking DNA under her nails, so again, I knocked them shits away. She was so wet that her secretions slapped on my stomach each time I entered her. Her face had gone from a shiny black to a bluish-ash pale, but she was still holding on.

"I told you what the fuck it was, Bahati. I'm a fucking king, baby. You never had a fucking chance... You should have just stood down—sucked my dick, got this bread, and enjoy your fucking time. But you had to go and put a bug in your papa's ear... playing with my bread. I'm indebted to no one, baby. Can't no muthafuckas say they have the power to feed or starve me. The last niggas that did are six feet under, lined up in a row with dusty-ass gravel above them."

Her gasps were drowned out by the music, but I could hear them. I could hear her going home to glory, along with the slickness of my dick still slamming into her pussy. It sent me on a euphoric high, knowing the last person who played with me would be the last person to play with anybody. Her father? He'd get by but never away. The loss of his freaky-ass daughter would be enough to send his ass back packing to Africa.

Taking my eyes off Bahati, I looked down at the beautiful mess our body parts made. My dick was glistening with her juices. Bahati was a good time. The same way she danced all over the internet for her couple of hundred followers to see, she'd done on this dick multiple occasions. She was good until she wasn't. I was not ready to commit myself to a woman. How could I when I was committed to getting my family out of the dark hold our forefathers had tossed us in? She knew I wasn't on that with her, but every time I didn't answer her phone calls or come over, magically, our supply was either short or nonexistent. I couldn't have that shit. So, as fine as she was and as good as her pussy was, she had to fucking go.

Her face was now completely blue. She'd become weaker, and when I decided the sex felt too much like I was taking advantage of her, even though she initiated, the blood rushed to my dick, and I exploded inside her slippery tunnels.

Her eyes closed, and a tear slipped from them involuntarily. A glow flared beside me, and I turned to see while releasing her from my grip. I went tone deaf instantly. The only thing that could be heard was the thudding of my heart while I stared at the bright screen. The man, who had pieced the woman—who had all of my heart—back together, stood there, frozen in time, arms stretched wide. I'd just committed several acts of sin, not even ten minutes after hearing his message.

Pulling my pants up, I snatched my keys and scanned the room for any evidence of me being there. Taking one last look at the screen, for the first time in the years that he'd been with my mother, I had to disagree with the pastor.

I wanted more, and I would have more. There was no

contentment.

I wanted more. I would have more. No room for anything else.

More money. More cars. More clothes. More books. More jewelry. I would have it all because a king is entitled to his possessions, and I would get it. But in my kingdom, we had several rulers who all wore a crown. Ezio Cuppacio. Metavello Cuppacio. Renello Cuppacio. And when the little Cuppacios were of age, the crowns would be passed down to them.

Stopping at the door of Bahati's bedroom, I kept my back facing her limp body.

"I don't have more money than your papa yet, but soon I will, love."

There was nothing on this earth that could stop me from taking what we were owed. Anybody in my way was seen as a threat, and I didn't care if they bled every month. Men and women could die slowly fucking with me. When it came to my family, all morality went out the fucking window.

I'm Shio Cuppacio, and any man or woman who threatens the last name would be sent to visit the first batch of Cuppacio niggas. This was the new age where you either got down or got laid down—on foe 'nem.

Chicago, before moving to Jagoda Bay

"HONOR your father and your mother, so that you may have a long life in the land that the Lord your God is giving you. Exodus twenty, twelve."

Pausing, I waited for the word "father" to sour my taste buds. Instead of doing so, my tongue continued to hold the minty flavor of the peppermint I'd plucked from the crystal plate resting on a long, dark wood table in the narthex, and I resumed prayer.

"I honor my mother. Shannon is a good woman; a saved and spoiled woman that did the best to instill love and respect in a nigga. So, for that, I honor her to the fullest. She will never want for shit. *Ever*. If she asks for the fucking continent, I'm handing it over on a diamond platter without blinking. But with the way those Cuppacio boys are working her nerves, I know fo' sho' they're going to have to find another place to stay." I sniggered.

Polished wood and the mix of rich, smoky, and sweet fragrances filled the air as I sat in the middle of the pew in the most sacred part of Metro Chapel Church: the sanctuary. My eyes scanned the empty pulpit, which in a few days would be swarming with sinners, hypocrites, and some of the worst motherfuckers in the world, hoping and praying that their presence and hefty offering would be seen as good enough for the big nigga upstairs to forgive all the fucked up shit they've done in the world. Motherfuckers like me.

Lowering my head, the Jesus piece resting on my chest felt like an anchor, even though it was the lightest and most subtle chain I owned. I've been debating having the jeweler make me something a little more flamboyant, flashy, and icy. But I hadn't had the chance to get around to it yet.

"You can be the worst person in the world. Do so much unforgiving shit. Then you do some good, but that's all washed out because you've done a plethora of bad. That was my father."

Rubbing my hand down my wavy head, I licked my bottom lip. When I woke up this morning, I felt the weight of an elephant on my chest. It felt like I couldn't fucking breathe. Even after saying my morning prayer, working out, and taking another jog around Ezio's neighborhood, I still couldn't get my mind right. So, I got dressed and came here. Now, in my stepfather's church, I was asking for a sign.

"I guess you wondering why is this black-ass nigga in my fucking house talking in circles? Truth be told, I don't even fucking know."

Gripping the chipped wood of the pew before me, I squeezed the polished finish and attempted to stand. Feeling a small hand on my shoulder, and her sweet perfume tickling my nostrils, I paused and dropped my head further.

"Son. Tell me what's wrong?"

Shannon Washington. The woman, who not only gave me life but also showed me enough love to fill this church and the one down the block, stood over me as if she were six feet tall instead of the five feet, four inches that she is.

"What are you doing here, Ma?"

"Well, besides the fact that this is my husband's church... I saw you on the camera and wanted to stop by and check on you."

Shannon Washington. The First Lady. The strongest woman I knew, and saying that was a lot because I knew plenty of strong women. To be attached to a Cuppacio, you had to be strong. You had to be strong or you wouldn't survive.

"I'm good—" I started to lie before she cut me off.

"Don't lie. Don't sin in the Lord's house."

Sighing, I sat back and held her gaze. Our chocolate eyes mirrored. I also stole her dark skin and thick, coarse, wavy hair, which traced back to her Somalian roots. All of my other features, including the sharp noses that my cousins and I shared, came from our Italian lineage. Some days, I hated that I looked like that nigga, and others, I didn't mind. Shit had me confused as fuck that on most days I didn't hold the same sentiments as my cousins when it came to the niggas whose sacks we were formed from. Then, there were days when I hated my father just as much as they did.

"I been thinking..." I held eye contact with the most beautiful woman I knew.

She'd been through a lot—more than most her age. I didn't know a woman on this earth who had endured what Shannon had, and for her survival, I would always and forever give her anything and everything her heart desired. As a certified mama's boy, her feelings would always matter above my own. Even though I was in this church, her response to my dilemma would be the be-all. If my mama wasn't feeling it, then this shit would be pushed to the furthest portion of my mind to never be explored again.

Her sepia orbs held a soft gaze as she continued to wait for my response. She was patient—my mother had always been patient. Peering at my twin, I had to fight the emotions coursing through me. It should be a crime the way I loved this woman. She was everything to me, and the mere thought of hurting her caused a pang in my chest, one I had to fight to not reach up and soothe.

"I been thinking about reaching out to Sandro's other son."

I'd never been the one to beat around the bush. I didn't like to leave people guessing. I was a straight shooter. I meant what I said and said what I meant, holding nothing back. Games were for children, and even when I was a jit, I'd been a grown-ass man. Being forced to grow up way before my time would do that to you. When I should have been running in the grass and scraping my knees, I was learning to cook dope and clean bullet wounds.

Studying her expression, I was waiting quietly for the faintest of hesitation. If Shannon said no, then that's what it was. Didn't too much shit move in my world without her blessing.

"Sandro's other son…" she spoke just above a whisper.

Sandro Cuppacio.

The man she'd gone half with to create me. The man who I hated out loud most days, but missed in private on others. The Cuppacio Mob had been a ruthless and heartless organization, and while Sandro was just as vindictive as his family members, he lived a whole other life that many were oblivious to. He'd fathered a child outside of the organization. One that I vaguely remembered, even though I'd only seen him once during my childhood.

"You not with it, hunh?" I asked.

Shaking my head, I knew better than to bring up old wounds with my mother. She was a saved woman and had done well for herself. She'd married a preacher even though her son and nephews did ungodly things by the hour.

"Son." My mother reached for my face, held my chin in her soft, warm hands, and gave a half smile. "You're such a good man," she cooed.

"But I'm not, Mama. I'm not good. I don't think I'll ever be good."

And I was okay with that. I'd done some sinful shit, and I was far from being done with sinning. That shit was just in me.

"Shio, doing bad things doesn't make you a bad person. Sinning doesn't make you a sinner. Your intentions do. You always lead with pure intentions, son. You do the right thing even when no one else is looking. You stand behind your family no matter what, and you still have room to accept Jesus as your Lord and Savior. That is what makes you a good man, son."

Standing, I towered over her and swept her up into my embrace. Her gorgeous face barely reached my chin. My mother knew all the right things to say to make me feel whole when a nigga always felt empty. What she said next brought a different feeling, though—one of approval and acceptance of my circumstances.

"Go get Tunan. After all, he is your brother."

THE NIGHT of Neltz's Birthday Party

PEELING MY GLOVES OFF, I tossed them into the fire sitting in the middle of a vacant field just outside the city limits. A warm, orange glow illuminated my face from the flames, which were eating away at the green, rustic Ford Explorer until it was just a shell. My clothes were next, even the shoes, and when I was sure that the clothes had fed the fire, I unzipped the duffle and pulled out my change of clothes. By the time I was dressed, the fire had grown wild, so I jogged to my vehicle parked a few feet away. The heat burned my back, but it wasn't enough to be painful. Tossing the duffle onto the bed of my truck, I hopped into the driver's seat and took off.

Keep Hobo alive.

That was yet another thing added to my extensive list, which had grown over the months since we settled in Jagoda Bay. But, for Neltz, I would do it. Ever since I caught wind of those little niggas planning Hobo's demise, I knew I had to intervene. Their plan was too fucking flawed. They hadn't fact-checked shit. Had I let them go through with their little mission, that would have been just extra shit for us Cuppacios to clean up. With Ezio having a new baby and being a fucking newlywed, Renello planning a wedding, and Metavello preparing for twins, I was the most available man, so that automatically made me responsible for all these little niggas.

It was cool, though. I'd always been the fucking fixer of the bunch and had grown used to doing what I had to do to make sure everyone around me was okay mentally and physically. Nonetheless, my plate was past full. I couldn't even fit a fucking dinner roll on it, and Neltz, along with Italian, getting caught up in some bullshit would push my food onto the floor. I couldn't have that. A nigga was hungry more than ever now that we'd tasted the good shit since leaving Chicago.

We hadn't killed Hobo, but I needed all of our DNA from today's events destroyed. One day, he would meet his end when Neltz was strong enough to stomach it, and when that time came, I didn't need some detective that took his job a little too seriously to come and try to piece together some shit that was handled sloppily. Neltz still had eight years until he turned eighteen, but the law has been known to dig up evidence from fifty years ago. Scientists have been cloning Saber-tooth tigers with DNA from millions of years ago, so I didn't put anything above the government. If a person wanted to know something, they could dig until they found out, but with me, you'd be digging until you reached the core of the fucking earth before I was caught slipping.

I waited until I was about an hour outside of Jagoda Bay before I turned my phones on. There was no need for GPS because I knew exactly where I was headed. I'd only made the drive once, and that was nearly a year ago. Still, I knew it by heart. I'd been putting this shit off long enough. I'd passed the ball, waiting for a nigga to pick it up and make a play, but that shit had just been rolling around on the court. Now it was time for me to show my face.

When both of my phones powered on, the one I used for personal interactions connected to the radio, and Lana Del Ray's "West Coast" rattled through the speakers. One day, I'd stumbled across her music during my workouts, and she had a nigga hooked. Them Cuppacio boys clowned me anytime I wasn't playing rap, R&B, or Selena. I enjoyed all types of music, though. Classical, jazz, and gospel were amongst my favorites, but rap, especially my boy, Essex, was the most relatable to me, so it got the most play.

Bobbing my head to her whisper-like chords, a text came through on my personal iPhone. Picking up the overused device, my thumb swiped the screen, not stopping until I reached my messages.

> GLOW
>
> Yes, I'm good. Just leaving Neltz's party. I'm calling it a night early.

READING Glow's response to a message I sent right after I slipped away, I waited for the butterflies to flutter in my belly and for my heart to skip a beat. All of that good shit I know my family was experiencing, I paused for it to hit me. When it didn't come, I shifted my eyes to the open road in front of me before typing out a reply.

> You got that breakfast video to film tomorrow, right?

GLOW HAD CAUGHT my eye from the moment I set foot in Jisei's yard. Usually, I liked my women with a bit more melanin in their skin, but the light-skinned beauty had me intrigued. She was slim, almost too slim, but she had enough ass to declare her slim-thick. We'd been texting mostly because my life wasn't set up enough to date. Ironically, I didn't have the time to entertain a woman, but acquiring a wife was on my priority list. Had it not been for my hectic lifestyle, I would have long ago swooped Glow off her feet. But time hadn't been on my side.

With Demise hovering over us with our pending

23

marriages, I knew my time frame for crowning a queen was something that I couldn't delay much longer. However, every time I planned on getting up with Glow, some bullshit fell in my path that I had to clean up. The twins had finally gotten it right. Vello wasn't engaged yet, but I knew it was coming soon. I was the last one left, and instead of stressing everyone the fuck out, I was just going to propose to Glow.

On paper, Glow was perfect for me. Shit, she was perfect for any nigga. Not only was she pretty, but she was successful. She'd made a killing off of doing food reviews all over the city. Who would have known motherfuckers would get a kick out of watching someone suck on a crab leg, but with how fucking attractive she was, I would watch anything she put in her mouth too. Instead of continuing to waste her time with small talk, I hit the plus sign on the bottom left side of the screen, selected the Apple Cash icon, and sent her a stack. I didn't know how much the breakfast food would cost, but I knew she ordered a plethora of shit to try out just by watching a few of her videos. When the money went through, seconds later, bubbles formed at the bottom of the screen.

GLOW

Shio! Thank you so much! But you did not have to send me that!

It's all good.

THE HIGHWAY SPLIT into two sections, and instead of merging to the right, which led to Sparkling City, I ventured to the left lane.

24

GLOW

You always say that. I feel like I have to do something for you. Outside of holidays and events with your family we haven't even seen each other. No date or anything. I gotta take you out.

READING HER MESSAGE, discomfort settled in my chest, causing me to grip the stirring wheel. It would be a cold day in hell before I allowed a woman to take me out. Not that I was a sexist or no shit like that, but I did the fucking courting, and I paid the fucking tab. My woman could make all the money in the world, but I didn't need her spending hers on me. She could blow hers like a fan, and then come and blow mine, and it still wouldn't put a dent in my pockets. All it would do is make my dick stiff.

Glow and I made sense. She was one of Jisei's best friends and was versed in my lifestyle. Granted, she wasn't mob-affiliated by blood or marriage, but she'd been around us long enough to know that we weren't regular niggas. Plus, she'd heard us call Demise Don enough times to put two and two together. I'd looked into Glow before I called myself pursuing her, and her background was clean. A few sucker-ass boyfriends, a divorced pair of parents who were still in her life, and a little sister who was a little older than Pearla is what she came with. Even though she was a content creator garnering millions of views with her food reviews, she hadn't told a soul about who we were or what we did. I knew because I'd looked into that too. Whenever I made the time to get her to my fucking self, she was going to make the perfect bride for me. First, I had to handle *this*, though.

After wishing Glow a good night, I switched the radio from Lana to Sonder. My boy, Brent Faiyaz, was in his bag when he was part of a group. I still fuck with his new shit, but I vibed with his old shit heavy.

Things have been quiet with the mob. Everyone seemed to be settled, and these days, the only issue we had hovering over us was Grind still being in a coma. Other than that, we'd all just been playing our roles and getting this paper. Hopefully, things could stay calm so that I could seal my deal and have Don not side-eyeing me every time we were in the same room.

I'd had a long-ass day wrestling with Hobo's big ass, and now, I had a long-ass drive. I wouldn't be at my destination for another five hours, so I locked in, blasted my music, and enjoyed the wide open road.

CHAPTER 1
TUNAN "TUNE" PAYNE

"Payne! Be ready in ten!"

The guard hadn't waited for my response; instead, he went to make his walk-through around the pod. Rubbing my hand down my face, I peered at the pile of neatly folded items. There was my extra bedding, crisp olive green jumpsuits that made up the uniform we were required to wear, and two pairs of sneakers—one being Jordan 4s and the other, all-white Forces that still looked brand new and cost a fortune to have smuggled in here. There were boxes of leftover candies and snacks.

Walking over to the pile, I picked up the only thing I would be taking with me. It was a picture that had been getting me through this one-year stint. A bright smile and a pretty face, frozen in a Kodak moment, had my heart fluttering. I hadn't loved a woman like I loved Tuscany Payne Cherman, ever. Not even my mother received the love I had for my sister. She'd stepped up and sacrificed so much for us, and for that, I would never forget. She was my everything, and seeing her hold her second son, who looked just like his big-headed-ass daddy, got me through my darkest days in here. With his arm wrapped around her waist was her oldest son, my nephew, Tulsaire. I loved that young nigga with my whole heart and couldn't wait to hear what he'd been up to. One stipulation of my being behind bars was that I only conversed with my brothers. I didn't want my sister and nephews anywhere near this place, even if it was just a phone call. I didn't even accept letters from Tuscany.

I knew my sister was disappointed in me. I had no reason to be in this musty-ass jail serving a year's sentence. I knew my brother, Tulscan, was outside the gates waiting for me, and I knew he would take me straight to our big sister, so she could cuss me the hell out. I was ready for that shit, too, because I knew I deserved it.

"So you out this bitch today, hunh?"

Snatching me from my thoughts as I leaned against the concrete wall with my knee bent so that my foot was planted on the peeling paint while the other was on the dirty-ass ground, I eyed my cellie. With his elbows resting on his knees, he had the look of defeat on his face, and I knew it had nothing to do with my release.

"Hell yeah," I answered truthfully.

Typically, one wouldn't tell an inmate that he was going home. Niggas were so slimy that they'd sabotage your chance at freedom. I didn't fuck with too many outside of my brothers, but my cellie was cool. He was in this bitch pending sentencing. He'd undergone a speedy trial and was convicted on all charges. Now, he was just waiting for the pussy-ass judge to hand him his time.

"You know I'ma be in this bitch for a minute. Ion wanna see you come back through here."

More than likely, when Leader was given his time, he would be moved to a federal institution. This jail was simply a placeholder. But I got his message loud and clear. He wouldn't have to worry about seeing my face in this hoe ever again.

"I ain't coming back in this bitch, at all. I can promise you that."

Leader searched my eyes for what I assume was the truth, and when he got what he was looking for, he pulled a pack of index cards out of his jumpsuit pocket. When he showed up a few months ago, I had already taken the top bunk because I knew I wouldn't be in this bitch long. I had no plans on getting comfortable. He wasn't getting out anytime soon, so it was only right that he got the bottom bed. The nigga was only twenty-two and was facing hardcore time. I'd heard of him and his brother, Emperor, and those young niggas were moving plenty of weight in Cove City, which wasn't too far from the A. Grown-man time was a possibility when you made grown-man money. That young nigga had run up numbers I hadn't even seen yet. He was a product of his environment, as his father had been heavily involved in the streets at one time.

With his knowledge of the system and how the odds were never in a Black man's favor, he knew that a lifelong sentence could be the outcome of his illegal doings. Leader wasn't defeated because he was facing fifteen years. This young nigga was defeated because he had some shit he had to let go on the other side of the gates. More than likely, it was a bitch.

It was always a bitch.

"Aye, what's on them index cards?" I jutted my chin.

He studied them bitches religiously. You would think he was preparing for an exam with the way he flipped through them motherfuckers day in and day out.

Slapping the stack against his palm, he placed them back in his pocket before standing. "You ever met the perfect girl?"

We'd talked about surface shit in the last few months, mostly regarding niggas we knew in the streets and family and shit. I knew about his son, his mama, and his siblings. I knew his daddy was dead. He knew I didn't hold my fuck-ass pops in the same regard as he did his, and he knew about my siblings and nephews. I knew his baby mama was the reason he was in this bitch, and just like him, he knew I was in this mother-fucker because of a bitch too.

"Hell nawl. I ain't never met the perfect girl."

Even my sister had her faults, and she was my world. I'd never met nothing close to perfect, and if she was out there, I damn sure didn't want her. I was good on these hoes.

"I did."

Just like I suspected. That nigga spent most of his time staring at those cards and working out. He was going to be swole as fuck when he got up out of this bitch if he kept it up.

"She forbidden fruit, though." His eyes lowered, and his shoulders slumped.

"Aye..." I tapped his chest with the back of my hand. "Chin up, nigga. You waiting on yo' sentencing, but however this shit go, you ain't gone get life. Do your fucking time like a G and get home to her."

Leader squared his shoulders and lifted his head. "She got a future and shit. I should have never fucking touched her. She was pure. Still pure. Fuck a doctor going to do with a dope boy?"

I didn't know much about his baby mama, but I'd heard him fussing on the phone we had illegally stashed in the wall behind the toilet with her a time or two. From those conversations, I knew she was just the type street niggas went after. Sack chasers with nothing to offer but pussy and problems. Had it been me getting caught with bricks in the car, her ass would have had to take that charge on the chin. How the fuck the provider going to do the time? Hearing that he'd cuffed something with a future made me smile inwardly.

"Nigga, she knew you was in the streets when she got with you, just like you knew she was in school to be a doctor. It takes like, what? Fifteen years to be a physician, right?"

He nodded.

"Aite then. Whenever you get out, because you *will* be walking out of this bitch one day, it's going to line up with her being done with school. Divine timing. You got this nigga."

Leader slapped hands with me and slapped my back in a brotherly hug, holding me in place. "I'ma get my brother to hand you a lil' something. Stay up, nigga. I want to see you shining when I touchdown—legally." He lowered his voice so that his words would only be heard by me and not the prying-ass COs.

I slapped Leader's back and nodded. "Say less, nigga. I'ma hit the phone when I get one so we can stay in contact."

"Love, bruh."

When the guard showed up at the cell, he glanced past Leader and me to my pile of belongings with a questioning look. Instead of elaborating on our moment or telling him that I wasn't taking any of that shit with me, I held my arms out so he could put the cuffs on. He didn't need to know I was leaving all that shit for my cellie, even though Leader didn't need it.

"Leader, you ain't got life, nigga. Remember that shit!" I reiterated as I stepped out into the prison corridor. This would be my very last time walking through these stale-ass halls, and he couldn't direct a nigga fast enough.

My young cellie nodded, and I felt a sense of sadness wash over me even though it was supposed to be one of the happiest days of my life. I'd done this time alone. I told myself I wouldn't form any bonds because I was never looking back. Plus, these niggas in here were either gay as fuck, grimy as fuck, or weak as fuck. But Leader was as solid as they came, and the talks we had distracted a nigga from being so upset that I'd been placed in this bitch to begin with. I hoped he didn't lose his mind behind these walls. I was going to hit him up as soon as I got situated to check in. I appreciated his offer to let his brother break me off, but I was good on receiving anything that wasn't from my brothers. I wasn't opposed to help, but whatever they didn't have for me, I would figure out the shit myself.

I was led past the empty-ass pods, and with each step I took, my spirits lifted higher. It was yard time, so there was no one in the cells we passed. Everyone had probably run outside, wanting to feel some fresh air and soak in some sunlight. I was one of them niggas just yesterday, but today, my time was up in this motherfucker.

Three hundred and forty days. This jail had been my home for the last three hundred and forty fucking days. Seeing the same niggas every single fucking day that didn't share blood with you made you never want to do illegal shit ever again. Dealing with these lowdown, dirty-ass CO's made you want to get out, find their asses, and beat the fuck out of them to see if they could really back up all that tough shit they spat inside these walls. Three hundred and forty days of my freedom were taken from me, and another felony was added to my record. Three hundred and forty days of sharing dirty showers, surviving on oodles and noodles, missing holidays, and missing time with my family. All because of one bad decision. Not only did I miss my family, but I'd gone a year without pussy. I had the opportunity to knock some of these BBL bandit-ass COs off, but with how I was feeling, I was staying far away from these bitches in and outside of prison. If I hadn't learned shit else in this motherfucker, I'd learned discipline.

The guard removed the cuffs from my wrist, and I refrained from rubbing them. He'd had them way too tight, but that wasn't nothing new. Lowdown COs made my fucking ass itch.

They'd better hope I didn't catch their asses on the streets. I was walking a straight and narrow, but I could maybe risk freedom one more time to beat their asses.

The lady behind the discharge glass gave me "fuck me" eyes, even though she was old enough to be my mama. Ignoring her advances, I waited for her to hand me my check. I wasn't expecting it to be the eight bands I'd had in my pocket when I arrived, but if it was anything less than six, I was acting a damn fool. I didn't give a fuck if it was my first day out; stealing from me was some shit that I didn't tolerate.

Snatching the check from the small gap in the glass that separated us, I was shocked to see that it was for the entire eight grand. She'd said something to me, but I walked off, waiting to be buzzed out as I placed the check in my pocket. My brother, Turo, had dropped off a Nike set with socks, underwear, a white beater, and Jordan 1s days ago. It felt good to be out of those dingy-ass prison clothing and would feel even better when they opened this door so I could all but run to my brother, Tulscan.

Baaaaaannnng

The door swung open, and instead of sunlight, I was greeted by gray skies. I knew them niggas outside were mad as fuck that the clouds were blocking the sun during their free time. Looking from the sky to the guards to the rusty gates that surrounded the building, I inhaled the damp air. I had replayed this day in my head over a million times in the past year, but not once did I imagine it being all dark and gloomy. In my dreams, the sun was shining as I skipped to my brother's ride. I didn't give a damn if there had been a tornado outside—as long as I was out of this place, I was cool.

The fresh air did something to my soul, producing a broad smile on my face. I didn't care what anybody said, even in the yard, the air was tainted. It didn't breathe the same. As I

LISA AUSTIN

walked through the gates and made a right, the view of the parking lot had me quickening my steps. When I didn't spot Tulscan's G-Wagon, my smile dropped. I'd talked to that nigga every day this week, multiple times a day, about the time I was being released. I scanned the parking lot one more time just to make sure I hadn't missed his car. I didn't have a phone because it hadn't been on me when I got locked up. There was no way in hell I was turning my ass back around and asking to use their phone. I would walk if I had to. I was two hours outside of Atlanta, but I'd take the bus if need be. But shit, I didn't have no bus funding since I declined the jail's offer for the MetroCard when they presented it in anticipation of today. I also didn't have an ID on me to be able to cash the damn check.

Fuck it.

I decided I would walk because all that mattered was my freedom. Freedom, family, and this eight-thousand-dollar check were all I had, but that was more than ninety percent of those niggas behind bars had.

"Damn, it's been that long that you don't recognize your brother?"

Pausing in my stride, I turned to see a dark-skinned nigga leaning against a big-ass, tricked-out pickup truck. My brothers and I shared the exact same face. I got a bit lighter than them during the winter months, like now, with it being February. This nigga, though. He and I shared a handful of features. Our nose, eyes, and lip shape were identical, but he didn't look like a Payne. Still, my mother had confirmed he was indeed *my* brother.

With a neutral expression on my face, I approached him. His hand was crossed at his belt, and there was a Jesus piece on his neck. I didn't know what cologne he was wearing, but that shit greeted me before I even got within an inch of him. He was going to have to pass the name of that to me, and when I got back straight, I would add it to my collection. As for now, I wasn't buying shit that wasn't a necessity. Instead of slapping his hand, I stood an arm's length away from him and waited for him to tell me why he was here instead of my brother, my *real* brother.

"First day out. I hope it's yo' last one."

Chuckling, I couldn't even check him about getting on me. I was too damn old to be up in here on bullshit-ass charges. So, I would give him that because if I could help it, I wouldn't be in this bitch ever again.

"Hell yeah, it is."

We both glared at each other. The last time I'd seen this nigga was when I sold him a painting Turo had stolen while on a mission with the Navarros. This nigga had paid a grip for that bitch, and when he revealed that he was my brother, I knew it was the only reason he'd gotten the painting up off me. We exchanged numbers, and he'd propositioned me to join the mob. After our first conversation, we hadn't made a move beyond that. I was skeptical about the shit, but when my mama confirmed he was indeed my brother, I decided, as long as it was getting me rich, I was joining whatever the fuck it was he wanted me to join. My mother's sons didn't agree with the shit, but I was past whatever they were talking about. Before I could reach back out to the nigga since it had taken him so long to reach out to me, I'd caught a charge and had been in this bitch ever since. I hadn't even thought about his ass once while doing my bid, so seeing him out here was shocking, to say the least.

"You not fucking with me," my *daddy's* son rubbed his hand down his goatee.

"I'm just tryna see what you on. Why you here?"

"Shit, why you here?" he retorted.

My expression hardened. "Because I put my trust in the wrong muthafucka."

"You here on domestic violence charges. Let's call it what the fuck it is. You put your trust in the wrong *bitch*."

His words stung. But the shit was true.

I'd been a fucking player; fucking women by the boatloads. I was a young turnt nigga. Many of my brothers had settled down. Tulscan was the latest one to do so, wifing up a fine-ass real estate agent from the Bay. But me? I was having my fucking way. I told my brother that I was moving from the A to Jagoda Bay. I was excited to not only be in the same city as my sister and nephews, but was glad to be thrown into a world of new fine-ass women.

While visiting for Tuscany's baby shower, I was able to get a glimpse of just how Jagoda Bay gave it up. The women there were top-fucking tier. Right when I was about to have my newest sister-in-law find me a spot in her city, I let her and my brother's lovey-dovey shit rub off on me. I met a bitch, fell for her, and moved her in. That shit not only halted my move, but also ruined my fucking life. As fine as Stella was, the bitch was equally toxic. All we did was fuck and fight. The shit had never been physical, though. Not until I caught her stank pussy ass in my bed fucking another nigga. I don't even put my hands on women, but I tried to murk her and that nigga. Due to the neighborhood I lived in, my black ass was hauled to jail and has been here ever since. Stella was the reason I'd turned down many of the fine-ass COs who tried to get this pressure up out of me. I was good on pussy for now. I just wanted to get my shit back in order.

"Aye, I'm not here to kick you while you down." My daddy's son brought me back from taking a walk down memory lane.

"Couldn't fool me," I replied, my face still neutral.

Even though this nigga was dressed plainly in a navy hoodie, matching sweats, and white Forces, I could tell that his life had elevated since he'd bought the portrait. He had to have some money at the time to drop a ticket on the painting, but now, I could tell he was really holding from his truck to his demeanor. He wasn't flashy and didn't have on any jewelry outside of the gold Jesus piece, but his aura gave off that he was caked up. I wasn't counting no other niggas pockets, though, even if we came from the same nutsack. I just wanted to know what the fuck this nigga wanted so I could be on my merry way.

"We come from the same man," he flatly stated. He didn't seem to be too enthusiastic about what he'd just said, further confusing me.

"That nigga wasn't shit to me. My mama had a house full of kids. I got four brothers and a sister. I was born in this world with brothers, and we were poor as fuck too. My mama had mentally checked out on us, leaving her only daughter to raise us. My sister had to sell her body to a sick-ass nigga that kept his foot up her ass and was old enough to be her granddaddy. Where the fuck was our daddy then? Ion give a fuck about that nigga. Even if he was alive, I wouldn't give a fuck about him," I said, the anger evident in my tone as I spat the words out.

Shio watched me, and I watched his ass right back. If he thought we were going to bond over stories of our Casper-ass daddy, he was sadly mistaken. My mama eventually came around and got herself together, but having all those babies by different men messed with her mind. We drove her crazy, and when we got older and some of us started choosing the streets and catching charges, we really pushed her over the edge. Luckily, we all made a life for ourselves, and a sperm donor had nothing to do with it. Unless he could find our pappy, bring him back to pay child support, and go back in time to stop

Gilberto's foul ass from messing with my sister, there was nothing he could say about Sandro Cuppacio.

"You put some thought into what I asked you about last time we rapped lately?"

Bruh and I talked over a year ago. Hell nah, I hadn't put no thought into the shit, especially not recently. At the time, I'd thought about entertaining it, particularly since he was in Jagoda Bay, the city where I was supposed to be moving to. Once I got locked up, he, the mafia, and Jagoda Bay were not on my list of priorities.

"As you can see..." I gestured behind me. "I've been occupied."

Shio grumbled. "Yeah, I see."

"What you want from me, Shio?"

I could see that he was processing my answer. "Listen to your father's instruction and don't reject your mother's teaching, for they will be a garland of favor on your head and pendants around your neck."

Scraping my bottom lip with my teeth, I stiffened. "Proverbs chapter one, verse eight and nine," I said as if he'd asked a question.

Shio looked impressed. "You know the word?"

"Yeah... Well, when I learned the urban fiction section books by heart, I figured if I could read fake niggas living fake lives, I could dive into the Bible. To be honest, that book more ruthless than the urban and street lit I consumed."

I'd been dragged to church by a few of the older ladies in the hood growing up, and I knew I believed in God. However, I had never been deep into Christianity like that because I was too much of a fucking heathen and had no plans to fix my ways. But when you didn't have shit else to do, shit changed. I was still very much a demon, but I knew the word now.

"That's what's up. I'ma have to bring you to my stepfather's church."

I didn't know how I felt about that, so I didn't respond to it. I was still confused as to why this nigga was standing in front of me.

"To be honest, I don't know what the fuck I'm doing here. All I know is that you my brother, and I want us to have a relationship. I know you were doing your thing before you got locked up, but—"

"But you know that hoe bled me dry, hunh?" My cheeks warmed in embarrassment. I wasn't the motherfucker that was easily shamed, but letting Stella take my freedom and my gwap was enough to make me want to kick my own ass.

That was another reason I didn't want to talk to my sister and refused her letters when I was locked up. She met Stella once and told me to leave that hoe in the streets of the A. I didn't listen, though. She got with one of the many scammers living in Atlanta, not even a week after I was locked up. A whole other nigga from the one I caught her with was balling out with that bitch on my dime. She'd taken me for everything I had. No lie, it was the first time I came close to shedding a tear behind a female. It wasn't because I'd lost, but more so, I should have never let her in my space in the first place. The bitch didn't even have access to my accounts or the passcodes to my phone, but that didn't stop her scammer from robbing the fuck out of me. My brothers were just as pissed as I was and had been searching for the bitch, but she had to have been living under a rock because they had been unsuccessful in locating her.

I was raised by women, so Stella didn't leave me with a bad taste regarding the opposite sex. Plus, my forgiving-ass ways couldn't allow me to dump my insecurities on another woman. I did know that I wouldn't be entertaining another female until I got my shit together, and even then, I didn't want nobody that wasn't already bossed up in their own right. I'd fallen for that sickly bitch. She'd gone through breast cancer and everything that came with that. During that time, I had to nurse her back to health, pay for treatments, and more. So much had happened in the nine months we'd been dating that the relationship felt like it had been going on for years. As sick as she was, her one titty ass still fucked another nigga and ran off with my shit. When I did get myself a new bitch, she had to be a hundred percent healthy and paid. I was no longer in the business of reviving bitches from their deathbeds. I needed mine with a clean bill of health and her own wealth.

"We can't change the past. I even looked into finding Stella, but that scammer she was with must have given her a new identity. At this point, leave it in God's hands. I can't fix the past, but I can offer you a brighter future. I really don't know what the fuck I'm doing out here, but I do know I can't go another day without having a relationship with my brother. Join us." He stood taller.

"The mob?"

"Yes, the mob. Join the mob. In Jagoda Bay. It ain't what you think. That TV shit? Some of it is true, but we coming different."

"So, you saying y'all better than the Godfather shit I've seen?"

Shio flicked the tip of his nose with his thumb. "Nah, I'm saying we worse. Joining the Rinaldi Mob has been the hardest shit I've ever done, and it ain't got nothing to do with the missions."

"Missions?"

"You'll see." He chuckled barely, but I heard it. "It's fucked up most of the time, but at the same time, it's rewarding too. I know you have other brothers, but you *my* brother. I want you to live life like a fucking king."

"So it's gone make me rich?"

"It is."

"On God?"

"On foe 'nem."

"Count me in then." I grinned mischievously while rubbing my hands together like Birdman.

"It's stipulations, though. You have to get m—"

"Ion give a fuck. The stipulations don't matter. I'm in." Using the back of my hand, I tapped his chest and walked around him to the driver's side. "Come on, I'm driving."

Hopping in the big-ass truck, fresh leather and black cherry filled my nostrils. The display stretched across the entire dashboard and lit up dimly. I hadn't expected a pickup truck to be this luxurious, but I was fucking with it. Resting on the middle console was a mountain of rubber-band money.

Shio eased into the passenger seat. "Welcome to the mob, nigga. It's more where that comes from."

"Shit, say less."

I was all for the mullah. I didn't give a fuck what I had to do as long as that shit wasn't degrading, didn't test my manhood, and didn't get me locked the fuck back up. Show me the fucking money! Stella had taken me for everything I had, but my first day out, my dear ole brother had come through in a major way. I would entertain this brotherhood, but I wasn't staying with that nigga when we got to the city. I had a sister and a brother I could house with.

Jagoda Bay, here comes a fucking goonie.

CHAPTER 2
GLOW

"He's just so damn cute! Ughhh! I hate that you don't live next door to me anymore! I'd literally be your in-house babysitter."

Baby Ezee smiled up at me as if he knew what I was saying while I held him in my arms. He was so damn long, which was to be expected since his daddy was tall. His height wasn't the only thing he'd inherited from his father. Baby Ezee's cheeks were flushed red, mainly because he'd just woken up and still had the pressure from the crib mattress on his face. He was so light-skinned, you could touch him, and he would change colors. Still, he was the most handsome baby I'd ever held. His amber-colored eyes were the icing on the cake. Jisei complained that her baby not only gave her stretch marks but forty pounds, but I'd say this handsome bundle was worth it.

"I know... I miss my townhouse sometimes." Jisei plopped down next to me.

What was supposed to be a night inside, editing content, turned into me getting dressed up and coming to Dasani and

Demise's estate. Dasani had called the bartender and caterer over and insisted that all the ladies show up, according to Jisei I hadn't been here a good ten minutes before I was asking where Baby Ezee was.

"Ain't no fucking way I would want to still live in a place I overdosed at."

Pia entered the room with her small belly that seemed to appear out of nowhere. The last time I saw her, which was at Neltz's party, there was no signs of pregnancy. I knew she was expecting because I was in one of the ladies' group chats. I say one because I knew there was another one I couldn't be a part of since I wasn't officially *in the family*.

Nel entered shortly after Pia, and he was the one to make the remark about my friend's overdose. When I first started hanging around, everyone's dark humor used to leave me frizzled until I learned this was just how they were. Now, I laugh it off like everyone else.

"Damn, Nel! You may as well carry Princess P inside with the way you be on her ass," Mocha said, smacking her lips, as she took a sip of the green cocktail the maid had passed out. Mine was resting on the table in front of me. I wasn't much of a drinker. Actually, I didn't drink at all. The most I did was sip, but I could count on one hand the amount of times I'd gotten drunk. Tipsy often? Yes. Sloppy? No. It wasn't against my religion or anything like that; I just hadn't been one to indulge.

"Heyyy," I said to the couple as Nel helped Pia onto the couch across from me.

No matter how many times I had been in Dasani's get-ready room, I still couldn't get over it. It was so pink and Parisian. From the moment you walked in, it screamed luxury. The room was equipped with everything to pamper a girl, including massage beds, shampoo bowls, styling stations, and a manicurist station. Dasani, like all the women in the room, was spoiled rotten. If I hadn't learned anything else, I learned that the men in this family loved their women out loud and had no problem turning their pockets inside out for them.

"Wassup, Mocha? You not playing Camp Leader Mocha today? Should I have brought my permission slip?" Nel cocked his head and folded his arms into his armpits.

"Un hunh! Stand down when it comes to my child," Azure, Mocha's very young mother, scolded.

"Periodt, pooh! You stay bringing up old shit, Nel. But did you die?"

"Watch ya mouth, Mocha." Azure turned to face Mocha, who shied away in response.

"Nel messy self always starting stuff. Why he here, anyway? This is ladies' night!" She rolled her eyes again.

"Not too much on my fiancé. He just wanted to make sure I got in good."

"Facts, baby." Nel bent down with his dreads hanging in his woman's face and placed a wet kiss on Pia's lips, who, in turn, looked at him with enough love to fill a stadium.

All of these couples were undeniably in love, but if I could be a fly on the wall with any couple, it would be them. With the way they were infatuated with one another, I just knew their sex life was super intense. Plus, both of them were attractive as hell. Even when she's relaxed, Pia's bare chocolate skin looks better than a full beat. She was dressed comfortably in a red tennis skirt with a matching tank top that revealed her belly. On her feet were white Chanel sneakers, and across her body was the matching Chanel Boy bag. Her outfit matched the red engagement ring on her finger, and her long hair was pulled back in her signature ponytail. Her skin had a bright glow, and the jewelry on her neck and wrist showed her man had money. Nel was in designer clothes with heavy jewelry and looked just as good as his bride-to-be.

"I love you, Nel, but you gotta roll." Dasani waltzed back into the room.

She was rocking denim shorts that her thick thighs nearly swallowed up. Her stomach was out due to the navy halter top, which only concealed her small, perky breasts. On her feet were a pair of blue Hermes sandals. The only jewelry she was wearing was her boulder of a wedding ring and a diamond choker around her neck. Her hair seemed to be freshly done as it was pressed and hung down her back.

I always made sure to look my best around these ladies because they never took a day off from looking like royalty. Mocha was always looking like she stepped off a runway, and it made me sick to my stomach to think about how much she'd probably spent on her wardrobe, or should I say, how much her husband spent. Jisei was normally in something chill since she was still getting used to her post-baby body. Today, she was in an oversized diesel T-shirt dress that she paired with matching sneakers, but she was still iced out and looking pretty as ever. I didn't have half the brands that these women had, but I did what I could to look the part. I couldn't lie as if I hadn't stepped my game up since I'd been around them because I had. They never made me feel unwelcome or like an outsider, but what the hell did I look like dressing like a cheap hoe when they were in the finest?

I made good money in my profession, but not enough to be dressed in designer clothes every day. Still, I looked cute in my gold Nike Vomeros, white Nike shorts, and a matching fitted white T-shirt. I added gold jewelry and an oversized light denim jacket to layer my look, and my blonde and brown mix knotless braids hung down my back, which were freshly done. That was the vlog I was supposed to be editing.

I'd been invited to a brand-new braiding salon in Shirah, and in return for a free service, I agreed to make a vlog post. I could have easily negotiated for a free style and been paid for my video, but I loved supporting Black-owned businesses. Seeing an all-African American braiding salon was unheard of; not only was the salon gorgeous, but the service was top-tier, and they had slayed my braids. With my light skin, I usually shy away from blonde shades of hair because they tend to wash me out, but the 27/4/613 color combo looked perfect against my skin. I couldn't wait to post it on my social media and hoped it would generate lots of business.

Nel finally swaggered out of the room, and everyone had a drink in hand except Pia and me, since I was holding the baby, and she was pregnant. The vibes were immaculate, as always.

"Your hair is so damn pretty, Glow. I can't wait to see the vlog."

Pretty-ass Scarlett was forever giving me praises. She'd come in a few minutes after Nel left and right after her, Daylani, Dasani's sister. Daylani and Pia were off in the corner, going over wedding details that I found to be adorable. I couldn't wait to attend. I knew Nel was going to break the bank for her.

"Thank you. You should definitely try it out. You will love it there."

"I most definitely will. It's getting way too hot out for anything other than braids," Scarlett said before placing her drink to her lips.

I had to agree; it was one of the reasons I accepted the owners' offer when they messaged me. I loved it when Dasani invited us all over and let her team style us for free, but keeping up with extensions was still high maintenance. These braids would give me the energy I needed to get through my upcoming videos.

"That pizza place you went to the other day? That looked sooo good. Reminded me of when my husband took me to

Chicago. I nearly hurt myself eating in the Windy City."

Azure agreed with Dasani. "Chicago has the best food!"

"Paola's was fire. All the food was hot and fresh too. Y'all would love it."

"They had drinks?" Jisei asked. She was breastfeeding, but that didn't stop her from having a drink when she wanted. My friend said she'd gone nearly ten months without alcohol, so now she made sure she indulged every chance she could.

"Baby... the way you eat all that good shit and still manage to stay fine, I want to be like you when I grow up!" Azure raised her glass, and the ladies all agreed.

My cheeks flushed red, and instead of replying, I rubbed my nose against the baby's, who was already on his way back to sleep. He was so fly in his Burberry sleeper, and knowing he was wearing my baby shower gift had me snapping pictures and uploading them on my story. I was careful to only get the baby in the shot. I wouldn't dare upload Dasani or any of these ladies' homes.

When Jisei moved next door to me, the most we did was speak to one another. Mr. Joe across the street looked out for us both, and in turn, we started looking out for each other. When I started seeing all the fancy cars that would pull up, I just thought my girl had a lot of motion. I was happy for her since I didn't have an ounce of it myself. Then, we started talking, and before I knew it, I was being invited to all of these big-ass mansions where these fine-ass niggas with these beautiful-ass women resided. The men called Dasani's husband *Don*, and he was also Jisei's brother. It didn't take me long to realize my best friend was a mafia princess. I didn't know how I got tied in with this family, but I had to be one of God's favorites. My life was nothing more than work and no play until Jisei came along. I did hang out with my mom and sister from time to time, but my mom lived way in Sparkling City, and my sister was away at college.

I'd been born and raised in Jagoda Bay, but when my parents divorced while I was in fifth grade and my sister was in kindergarten, my mother got a job out in Sparkling City, where she's been ever since. Sparkling City was cool. It was pretty, had a slower pace of life than Jagoda Bay, and was a lake town. Even though I made great memories living there, I also went through some tough phases. I knew college wasn't for me, so I found a job here in Jagoda Bay and moved in with my dad for a while. When I grew tired of his and his wife's constant prodding about doing something with my life, I moved back in with my mom, quit my lousy-paying job, and spent a miserable day eating at a new diner by myself—that I happened to record—which turned into a whole new career. I immediately moved my ass back to Jagoda Bay, and after two years of consistent posting, I bought my dream townhouse. I now have over three million followers across all platforms and got paid to eat while documenting it. Even though I made money and became somewhat locally famous, I still found myself yearning for something more. I knew I didn't want a man, since the two guys I dated back in Sparkling City did a number on me, but I was missing something. I'd tried to make friends, but all of that backfired. Since then, I've been skeptical about the company I keep, as people often want to hang out with me because of my growing platforms.

Jisei was literally a gift. I'd gone from being afraid to let people into my circle to being scared I wasn't good enough for hers. Next to these women, my little three million followers meant nothing when they had millions of dollars within reach. What I loved most about them was that I wasn't the center of attention. You'd think I loved the fame, but I was the opposite. In real life, I'm laid-back and chill. On camera, I was Glow— the Pretty Eater that everyone loved and wanted to be like.

People idolized me, but they didn't know that the women I idolized were married to men involved in organized crime.

The nanny had to pry little Ezio from my fingers, and only then did I pick up my drink and take a sip. It was sweet and fruity, and I knew then that it would be the only sip I took. Jisei would drink it down quickly, just like she always did whenever we had drinks.

"You shol' won't let that baby go. Let me find out you next!" Pia yelled across the room, finally coming out of wedding planning mode.

Daylani was still glued to her laptop, stopping to sip her drink every now and then. She and her sister were twins, with their hair color being the only thing that set them apart. The women came in all shapes and sizes, but they all were equally stunning. They had raised my standards in everything related to daily living. I loved my townhouse and my little Lexus, but now I was aiming for a big mansion and a hundred-thousand-dollar car. I'd have to eat a lot more calories to get there, but I was committed. There was no way I could live basic after partying with the rich. Hell no. I don't blame Jisei one bit for moving out of that townhouse after her husband bought her that huge house. I would have done the same.

Jisei bumped my shoulder.

"You got baby fever?"

"Who? Me?" All eyes were on me as the ladies drank. "Oh no. Have a baby with who? This well is dry-dry. I don't have anyone to procreate with."

"Girl, please. There is a certain *Cuppacio* that has been sniffing behind you. Let me find out y'all gone have a lil' chocolate baby... or a light bright like Lil Ezee!"

Jisei smiled at Mocha, referencing my little infant boo. She was so in love with being a first-time mommy, and it was such a beautiful thing to see.

I took another sip at the thought of Shio. Like all the men, he was fine as hell. His chocolate skin was smooth like leather, and he always smelled like money, high class, and bad decisions. He didn't talk much when everyone was grouped up, but through texts, he asked questions and was attentive to anything I told him. He'd even given me money on a few occasions, just because. Just by looking at Shio, he made me want to jump his bones and end my drought. But, in reality, he wasn't really checking for me like that. He was polite and had good listening skills—well, reading skills since we'd only been texting—but that was pretty much it. It had been months, and I didn't know anything about Shio outside of the surface shit. I knew they had to keep me at arm's length due to their occupations, but I wasn't stupid. I kept my mouth shut, but it wouldn't matter if I didn't because I had no one to tell besides my sister. Glee had inquired about my new group of friends, but I didn't mumble a word because I loved and respected these ladies' privacy just as much as I loved them.

I was trying to get like them; have my feet kicked up while being fed grapes by a big dick king. And I wasn't assuming about these men having big dicks. One night, these ladies got too lit and had a "my husband's dick is the biggest" contest. Discover was on bed rest and wasn't at our gathering—as she still is—but when Pia showed Nel's gigantic dick, I just pictured Vello's being the same as his identical twin. I went home and masturbated to the images that were planted in my head forever. I still didn't know who won, but my God, they were all blessed. I didn't know how those dicks fit inside these prissy-ass women, but shit, I know my ass would be taking it, so I had no choice but to assume my ladies were too.

"Shio is a busy man, but I don't think he likes me like that," I admitted for the first time out loud.

The way the women gave me looks of pity had my cheeks

burning with embarrassment for the second time today. It was what it was. Shio was fine as hell, had money, and I'm sure his dick was just as big as the rest of the men, but he wasn't assertive enough with me. Hell, he wasn't even aggressive enough. He used his manners, wasn't all loud and rambunctious like the rest of the men, and sadly, I think that's what I was now attracted to. I'm not saying that I wanted anybody's husband, because I would never! I'm only appreciating how fine these men are, and how I love the way they loved their women. I had no plans to become somebody's side chick in this grouping of friends. Honestly, the men barely gave me a second glance, so they had no plans on fucking off anyhow. All they saw were their wives, and I'm sure that's the way it would stay whether Shio and I got together or not.

"Shio is..." Pia looked away as if searching for the right words.

I understood it was probably difficult trying to describe him without implicating the men in my presence. I was tired of them hiding their truth around me, but at the same time, I got it. Regardless of what Pia was trying to say, Shio didn't want me, so I was afraid I'd never be part of this internal club of mob wives. I could wait for one of the little Cuppacios to pick me, but that was laughable. I'd never date teenagers. Even when the little Cuppacios became adults, they would always be kids to me, and the thought of anything more felt disgusting.

There was no other "in" to be included in this lifestyle because all of the men were either engaged or married. I wasn't really looking for a man. Still, I was definitely hoping for a Rinaldi mobster, so I could finally *belong* with my girls, get spoiled rotten, and have big dick for breakfast, lunch, and dinner. I'd overheard Demise scolding the men about marriages once or twice, so I figured you had to be married to join the organization. My luck was shot to hell, but I refused to force something that wasn't meant to be. And from the looks of things, Shio and I were not compatible.

"Shio is different. Not different in a way that he isn't normal, but just different from all the other men," Pia stated finally, breaking me from my mindless thoughts. "He's calculated, intelligent, educated, and a straight shooter. Even when we were kids, he had it all figured out. The problem with a man that's well-versed is that he tends to have to get things in line with those around him. His life takes a back seat more than it should because he's always being the "clean-up" man. But don't underestimate him; he knows exactly what he's doing. He always does." Satisfied with her non-incriminating answer, Pia nodded and took a sip of her sparkling water. Her nose was starting to spread and was shinier than usual. The pregnancy was doing wonders for her skin, though.

"Well, he is fine as hell! I tell you that," Azure blurted.

Everyone's eyes shifted to her, and I held in my chuckle.

"Mama, really? I'm telling Big Zan."

"Girl, I love your daddy, but I ain't blind. That man is fine as hell! And he has manners too. It's something about the way he stands back and assess everything that lets me know he's a certified—"

"Ahem!" Dasani cleared her throat, causing Azure to shut up and sip from her glass.

There they were again, shutting me out.

"She didn't tell not one lie, though. My cousin is fine," Scarlett said, breaking the moment of awkwardness.

"As hell!" Daylani yelled from her laptop, and all of the girls burst into laughter. I even joined in because it was true. He was fine as hell; a blind woman could see that.

"So what you saying is, even as a kid, Shio was the man with the plan?" I shifted my gaze from Scarlett to Pia since they'd grown up with him.

Pia leaned in like she was about to reveal a secret, and that had me scooting to the edge of my seat.

"I'm saying... Shio is the nigga that shows up after having studied everyone else's plan. Plans they didn't even know they had, so they damn sho' didn't know *he* had 'em. After learning everyone else's moves, only then does he formulate his own, and I guarantee you... it's no flaws in his. Give it time. I can promise you that the woman he ends up with is going to get the absolute best Cuppacio experience. Don't tell Nel's jealous ass I told you that." Pia winked and sat back in her seat like she hadn't caused me to shudder in mine.

Just as the subject shifted from Shio, my phone buzzed.

It was a text from the man of the hour. I'd never opened his text so fast before a day in my life.

SHIO
You good?

Yes. You?

SHIO
Always. You got plans next weekend?

Nope.

SHIO
You do now. Be ready at seven.

I guess there was still hope for me to join the mob wives after all.

CHAPTER 3
SHIO CUPPACIO

"Married? Nigga, why the fuck didn't you tell me this shit before setting up a meeting?"

Tunan unbuttoned the jacket to his tailored suit and hopped in the driver's side of my truck. I didn't know why the fuck he hadn't bought himself one yet because he was forever driving my shit when we were together. I preferred to drive myself, but if my little brother wanted to chauffeur his big brother, who was I to interfere?

Tunan had been in Jagoda Bay for about a month, and I'd finally been able to convince Don to sit down and have a meeting with him. When we arrived at the Dungeon, Don sent a last-minute text saying something had come up and he would have to postpone. Peeling out of the Dungeon parking lot, Tunan shifted his focus from the road to the streets.

I still hadn't had the chance to introduce my brother to my cousins, mainly because those niggas were too pussy whipped these days. I wasn't complaining about those irresponsible niggas, though. Not one bit. In fact, I encouraged the new leashes they were rocking. However, Ezio had yet to resume his role of meeting with Goal every month to get our product. While I couldn't duplicate myself, I knew Tunan would step in and help because he was hungry for security. I'd been trying to get Don to add the last Cuppacio to the roster, but the nigga had been acting petty. According to Reuchie's laws, Tunan was in, whether Don met with him or not. I was trying to be courteous and respect his position by getting his approval. But Tunan was a Cuppacio just as much as my cousins and me. Don knew that, but he just wanted to be an asshole.

When Don canceled, I at least wanted to put Tunan on game of what was to be expected of him since I'd waited long enough for Don to do it. Telling him marriage was a high priority had this nigga acting like I'd just told him he had to cut off his left leg.

"I tried to tell you, Tune..."

With my phone in hand, I texted my pilot to confirm our plans for next Friday. It wasn't often that I chartered a jet, but for quick and guaranteed trips, I was willing to spend the money. With these airlines frequently delaying flights, I needed to be sure I could get to my destination and back before my date with Glow on Friday night. My current itinerary had me flying out at six in the morning, handling my business, and returning to Jagoda Bay by four in the evening. That would give me enough time to shower, change, and arrive at Glow's house with some time to spare.

"When? Hunh? Cuz I been here a month and not once did you say, '*I can get you rich, but you gotta get married.*' What type of shit is this? Nigga this ain't the Middle East! Fuck! I should have listened to my brother," he said in a groan.

"I am yo' brother."

"Nigga, my REAL BROTHER! He told me you mobbing-ass niggas was gone get me tied into some shit, on my soul! Cancel the meeting. With the way that nigga canceled on us last minute, he don't want me in the shit, no way. I'm super straight. "

"Aye, stop putting shit *on your soul*. You in a new city, you not hurting for no bread, we good looking niggas, so what's the problem?"

Even though Tunan was talking his shit, his demeanor was cool, and that let me know he wasn't as fucked up as he was portraying to be about getting married. He knew how this mob shit went. Either he'd done his research, or he'd heard some shit from one of these groupie-ass niggas around Jagoda Bay. Marriage was inevitable, and I wanted him in, so he was going to have to do what everyone else had done: suck that shit up and find the best woman for the job.

Pulling a blunt from the middle console, I lit it and let the exotic Kush suffocate my lungs. Pills and syrup used to be a part of my guilty pleasures, but I never got hooked on the shit like Ezio had been. When I saw my right hand go through what he did, I had to fall the fuck back. Now, I smoked a daily blunt, refraining from indulging on Wednesdays and Sundays. On those days, I preferred to remain sober.

Once my body relaxed from the potent drug attacking my nervous system, I handed the blunt to Tunan. He'd done his time and wasn't on probation, so he, too, fucked up his lungs with recreational smoking.

"I'm just saying. That shit caught me off guard, G."

I nodded. The rest of us were also caught off guard by the obligation.

When we found out we had to be wed in order to officially join the mob, it threw us for a loop. It was what it was, though. If everything went well next Friday, I would have me a blushing bride and would be able to put that behind me.

"Yeah, well... You in a city full of beautiful women. Take your pick. Choose wisely, though," I let him know as he passed me back the blunt. I had to crack the window due to the funky fog the weed had created in the truck. I needed Tune to be able to see. Being wrapped around a pole wasn't on my bingo card for the year.

"So, where yours at?"

I could feel him side-eyeing me as I stared straight ahead while getting my fix. It was still early, only being noon, and I had a taste for a Caesar salad, so unbeknownst to Tunan, we were headed to lunch. I had about two hours to spare before I had to meet Nel at one of the stash houses for a count. Ever since our shit came up short that time, we do triple-fucking counts. After the money got handled, I had to go check a few of our customers' traps. We didn't personally give a fuck what the niggas did with the dope when they copped it from us, but knowing their shit ran smooth was important to me. I liked to see how a man treated those working for him because if he was a shitty boss, that said more than enough about who he was as a person and as a businessman. If you can't respect the niggas that are keeping your belly fed, then you aren't fit to be fucked with—or in my case, served.

Once that was handled, it would be in the wee hours of the morning. I had to find time to pencil in visiting the cabin because I hadn't fed the Hobo nigga in two days. I couldn't have him dying on me before my nephew turned eighteen.

"Aye, bust this left right here."

Tunan made the turn, but continued to glare at me. "Where yours at?"

"I heard you the first time, Tune."

"Well, shit... answer, nigga."

I tried handing him back the blunt, but he declined, so I put it out in the ashtray and tossed it out the window. The blunt was still three-quarters full, but there was more where that came from.

"You rich-ass niggas just be wasting the weed. I could have took that lil' piece of blunt with me and had it for the morning."

I chuckled. "Tune, it ain't that deep."

"And that's another thing. You always hollering about shit not being *that* deep."

"Cuz it's not. Shit be surface as fuck." I shrugged while confirming details with the pilot so I could wire him the twenty bands it would cost for him to get me to and from my destination.

"Yeah?" Tunan cut his eyes at me and smirked. "Aite den."

"To answer your question, I haven't really had the time to find a wife. I'm not putting much thought into it like that, though."

My finger hovered over Glow's message thread, but I hesitated. I hadn't had the time to pursue her like she deserved, but if she so happened to take the Cuppacio last name, it would make up for all of my mishaps. At one point, I had a few women I kept on my roster for those nights I needed to feel something soft. In recent months, I'd narrowed it down to one. However, none of them was fit to take the Cuppacio last name. They were good for a few orgasms, and that was it. Glow, though—she had the potential to be all that and more. Time just wasn't on my fucking side.

"So you not putting much thought into the bitch that's supposed to be your wife? Your *wife*, nigga?"

"Nah. I'm not."

"So you'll marry a bitch with one leg, teeth missing, and deaf in one ear? Since it ain't that deep and you not putting that much thought into a wife, you just gone marry anything out here?"

Rubbing my hand down my mouth, I locked my screen and stuffed it in the pocket of my slacks. "As long as she's loyal, honest, kind, can take dick, and spend my money like I print it, I don't give a fuck what she looks like," I spoke the honest God truth. I didn't have a type.

Granted, most of the women I'd bedded hadn't been as light as Glow, so I did prefer a chocolate woman. I also preferred one that was of African American descent, but I didn't have a type per se.

"Yeah, you must gone cheat?"

"No. I'm not. When I take a wife, she'll be the last person I lie with."

"Forever?"

"Yeah, Tune. Forever. When I said I want a woman that's loyal, I meant that. I can't expect her to give me some shit I don't give in return. Won't be any cheating going on."

Tune stared at my side profile until he had to focus on the road again.

"Take this right," I instructed.

Finding a comfortable speed on the new road, Tunan started back up with the questions. "So, Ezio is married, Nel is engaged... that means it's just you and his twin brother left, right?"

He hadn't met the rest of the Cuppacios just yet, but I'd told him about them. Them boys were my bloodlines, plus at least one of them called anytime I was around Tunan.

He'd been staying with his sister, Tuscany, since he'd gotten out. With the money I gave him, plus his other brothers, Tunan was sitting with more than he had before, and he wasn't no broke-ass nigga before his jail stint. Even without the mob, he was good. Stella running off with his riches hadn't even crossed his damn mind, and it shouldn't. He couldn't be crying over spilled milk when he'd left his fridge open.

He had the means to get his own spot, but I understood him wanting to be around the people he'd thugged it out in the trenches with. I noticed the Paynes were a close-knit family, and those boys didn't play about their sister. She was pretty as fuck, so I didn't blame them. She was also a married woman, and I didn't plan to even attempt to look at her any other way than as my brother's sister. Not a nigga on God's green earth was going to have me out here like Metavello's ass. That shit he pulled could have ended bad as fuck for him, but thankfully it worked out.

"Metavello ain't got too long. I'm really the last man standing. Well, now you…" I grinned.

"Nah, just you. You the last man. I haven't signed my name on shit, and the nigga canceled the meeting."

I laughed. The nigga low-key reminded me of Vello with his smart-ass mouth. "Aite, Tune."

The restaurant came into view, and Tunan pulled in the long valet line. Vines was an upscale Italian spot that had some of the freshest salads. You'd think they grew the Roman lettuces in the back of the building. Their pasta was next level too. I frequented it several times a month because they consistently delivered on what you expected. At first, I thought moving to Jagoda Bay would be a let-down for my taste buds, but so far, they've been giving Chicago a run for its money. Still, there was no place like home.

"Why you so adamant on this?"

"What? You joining the mob?"

Tunan nodded, and I sighed because I didn't have a direct answer.

I asked myself the same shit so many times over the last few weeks. On one hand, Tunan was an affair baby. I still remember how hard my mama cried when my pops revealed he had an outside baby. Tunan was a reminder of the pain my mama went through when she learned of his existence. But he was a Cuppacio. He deserved to be brought into the organization just as much as the rest of us. It was his birthright, and he was my brother. If I was out here eating, I needed my sibling on the same shit.

"I got something lined up," I said, changing the subject.

A slow smile spread across Tunan's face, and for the nigga to look like his other brothers, he looked just like me too. It was crazy seeing his features mirror mine.

He raised his eyebrows. "You got a potential?"

"We are supposed to have dinner next Friday. She's already cool with the wives, so she's hip to the lifestyle, to some degree."

As the valet approached the truck, I opened my own door. I leaned in so that his ears alone could hear what I had to say. "Leave it up front and keep the keys inside."

He nodded, and I bumped forearms with the young boy, who looked like he'd been on a high all day from driving fancy cars.

Standing in the line with Tunan beside me, we caught the lusty glances of a few women. Many of them were good-looking, no doubt, but I had to see how next Friday went before I entertained another. The one I was sticking dick in on the regular was plenty enough for now.

"Damn! Jagoda Bay don't play fair." Tunan grunted, loving what he saw.

I don't count the next niggas nuts—brother or not—but Tunan claimed he hadn't been focused on women since being released, which was good for him. If he could go a year without fucking, he could keep going until he found his forever. As I'd attempted to preach the same shit to my cousins before they settled down, dealing with multiple women was not only a headache but a recipe for disaster. Women could genuinely be your come-up or your downfall. Tunan had already seen this to be true from his situation with Stella, so I was hoping I wouldn't need to stay on this nigga if he started entertaining.

"At all," I agreed. Joining Tunan in enjoying the eye candy, I gave a wink to something thick and chocolate who was snickering with her friend. "It's going to be real hard to stay faithful."

We moved up in line, and I continued, "But nah. You got it. Just like you ain't fucked nothing since you been out, or how you ain't fucked on none of those guards, use the same restraints when you lock your wife down."

"I guess. So what's yo' goal next week? After your date and shit? You gone tell her your intentions, or you gone court her and shit a bit?"

I didn't tell Tunan that I've had more than enough time to court Glow, but I hadn't prioritize the time. Instead, I moved up in line, stuck my hands in my pockets, and smiled at the hostess as we approached her.

"Shio! You didn't have to stand in line. I could have escorted you to your table without the wait." Jasmine batted her thick lashes while discreetly running her hand down the waist of her black dress. Vine had a strict dress code for their staff, so her job to remain primmed and prepped at all times was necessary. Jasmine was pretty. Every time I was in here, I could see the mental battle of keeping her job or trying her luck at bagging a nigga with some paper. She was still employed, which meant so far, she hadn't lost the fight. As I assessed her medium-built frame, her honey-hued cheeks warmed as she fumbled with the iPad she used to check customers in.

"I didn't mind waiting, Jasmine. I appreciate it, though. You good?"

She nodded feverishly, her shoulder-length hair bouncing with each motion. "I'm great. Thank you again for putting the word in with the nursing home. They were able to get my nanna in, and she loves it. I still can't believe they accepted her insurance. That place is the elite choice of nursing homes."

"God was on your side, beautiful."

She fumbled with the menus and motioned for us to follow her.

Both Tunan and my eyes went right to her backside. Jasmine had enough ass for a nigga to grip on, so it filled out her dress nicely. As we walked through the restaurant, I glanced at the murals featured on the walls mimicking an Italian countryside with rich vineyards, deep hues of mahogany and green, I listened as she ranted more about the facility her grandmother was in.

She was in disbelief that they had accepted her insurance because it was out-of-network when she was researching the best place for her grandmother. During one of my visits, which was on a slower day, she mentioned that her nanna was being kicked out of her current nursing home because they no longer accepted Medicaid. I made a call, and they had a room ready for her within the hour. I'd never take it there with Jasmine because I appreciated seeing her pretty face anytime I was in here, and I didn't want to confuse anything. My actions were because I had the means to help, so I couldn't help but to do her a solid.

"I've never seen you before. You're his brother? I'm Jasmine."

Jasmine held her hand out for Tunan, and his foolish ass just nodded at her, making her retract her hand in embarrassment.

"I'm Tune, the brother from another mother. How you doin', Ms. Jasmine?" His words softened the blow because Jasmine was cheesing like she hadn't been looking like she was about to run just seconds ago.

Tunan showed all of his teeth in his mouth, and Jasmine

was eating that shit up. "No offense; ion shake hands. I'm 'bout to eat, and a nigga just got out." He tapped his temple with his middle finger. "A nigga still institutionalized."

Letting him do his thing, I opened the menu, even though I knew what I wanted. I wanted to look occupied, giving them space to continue their banter.

"Got out? You were in jail? For what?" she asked with amusement as if he'd just revealed he'd gotten his master's degree. The good girls always fell for the bad boys; it was a tale as old as time.

Locking his fingers, Tunan rested his arms on the table and leaned in. "For Ike Turner-ing a bitch for playin' with me. Move 'round, Jasmine. This dick gets aggressive when I'm fucked over," he spoke with a straight face.

Jasmine's body stiffened, and she tugged at the collar of her black dress. "I... uh... Your waiter will be here shortly." She gave me one last farewell before she nearly sprinted back to the hostess stand, where she had a line of motherfuckers waiting.

"Leave Jasmine alone, Tune."

Tunan kept his arms folded atop the menu and grinned. "You got me out here in this tight-ass suit, and now you mad that your hoes on my jock? How that work?" he taunted.

"It's tailored, not tight. And Jasmine isn't mine."

"Jasmine isn't mine—ole deep voice-ass nigga."

With Tunan's Memphis accent, he sounded as if he were pronouncing her name without the S. *Jaaamine.* I was still getting used to his lingo. Even though he'd spent years building a life in Atlanta, the M-Town hadn't come up out of him. I thought we Chicago niggas be saying some shit. We didn't have nothing on Memphis Tennakey.

"You can relax, Professor Oglevee. I told you... I'm not studdin' these females. I'm trying to run my bands up. That's why this marriage shit throwing me for a fucking loop." He sighed while peeling open the menu. "Ion know what half of this shit even says on this long-ass menu." Tunan tossed his menu.

I chuckled. "Get the steak... butterflied, a Caesar salad, and depending on how big your appetite is, the prawn pasta is good."

"Yeah, I'll take all that." He sat back in his seat just as the waitress came to fill our water glasses.

"So, back to this date on Friday with ole girl."

"Glow."

"Yeah. Glow. You never answered on if you gone let her know wassup or not."

Leaning back in my chair, I used my thumb to twist the ring on my index finger. Tunan waited impatiently for me to answer. Next Friday would change my life forever, that much I knew. I felt it. Anytime something drastic was about to occur, my body would hint it to me before my mind processed it. That's the way it had always been.

"Just know, by the time the date is over next week, she will be stamped as a Cuppacio fiancée." I smirk at my brother, feeling good about what was to come.

Going through my to-do list mentally, I sat back and waited for the waitress to walk by so I could request another drink.

God first.

Make sure the family good.

Eye them Cuppacio boys, the little and the big ones.

Build a relationship with my brother.

Get my brother rich.

Health and wellness.

Stay on top of my mob shit.

Keep Hobo alive.

Find a wife.

CHAPTER 4
SHIO CUPPACIO

P ain radiated in my legs, arms, and seemed to intensify behind my cranium. At my age, there was no way I should be experiencing this type of pain unless I'd been pushed too hard on someone's peewee team. But there was no peewee, there was no team, and there weren't any limits. Day after day, I'd been dragged from my home to endure one ridiculous thing after the next, and all I could do was obey. The only thing that kept me going was what happened at the end of the day. No matter how hard I was beaten, degraded, or mistreated, none of that mattered when I got home.

"Corinthians 16:13-14. We studied that last week. Recite it."

My chest was on fire from Niccoli punching me in it one too many times yesterday, just because he could. Bendino, my little cousin Scarlett's father and the Don of the Cuppacios, was away on business. He'd made it clear that we wouldn't be having any "mafia training" while he was gone, so the plan was to go to Nel and Vello's house since they lived the closest to me, and the three of us would spend the night at Ezio's house. I was supposed to be on my way out the door, but I'd been stopped as soon as I left my bedroom.

66

My mother appeared in the hallway. "Sandro, let him go. He is going over Enri's to hang out with his cousins."

She'd just showered, so she was wrapped in her favorite green silk robe that stopped at her calves. The sweet smell of her body wash danced in the air while she stood next to the man with whom she'd gone half to create me. Turning slightly so I could see the beautiful face of my favorite person on the planet, I noticed that she'd washed her hair. Water droplets landed on her shoulders as her wavy hair glistened underneath the dull hall lighting.

My father faced my mother, and the serious expression he'd been harboring vanished with one look at her. She shrank just from his glare alone. In this home, when it was just the three of us, my father treated my mother as if she were the only soul who mattered to him. One could believe from seeing his expressions toward her that she was the only woman he'd ever loved; I believed she was.

"I just want to make sure he pays attention to his old man. Nothing more, sweetheart," he assured.

My mother's smile dropped, and her body went stiff. That was another thing I'd been beginning to notice. They'd be so in love, and all of a sudden, my mother would pull back out of nowhere. When I was much younger, their emotions would give me whiplash. But now that I was getting older, I knew the reason. I'd seen the reason countless times.

My mother still wasn't convinced, so my father pulled her to his side and placed a gentle kiss on her forehead, causing her to sigh and retreat.

"I can't teach him how to be a Black man. I'll never know what that feels like. What I can do is teach him how to have a relationship with God, and with the Higher up on his side, it will make his journey outside of these walls an easier one," my father explained to my mother while running the back of his knuckles down her cheek.

Had it not been for the actions I'd seen in this house, I wouldn't know what love was or what it looked like. Here in this home, when it was just our trio, my father loved my mother as if his life depended on it. An Italian man had married a Black woman. My skin was the color of melted dark chocolate, and my father's was the opposite, holding no pigment, even when he'd go away on business trips and return with a sunburn. I'd been born to a man who hadn't experienced the dangers men like me faced in the real world. God was a big part of our homelife when it was just us because, let my father tell it, God was the only way I'd be able to get through the hell that resided on the opposite side of the door. At first, I thought it was all smoke and mirrors. There was no way a man in the sky who no one has ever seen or met had these set of rules we had to obey, or else we were deemed to Hell.

Do good and God does unto you.

I didn't believe a word of it. But, after years of abuse and my cousins and I still being able to stand and breathe, I knew it had to be God.

"You're a good woman, Shannon, and you deserve so much more."

With my mother still in his arms, my father looked at me. He wasn't in his usual suit and tie. Instead, he was clothed in black slacks, a white dress shirt that he had rolled at the sleeves with the first three buttons undone, and a pair of house shoes that he'd probably stuffed his feet in after taking off his loafers.

"Shio. You still have some good in you. Hold on to it."

My father was always pouring into us and saying the most bizarre things. This was another common occurrence in our house. I didn't acknowledge his request; I just stood in the hallway, ready to move around them so I could go play, but I knew better than to voice that.

It took more forehead kisses and body rubs for my mother to surrender and return to her other self. Another thing I'd learned from my parents, which I knew for a fact they didn't mean to teach me, was that most people, if not all, wore two masks. Both Shannon and Sandro did.

Boom Boom Boom Boom Boom

My mother stiffened again, and instead of my father comforting her, he almost pushed her out of his arms as if he was allergic and whoever was on the other side of the door would shoot him dead if they'd witnessed him loving on his wife. Sandro's expression hardened, and he didn't spare her a second glance as he turned on his heels and walked to the door. Before he could reach the front door, he stopped at the slender hall table and removed the top from the only item resting on it. I sucked in a wad of air as I watched him pull out the white baggie full of devil's powder. When I first witnessed the substance, I thought it was baby powder. But people didn't chop baby powder up on a surface and stuff it up their noses. My mother held her arms out, and I slowly walked into them, keeping my eyes on my father. My heart started to race, and my fingers twitched. My cousins were expecting me, not the other way around, so I knew it wasn't them at the door.

Grabbing my face, my mother placed a kiss on my jaw, then the other, before tucking me behind her. Even at seven years old, I was up to her shoulders. My father was six feet and three to four inches on a good day, and I was proving I'd take after his height. It was all I had from him—everything else was Shannon.

Where we stood, I had a clear shot of my father's side and the door. My mother was trying to shield my view and guard me from the viewer, but it was inevitable. Even if I'd been locked in my room, I'd have to answer to whatever it was demanded of me when it came to the guests we'd get. I blinked hard, watching my father take a long sniff of the drug that turned him into the person I despised as the doorbell continued to chime. My mother was trembling and praying under her breath while my father pinched his nostrils as the drug took him to a new height.

My father opened the door, and one of the people I dreamed about killing appeared. My father started unrolling his sleeves and straightening his posture. Just that fast, he'd gone from loving husband and doting father to mobster. The drug and the mob did that to him.

"Family! You're good in here?" Niccoli, with his piercing blue eyes, looked past my father, making my mother push me further behind her. I could still feel her shaking and hated that I couldn't do anything about it.

"Yes, cousin. I'm good here. Is everything all right with Don?"

Niccoli didn't take his eyes from where he knew I was, which was behind my mother. "All good. I need the boys. All of them."

Sprinting as if she'd drunk seven energy drinks, my mother appeared on the side of my father, leaving me standing in the hall. "Don says they have no training while he is away. He's not coming anywhere with you."

Niccoli's smile dropped, and he looked at my mother with sheer and utter disgust. All of the Cuppacio men were ruthless, greedy, and evil, but Niccoli was the worst because he was a snake. The mob seemed to look past his slithering ways, but my cousins and I didn't. We saw him for exactly who he was.

"Sandro, you're going to let your whore talk to me in this way?"

I could see my father's shoulder tense.

"Slap that bitch before I do it!" Niccoli barked.

Before he could walk into our home, my father slammed the door in his face and rushed my mother. Before he could lay a hand on her, I was pulling the back of his shirt. He'd forced her against the wall and punched above her head. She didn't scream. She didn't yell. She simply glared at my father with weary and tired eyes.

"You have to act like I've hit you when I open the door," he said through clenched teeth.

Reaching behind him, he snatched me to his side. The two of us locked eyes. He let my mother go, kept his grip firm on my shoulder, and opened the door back.

My mother pressed her hand against her face and cried as if

she'd gotten hit just as my father had instructed.

Me, though? There was no pretending. There was no one on the planet I hated more than Niccoli, and that said a lot since I hated all the Cuppacio men. There were times like this when I even hated my father. The good he did when no one was looking meant nothing if he was Satan anytime there was an audience.

"Shio fucking Cuppacio. Ready to die?" Niccoli grinned sneakily as if he were talking to his enemy instead of a child, who had only been able to read for three years.

Snatching away from my father, I stepped out of the door, where there was some form of love, into the real world and next to the snake.

My mother was still pretending, but was focused on me. Niccoli nudged me aggressively with his shoulder, but I kept my sights on Sandro. My mother's cries intensified, and I knew that she'd gone from faking it to weeping in real life. She knew what happened anytime I was not under the protection that our roof provided, only when it was just us three.

My father could console and pour into us behind closed doors, but he couldn't and wouldn't protect us from his own family, so I knew that in the real world, he'd leave me out to drown just the same. It was then that I concluded that if someone couldn't love me fully, wholly, and out loud, they couldn't love me at all. If I had no intention of loving someone, I wouldn't give them a false sense of hope that I would. Because that was what my father was to us. A temporary relief. A false sense of hope.

Unblinking, I used the back of my hand to swipe at my nose. My father was such a great pretender that the hateful glare he shot me almost seemed real. Maybe it was—maybe he really did hate us, but pretended he loved us. Either way, I was done with the whiplash. He was right; my mother deserved better, and even if it took my last breath, she'd get it.

"Be watchful, stand firm in the faith; be men of courage; be

strong. Let all that you do be done in love. Corinthians 16:13-14. I'm always listening, father."

Grabbing my shirt, Niccoli dragged me away, and I kept my eyes locked on my father until my home was no longer in view.

I HADN'T BEEN HERE in a while. Truth be told, I didn't know why the fuck I was here to begin with. This was grave number two of two. Five or so miles back, you could find my father's original resting spot. When Don killed all of the men, we were young as fuck. Although we couldn't be happier that the Cuppacios' reign had ended, we were still faced with a few fears. We'd been stuck with women and children to provide for, and we'd barely had hair on our dicks. Then, we had to bury all of these men.

Ezio had stumbled upon some safes, and after paying a few of the women who wanted to leave, we bought the cheapest plots available and buried them niggas in a row. They had inexpensive gray headstones above the ground, which had been a requirement of the gravesite, and their caskets were no more than cheap pine boxes. Hell, we'd even buried them in suits from their closets. They didn't deserve proper burials, but we had to lay them to rest at the very least. Now, here I was, on a gloomy day with gray clouds hovering above in my windy-ass city, staring at the granite like it was about to talk back.

Lifting my head, I popped my neck and sighed. Grabbing my left wrist with my right palm, I crossed my arms in front of me. "What the fuck done happened now?"

"I'm surprised I didn't find you with your dick out, using this muthafucka as your personal toilet," his voice sounded as his body appeared to the right of me.

I angled my head to get a good look at the only person on this planet who could have found me. Scoffing, I looked back at the four-foot-tall black granite slab that displayed his name, birth date, and death date. I couldn't bring myself to have "loving father and husband" engraved on it because that would have been a lie.

"How the fuck you find me, *Don*?" I asked again.

Doing a one-eighty, I faced Demise Rinaldi completely. Just as I was in a suit and tie, so was Demise. It was rare that you caught that nigga in street clothes these days, and as of late, I'd been in my mafia attire more than normal.

The left side of his mouth curved up, and I knew this nigga was about to come out of his mouth with some slick shit. That was Don, though. He either said some shit that made you want to beat his ass or kill his ass. There was no in between. The nigga didn't know when to turn his ignorance off to save his fucking life.

Sizing him up, I swiped my thumb across my nose, getting annoyed with his silence. "What the fuck you want, Don?"

He took a step closer in my direction, and I didn't know who the fuck this nigga thought he was intimidating, but it damn sure wasn't me. Often, Don was granted approbation from a nigga because, technically, he was my boss and was responsible for how my family ate. But us Cuppacios had been handling shit for a long time before he brought his ass around. He had a lot of shit with him, but he hadn't dangled any bread and butter over our faces, and that kept him on this side of the earth because we didn't give a fuck.

Nevertheless, I had a lot of respect for Don, even though on most days I wanted to put him in a pine box. He'd single-handedly dismantled not only his own mob by killing his father, but our mob as well by killing ours. He saved my mama and 'nem. For that, I gave his ass more grace than normal. Because make no mistake, with or without him, I was getting to the paper.

"You know, you Cuppacios the only niggas on the planet

that talk slick and still got your life. I wonder why that is..." He gave me a teasing smirk.

"Because us Cuppacio niggas will go toe to toe with you, win or draw, because it fasho ain't no losing. Now, again... what can I do for you?"

Don broke out in a full-on grin, making his ass look just as crazy as Matteo. "I want to kill y'all so damn bad, but I'm man enough to admit that I just might shed a half a tear behind you niggas. I don't know why, but I've grown fond of you hard-headed, disrespectful muthafuckas."

We engaged in a stare off before Don turned to face my father's tomb and continued, "Of all the Cuppacios... I think I fuck with you the hardest. You know why?"

"I still don't know why you here, so let's answer that question before I answer any of yours."

Don snapped his head at me while keeping his body facing forward. "Hold the fuck up, muthafucka! You gone let me get to it, all right? Impatient as fuck, damn!" He faced forward again. "Anyway, as I was saying... I fuck with you the hardest because, you unpredictable. Everything those other niggas did, I was hip to it before it occurred."

My brow rose. "So you knew Ezio was going to nearly kill your sister by allowing her to overdose?"

"Nigga, no! That shit threw me for a fucking loop. I'm still surprised I let that muthafucka breathe after that bullshit. I've killed niggas for way less."

I shrugged because, had my nonexistent sister overdosed because of a nigga, it would've been lights out for that nigga. Fuck rules. However, I had no response for Don, so I waited. He would get to the real reason for coming all the way to Chicago to find me eventually. That nigga called me impatient, but he was really talking about his fucking self. Had I shown up to the Dungeon wanting to rap, he would've given me all of sixty seconds to speak my piece.

"Them other niggas act like they don't like me, but they really do. I may even step out on a limb and say, they love me. But, you? You'd kill me without blinking. You're probably the only nigga that got the balls to do it. My own uncle couldn't even kill me after knowing I'd blown his brother's brains out. But, you? You'd do it swifter than these winds." He held his hand up, spreading his fingers, letting the wind course through.

My trigger finger twitched, forcing me to resist the urge to pull the gun from my waist and show Don just how factual he was. But I still had no words for him. I would neither confirm nor deny the allegations.

"I'm here because... I need a favor from you."

Chuckling, I shook my head. "Get the fuck outta here. You pop up in Chicago because you need me? You the Don—all you had to do was summon me, and I would have had no choice but to come. You never had a problem with forcing us to do some shit we wouldn't if a muthafucka paid us too. So, cut the shit. The Don don't do favors."

He'd just cancel a meeting I requested over some petty stuff, and now he's here like he's Timmy and I'm one of the Fairy OddParents granting wishes and shit.

"You right. The Don doesn't do favors. But *Demise* Rinaldi does."

If Don was here asking me to handle some shit for him, it had to have been something I one thousand percent wouldn't want to do. My plate was too full already. I couldn't add shit else to it except my current plans to finalize this marriage shit. Outside of the tasks being a duty, I was a lonely fucking king. I had my brother, my cousins, my family—a full court, but the throne was empty. I'd put off filling her seat long enough. It was time for me to add that missing element in my life. That was all I was able to make room for: crowning my queen.

My mind screamed at me to tell his ass, "No."

But, I found myself asking, "What you need, Don?" with as much enthusiasm as a tired toddler.

"I need you down in CDMX."

I couldn't travel until at least another six weeks, especially out of the country. I still asked "When?"

Don cocked his head. "Do you know what CDMX is?"

Peering at him, I grunted. That was the only response to that question he was getting.

"And you doubt that I fuck with you the toughest. You hadn't even asked what I needed you down there for—just when. Hmmph." Don taunted.

"Don—"

"Aite, aite! Ole serious-ass nigga. First, I'll tell you what it's for. I need you to go to a dinner party."

Again. I gave nothing.

"Ines Ledesma," he said as if the name wasn't alarming.

I waited for Don's playful grin, but it hadn't made its usual appearance. No man put fear in my heart, but there were some I had to put extra planning and thought into going against, and Ines Ledesma was one.

At one point, he was something like a legend. I'd heard tales of the Ledesma Family growing up, and like the Cuppacio men that came before me, nothing was good. There were claims floating around about the Cuppacio, and while some of it was false, most of it was true, so I knew most of what I heard about the Ledesma Cartel held some truths as well. Still, I was a man who believed none of what I heard and only a fraction of what I saw. If I were the type to believe what I heard, then I would say that the Ledesmas made the Cuppacio look like play toys.

They were ruthless and, some years ago, had been responsible for the rising crime in Mexico City. It was so bad that you had to be vetted before stepping off the plane. Even if you were just a tourist, you had to check in or you'd find yourself with your wig blown back before you could snatch your luggage from baggage claim. That was back then, though. These days, the gossiping-ass niggas in the streets claimed that the Ledesmas were being bitched out by a younger, more ruthless, and deadlier familia: The Rodríguezes.

Even though I didn't believe most of that shit, I knew that Don's little pop-up was more than a favor. It was like risking death by putting me at the table with a shark.

"We already got a cartel locked in," I said, more so to myself.

We had the Navarro Cartel, and I fucked with Goal and looked forward to my pickups. The nigga was a fool, even though he had me side-eyeing him for lending Don his aquarium for our last mission. From what I know, Ines Ledesma also moved cocaine and owned coca farms just like the Navarros.

"I don't need him for his work. If you're not a friend of the Rinaldis, you a foe. That nigga claims he wants to be a friend. I want you to see what the fuck he's offering, and if the offer is even worth my time. If it is, you come back and report that shit."

"And if it isn't?"

"Look, I need you on this." A vein appeared down the center of Don's forehead as he stuffed his hands in the pockets of his pants. For the first time since I'd met him, Don looked stressed. This nigga was always popping off at the mouth, so seeing his face tight almost threw me for a loop. Still, I stood idle.

"You couldn't send Reuchie? Where the fuck he at?"

"Reuchie on a... extended leave of absence. According to his son, that shit is indefinite. You the only man on my team that can get this done. I trust you with this." Don was on a roll today because his trusting me with anything was a new one.

"You just admitted that I was unpredictable, but now you trust me?"

"I said I trust you with *this*. I didn't say I trusted *you*. Trust is earned, and just as I haven't earned yours, you ain't earned mine."

"Aite."

"Aite?"

"Yeah, Don. Aite, I'll do it," I agreed while mentally assessing my plate, trying to figure out where I would fit this in. Once he gave me a date, I'd move around whatever was scheduled at the same time to make it to this dinner party.

"You know..." Don reached forward, knocking dust off the tombstone. "You loved your pops. That's why you upgraded his grave unbeknownst to your cousins. They think he still lined alongside their bitch-ass pops, but little do they know, he way back here, resting eternally in luxury. The grass is greener, the trees are shadier, and the tombstones are taller in this area."

My body tensed at his revelation.

"You leave in the next hour."

My head whipped so fast that it sent a pain down my spine. "What?"

"I've already given your pilot the new course. He's to take you straight to Mexico City. And don't worry, he's being billed to me."

"I ain't worried about no fucking bill. If I couldn't afford it, I wouldn't have charted him to begin with."

"Nigga, I know you keep his ass on speed dial. Having him charter you to see a dead nigga that ain't worth yo' sympathy seems like a waste, though."

I sighed, not giving a fuck about his opinion. Tonight was my date with Glow. I hadn't even brought my main phone with me because this visit was supposed to be in and out. The phone I had on me only had Ezio's and Tune's numbers stored in it. I could have easily called Ezio and had him ask Jisei for Glow's number since I didn't know it by heart, but she deserved better than that.

Don looked down at his Ademar. "You got about fifty-five more minutes to get to the hangar."

"You still haven't told me what to do if his plan for *friend-ship* ain't presentable, for lack of better words."

Don shrugged and turned to walk away. "Kill that nigga and pray to God you make it past his guards so that you can bring yo' ass back home. Hopefully, it won't come to that."

Don took some steps, and only then did I notice his driver in the distance, along with two guards outside a white Phantom.

"After I do this, have the meeting with me, Don."

The quicker I sat down with Don, the quicker my brother could get his ass in. I could have brought it up while I had Don alone, but this wasn't the time nor the place. Plus, I wanted Tunan present so he could speak on his own behalf. Don already knew what the meeting was about. That nigga had more eyes than the alphabet boys; he was just being lowdown, a favorite pastime of his.

Don waved me off, walked a few paces, but then stopped. "Oh, and Shio?" he called over his shoulder.

"What?"

"You're unpredictable because you're battling your emotions. You discreetly loved yo' daddy—still do. You want nothing more than to avenge his death, and what better way to do it than to off the nigga who killed him? Just make sure you keep *battling* those emotions. I would hate to have to do you, and have your family on some 'slow singing and flower bringing' type shit." A grin stretched across his face before he started chuckling.

Running my tongue across my teeth, I blinked. This man was psychotic, and I knew this because I could meet him where he was if I wanted. Instead, I keep it cool because it wasn't worth the blowup that would happen if I killed his ass.

With the same neutral face I'd had this whole encounter, I replied, "You don't even believe that shit."

Don continued his pace and held up a middle finger. "Forty-eight minutes."

"Fuck!" I barked out before fishing my phone out of my pocket. I went to my dial log and hit the name. Placing the phone to my ear, I waited until it rang.

"Married, though?" was Tunan's greeting.

"Aye, get the fuck over that shit. You ain't even had the meeting yet and you crying about some shit you can't change. I need a favor, though."

"What is it, *big bro*?"

After giving Tunan instructions, I ended the call.

Mexico City, though? What the fuck Don got me getting involved with?

I took a deep breath knowing my frustrations wouldn't do me any good. Running through my ever-growing list, I turned and walked away without speaking a word to my father's tombstone.

God first.

Make sure the family good.

Eye them Cuppacio boys, the little and the big ones.

Build a relationship with my brother.

Get my brother rich.

Health and wellness.

Stay on top of my mob shit.

Keep Hobo alive.
Get through the meeting with Ines Ledesma.
Find a wife.

CHAPTER 5
TUNAN "TUNE" PAYNE

"Uncle, yo' surroundings don't look like you at GameStop."

Tulsaire spoke through the Bluetooth even though I had him on FaceTime as I pulled up to the restaurant. The valet line was too fucking long for my liking, plus I had way too much money in the whip to be handing one of those preppy boys my keys.

I backed into the parking spot with precision but left the car running. Now that I was parked, I was able to get a good look at my nephew since I'd answered the call while my eyes was driving. I had to fight back emotions once I saw my nephew through the rectangular screen. This boy was growing up on me. His voice had dropped an octave, and his hair had grown. He kept it in a curly high-top fade with a crisp line, which looked like he'd just gotten it done today.

I smiled. "That's because I'm not at GameStop, youngin'."

Tulsaire was engrossed in his gaming system, LED lights illuminating on his golden skin as his eyes shifted from the TV in front of him to me.

"Well, I hope you plan on going when you finish doing whatever it is you're doing. You've got clothes on, and it's late evening. Even got ya lil' chain on. You must be going to the club?"

"*Lil'* chain, nigga?" Chuckling at him dissing the only jewelry I had to my name, I continued to watch him as he swore under his breath like I couldn't hear him.

He'd better be glad he wasn't home because Tuscany had ears like a bat. My sister was crazy about her firstborn but wouldn't hesitate to get in his ass. He was a good kid, though; he just let that damn game get the best of him.

Turning my eyes from the phone to the white brick building in front of me, I bit down on my bottom lip. "Nah. I ain't goin' to the club."

"You getting up with a girl then?"

Cutting my eyes back at my nephew, I couldn't help but grin. "What you know 'bout gettin' up with some girls?"

"Do you see me, Unc? I'm a Payne-Navarro. I can't keep these girls up out of my face."

Tossing my head back, I laughed. That little nigga was indeed handsome. He was going to give my sister a run for her money, for sure. He had too many real niggas in his corner who were going to make sure he was a beast. He had already started his coming-of-age quest because I'd been staying with my sister for a little over a month, and he hadn't shown his face once. Since it was nearing the end of the school year, he'd been planning on spending his time with his big brother, Goal, and his other brother, Gage. Outside of the pictures my sister had around her enormous-ass house, I hadn't seen my oldest nephew since I'd made it home. The baby, on the other hand, had been glued to my leg if he wasn't hanging on my sister's breast with his greedy ass.

"Well, that's all they better do. Look... You got plenty of

times for girls. Right now, they are not worth the trouble they come with."

Tulsaire toggled his eyes from me to his TV. "Are you saying that because Stella ran off with all your stuff?"

Again, I tossed my head back in laughter. This little nigga was funny without even trying. "Mane... I'm off dat. Unc on to bigger and better. Can't cry over spilled milk. Obviously, she needed it more dan me."

"I guess." He shrugged. "If you need to get back straight, just know your nephew got you!" Tulsaire puffed his chest out.

"The same nephew that's hounding me 'bout GameStop? Can't be *that* nephew."

Tulsaire pressed a few more buttons on his controller before standing. He picked up his phone and walked to the opposite side of his bedroom, which looked more like a mini-apartment. It was his room at Goal's house, and it proved my nephew was spoiled as fuck by everyone. Even my mama was crazy about him. He was her first grandson, and she'd give him the world if he asked. He planned on spending his last two weeks of summer break with her. I was skeptical, though. Even though we'd put our mother up in a nice home, she still lived in Memphis. We'd renovated the house we grew up in, and I was starting to regret that shit because she spent most of her time in the hood at that one than the one in the suburbs. My city was a war zone, and if one of them young niggas tried my nephew, I was painting that whole town red.

When my sister became pregnant with him, it was only then that my mama stepped up and took on her role as a mother. Tuscany had held that responsibility for years, so I support the change in command. She needed to bring her ass on to the Bay because if she wanted Tulsaire to keep visiting, she had to make a choice about living in Memphis. We were past that now.

Tulsaire laid the phone down so that I could see his room ceiling. I was looking at a Maybach roof on my nephew's bedroom ceiling. I don't know whose idea that was, but the visual I was seeing went hard. I could hear him pressing buttons before he picked the phone up, and smiled into the camera right before flipping it. In a small safe, there were numerous piles of money to the point that he couldn't fit anything else in it. There was also what appeared to be a passport that I knew had to have more stamps in than a bitch with nine kids on her welfare case.

"You holding like that, but you hounding me about Game-Stop. Shit, you got GameStop money."

Tulsaire closed the safe and then sat back in front of the TV, propping up his phone. With the angle he now had, I could see a Navarro chain resting on top of the muscle shirt he was wearing.

"I'm not trying to spend mine. I want you to spend yours. Ain't that what uncles are for?"

"Damn, 'Phew. I just got out. You just said yourself the girl done cleaned me out."

Tulsaire crinkled his nose. "You not mad about that, for real. If you were, you would be in Atlanta looking for her instead of here in the Bay."

My nephew hadn't lied. I wasn't the least bit worried about Stella's ass. I had more pressing matters at hand. I'd told myself I wasn't studying these bitches and that I was putting this dick on lockdown, and come to find out, I got to get fucking married if I'm to be in this mob shit. Stella scamming me out of my riches was at the back of my mind. If I brought that shit to the front, I was liable to get pissed, and a pissed Tunan was criminal. I'd told not only my cellie, Leader, but my brothers, too, that I wasn't going to see a cage no more. I especially wasn't going behind a bitch, and I meant that. I was staying away from these whores, but I didn't know how in the hell I was supposed to do that if I had to give one my last name.

"How you like living in my house? What my mama 'nem been doing?" Tulsaire shook me from my thoughts.

"Stop acting like Tuscany Cherman doesn't call you every day."

"Facts..." He smiled. That boy was everywhere with everybody because we all wanted to soak up his energy, but he was obsessed with his mama, just like we'd been our whole lives.

"Athena be getting all my money. I ain't gone have none fucking with her." I shook my head.

"Fall up off my sister. You sick of eating crab legs yet?"

"Mane, am I?"

Athena and Tulsaire had basically been kidnapped together. Baguette, my sister's husband, was hustling hard and getting his product from an old head named Gilberto Navarro. Gilberto was a motherfucker, and everyone knew it because his old ass stayed doing fucked up shit. When Baguette no longer wanted to do business with Gilberto and switched over to copping product from Goal, that motherfucker kidnapped Baguette's daughter, Athena, whom he shared with his first love. Gilberto had already been raising Tulsaire, whom he fathered with my sister on some manipulative shit. Once he stole Athena, he raised them together up until his ass was killed. When they found Athena, they took Tulsaire too. My nephew ain't been out of our sight since. Goal being Gilberto's son was crazy to me because that was who Athena's mama had been fucking with while she was missing. That whole situation was wild as hell. All the bodies we had to drop behind it still made me shake my head. Honestly, that time period was chaotic as hell for everybody, but low-key exhilarating.

Everybody welcomed Athena with open arms, and now, she was even more spoiled than my nephews. I'd come home from jail and gained a whole new niece. Being surrounded by so many kids had me wondering when I would have one myself. But if a bitch ran off with my kid like the last one had done my money, it was really going to be lights out.

"On the real, though, Unc. If you need some money, I got you."

Smiling at my nephew, I couldn't help but miss that boy badly. He was one of my best friends, which was sad because he was only twelve. "I can assure you, Unc is good, Neph'. You know I'ma get to it regardless."

We didn't keep Tulsaire sheltered because he'd grown up with a cartel boss for a father, and since Gilberto was ignorant as hell, we knew he'd seen more than he should've. We didn't discuss business with him, but one day, he would lead the Navarro Cartel, so there was no reason to hide anything around him. He knew what his brothers and uncles did, and even then, he still had his innocence.

"Well, if you getting to it, you need to be getting you a new car." He frowned. "You got the raggediest car in the neighborhood. It's embarrassing."

Again, I was laughing my ass off. Stella hadn't taken my gold Cuban that I was now wearing because it was at the cleaners, nor had she taken this Infinity. It was ten years old, and I'd been using it to make plays in before I got sent to the slammer. Not only was the inside of the roof ripped, but it had more miles on it than a hoe on the street. It needed a paint job, and the bumper was dented, but for now, it was getting me where I needed to go. Most of the time, I used my sister's car since she always sent me on errands, or I was in the car with one of my brothers—Shio included. A car wasn't high on my priority list. If I needed one that bad, I'd probably get one from a chop shop before I went to a dealership. I didn't have any bills, I was living with my sister and had my own space, and I had about a hundred thousand in the tuck. I was doing well financially for someone who had come home to only eight bands. And now that I had the mob hanging over my head, I knew money was really about to start pouring in. I was just enjoying my freedom and figuring out where the hell Shio and I's relationship was going.

The more I said I didn't want to be like that with the nigga because I didn't know or fuck with our pops, the more he grew on me by the day. Shio was quiet, but when he did speak, it was always with some knowledge or some game. He'd kept it realer than most. I only really fucked with my mother's sons, but I did have a few associates. Not one of them niggas had reached out to even say hello since I'd been out. I was a grown man, so another nigga didn't owe me shit, but as much money I've put in niggas hands and on lawyers over the years, and to see that shit not be reciprocated had me letting my guard down with Shio. So far, bro was aite.

"This car getting me where I got to go, nephew. Just know—"

I reached inside my glove compartment, and my grill was the first thing to pop out. I'd forgotten I'd placed it there, so I popped it in my mouth and grabbed a stack of money. Holding up the bands next to my head, I used the pinky of my left hand to open my mouth further to shine my teeth at the camera.

"Just know I'm still him, neph'! Where you think you get it from? Them Navarro niggas just now coming in the picture."

Tulsaire mimicked me, handcuffed as if he was holding a Polaroid camera, but he was holding up air and flashing me his pearly white teeth.

"Ugh ugh ugh ugh!" I did my best Money Bagg Yo impression.

"I see ya, Unc'. Now, make sure you head to GameStop first thing in the morning. I want them games in my room by the time I come home next week."

Laughing again, I folded two wads of the money and stuffed them in both my pants pockets before placing the rest back in the compartment. Standing from the car, I checked my surroundings, and the couples entering the restaurant eyed me skeptically. The car didn't match the swag, or maybe it did, but I wasn't wearing slacks and dress shoes like the rest of the men who were coming and going from the restaurant. I was fly as fuck in Evisu jeans, a white matching tee, and some white Jordan 11s. I was more than likely out of dress code, but I'd slide the hostess a big face to get through the door.

"Let me hit you back, nephew."

"Aite. Stay dangerous," he said.

"Bye, lil' boy!" I smiled and hung up the phone.

Noticing the time, I grabbed the crotch area in between my legs so I could jog without the weight of my gun and money pulling my pants down. I'd caught the door just as an elderly Asian couple walked in. The husband turned his nose up at me as the wife acted as if *we* weren't the ones making whatever business they had, whether it be a fried rice house, a nail salon, or a beauty supply store, rich. Instead of cursing them the fuck out, I flashed my solid gold grill at them.

The fuck they think this shit is?

I was planning to be a gentleman, but I walked past their asses and approached the hostess stand. A cute, strawberry-blonde-haired chick was standing behind the stand. She took one look at my attire and opened her mouth as if to turn me around. I reached into my pocket and pulled out two hundred-dollar bills. One probably wouldn't be enough to get her to let me inside this establishment.

She snatched up the money so fast that I was sure she chipped her French manicured nails. "Welcome to Capital Grill. Table for one?"

Licking my lips, I scanned the restaurant. It was dimly lit and intimate but lively. I was underdressed like a bitch, but fuck it; this was the best I could do at the last minute. "I have a reservation for two already. Under Shio Cuppacio."

She scrolled on the iPad before nodding. "Your date is already here. She arrived earlier than the reservation but insisted I sit her. Right this way."

I was thirty minutes early, and I would have been even earlier if I hadn't spent time on the phone with Tulsaire. I hadn't seen anyone young or single walking in while I was chopping it up with my nephew, so it had me wondering how long *my date* had been waiting.

"Here we are."

I could only see the back of her, but the blonde and brown braids that flowed down the back of the chair looked good. I could also see that she was in a halter dress that showed all of her fucking back. I hadn't thought about a woman, but seeing her silhouette and knowing if she stood up, I could possibly see the crack of her ass or her thong had my dick stiff. She reached for a glass of what appeared to be water, and a stack of gold bracelets decorating her arm clanked. I immediately had the urge to fill her wrist with a Cartier bracelet, a Hermes one, and a fucking rollie since those were absent. I hadn't seen her face and was already wanting to trick my little money on her. The glow of her skin and scent of her sweet perfume had me folding, and I didn't even know if she had a beak for a face or not.

So much for my "fuck these bitches" motto.

She'd taken the seat facing away from the door, and for that, I applauded her. I'd already found the blueprints of the restaurant online, so I knew all the exits; plus, I'd visibly seen them when I came in. Still, I needed to face the door. You can take the nigga out of the streets, but never the streets out of the nigga.

I felt someone looking at me. Following the heat of the stare, I was met with an older Black woman holding a wine glass, her nose turned up at me. Not wanting to show my ass in these folks' place of business, I rounded the table and took a seat instead of giving the old bird a piece of my mind.

Gotdamn!

Her eyes ballooned, and at the same time, she began coughing.

Reaching my arm over, I tried patting her back, but she held her hand up. While she composed herself, I raked my eyes over what I could see of her frame. Little baby was gorgeous. If I could use one word to describe her little ass, it'd be soft. Not in the sense of touch, although I'm sure everything was indeed as lush as it looked, but soft in the context of living. It looked like she'd never known a bad day, an inconvenience, or a hard time in her life.

I'd had my fair share of women, but I steered away from the ones that looked like this one across from me. It was true that good girls liked bad boys, but she was more than good. She screamed saditty and high maintenance, and those were the ones that I looked at but didn't fucking touch. The old me needed a woman who could fit into my lifestyle. I didn't need a person trying to convince me to punch a clock because it was what her daddy had done for the last thirty years. Internally chuckling, I realized I was doing the very thing these motherfuckers in this restaurant had been doing to me since I pulled up, but I couldn't help but to judge her pretty ass.

Not my type, but damn sure every niggas type.

"I'm good. Thanks. Who are you, and why are you at my table?"

Even though I'd startled her, I could see that she was checking a nigga out just as I was checking her out. The front of her dress was a V-cut, showing enough cleavage so that I could pinpoint her cup size. She was about a 34B, but still, they were good and perky. Whatever shimmery shit she'd used on her back, she used it on her front as well, and in the crest of her breast, there was a long, gold chain dangling. On the table beside her silverware was a Louis Vuitton handbag that went well with her look, but a Chanel would have been more fitting.

She needs a fucking Chanel.

Here I was saying what she needed as if I'd bought one before for anyone outside of my sister. Them shits were like ten bands, and at the moment, I only had ten of ten bands, so I had to fucking cool it with the imaginary tricking.

In ten seconds, I had every feature on her pretty-ass face memorized. Her nose was on the larger side, but it went well with her facial structure. Her eyes were spaced apart like Halle Bailey's, but again, that shit gave her a unique look. Her lips were plump and lined in brown with nude coloring in the center, and I imagined them wrapped around my dick with that shit smeared all over her stunning face. She looked like she needed to be on a fucking island getting some tan on her light-ass skin, and her look of the night matched the tropic aesthetic, and the way her hair was styled added to her attire. Yet, we were in the middle of a restaurant in Jagoda Bay.

I'd noticed that the women here didn't play around with their appearance. In the month I'd been here, I'd seen women of all shapes, sizes, and nationalities and hadn't come across a lemon yet. Of course, I only looked briefly because I wasn't on that, but damn, Jagoda Bay had to be heaven for niggas. Being from Memphis and then moving to the A, I wasn't new to bad bitches, but damn, Jagoda Bay was different, and so far, miss lady was leading the fucking pack.

She had a beauty mark near the outer corner of her left eye and a birthmark on the same side near her chin. Both were the kind she would've had to work around not to cover because whenever Tuscany did her makeup routine, all her markings and moles disappeared. I wasn't the type of nigga that hated makeup—I actually loved that shit. Anything that enhanced a woman and made them even more beautiful, I was down for. But then again, I was biased because I'd grown up with a sister and had sat on FaceTime way too many times while Tuscany *beat her face*, even in adulthood.

"Excuse me? Could you leave?" Her mouth was saying for me to get the fuck out of her face, but the way her taut nipples were poking through the thin fabric of her dress said another.

Slouching in my chair, I licked my lips. "Nah."

The frown on her pretty face deepened, and even under her heavy makeup, I could see her cheeks redden. She was flushed, and I was happy to see it. With the way she had my dick fighting for his motherfucking life in my jeans, she ought to feel something.

Her eyes scanned the restaurant. She was looking for security, the manager, a waitress, hell, a patron would do if they could get me away from this table. But that shit would be in vain. Wasn't a soul in the restaurant that could go toe to toe with me, and I didn't need the heat tucked in my pants to prove that point. I was like that and dared a nigga to try me.

"No?"

Leaning back further in my seat, I eased my arm slightly over the backrest, making myself comfortable, and looked into her dark eyes. I wouldn't repeat myself, but she'd understood the message by the way I relaxed into the chair.

"I have a date that's showing up soon."

Holding my phone up, I displayed the time since my wrist was bare. Thinking about my watches I'd left at the crib back in the A before I got locked up, I started to cuss. Instead, I looked at the fine ass in front of me. "That nigga shouldn't be showin' up at all if he's ten minutes late, and if he did, you should make him pay you for your wasted time and get the fuck outta dodge, my baby."

"Your baby?"

I nodded.

A chuckle escaped her lips. Her eyes roamed as far as she could see, and mine did the same. A comfortable silence blanketed us even though the restaurant was buzzing with quiet conversations and a live singer playing the piano somewhere in the distance. Her pink tongue swept over her lips, and she used her hand to toss her long-ass braids over her shoulder. "He sent you, didn't he?"

"He did."

"Fuuuuuck!" she silently cursed. When her hand pounded the table in a mini-crashout, I was no more good. She all but groaned, continuing her tantrum. "Ohmyfuckinggod! I'm never getting in the circle."

"The circle?"

"Fuck, fuck, fuck! I said he wasn't doing enough, and then as soon as I put all that aside to see where this went, he sends his fucking store runner."

I sat up so fast in my seat, my back popped as I interjected, "Hold up now, my baby. The store runner?"

She glared at me as if I were the one who had offended her. When her glare didn't faze or illicit a response from me, she answered, "The flunkie, store runner, do boy... whatever it is they call your type these days. That's no disrespect to you because, I'm sure you don't give a damn what the loser bitch that got stood up thinks. I'm just... I apologize. I didn't mean to offend you."

Holding my hands up, I sat back in my seat. "None taken, my baby."

She began rubbing her temples as her elbows rested on top of the white-clothed table. She was doing that thing again, where she quietly cursed to herself, and it took everything in me not to laugh. Although she'd put a title on me that I've never worn and never would, I didn't want to add insult to injury by embarrassing her and laughing in her face.

After a few minutes, she stopped rubbing her temples with her milky-white manicured, oval-shaped nails, which had an assortment of gold rings decorating her fingers, and sighed. When I saw her gather her bag, I sat back up.

"I'm so sorry about this. Again, I meant no offense. I just thought that I would—"

"Be gettin' in the circle?" I threw her words back at her.

She squinted her eyes at me in a scolding manner. Hell, she was the one who'd said it; I was just repeating it.

"Yeah. That. Forget you even heard that. Enjoy a meal on me." She reached into her purse, and I didn't know what she thought this was, but I reached over and covered her hands with mine. I didn't know if it was the linen from the table, but the zap had us both flinching on impact.

"My bad," I apologized for shocking her. "But Shio had some shit that came up and sent me in his place. There's no reason for you to waste a perfect-ass outfit for nuttin'. Have a steak witcha boy, and a few of them fruity-ass lime drinks y'all women like to toss back."

She squinted her eyes again. "You mean Lemon Drops?"

"Yeah, them. Have as many of those as you can take down. But my treat... I appreciate your *generosity*, but I think I can scrape up enough to feed us both."

She ran her hand down her braids again while scanning the restaurant.

My eyes couldn't help but to go back to her cleavage. Her shit was just sitting so perfectly. I could tell that she was about to turn me down, so I spoke up again. "Aye. Whatchu got to lose?"

"Hunh?"

"Havin' dinner with me. Whatchu got to lose from it?"

"Time. I have work to do that I put off for this date."

"Cap. He planned this date last week. I was with him when he was textin' you the details. Whatever work you had to do, you either already did it or rearranged your schedule because you knew you weren't gettin' to that shit today."

Her mouth shut tight, and I knew then I had her. She wouldn't be getting her pretty ass away from me just yet. At least not before I fed her and had a conversation with her.

"Okay... you got me there. I'll stay, but under one condition..."

"What's that?" I ignored my racing heart, trying to play it cool, knowing damn well I was going to agree to whatever she tossed out as long as she would stay with me.

"You don't mind that I work here."

Confusion plagued me. I didn't know what type of work she did, and I knew I wasn't dressed for the occasion, but I was almost certain she couldn't break out a laptop over a candlelit dinner. A grin broke out over her face, showing her stark white teeth. I was a sucker for pretty teeth and pretty feet. Those two were my fucking weakness.

"I use my phone for work." She held her device up. "I'm a food vlogger. I go to different restaurants around the city and give reviews."

"So you one of dem greedy muthafuckas that be eating seventy pieces of fried chicken, lookin' like you 'bout to pass out on camera?"

Her head flew back in laughter, and when she snorted like a fucking pig, I chuckled too.

"Yeah, something like that. So I need to order more than usual. This restaurant is fancy, and people are already looking at us due to my embarrassing-ass laugh, so I won't order too much. That's why I don't mind paying. I can swipe it on my business debit card and use it as a tax write-off."

"Mane, fuck these folks. You laugh as loud as you want to. And I respect the hustle, my baby, but still, you'll never fork over some money for anything when with me. I can pay in cash and give you the receipt, though; that way, you can still write it off."

Cash was the only option, regardless of whether she needed the receipt or not. Stella had run my fucking credit to the ceiling before my brother had a block put on my social security number and a fraud alert on the one bank card and one credit card I had before going in. Shaking that sour bitch from my thoughts, I focused back on the fine-ass woman in my space.

She debated internally just as the waitress arrived.

The ball was in her court, and I locked my eyes on her as she continued to ponder. "What we doing, my baby? You gone fuck witcha boy?"

She cleared her throat and nodded. "We can stay."

I hadn't been happier since the day I got out. I ain't lying. Smiling, I picked up the menu and scanned it as she gave her order to the waiting waitress.

I hadn't been here before, but all these fancy-ass places were the same. Steak and potatoes with a green veggie were all I needed, and maybe a shot of yak.

"By the way, I'm Glow."

"Glow, hunh? Well, it's nice to meet your pretty ass, Glow. I'm Tunan."

"OH MY GOD! Those drinks were strong!"

Glow was leaning on me as I ushered her through the

restaurant. She wasn't drunk at all. She had only taken one sip from each of the Lemon Drops I ordered her. Her fucking feet were hurting, and she was wobbling in those heels and trying to pull the drunk card as an excuse to lean on a nigga. Her body was so soft and velvety that I didn't mind her invading my space.

We'd stayed at the restaurant way past closing, so we were the last to leave. Glow had shown me her social media accounts, and when I saw how much of a big deal she was, I ordered more food. When it all came out, she convinced me to put my chair beside hers while she recorded us both trying the food. I'd eaten more than she had. I didn't know if she was one of those girls who hated to eat in front of niggas, but she took a bite of everything—just enough for the camera. As soon as she cut the scene, she was done with that particular dish and ready to move on to the next one.

We left so much food on the table that it was ridiculous. Some foods she hadn't even gotten to try. Still, to be able to sit by her pretty ass all night was good enough for me. I even interacted with her audience when she cut the camera and went live. They were on a nigga bad, causing her ass to end it. She had over ten thousand people watching, and that shit was wild to me. I was glad she'd ended it because having so many people watching me gave police vibes like a motherfucker. Glow was a big-ass deal in the food reviewing world. The people loved the fuck out of her and had been sending all types of monetary gifts the whole time we were on live. I nearly got on someone's ass for putting a fucking rainbow over my head until Glow explained that it was money. The longer she was on live, the more people joined and the more money she earned. People were real-life giving strangers their money just for talking to the camera. However, I couldn't even blame them; she was worth watching and tricking on.

Fine ass.

"You didn't valet?" She looked at the valent tenant, who was leaning against the podium, scrolling his phone.

"Nah. Come on."

Without another word, I scooped her up in my arms, and a yelp squealed from her throat. She placed her hand on her ass so her panties wouldn't show since she was wearing a dress as I carried her further into the parking lot. She was heavier than she looked, and I liked that shit. I benched more than Glow, so I was able to cradle her in my arms with ease. Her free arm went around my neck, and her perfume danced up my nostrils as I carried her to my car.

When we got to my whip, I bent down and opened the door to place her inside, not wanting her pretty ass feet to hit the ground. The door cracked open, and even though my car fit the description of who she thought I was—the store runner— she didn't act too good to be in the passenger seat in an old-ass car. She'd taken an Uber to dinner, and I knew it was because she'd had plans to go home with Shio. From the amount of martini glasses left on the table that were all full, Glow was no drinker, so the Uber was a tell-tale. I jogged around my side of the car and peeled out of the parking lot. She hadn't given me her address, and I didn't have a home of my own to take her to, so we just rode the city with no destination in mind.

"Tunan... You've been listening to me do boring food reviews all night. Tell me something about you." Her head was leaning against the peeling leather of the seat, and yet, she was as comfortable as ever. She'd kicked her heels off and had her legs folded as she watched my side profile.

"Seeing you in your element wasn't boring. Interesting, yeah. But boring? Nah. Your profession is different, but I fucks with it."

She blinked her wispy lashes, but took a beat before

responding.

You could make money in all types of ways these days. It was money in anything, you just had to find your lane and capitalize, and then scale that shit up. I'd never wanted to do anything but get money out on the streets, so I applauded folks like Glow.

"I appreciate that, Tunan. The girls are going to go crazy when they see you on my vlog. They already did the most on live." She rolled her eyes and sighed. "I can't believe you don't have any social media."

She'd made a big-ass deal when people in the comments were asking me about my social handles, and I replied that I didn't have any. It was as if that was unheard of, but it just showed that Glow and her followers were green as hell.

"I have an Instagram that I haven't been on in damn near a year. But I don't have a TikTok. I thought that shit was for kids and dancin'."

Glow showed me her TikTok profile once she ended the live, and I was in awe. It felt like I'd missed so much in a year because I swore that was a dancing app.

"It's come a long way from that."

"Shit, I see." I licked my lips as I looked over at her.

Fine-ass Glow.

"Okay, tell me something..."

"I mean, it ain't much to tell. Old enough, and I got a slew of fucking brothers and one sister."

"Where are you from?"

I grinned. "Atlanta."

"Lie. You sound like Glorilla a lil' bit when you talk."

"Damn! You sayin' I sound like a female?"

"Nooo! Well, I should have said Money Bagg Yo or Yo Gotti. You use the same slang as them. Plus, I've been on 901 TikTok more than I care to admit. You may have lived in Atlanta, but you're from Memphis."

Glow was a lot smarter than she looked, but I peeped that back in the restaurant. She was observant as fuck too. I didn't think I had an accent for the longest time until I moved to the A. Those niggas were forever telling me I was country as hell—like they asses could talk.

"Yeah, I'm from the M—born and raised."

"Fasho," she replied, making me laugh hard as hell.

"Naw, mane. So you trying to take my lingo now?"

"Yeah, mayne. I wish I had an accent."

"You do have an accent, my baby. Take that 'Y' up outta *mane* too. You make a nigga sound like he from the backwoods of Mississippi or some shit."

"Yeah, but it's not as cool as yours. I want to sound like a down South rapper!" she whined. "And I thought Memphis was considered Mississippi. They run into each other, don't they?"

"Nah. Dat shit totally different. We ain't on no horses or in corn fields and shit. We the trenches, my baby. Sayin' Memphis and Mississippi is the same place is the same thing as sayin' Jagoda Bay and Sparkling City are the same place. They close to each other, but the culture ain't the same. If you wanna accent like mine, spend a year or two in the M. You'll catch on."

"All that killing they do out there? I'm not trying to get robbed or worse. I'll just study the TikToks." She chuckled and swept her neatly done braids over her shoulders to rest on her chest. "You got a big family, Tunan. I know that was crowded growing up, but that's still cool. I never wanted a lot of siblings, so I can't even imagine. Tell me something else."

Crowded was an understatement, but I nodded instead of going into details. We had a two-bedroom home growing up, and were spread out everywhere so that we wouldn't be on top of one another. One of my brothers even slept in the kitchen.

We thought the nigga was going to grow up and be a chef.

"I just got out," I said, breaking the brief silence.

I wasn't ashamed of my record. Just like I wasn't ashamed of my whip. If she was going to fuck with me, she may as well have all the facts at her feet. There was no cap in my rap. My life was just that, and I was a man before anything, so lying to women was not my speed.

"How long did you do?" she asked, unfazed.

"A year. Been out a lil' over forty days."

"Was it justified? What you did... the crime... Was it justified?"

Thinking back to how I'd nursed Stella back to life and she fucked a nigga in my bed, I nodded. "Yeah, it was. I just wish I handled shit a lil' differently lookin' back."

"How does it feel to be a free man?"

"Shit feels too good, Glow."

She smiled, and my heart did that thing it shouldn't be doing. I was only a stand-in for Shio tonight, and I didn't have anything to offer a woman. Even though I was forgiving and didn't consider the opposite sex to be hell, I also wasn't in the right mindset to do anything with a woman other than what I was doing now. Hell, I was so put off by what Stella had done that I hadn't even thought about getting my dick wet until I carried my ass into the restaurant and sat across from a certain pretty food vlogger.

"I know it does. Was I your first date?" Glow asked with low eyes, even though she wasn't drunk. I, on the other hand, had a couple shots of overpriced Cognac, so I was feeling the fuck out of my liquor.

Blinking, I came to a red light that I was inclined to run, but since I was intoxicated and riding with a pistol, I didn't want the laws to get behind a nigga. I'd have to put them on a high-speed chase and scare the fuck out of little miss saditty if I acted on my impulses.

"You was," I replied while stealing a glance at her as I waited for the light to change back to green.

"I popped your cherry then."

She caught me off guard with that shit. My stomach muscles clenched as laughter erupted from my belly. I laughed so hard, I nearly took my foot off the brake. A motherfucker ain't never popped my cherry. Even when I had sex for the first time, I didn't get fucked. I did the fucking.

"You wild as hell, my baby."

"Even though I got stood up, I'm glad it was you, Tunan." Her sleek eyes were bright with innocence and amusement, almost making her look like an animated character.

Licking my lips, I jutted my chin. "Yeah, Glow. I'm glad it was me too."

She still hadn't given me an address, and I didn't know her well enough to take her back to my sister's spot. I had a good time with Glow, but my sister's husband was a retired street nigga, and her best friend was married to a cartel leader. I didn't like everybody knowing where I stayed when I had my own spot, so I wouldn't dare disrespect their space like that. I'd seen how pretty faces came around and brought down whole empires by running their mouths. If Shio had been pursuing her, I knew she was vetted because dude was on that type of shit. Still, I wasn't bringing her to Tuscany's house.

Looking over at her, she was pulling her braids down the side of her neck again and running her fingers through them. Her gold jewelry glistened, even though little light could reach the car from the moon and street lamps due to the five percent tint on my windows. Glow was mesmerizing, and even though I knew her pretty ass was still hungry, she'd been a good first date. She'd been the best date I had been on in all my dating years, but I wasn't going to tell her ass that. Bad enough she thought a nigga was the store runner.

Jagoda Bay was lit up at night, and the streets were half as full as they were during the day. Traffic out here could be hell, but I'd seen nothing worse than traffic in the A. I pulled into a parking lot area that overlooked the water that I'd seen riding with Shio a few days ago. It wasn't far from the restaurant, so it confirmed to my tipsy ass that we hadn't been riding around for that long. Shio told me this was the Bayside Shoppes area, and even though I had visited Jagoda Bay before my sentencing, I hadn't explored many parts of it before my stint. The more I rode through the city, the more I approved of my plans to settle here.

Parking in the empty lot, I adjusted my rearview mirror to see the traffic behind us before looking out at the water. Glow had pulled out her phone, and while she was momentarily distracted, I removed my gun from my waistband and tucked it under the seat. I could see she was still scrolling from the corner of my eye, so I reached for the bag of weed and backwoods I had in the middle console.

"I'ma roll up, but I ain't gone smoke if it bothers you."

Unrolling the Backwoods, I made sure it was flat before I started sprinkling Kush on top. Like its women, Jagoda Bay's weed was premium. I started to go without weed like I was doing pussy, but the first day out, my brothers had smoked me the fuck out, and I was back like I hadn't ever left. Wasn't shit wrong with smoking a little weed, anyhow. It was better to smoke than walk around ready to shoot motherfuckers that pissed you off.

Locking her screen, she slid her phone in her purse and turned her body to face me. She had her legs folded in a way that I couldn't see her panties, which I appreciated. I was already repeatedly telling my dick that this wasn't that type of party.

"You can smoke. Had I had my bundles in? Hell no." She tossed her hair back over her other shoulder.

Baguette smoked with my sister no matter what type of hair she had, but then again, Tuscany changed her styles like I did socks, so she probably didn't care if her bundles held a hint of smoke.

Licking the blunt to seal it, I nodded. "I gotcha."

"Ohhh! I love this song!"

I'd forgotten all about the radio playing since I'd removed my phone from Bluetooth. I had the car programmed to ATL's hip-hop station, but I assumed it station was a pop station out here, based on the song playing.

"Like you, like you, I find it hard to find someone like youuuu!"

Using the lighter, I ran it down the length of the blunt. "Yeah, stick to food reviews, my baby."

Glow's mouth dropped open, and she reached over and shoved my shoulder.

I nearly burned my damn thumb from trying to dodge her little pretty ass. "Watch out!" I smiled at her playfulness.

"Shut up. It's because I had those Lemon Drops. I do *not* drink. I wouldn't dare sing in front of a boy. Hopefully, I don't remember this tomorrow, or I'm going to be too embarrassed." She shook her head, but the grin on her face told me that she wasn't regretting those cracked-ass vocal chords.

"You had three sips and four bites of food. Yo' ass not drunk, and I bet you hungry as shit."

Snapping her fingers and bobbing her head, she ignored my statement. "Doja Cat be talking that talk."

"That's who that is?"

I wasn't into pop, but I could have sworn the girl she mentioned was a rapper. On this track, she was rapping and singing, and the shit sounded fire.

"Yeap. My girl. I gotta go see her in concert," she said more to herself than me.

Letting the Kush suffocate my lungs, I thought back to what she'd said before I commented on her flat-ass singing. "So that's what you on?" My voice rose an octave.

"Hmm?" She was still snapping her fingers, gold bangles just clanking and shit.

Exhaling the smoke at the same time, I replied, "Not remembering our date tonight. Is that what type of shit you on?"

She stopped snapping her fingers and grinned. Just as quickly as it appeared on her face, it vanished. The lake in front of us looked like specks of glitter were scattered across it, with the moon above. In this setting, she looked more desirable than she had back at the restaurant. It could have been the weed or the yak, but Glow was too fucking fine.

"I'm going to remember the date, Tunan. It's what I do *after* the date that I don't want to remember," she replied bashfully.

Taking a pull from the weed again, I drew so damn hard that it felt like my chest was about to cave in. I hadn't fucked anyone in a year and had no plans to do so either. That's why the mob wife shit was throwing the fuck out of me. I'd been beating my dick in the shower like I did for the last twelve months in prison, but with this soft-ass woman next to me, all of my sworn-off-women talk blew into the dust.

"Is dat rite?"

I wouldn't initiate shit. I had no plans on fucking, but who the fuck was I to deny a pretty girl a nut? If Glow was big and bad, she'd come over here and take what the fuck she wanted. But if she wanted to stay in the playground, that was cool too. I'd finish my blunt, watch her croak to a few more of these bubble gum-ass songs, and then take her home.

"I'm your first date out. So that means you haven't had...

sex."

Blowing smoke away from her face, another song came on, and I actually recognized this one. I fucked with The Neighborhood—"Sweater Weather" was every hood person's song.

"Are you askin' me or tellin' me?" I raised one eyebrow.

Gnawing on her bottom lip, she shrugged. "Asking."

"You know a nigga don't have to spend two bands at a steakhouse in order to get some pussy, right?" I chuckled at her rationale.

She shrugged again, comfortably bundled in the passenger seat.

Her thinking I had to wine and dine for pussy was cute. If I wanted some pussy, all I had to do was walk outside. I could have done that shit in the green Georgia corrections jumpsuit with the stench of the jail on my nuts, and pretty women would still flock to ride my dick. I'd fucked women for nothing. Just breathing has gotten me pussy. Still, I answered her truthfully.

"But, nah, my baby. I'm chilling. I haven't had sex," I admitted.

Again, it could have been the weed, but it looked like she had visibly relaxed. Licking her lips, she lifted in her seat.

"Glow..." Her name came out more guttural than I intended it to.

"Tunan."

"If you bring yo' pretty ass over here, I'm not fuckin' you like you think I am."

Confusion sat on her pretty-ass face.

My little baby green as hell.

"I'm fresh out the pen, my baby. All that quick pumping and missionary shit that I'm sure you used to ain't gone fly 'round here. I haven't fucked in *a year*. I'm giving out nuttin' but hard dick. Ain't shit gone be pretty 'bout it if I get up in it tonight."

She could do with that information as she pleases. I expected her to sit her fine ass back, sing, and vibe, but Glow wasn't as *good* as I thought she was. She hoisted her knee over the center console, giving me a glimpse of her nude silk thong. Once she was seated on my lap, my dick was fighting against my jeans again, and I was blowing smoke in her face.

"I haven't fucked in two. Luckily, for you, I don't do *pretty* in that context."

I highly fucking doubted that. I knew that even her sex was pretty, and with the way her arousal was smelling, even that shit was pretty. I meant what I said. If she wanted it, she could take it, so I lifted the middle console. There was an unopened box of Magnums in it that I prayed wasn't expired. I'd been with Stella for those short months, but I hadn't let my promiscuous ways go for her. I kept some rubbers because I wasn't running in shit raw—not Stella or them whores.

Handing her the box, I checked the surroundings one more time before letting the seat all the way back. The way her chest was rising and falling, and how she was holding the condoms like it was a foreign object, was almost comical. Still, I kept my cool because now I was horny and high as fuck.

Pulling from the blunt again, I waited to see if she was really about it. After another few seconds, I hit he blunt and reached for the box. "We ain't gotta do this shit, Glow. I'm just enjoying your company, my baby. You can keep your spot right here, though. I fucks with the view."

And I did. I was able to get a front row seat to her cleavage and that luminous shit she had on her skin. Her braids cascaded down each side of her neck and landed on my jeans. I hadn't realized they were that long.

"I'm horny, Tunan."

Those three words. Those three fucking words had me

switching mindsets immediately. Ashing the blunt in the tray, I grabbed the hand sanitizer and doused my hand before rubbing the liquid all over both. When they were dry, I pulled her panties aside, and her bald, yellow, glistening pussy stared back at me.

Using my thumb, I circled her clit, and her body shuddered as she tossed her head back. Her pussy, like the rest of her, was pretty. Clean, waxed, and fat—even though she was petite. She had a whole moose knuckle in her panties, and this mother-fucker was juicy too.

She dropped the box of condoms on my chest, and using my free hand and teeth, I opened the box and pulled a condom out. Not missing a beat from stimulating her, I pulled my dick out, sheathed it, and let it smack the side of her thigh. She still had her face toward the ceiling and was growing wetter by the second. I didn't think I'd end this stand-in date buried in pussy, but here we were.

"Glow, look at me, my baby."

Her body shook again, but not from an orgasm because I hadn't taken her there yet. She was shaking from the sheer pleasure produced by my thumb. When her eyes met mine, she looked so fucking sexy that I had to look away so I wouldn't bust.

"Touch it. Is it too much for you, my baby?"

Her eyes traveled down as her small hands grabbed my dick, and that shit felt better than I thought it would. I could feel everything, including the cool metal from the gold rings on her finger. Her eyes bulged as she motioned up and down my length. I was blessed but knew that all women's tolerance levels were different. I'd had women who passed up on me because of my length, and others who accepted the challenge. Glow not fucking in two years would definitely pose a challenge for her, not me.

"It is... b...but, maybe you can get on top?"

This car wasn't made for shit like this, but my dick was out and eager, so I would make it work. Grabbing her waist, I slid us to the backseat, nearly breaking my fucking arm, and flipped us around. I was still too damn tall for this shit, but I was going to make it work.

As she lay on the back seat, she slid her dress off her body, and when it reached her thighs, I assisted her in removing it. Her panties were next to go. I was fully clothed, and here she was ass naked. Her pussy was soaking and looked better than anything we had on the table back at the restaurant. But I didn't know her like that, so I wasn't eating shit no matter how bad my mouth watered for me to.

Hooking her thighs in my arms, I placed my dick at her opening. Tucking my lip in my mouth, I eased inside of her. "Fuck."

She was tight. Virgin fucking tight, but with the way she was taking it, I knew she'd been broken off before.

"Oh God!" she moaned out.

Before I could even get all of my inches in, she was shaking and coming all over my dick. That shit was an ego boost like a motherfucker. I hadn't fucked in a year, and all I had to do was slide the dick in, and she was nutting up.

"Tunnnnaaaannnn!"

"Take dis dick, my baby." I wasn't a talker during sex, but I needed her to keep doing everything she was doing.

Once my dick was snugged inside fully, I had to pause and catch my fucking breath. The pussy had knocked the fucking wind out of me. Even behind a rubber, Glow had the best pussy I'd been inside of, and it wasn't no prison talk or shit like that. Her pussy was snug, wet, warm, and deep. It was so fucking deep for her to be so little that if I wasn't in it, I would have thought I'd dreamt this shit. But I'd promised a fuck, so that's what the fuck I was going to do. Glow and I didn't know each other, so romance was out the window. She was horny, so I was going to give her pretty ass what she asked for.

Pulling out, I rammed back in, and Glow lifted her whole body from the seat. Her arms went around my neck as my chain brushed her face. Leaning in, she latched onto my ear, and then she started sucking on that shit.

A moan escaped my lips. That shit felt so fucking good, all I could do was increase the pacing. The car rocked as I bottomed her pussy out while our moans mixed in with the bullshit playing on the radio.

"Ummmmmmm! This feels so gooooood, Tunan!"

It felt good to her, but heavenly as fuck to me. Glow had gone from sucking on my ear to my neck, and I knew by the time she was done, I'd be marked up like a vampire's victim. I had never in my life had a fucking hickey, but I let her rock. Good pussy and good vibes got you your way with me. She could have whatever and do whatever as long as she let me keep drilling her ass.

I felt the electricity of her touch the same way we did when we first touched at the restaurant. My heart thumped ecstatically as she made my body feel the fucking best it ever had. I wanted to kiss her, wanted to let her know that her pussy was the best and that I'd go to sleep in this shit every day and wake up in it if she let me, but the only thing I did was continue to fuck her and grunt occasionally.

Her pussy got wetter, and my balls tightened more. Fucking Stella. Had it not been for her conniving ass, I could have really turned Glow up in this bitch. But I had to protect myself and not just my dick. I wasn't putting my mouth on a woman, no matter how pretty she was, until I knew more about her. And right now, I have no interest in knowing shit about anyone who wasn't Benjamin. But dick? Dick, I could give her, and with the way she had this Super Soaker between her thighs, she could get it over and over again.

Glow had sucked on every part of my neck, leaving behind sticky wetness. She tried to push up, but the constricted space and the door kept her in place.

"Not you tryna run from the store runner. Take this dick, Glow. You horny, right?"

"Ye... Yeaaaaassssss! Fuuuuck, yesssss!"

Her back lifted again, jutting her chin upwards. She looked so damn sexy that I couldn't help but lower myself and nibble on it. Keeping her chin in my mouth, I increased my speed until my whole body rushed and tingled as hers did the same.

"Fuuuuuck."

Pulling out, I snatched the condom off and spat warm, milky nut into my hand. The shit was never-ending, so some spilled off onto Glow's legs and on the seat. Looking up, she was watching me while catching her breath, and being freshly fucked looked so good on her. Using her right arm, she covered her breasts as if I hadn't already seen them.

Cute, my baby.

Taking my shirt off but keeping my wife beater in place, I wiped in between her legs first, and then cleaned my nut. Once the seat was dry and my hands were free of "my kids," I sat back on the seat to catch my breath. Leaning my head back, I closed my eyes as I tried to steady my heartbeat and my breathing. First month out pussy had hit so fucking different that I was glad I hadn't fucked any of them run-through-ass COs.

Hearing the clanking of her bangles, I turned to see Glow sliding in her dress. She didn't have one fucking roll in her back. Everything about this woman was perfection, even her wet, tight-ass pussy.

Then, it dawned on me.

I'd fucked my brother's potential wife. Shio had been nothing but welcoming, and even though I hadn't met with Don yet, my father's son had changed my life in a month's time. To repay the nigga back, I fucked his official ticket in. But, damn. He knew better than to send a fucking savage to his dinner table. Because, regardless of whose table I was pulling up to, I was going to eat.

CHAPTER 6
SHIO CUPPACIO

eep Beep Beep

    Blindly reaching for my phone, I hit the snooze button and stretched my limbs. As I sat up in bed, the cream silk sheets gathered at my waist. As I rubbed the sleep out of my eyes, I was hit with the smell of heat and tainted air, reminding me that I wasn't in Jagoda Bay anymore.

My thudding bladder led me from the bed, across the cool marble floors, to the toilet. I hit the light on my way inside, and the Dove body wash on the side of the garden-style tub was an indication that I'd taken a long, hot bath hours ago.

Late last night, I arrived in the beautiful land of Mexico City. Even in the dark, the streets reeked of culture. Spices filled the air from the street hustlers, and bold, bright colors were everywhere I looked. This land was filled with history. If I'd had the time, I would have checked out a few of the many museums, visited at least one of the cathedrals, and made my way to Teotihuacán to walk the land that holds the Pyramid of the Sun and the Pyramid of the Moon. They were just as fascinating as the land they were built on, since the pyramids were used for rituals, offerings, and sacrifices. I knew the energy, along with the architecture, was worth experiencing.

There was so much to do here, and the shopping was like no other. I don't know what the fuck they had going on in the States, but Mexico's malls were on steroids. All of them were luxurious and filled with shit you couldn't get back home, no matter how much paper you had. I wasn't here for all that, though. And had I been, I would have preferred something soft by my side, so I could drop some bread on her while showing her a new world. That shit wasn't an option, for now.

Although I was clear across the country, my routine was still one that I had to abide by. After shaking the piss from my dick, I stood at the his-and-hers sink. Looking to the right of me, I saw no feminine products taking up space on the counter, which had me biting down on my molars. I'd stood my date up, but hopefully Tunan was able to show her a good time. She deserved that much, and he needed to get out as well. He'd been spending all his time with his other siblings and me, so some interaction with someone who didn't share the same blood as him would do him some good.

The electric toothbrush tickled my gums as it worked its magic to remove any plaque that may have formed overnight. After spitting the toothpaste residue mixed with my saliva into the running water, I flossed, washed my face, added moisturizer, and then sunscreen. Folks thought that since we were black, we didn't need protecting from the sun. I thought that too at one point until my dermatologist put me on a few years ago. Now, I incorporate it into my daily skincare routine, and I look forward to seeing the results over the next few years.

Seafoam green Nike running shorts that stopped at my upper thigh, matching Nike sneakers, and my Apple Watch were all I took with me out the door. The ride from the elevator to the lobby was a short one, and as soon as I made my way through the semi-busy lobby, my heart accelerated. Ignoring lusty looks from employees and lodgers alike, I removed my Nike top and sprinted from the pavement to the trail.

Mexico City was in its rainy season. With its location being in a valley and surrounded by nothing but mountains, the terrain traps moisture, creating cooler environments that lead to showers. Of all the seasons, it rained most of spring, all of summer, and part of fall. Today, though, Mother Nature must've been on my side because it was hotter than a bitch, and the sun was blazing high in the sky with not a cloud in sight. Trees covering the trail would shield me from the sun, but a nigga could use a nice breeze during my run.

A five-mile trek was my normal day-to-day routine, but today I was doubling it. Don had me clear across the fucking world on a suicide mission, and my brain had been putting in overtime, coming up with a million ways this shit could go bad. Exercise and what I put into my body played a major role in how my day-to-day went. I was hoping that if I knocked out my run early, everything would go smoothly.

I'd been preaching to my cousins about finding better routines to keep their health in tip-top shape. We, as humans, consume so much bullshit. The food and energy of the world were deteriorating us, and we were failing to realize how big of an impact they both had on speeding up the rate of our deaths. That's why, when it came to problems, I tried my best to solve them instead of letting that shit linger and boil into a pot of mess. Holding feelings and opinions hostage created nothing but quiet frustration, and I ain't have time for that. If people had an issue, their best bet would be to solve it on their own before fucking up somebody else's day.

As for food, I loved carbs and fried foods just as much as the next person. I just knew how much of the shit to consume. During the holidays, I had one plate and a few desserts and left it at that. I ate until I was satisfied—not stuffed—and protein was a huge part of my diet. Above all, I drank my water and minded my fucking business unless it involved a Cuppacio.

Instead of letting my mind wander off into places that would take an additional ten miles to clear out, I focused on the empty path ahead of me. As sweat poured from my pores, I mentally recanted my personal to-do list a few more times.

"Time to check off one of these shits. Fucking Mexico City, let's do this."

"So, Demise Rinaldi can send *one* of his henchmen but can't come face me himself?"

METAL CLINKED against the ceramic plates as Ines's family stuffed their faces. He sat at the head of the table with his wife at the far end, who had yet to wipe the snarl off her face. Three of his oldest children, all boys, sat on the left side of the table, and three of his youngest children, again all boys, sat on the right side. I was seated on the side with the younger children, but I didn't give a fuck as long as I could see every door in the room. The younger children—all of whom were Hispanic like their parents—either had their heads in a tablet or a phone. It wasn't much different on the left side. They, too, were all occupied with their electronic devices, looking like they wanted to be anywhere but here. Ines's wife, Maura, hadn't spoken up once about her children having distractions at the dinner table. She only smiled at them when her gaze landed on any of the six, but when she cut her eyes to me, her lips instantly went upside down again. It was such a shame, too, with her being a beautiful woman. Had she known her filler shifted every time she frowned, she might have thought twice about that.

Ines Ledesma waited impatiently for me to answer. But he would be waiting until his food got cold because I had no intention of answering anything rhetorical. With the way his belly was protruding, he needed to push back from the plate any fucking way. I had a wellness and fitness plan that would have him in top shape in no time, especially since he was slim everywhere else except his midsection.

"Henchmen are errand boys now?" His Mexico City accent was so thick that his English ran all together.

My ear perked up at the screeching sound of his wife's laughter. Instead of returning the scowl she'd been tossing me all evening, I stared straight ahead at the empty chair in front of me. The older children hadn't given the vacant chair a second glance. The house was fully staffed with not only guards at every entrance, but also three strategically placed in the dining room, where we were attempting to have dinner. The chair wouldn't have been left there if it were meant to be empty. I could tell with the way the staff had been scrubbing the nonexistent dust upon entry that Cruella here liked for everything to be perfect. The inside of the mansion was just as colorful as one would expect from a rich Hispanic family. The casita was beautiful, but that's all it was. The energy was fucked up in the motherfucker, and I was about ready to get the fuck on.

"Are we expecting another guest?" I asked no one in particular.

A snort sounded from Maura Ledesma, making her husband shift his dark eyes from me to her. Had his orbs been a bullet, his wife would have been shot dead. Shifting in her chair was an indicator that she was now uncomfortable and knew she'd stepped out of line. Instead of backing down, she picked up her champagne flute, placed it to her burgundy-hued lips, and took a sip, leaving the rim stained.

For her to be so snooty, you'd think she had access to a professional makeup artist who would've told her the lip color choice was a bust. The shit did nothing for her complexion, making her look like she'd been left in the tanning bed two hours longer than needed. She resembled a tortilla that had been dipped in birria consomé.

The child next to me placed his iPad down and turned in his seat to face me. Keeping my posture toward the seat across from me, I turned my neck and looked down at the child who looked much like his father. In fact, all the children, young and old, looked like either Ines, Maura, or a combination of the two. There were no outliers among the bunch.

The child gazed at me curiously as if he'd just noticed me for the first time. Like the rest of his younger siblings, he was in khaki Chino pants, a white linen shirt, and loafers. The older sons looked as if they were headed to the club after this. Each of them was in black with gold chains around their necks. Ines was in a suit, and his wife complimented him in a long, flowy blue dress.

"Your skin. It's... really dark."

"It is," I answered without offense.

I've been dark all my life, and I love every bit of it. My mother taught me the importance of both of her heritages. She was half Melanesian and half Black American, and knew of her family's history in the Solomon Islands and in America. She and a full-blooded Italian man produced a Black-ass nigga, and I wouldn't have that shit any other way. Ezio can have that light-skinned, mixed-boy, pretty-eye shit. I cherish being Black.

"Are you African or some type of black or something?"

The older Ledesmas doubled over in laughter as if they were the same age as the younger ones instead of grown-ass men. My eyes burning through the three of them had their asses tightening right on up and clearing their throats. Ines shifted his gaze to his oldest children and, seeing how their heads were now back buried in the phones, looking like they didn't want any fucking smoke, he frowned.

"I'm not being... racist. Your surname is Italian. But you're so dark... I'm sorry." He picked up his iPad, his brown skin flushing red. Placing my hand on the iPad, I pressed it back into the table.

"It's okay to ask questions. To answer yours, I am Black. My skin is dark because of the Melanesian blood flowing through my veins. I had an Italian father, but I don't identify myself as such."

"I... identify?"

With the way the child was constantly stumbling over his words, I could tell he struggled with comprehending English as a native Spanish speaker. The entire family was fluent in English, but that didn't mean their English vocabulary was also adequate. They were whispering amongst themselves ever so often as to hide the fact that their English vocabulary was limited.

"Yes, identify. The fact of being who or what a person is. I'm a Black man. I identify as Black."

The child smiled. "I understand now. Thank you."

"You're welcome. Now, who is that seat for?"

The child picked up his fork and stuffed the steak inside his mouth. "My sister."

"Shio Cuppacio. Tell me... Why should I consider doing business with Demise when he won't even show his face? Last I checked, you're not even officially a part of his organization. You have yet to secure a wife."

"So, you've done your research..." I stated, slowly.

Even though I knew he had, my pointing out the obvious was to make his ass feel stupid for trying to insult me by calling me a fucking henchman. I was no one's errand boy.

"I've done a little." Ines picked up his glass of Cognac and took a sip. "You've done yours?"

Nodding, I twisted the ring on my middle finger using my thumb. My hands were folded in my lap, shielded by the fancy tablecloth.

"So tell me... ehhh... something that chu've learned." His thick accent gave way to amusement.

"I know that you shouldn't be eating steak with the blood pressure and cholesterol numbers you have. I know you can benefit from cleaning your gut out. I know that you in here questioning me, but you're in so much shit with the Feds and a neighboring cartel, and before shit comes crashing down onto you, you're scrambling to see who or where your sons, younger and older, can be placed so that they are protected instead of being sold off, killed, or made into someone's Mexican lover. I heard y'all be into castrating muhfuckas down here. But that's just some shit I heard, not a fact from my research. I know you need Don, and since you need him, *Demise* isn't a name you're granted to address him by. He's Don to you... to all y'all." I eyed each of the sons who nodded. I didn't bother looking at their mother because she would be on to the next rich Mexican if Ines didn't make it out of his jam.

Ines took another sip of his Cognac while his wife stood to her feet, chair hitting the mosaic tile with a thud. When her small fist came down on the table, knocking my bottled water over I'd yet to open, I simply sat it up.

"You're going to let him talk to you like this? In our home, telling lies? Guards, kill him! Now!"

"Madre—" one of the older boys attempted to speak up.

"Shut the fuck up! Now you want to speak up?" Maura whipped her head around, wondering why the guards hadn't moved an inch.

Ines held his hand up. "Maura, have a seat."

"Ugggh!" She obeyed her husband and downed her whole glass of bubbly.

"Shio. I'm flattered that you've done your duties to study me, but I'm afraid your facts aren't all facts. I have the Feds under control. The cartel, though... that one is tricky. I would like my sons to find a good place to continue life, and yes, the Rinaldi Mafia is one of a few I'm considering. All of my children have already established dual citizenship with America which is why I requested to meet with De—Don.

"Even though I love my children dearly, the trade-off of my resources is *far* more valuable than beings who came from my sperm. I'm not ready to hand over the keys to step down since they've become of age. I'd rather they be placed somewhere under strong leadership where they could live respectable lives. If and when I'm ready to hand over my organization, my wife and

I can make more children." He winked at Maura. Her anger had diminished, and now, she was blushing.

I waited for the sons to speak up, but crickets. Their father had just told me their lives weren't worth shit to him and that he wanted them far away from him so they didn't challenge his position, and they were all sitting here like fucking ducks. There was no way they'd stand a chance with us. Them Rinaldi niggas didn't have no fucking hearts, and us Cuppacio weren't any better.

"Well, it's settled then. Good luck with your troubles. I'll let Don know of your wishes." I straightened my tie to stand.

Ines Ledesma was playing games. His request didn't hardly make any sense. He wanted his sons to join another organization because he didn't want to kill them if they threatened his position. That was straight-up bullshit. He was being run out of his position in Mexico, and he didn't want his sons to become someone's bitch. I'd bet my next nut on that shit. They were already bitch-made, so the transition wouldn't be a hard task if shit collapsed before Ines could pawn them off on another organization.

Just as I went to stand, a loud scream erupted, followed by the clinking of heels. No one flinched, but I was on guard.

"¿Estás jodidamente seria en este momento?" (Are you fucking serious?) a feminine voice sounded off before we could see her.

A few more clicks of her heels against the marble floors, and she was now standing in the room. Taken aback by the woman in front of me, I settled back in my seat because I needed to see what this shit was about before I made my departure.

The only person who had his attention on her, besides me, was Ines. Her hair was pressed down her back and parted in the middle, and I was sure that if she turned around, it would sweep the top of her ass. Like the older sons, she was dressed as if she was headed to the club or had just come in from a day party, even though it was very early in the evening. The olive-colored two-piece set showcased every curve on her body. The top went around her neck, and the gold circle in the middle of the shirt gave a peek of her cleavage. Her breasts were perky, and her nipples were hardened. The shirt only covered three-fourths of her stomach, showing her sculpted abdomen.

The matching skirt slightly hung off her slim waist, more than likely due to her running inside the house like a madwoman. Her skin was just as dark as mine, making it hard for me to assess if she was a blood relative of the Ledesmas. She didn't look like she fit in, but the way she was screaming at these people had me thinking she had some rank in this mansion.

"Hola mi hermosa hija. ¿Cuál es el problema? (Hello, my beautiful daughter. What seems to be the problem?) Ines asked.

Daughter, huh? I thought to myself.

His daughter was an Afro-Mexican. I would have never fucking guessed this would be a scenario. Unlike with his other children, there was so much love in his eyes as he looked at and spoke to this woman. Now it made sense as to why he wanted his sons to join the Rinaldi Cartel. This nigga loved Black people!

¡Esta zorra me volvió a cortar la tarjeta! ¿Sabes lo vergonzoso que es? (This bitch cut off my credit card again! You know how embarrassing that shit is?) The beauty with the potty mouth pointed at Maura, who did nothing but hide her smirk behind a fresh glass of champagne.

"*Hija...* (Daughter), Ines sighed.

Clack

She stomped her heeled foot, and from her stance, I was assuming it was the right one. I was surprised the gold strappy heel hadn't broken with that stomp.

¡La zorra de tu esposa me está jodiendo otra vez! ¿Por qué? ¡Me mantengo alejado de ella! ¡Apenas estoy en casa! (Your bitch of a wife is fucking with me again! Why? I stay out of her way! I'm hardly home!)

Ines cleared his throat, smoothed his hand down his tie, and pushed out a heavy exhale again. This girl—his baby girl —was a beautiful, hot-ass mess. I could tell she had his ass by the balls.

"*Hija, estoy en una reunión muy importante. Esto tendrá que esperar. Siéntate. Cena con nosotros. Soy Shio Cuppacio.*" (Daughter. I'm in a meeting. A very important one. This will have to wait until later. Have a seat. Have dinner with us. This is Shio Cuppacio.)

Her dark brown eyes shifted to me, and that seemed to make her even madder. The frown on her pretty face deepened, and she stomped her fucking foot again while shouting, "*¡Que* *le den a este tipo! ¡Solo quiero que me devuelvan la tarjeta de crédito! ¡Me da igual esta reunión!"* (Fuck this guy! I just want my credit card turned back on! I couldn't care less about this meeting!)

Ines chuckled and reached into his pocket. I watched as he fished for a credit card and, instead of being satisfied that she'd gotten her way, she was still fuming like a brat.

"Puedes quedarte con mi tarjeta. Me has avergonzado, hija. Esto pudo haber esperado." (You can have my card. You have embarrassed me, daughter. This could have waited.)

Her focus went from her father to me. She licked her nude, glossed lips and spoke in her native language right at me.

"Me importa un bledo este americano. Que me bese el culo. Ahora, tarjeta, por favor." (I don't give a fuck about this American. He can kiss my ass. Now, card, please!)

Ines chuckled again, but with a red face as he held out his card. She switched to her father, but she had to pass me before she got to him. Looking her straight in the eyes, she paused in her stride.

"No tienes por qué importarte un comino, pero el negocio que tu padre y yo llevamos determinará si alguna vez podrás volver a usar alguna de sus tarjetas. Ahora siéntate y ven a cenar con nosotros antes de que cumpla tu oferta y te bese el trasero. Aunque no va a salir como quieres." (You don't have to give a fuck about me, but the business your father and I are conducting will determine if you'll ever be able to swipe one of his cards again. Now... sit the fuck down and join us for dinner before I make good on your offer and kiss your ass. Except it's not going to go the way you want it to go.)

Her chest inflated as her breathing heightened. All eyes were on us.

"O tal vez sucederá como quieres." (Or maybe... it will go the way *you* want it to go.)

I stated the last sentence lowly so that she and I were the only ones to hear it.

I could feel the heat radiating off her body, and although her hair smelled like hookah smoke, the oils and perfumes she used on her dark skin went well with the spicy attitude she came in here with.

Ines held out the card, and instead of taking it, she stomped to her seat and plopped down in it. No sooner than she was seated, the maid sprang into action. She turned the maid down politely when she offered up a plate, even though she was still shooting daggers at me. I didn't give a fuck, though. I didn't fuck with disrespect on any level.

"You speak fluent Spanish."

Only then did I turn my gaze from the spoiled one to her father. "You didn't find that out during your research?' I taunted.

"*Al igual que no descubriste que tenía una hija durante tu investigación. Supongo que todos tenemos nuestros secretos.*" (Just like you didn't find out I had a daughter during your research. I guess we all have our secrets.)

Rubbing my hand down my chin, I shifted my eyes from his daughter, who was all in our conversation, to the older kids, who were now tuned in too.

"*¿Secretos o debilidades?*" (Secrets or weaknesses?)

"*¿Que hables español con fluidez es una debilidad?*" (You being fluent in Spanish is a weakness?) His thick brow rose.

"Now that you're privy to it, yes."

"You're bilingual. Impressive."

"I'm not bilingual."

Ines stared me down, and I returned the jester before continuing with my leave. "I'm going to leave now. You folks enjoy your dinner."

I pushed the plate that I hadn't touched in front of spoiled ass. *"Comer.* (Eat)"

With a scowl on her face, she picked up the steak and chomped into it using her fingers. Juice dripped down her chin and into her cleavage.

"Fucking whore," one of the older brothers whispered before snickering.

Another look from me had him shutting up. "Guard," I spoke.

Confusion plagued Ines and Maura's faces.

"Ponle la pistola en la cabeza. (Put the gun to his head.)"

Without hesitation, one of the three guards marched forward and placed the gun on the back of Ines' son's head.

"What the fuck is this?" Ines roared.

"This is me not taking kindly to disrespect. You know my name, but you don't know *who* the fuck I am, Ines. Your son has three seconds to apologize, or the maids won't be cleaning just shells of lobster and half-eaten, overcooked steak from the table. One..."

"Cortez. Apologize to your sister."

"I'm sorry!" he immediately blurted out. The boy had probably pissed himself.

Nodding, the guard went right back to his post. This time, I stood for real. "Again, I'll tell Don your wishes."

I took one last look at the family, letting my eyes linger on the one devouring the steak with amusement in her eyes, and took my leave. I didn't get ten steps down the hall before I heard Ines running after me.

"Wait! Shio!"

He grabbed my shoulder, and that was the wrong move because I had my pistol underneath his chin before his next breath.

His hands went up with a smirk. "I see why he sent you now."

"What the fuck do you want, Ines?"

This pointless-ass dinner had gone on far too long, and I was ready to get the fuck back to the US. I had church on Sunday, and I had no plans on missing it.

"Please! Just hear me out!"

Shoving the gun further into his chin, I prompted him to speak.

"Take my daughter."

"Nigga, what? If I don't want your bitch-made-ass sons coming nowhere near my people, why in *the fuck* you think I want your daughter?"

"No, no... you have me all wrong. I'm not offering her up. I would like you to just take her and help her. She is the key to me ending this war with the Rodríguez Cartel. She is to marry his eldest son. However, she isn't quite ready to be a wife.

"Listen, she hears you. She did what you said back there. She's never done that before. I love my baby girl with my whole heart. She's my prized possession. It pains me to hand her over, but I have to consider it all for the sake of this organization. You see her. She's as stubborn and spoiled as she is beautiful. I just want you to mold her for me. I will have no say and stay out of the matters, if you agree. I want her to be able to get along well once she fulfills her duty. Her current ways will get her killed. You understand?"

"I'm not in the business of raising bitches. Do I look like a debutant academy?"

"Of course not. Well, at least take her to the Americas. Get her away from here for a while, while I get this all squared away. Tell Don, whatever he wants, it's his. He doesn't even have to take my sons in. I will find other placements."

I kissed my teeth. "We wasn't taking them bitch-made-ass niggas in no way."

"Do this for me, and I'll owe you a favor. I'll owe you and

Don a favor. Whatever Don needs. Whatever you need. Granted."

I should blow his head from his ass.

"*Papá, ¡no me voy a América! ¿Estás loco?*" (Daddy. I'm not going to America! Are you crazy?)

He jumped at the sound of her voice. Giving her one last look, he smiled before looking back at me. "Take her with you!"

"*¡Ni hablar! ¡No voy con él! ¿Estás sordo?*" (Hell no! I'm not going with him! Are you deaf?)

"Jagoda Bay. That's where you live now, right? Take her."

"NO—" She went to speak, but stopped.

There wasn't shit for me to say, so I left their casita. Pulling my phone out, I texted the pilot. By the time I made it back to the hotel, he was letting me know that the wheels could be up in the air in the next hour.

God first.

Make sure the family good.

Eye them Cuppacio boys, the little and the big ones.

Build a relationship with my brother.

Get my brother rich.

Health and Wellness.

Stay on top of my mob shit.

Keep Hobo alive.

~~Get through this meeting with Ines~~.

Find a wife.

AT LEAST I had one thing scratched off the list.

CHAPTER 7
DON DEMISE RINALDI

" Is everything set for this weekend?" I asked Rut, who was at my side as we approached the building.

As we walked through the double doors that provided a shield from the lingering eyes of the soundproof conference room, I took a seat across from Matteo while Rut sat next to him. Since it was Wednesday, we weren't on official mob business, so all three of us were dressed down in street clothing. Outside the doors was a large buzz of patrons spending their illegal money in my illegal underground casino, and I loved every bit of the scenario. The Dungeon was proving to be a fucking cash cow. I started the business as another way to wash all the fucking money the mob had been generating since I became Don. Eventually, it turned into the hot spot for all the fucking who's who of the underworld. You could walk in here with your last hundred G's—because you had to at least have that amount readily available to be granted access—and come all the way up. We had more than the basic fucking crap tables and slot machines. The Dungeon was full of connections, with the most powerful people in every sector of wealth and status you could think of. If you were lucky enough, you could meet the right person who could change your life for the better, or worse.

"Yeah, Lani says it's all good, " Rut responded as he swiped at his phone screen.

He and I were homies who'd met doing hard time together. Not only were we now in business together, but the women we married were sisters. I ain't like the shit, even though it made our close-knit circle tighter. Could you imagine your homie fucking someone who was basically identical to your wife? Dasani and Daylani couldn't deny their blood relation, even if they were strangers. Off that alone, I wanted to beat his ass sometimes.

"And she got that bread I wired?"

Daylani, being the best event planner the South has ever seen, was in charge of all of our parties. The upcoming celebration was for her sister and my wife. Dasani sold soaps, candles, and shit back when she thought she was going to be a single mama before I snatched her ass up—literally. Now that she had access to more money than she knew what the fuck to do with, she'd invested it in her own perfume line. We were still in the testing stages and had narrowed her favorite fragrances down to three. She was throwing a shindig at the crib and had appointed her sister to decorate, claiming she wanted something small. I'm not sure what her definition of "small" was because she was married to the biggest, and we knew nothing about playing it small. Big pockets, big connections, big talker, big walker, big dick—just big shit all the fucking way around the table.

"Yeah, nigga, she got the bread. She was fussing too. You know how she is about her big sister. She was insulted that you paid her." Rut chuckled while rubbing his head.

"Shit, I'm insulted that she thought we weren't paying her.

All this fucking bread; it's only right we fuck with our people and keep this money circulating in the family. Daylani runs a real business. Matter fact, I'ma let it be known that anybody utilizing her services in the mob needs to pay full strength."

Rut smirked. "Understood."

Giving my right hand my attention, I watched as he typed on his phone. Matteo's expression was neutral, meaning he was in a decent mood today. I'd been dealing with his moody ass since diapers because we were cousins raised together like brothers. If that nigga was frowning, I would have just let him be. I'd learned over the years that while I caused ruckus, Teo was the one to finish it.

After waiting for his eyes to finish rolling up and down his phone, I asked, "Teo. Where that nigga, Zo?"

Usually, Matteo and Lorenzo were tied at the fucking hip. For him to not be here had me wondering if everything was good. Lorenzo was more chill than Matteo, so I knew their partnership was hot and cold, but they were a good example of something that's not supposed to work, working. If I weren't so fucking busy, I'd probably be jealous of how close they were. Growing up, Matteo and I were just as close. Now that I'm running all this shit and in charge of all these niggas, I don't have as much time as I'd like to kick it with my day ones. That nigga had never been one to kick it, though. But when Lorenzo came along, he had a change of fucking heart. Now he "kicked it" like his ass was made of shoestrings.

Matteo lifted his head from his phone, and a scowl covered his face. There was the mean-ass nigga I knew.

"At the downtown restaurant. It was his turn to do inventory."

I just knew that nigga was about to come at me by saying something smart. A lot of shit has changed in the last two years. Not only was he married and a father, but he was also a big brother now. I still couldn't believe the shit that was exposed. Reuchie's bald-headed ass had shocked us all. Auntie still wasn't talking to his ass, but she had told Matteo she wanted to meet Pearla and Patty. Matteo wasn't going for shit his daddy had to say about being Pearla's biological father. He'd fired my uncle, and because I would forever be my cousin's keeper, I went with the move. It was time for Reuchie to sit his ass down any fucking way. Growing up, the Rinaldis put the mob before fatherhood, and knowing what I know now, I didn't understand that shit. The Cuppacios were terrorizing the fuck out of our organization under my father's leadership. And even with the threatening nature between the two mobs, Reuchie's ass was over there sticking dick in a Cuppacios' wife. I couldn't make that shit work in my mind, no matter how many times I scenarized it in my head. Teo was going to have to get answers for both of us sooner or later. As for the new seventeen-year-old family member, she would want for nothing for the rest of her days.

"How my girl Pea—"

The doors busted open, and it was as if I'd spoken them niggas up. The most tolerable of the rat pack walked in, and he wasn't alone. It seemed like everywhere I turned, these mob niggas' secret babies were turning up. My pops had made Jisei, Reuchie had made Pearla, and this Shio nigga, being accompanied by a lighter version of himself, gave away that the Cuppacios were on the same type of time.

"What the fuck you niggas want?" I asked before the doors closed behind them.

I felt a brewing headache as Shio walked in like his name was the one on the fucking bills. Ignoring me, he slapped hands with everyone in the room except for me, giving me a fucking head nod. It was cool, though. I didn't like touching niggas dick beaters no way.

"Every damn day I wonder... why I didn't lay the fucking kids down along with your sperm donors. Aye, Rut... that 'no discount' rule I was just telling you about. Make sure sis taxes *the fuck* out of the Cuppacios for their weddings and showers and whatever else these cheap-ass niggas throw in the near future. Their tough asses got it. These niggas moving big bricks."

Shio took a seat adjacent to me, and his brother sat next to him. Their resemblance was uncanny. It seemed like every fucking time I looked up, there was a fucking new sibling popping up. Them old-ass mobsters sure knew how to fucking get down. They couldn't keep their dicks in their pants for shit. Not only did I have a new sister, but so did Matteo, and now Shio with a brother. I didn't know how much more of this "secret baby" shit I could take. It felt like I was living in the middle of one of those urban, ghetto novels they used to pass around the jail.

Without changing his expression, Shio said, "Had you done that shit, we would have just been born again to give your ass even more hell. You ever heard of *reincarnation*?"

Frowning at Shio's smart ass, I scoffed. "You ever heard of *I would kill your reincarnated parts,* too, muthafucka?"

"Facts," Matteo cosigned, always having my back like I had his.

Turning my neck back in Shio's direction, my face hardened. "I assume you handled *that, choir boy,* being that you sitting here next to your brother breathing. What's the word?"

Shio held eye contact; the serious-ass nigga didn't waver at all. "Yeah, them people he trying to send yo' way? That's dead. He did have a proposition, though. For me, at least."

I trusted every man in this room, with the exception of the newcomer. Shio was still earning my full trust, but because of our business dealings, the trust was there to some extent. Still,

I appreciated him for not outright telling my business in front of everyone. This business with the Ledesmas was between us. Everybody had their part to play in the mob, and this Cuppacio in front of me was stepping into the role of his perfectly.

"You handling it. Right?"

"I'm handling it," Shio confirmed.

I was able to breathe a little easier, knowing he wasn't bluffing. I was leaving Ledesma's slick ass to Shio. Had Reuchie still been on board, that would have been his job. The game wasn't ending, though, just because one of my key players was down. Since he was out indefinitely, I had to move some pieces around the chessboard to ensure nothing was forgotten or left behind. Just had to fucking pivot at the last minute, but I was confident that Shio was the man for the job.

I nodded. "Now... Back to what the fuck you niggas doing back here."

"You canceled on us. We figured we'd catch you while you're available." This new nigga shrugged while leaning back in his chair, crossing his hands at his abdomen.

He was dressed down in gym shoes, denim shorts, and a sleeveless top. Belt chains hung decoratively on the right side of his shorts, and that shit must've been some Memphis or Atlanta shit because it damn sure wasn't the Bay. I couldn't remember which city the nigga was actually from, but he'd have to calm all that extra shit down. When his lanky ass showed up in a suit that was damn near too tight and nearly too fucking short, I immediately said, "Fuck no." I'd seen them on the camera and called a flag on the play. I also wasn't in the mood to hear what their asses had to say, so I texted Shio saying I'll catch them next time. If he was going to join my organization—because I'd already known that's what he wanted, just like I'd known he'd existed the whole time—he needed his shit to be cut and sewn correctly.

According to Uncle Reuchie's made-up ass rule book, I couldn't outright deny Tunan a seat at the table. As long as he met the requirements, he was in. But I didn't have the fucking time to keep playing matchmaker with these niggas. I couldn't for the life of me understand how hard it was for a nigga to get a hoe and put a ring on her. Jagoda Bay was crawling with bitches. Hell, if they couldn't find one in this city, it was hundreds, shit thousands, of other cities to choose from. The more connections I made, the more money I made, and the more money I made, the more money I had to fucking hide and invest. Time was money, and even though I'd grown a tad bit fond of these Cuppacio niggas, I'd invested way too much time into being the fucking love doctor since our families merged. Now here they were, back like I'd set up another time to meet, running down on a nigga and shit like that could make me move faster than I was ready to.

As I stared between the two, I tried to come up with at least one good reason to say, "Fuck no." I didn't have the patience for this shit here with these untamed Cuppacios. The deeper I get in this mob shit, the more I see why my deadass daddy let his men run amok. Overseeing the niggas was worse than managing a hundred toddlers. Then, I had to do this shit all over again in a couple of years when the little Cuppacios grew up. Yeah, nah. This shit was beyond me.

"The problem with you Cuppacio niggas is, I already have a whole slew of y'all that haven't fulfilled your duties to get married. Out of four niggas, only one of you done tied the fucking knot, and that shit damn near cost me my sister. I just want to shoot all you niggas dead and be done with it, but then ya done made babies and shit, and I'll have to repeat the killings when those muthafuckas get old enough to hold a fucking gun."

I paused. These niggas always managed to get me worked

up, and my usual way of dealing with people that made me uncomfortable wouldn't work in this situation. Teaching myself how to be a boss was draining a motherfucker. Inhaling quietly to myself, I looked up at Tunan.

"I like to give folks a fair shot, pun in-fucking-tended. The way I'm feeling, though... I don't want to add another Cuppacio to my roster."

No one spoke. Rut and Matteo looked damn near uninterested. Shio dropped his head, and I knew that nigga was plotting on how to make me change my mind. I watched Tunan intently in the silence. The nigga didn't wear his feelings on his face. He kept his expression neutral and his breathing even. He was hanging onto my words—I could tell by the way his eyes stared right back into mine.

I didn't know Tunan, per se. However, I'm familiar with his people. His sister's best friend was married to my homie, Goal, and I'd seen a few of Tunan's other brothers in passing. The Payne brothers were known to be solid. I felt I still needed to feel this one out, though. He wasn't thirsty to get in. He hadn't dick-rode his way into my space or had acted hard up to join our organization. He'd been out of jail more than a month, and the guys had all met up several times since his release just to kick shit. I'd only seen him twice: once when he showed up last week on the camera, and now. That shit spoke volumes without me knowing of him and his family.

"Aite. You in."

Shio lifted his head and his expression matched Tunan's, but I could see a half-grin form on Tunan's face before he said, "Cool," with his wannabe down ass.

"Slow down, lowdown. I wasn't finished. You in *only if* you can get married in—" I held my watch up to my face to look at the time. It was two hours until midnight on a Wednesday night. "Three weeks. Well, twenty days. You passed day one since it's nearly midnight."

"What?" both brothers yelped simultaneously.

Rut and Matteo were falling out laughing at this point, but I was deadass serious.

"How the fuck am I supposed to do that shit? Plus, ain't y'all got a rule that says no divorce? Three weeks not enough time to find a quality wife."

Shio placed his hand on his brother's chest, and they shared a look before standing.

"Yeah, take y'all asses on. Make sure you lose some money on the way out. My daughter needs a new pair of earrings."

Delicate Mafia didn't need shit; I just loved talking shit. She had enough jewelry to rock a different piece for three months straight. Still, I was buying my baby some new diamonds. She could get whatever the fuck she wanted with her pretty ass.

"Three weeks is more than enough time," I said as the pair walked toward the double doors. "I found my wife in a day on my first day out, got her pregnant, and popped up when the baby was due. I kidnapped her ass and forced her into signing papers she thought was from the mailman when, in reality, it was a marriage certificate. Her marriage certificate." I chuckled at the memories that felt so long ago. "You got an advantage, nigga. You Cuppacios niggas kind of slow, so I see now I gotta put time clocks on that ass. You either get married in two weeks, or you can't sit with us."

"You did what?" Tunan had stopped walking and looked so confused at my story.

I wasn't repeating a damn thing. I said what the fuck I said, and I ain't regret shit about how I'd locked Dasani down.

Tunan sneered after realizing what I said. "Hold up... Never mind that. You just said three weeks—"

"Yeah, well asking all them fucking questions made me lose my train of thought. We can make this shit a day if you want to keep going. Oh, and make sure you niggas at my house next Friday at six for my wife's Sniff-and-Sip party. Don't be late and don't come to my shit empty-handed. Matter of fact, bring a monetary gift for Mrs. Rinaldi." I flicked my wrist to emphasize jewelry or diamonds. These niggas know I didn't play about my Childish Titties.

"You dismissing us, gave me an impossible-ass timeframe to get married, and now you inviting us to a party? What the fuck is a sniff and sip? Ion do no drugs outside of weed," Tunan said in a harsh tone.

Matteo stood up. "Nigga, what the fuck you tryna say?"

"Do we look like we play with our fucking noses, nigga? Sniff and sip. My wife is launching a fragrance line, goofy. Now, get the fuck out! I need to be attending a wedding or shown a marriage certificate in the next thirteen days. I told these niggas they had to have weddings, but since I'm a nice guy, I'm granting you the *courtesy* of going to the courthouse. Plan a real wedding eventually, though. We likes to celebrate 'round this muthafucka. See y'all selves out, and don't forget... spend big before showing up at my house, niggas. Oh, and Tunan?"

Looking fed up with my shit, he asked, "Wassup?"

"Keep yo' hands to yourself. We don't beat bitches over this way; only the pussy. Adios."

When I saw that Tunan had served time due to domestic violence, I couldn't do shit but shake my fucking head. Those damn Memphis niggas were out of control.

"Bye, Ike," Matteo called out as they finally left the room.

"Aye, yo'! You wild as fuck." Rut chuckled at our antics.

"Wild as them animals Preston likes to foster. Them niggas know I ain't wrapped too tight."

Matteo was back on his phone, typing.

"How's Pearla?" I finally asked after we were interrupted by the Twin Towers brothers.

In the last few months, I've taken a liking to Pearla. She made her way into my heart, and I'd pulled down on her a few times. She was eating now, out of bed more, and looked like she wasn't losing any more weight, so that was a good sign. She was too fucking young to be down bad about a nigga. I didn't know if it was killing niggas, seeing Grind shot, or his marriage that had her hiding away from the world. She had us all wrapped around her damn finger, though. If she went too long without texting me, I would pull up on her at Rio's. Now I understand why Matteo had done the same with my sister back when shit was chaotic. It was family over everything.

"She good."

"Even if she's not, she will be," I assured. "That nigga, Grind?"

It wasn't much retaliation needed because Pearla had stepped for him. Even though that nigga was married, he better empty his fucking pockets for Pearla when he woke up, if he woke up. She was the reason why he had a fighting fucking chance. All a girl had was her innocence until she didn't. Once a good girl turned bad, it was no going back. Thankfully, Pearla was still a good girl, even though she and that little crew of hers were on some young and wild shit. Pearla has been too damn heartbroken to run the city with their asses lately, though. Her mood had forced all of them to sit the fuck down somewhere.

"Only reason I'm still spending my money on his hospital bills is because that nigga is showing signs of brain activity," Matteo responded with a scowl on his face.

I nodded, not ready to elaborate on my thoughts concerning Grind just yet.

In my opinion, there were two positives to this situation with Grind. The nigga was already married, so if I offered him a seat at the table, he wouldn't take me through loops and hoops like those fuck niggas from Chicago. And, he was still in a coma, so hopefully, he wouldn't wake up until Pearla was clear across the country, living her best life with her degree in hand. I think ten years of not communicating will do them both some good. The nigga was still expected to send her a hefty check for the rest of her life, even if he had to pass the money through us. He was forever indebted to my little cousin.

That hustling-ass nigga had fumbled the realest chick he would ever have by his side. But it was cool, though. Unlike the Cuppacio women, a Rinaldi woman didn't need a man for shit. Real talk.

Chuckling randomly, Rut switched the subject. "You really gave that nigga two weeks to find a wife, though?" Rut smiled in disbelief.

"Hell yeah, I did. He better pluck a bitch off the street and get that shit done. I should have did the rest of them niggas the same way. They popping out babies before rings; gone have us 'round here deep as fuck like the Brady Bunch. Have niggas calling us the fucking bastard bunch."

"You stupid. I'm 'bout to take Pearla some food before I take it in. Lil' Gas Station wanna paint together tomorrow, and a nigga need a good night's sleep."

Rut started laughing, while Matteo looked at him like he was crazy.

"Chill, Rut. Don't get his grumpy ass started," I said, hiding my smirk. I stood, grabbed my two phones, and looked at Teo. "I'm sliding, too, nigga. Rut gone make sure the spot stay hot. I need to chop it up with ole Pearla P and remind her niggas ain't shit."

"It's a school night, nigga." Matteo frowned with his territorial ass.

Ignoring him, I led the way. "It's Spring Break, nigga. Ain't no school. Now, come on before them worrisome-ass Cuppacio niggas come back in here. I can only take them niggas in doses."

"They don't die, but they damn sure do multiply," Matteo added.

"Shit. Tell me a fucking 'bout it."

CHAPTER 8

GLOW

"Where you going? Flip the camera around so I can see. I can tell you're in front of the mirror with the way you keep playing with your clothes. And since I don't see your bathroom in the background, I know you're in your full-length one."

Rolling my eyes at my very nosy and very bossy little sister, I stopped toying with my top so I could flip the camera. A face eerily similar to mine smiled back at the screen as she gave me a once-over. Her bedroom was dark, but I could see the poster behind her bed, adorned with the big-ass school's mascot: a fucking grizzly bear. Glee looked as comfortable as one could get. A bonnet was resting on her head, and I could see her natural baby hairs peeking from underneath the satin pink hair protector with a thick band. The glow from the television and LED light cast a shadow, but her pale skin shone through the phone screen easily.

She looked lighter than usual, even though it was nearing summer. I was sure having the flu and being on her way to a full recovery contributed too. Fighting the illness while taking her exams was probably kicking her ass, but my sister was the most determined person I knew. I was sure she'd ace her tests, even under the weather.

She told my mom and me on FaceTime last week that she would be coming straight home after her last exam. She was supposed to come stay with me for her summer break, but my mama insisted that she go home to Sparkling City first and spend some time with her. I was happy she accepted my mama's offer because, if she'd come straight here as planned, she may have brought her germs with her.

My townhouse had more than enough space, with three furnished bedrooms of the five total. I had converted the two rooms in the basement into a content room and a closet before my sister left for college. She always found her way into my bedroom despite having a room that she claimed as her own. She and our mom visited Jagoda Bay a lot in the summertime, but my sister only stayed the night with me three or four times.

Before we knew it, it was time for her to head out for her freshman year. I was so sad when it was time for her to start college, but my mom and I made sure to create a home away from home for her by decorating her room in their apartment. It was decorated in the same colors as her bedroom at my mom's and my townhome, royal blue and brown.

That was months ago, and my sister had now completed her first year at Blake University, an HBCU a few hours outside Atlanta in Cove City, Georgia. I was extremely proud of her, even though I never made it there to visit her. I'd been so busy working, and I felt bad about that now that the school year had ended. On the other hand, Glee didn't make a huge fuss about me not coming to visit. We went from talking every day to texting maybe once a week over the ten-month stay. Despite our lack of communication, I made regular deposits into her account and was still doing so even though the summer had arrived. I refuse to let my girl work because I know she needs the break. She ended the academic year on the Dean's List, so it was only right that I turned her and her hot-in-the-ass bestie up for the summer.

"Oh, okay. You looking pretty. Those jeans are making you look thick as ever. Let me find out *Glow Eats* been really eating good up in the Bay." She smiled, her chapped lips spreading, making her look even more sickly.

"What? Why you say that? I'm getting big?" My eyes expanded, and my heart pounded.

"Umm-hmm. Thick in them thighs, boo." She laughed, and at the same time, I sighed with relief.

I loved my current size, and even though I ate on camera for a living, I had no desire to gain weight. I had way too many clothes I hadn't worn yet. Especially the ones stacked to the brim in my content room that eager brands were waiting for me to wear. I had to get a move on it before they snatched those coins out of my creator fund.

"Where did you say you were going again?" Glee asked as I moved around, preparing to leave my townhouse.

"I didn't."

This time, Glee rolled her eyes. "You must be going with the boug-hetto girls that you can't speak of."

"The who?"

"The boug-hetto. They look and dress bougie as heck, but with the way I've seen them clown in the club on your Snap and theirs, I know they ghetto."

"Girl! You need to go to bed!" My head shook, braids moving as I chuckled through a grin.

The ladies weren't bougie or ghetto. I'd say they just didn't take no mess. I've never been confrontational, but I quickly learned to let that timid stuff go. You never know what will pop off when you're around them, and we've ended up in more than a few fights over the last two years. If anything, that was ghetto, but I can't lie—those were the best times. We didn't go around starting drama, but when the night ended with a few punches being thrown, I'd wake up the next day with belly soreness from laughing so hard. Good times.

"Un hunh... See, you're over there smiling. You done let the Kardashians turn you out."

"Kardashians, Glee. Really?"

Turning sideways, I inwardly praised myself for my look. It was one of my favorites this year, and even though I wasn't sure how this look would turn out with braids, I wouldn't want my hair styled any other way. My braids had been such a huge hit that I'd gone right back to the same braid shop and had them taken down and redone. This time, I did pay the ladies even though my review had gained them over twenty thousand new followers. They wanted to refuse, I simply left the money and all but ran out of the door. I respected what they were doing, and though I'd normally charge four figures to promote a brand, black businesses were a soft spot of mine.

When I got them done this second time, they had to open up overnight just so I could get on the schedule. I was happy for the ladies. Their work was good and consistent. These second set of braids looked exactly like the first set. Perfection.

"Yes, really. Those ladies drive six-figure cars, rock gigantic rings, and I think all of them have worn Crocodile Kelly bags. You know, they cost like a hundred grand? The Kardashians, they are. But seriously... You can tell me. Are they like some secret assassins or something? Is that why you can't talk about them?"

I laughed loudly into the phone. "Girl, what? Get off my phone, sis'. They have not turned me out. I just enjoy their company."

"And..?"

"And they are most definitely not assassins. They aren't even people you should compare to the Kardashians either."

"Oh, okay. Just asking. I thought that's why you don't go with them when they go out of town. Sometimes, they're out shopping and having brunch, and you aren't with them. I thought it's because they're out doing secret missions." Glee shrugged lazily.

"Wait. How do you know they be out?"

Glee yawned. "Mocha added me to her close friends. That girl can spend some money too. Her husband is really, really fine as hell. Chocolate men are my weakness." She fake shivered, and I chucked at her antics.

"Your weakness needs to be those books. Stay off that girl's page. I'ma tell her to block you."

"No! Don't do that. She's only a few years older than me, and I swear... she's living *the* life. That's how Blayke wants to be. Married young to a young, rich dude with a handsome son who looks just like him, so she can shop 'til she drops at breakfast time. Her words, not mine," Glee assured me.

Blayke had been my little sister's best friend since middle school. She was a pretty little thing with strict parents who were heavily involved in the church. She was supposed to attend a school in Jagoda Bay, but decided to follow my sister to Cove City. Those two were inseparable except when Blayke's parents had her holed up in the house with a Bible in her face. I had to talk on the phone with them for an entire hour, running down the summer plans for the girls, and the compromise was that I would come visit their church. They were something else, and I could see why Blayke was eager to get the hell out already, even though she'd been away at college for ten months. She was going to end up with a man they despised, despite their belief that Blayke was going to find a good Christian man. Blayke probably was at that college fucking out of both pants legs and dragging my sister right along with her. Glee was a virgin, but that didn't mean I thought she was all innocent.

"And how do you want your life to be?" Shifting my eyes from the mirror to the iPhone screen, I waited for Glee to answer.

My baby sister had a bright future. Unlike me at her age, she was confident about the life she wanted to build for herself. She was going to be a first-generation doctor, and even though I was beyond proud of her, I felt something had been bothering her lately. Something was going on, and I was missing it. I knew she wouldn't be my little baby forever, but I wanted Glee to hold onto her innocence for as long as possible. I didn't want her to get boy crazy and forget the plot. But something was nagging me that that had or was currently happening.

Glee's eyes migrated from the phone screen to the TV in front of her, as if she were shielding the truth from me. "I dunno. I just want to get through school so I can start the next one."

I was taken aback by her response. Blake University had always been my sister's dream school, so her readiness to be done there didn't make much sense. I grew tired of her and those annoying grizzly bears around the house during our adolescent years. Her entire dorm room was decorated in the college colors against my suggestions, so her love for Blake only grew strong as we aged. I wasn't sure what had happened since we dropped her off in June that caused this switch-up, and while it may be her current illness that had her so nonchalant, something was telling me that wasn't the case.

Glee had ghosted me after the first month or so at Blake. She'd text here and there after I'd blow her line up, but she wasn't consistent in communicating. I just knew she would be calling me every week to tell me all about the fun she was having at college. But the last few months, she wouldn't even answer my FaceTime's. She'd shut me out whenever I tried asking if something had happened; she would just assure me she was fine. Instead of continuing to badger her for answers, I decided to invite her to spend the summer with me. I knew school had probably kicked her ass, and my hope was that was the only thing that had been close to her ass. Pursuing a career as a doctor isn't easy, so my plan was to give her a summer she'd never forget. I knew I would have to figure out how to be a big sister to her, be available to my friends, and keep my influencer account up to date, but I had faith that everything would work out.

"Well, I'm proud of you, and we're going to have fun this summer."

"Blayke said as long as we can be around Mocha 'nem BDE men, it will *definitely* be a good summer." She grinned before bursting into giggles that immediately turned into coughs.

"See... the Lord hear you and Blayke being mannish. Bye, Glee! Tell Blayke she staying in Sparkling City. Not about to have her parents throwing me back in the water. Take some more elderberry before you call it a night."

I wanted to say that Lorenzo most definitely did have BDE because he had a big dick. I'd seen it when the ladies did the "my husband's dick is bigger than yours" contest. They shoved their phones in each other's faces for hours, displaying pictures and videos of their men's dingalings. I'd never seen a friendly competition like that and was shocked that they were engaging in such discussions with me present. It was hard to be around the men without thinking about their male parts before the "game," so composing myself afterwards took the strength of a single mom in a Tyler Perry movie. At the time, I'd been telling myself that they had scarred me for life. I remembered thinking there was no way that type of dick could fit inside of a woman's tiny hole, and I didn't want to find out. Unlucky for me, I'd fucked around and found out.

"Have fun. And snatch up one of their husbands' single friends. I know you tired of being the cat lady."

"I don't even have a cat, though."

"Not yet. It's coming if you don't put yourself out there. Blayke is calling. Love you. Byeee."

My sister disconnected the call, and I refocused on my outfit before my mind wandered to the unsavory things I'd done a few weeks ago. When the car scene came to mind, my coochie thudded in response like she still hadn't recovered from the pounding she'd endured. I still couldn't believe I'd had my first one-night stand after swearing celibacy, and all it took was a few sips of tequila. I'd made a note to myself to not even look at alcohol's way for a while. Nonetheless, had I been in possession of a picture of that man's dick, the ladies would have had to crown me.

Shit. This is gonna have to work.

This was my fifth time changing, and my closet was a mess because of it. If I didn't leave now, I would be late, and that was a no-no. I always tried to be early wherever I went because being late was disrespectful. Taking one final look at myself in the mirror, I felt confident in my presentation. Looking at the time on my phone once more, I decided to clean up my mess later when I got home.

Dasani was hosting a Sniff-and-Sip party at her and her husband's estate. I loved being invited to all of the ladies' homes, but theirs was my favorite. I still couldn't wrap my mind around them living the way they did. The invitation was wrapped in a big satin bow that smelled delightful, so that's what I chose to wear: bows. Knowing Daylani, who planned all the parties, that had to be the theme. Thankfully, I had plenty of items I could wear to fit the theme, but today's winner was a cream crop top that tied together into a giant satin bow pushing up my breasts. I paired it with form-fitting, high-waisted pants that stopped just past my knees and hugged my calves. On my feet were a pair of Betsy Johnson heels featuring a satin floral bow across the toe strap and ankle buckle. They were cute and comfortable, which was perfect for a mingling event like this.

The look was giving modern '50s pin-up girl, so I pulled my braids out of my face and let them hang down my back, clipping the braids together with a bow that matched my top. Two braids framed my face, drawing attention to my eyes. My makeup was beat, and the red matte Mac Ruby Woo set it off. Not having time to change my purse, I grabbed my white Louis Vuitton monogrammed Speedy 25, which already had my essentials, and headed out the door, hitting the lights along the way.

By the time I'd listened to The Weeknd's "The Birds, Part 2" seven times, I'd arrived at the Rinaldi estate. They'd pulled out all the stops, including valets parking the cars. I popped a peppermint in my mouth, even though I'd just brushed my teeth earlier when I answered Glee's FaceTime. Tossing my keys into the cupholder, I grabbed the envelope I brought for Dasani. I didn't know what to get her, so I chose a card with a personal note written inside and $300 in cash. With the way her immaculate home was lined with cars I couldn't even pronounce, and staffed with a full crew to run the event, I knew she didn't need my money. But I'd been taught to never arrive empty-handed at any gathering where someone was being celebrated.

The valet attendant helped me out of my car, and when I noticed that the light-skinned, handsome one looked familiar, I squinted, trying to see where I could place him.

"Pretty lady. You ready to let a real nigga in?"

Italian, Scarlett's little cousin, grinned while rubbing his gloved hands together. He, along with the other attendants that I was now able to identify as the rest of his passee, was all dressed in black down to the gloves.

"Italian, find you something to do. Like school."

He licked his lips. "I got that under control. Can't be that nigga if you dumb." He tapped the side of his head.

"I'm glad you know. But don't be playing in these cars."

I didn't have to warn him about mine because mine was the most modest of the lineup.

"Oh, Don done fucked up giving us this job. We 'bout to burn one of these bitches down to the rubber. As soon as they get full off that oil, we outchea." His swiveled his head, scanning the cars.

I looked over my shoulder down at my car and then back at him. He flashed his million-dollar smile, which would cause many girls' heartbreaks.

"Don't worry. You safe, pretty lady."

"Umm-hmm. Be safe." I knew if I lingered any longer, he'd continue to flirt as if he had a chance. Nodding, I hurried across the circular driveway, ignoring their inappropriate comments about my attire and figure. Italian Cuppacio was going to be someone's hell on wheels one day. That I was sure of.

Dasani had been raving about her perfumes and was excited to get back into entrepreneurship. I was so happy for her. She didn't *need* to launch a line, but it was her passion which fueled her to make it happen. I knew without a doubt her line would be a success—not just because of her and her husband's influence, but because of how she lit up every time her interest in fragrances came up.

Entrepreneurship is tough, but it gave me purpose too. As much as I longed to have a life like theirs, I loved that I had a thriving career as a content creator. It kept me busy and, with over three million followers, definitely entertained.

As soon as I walked through the open double doors, I smiled. I had guessed the theme correctly as bows greeted me from every angle. Large satin bows were tied at the end of the grand staircase, and large balloon arches shaped like bows were strategically placed throughout the space. A server handed me a champagne flute with a little bow tied to the stem and told me everyone was in the formal dining room.

"Glooooowwww! Look at youuuu, biiiitch!"

As Jisei greeted me, the rise of her chubby cheeks nearly made her eyes close, and her mink lashes were the best I'd seen. I made a mental note to ask her who'd done them because I was tired of fighting with my clusters. She was carrying her baby weight as if it was normal to be this round, and I couldn't help but wonder if she would immediately slim back down once she popped the baby out. I couldn't imagine gaining a whole bunch of weight and not being able to get rid of it as soon as I gave birth. I knew that was not only impossible and very unhealthy, but those were my feelings.

Someone else called out, happy to see me. I'd escaped inside my mind that quickly that I'd forgotten to speak. "Hey y'all! Everyone looks so cute."

As always, the ladies were on theme in expensive threads, tying the bow theme in perfectly. Each woman's style matched their personality, and I loved it. After giving everyone a hug, I handed Dasani her card.

"I didn't know what to bring since this is my first Sniff-and-Sip, but here you are, and congratulations! I know the business will thrive beautifully."

I loved the silver fitted tube dress Dasani was wearing. There was a large bow attached to the back, dragging the floor behind her. It was perfect. Her hair was pulled into a high ponytail with bangs, showcasing her almond-shaped eyes and highlighting her ethnicity.

Placing the envelope to her nose, she inhaled. "Ummm. It's moneyyyy in here! Thank ya, boo boo! I'm so happy you came."

I wouldn't be anywhere else. I wish y'all would invite me to everything, I said to myself, but to Dasani, I replied with a simple, "Of course."

The party continued with drinks and food being passed around. The sniff stations were absolutely adorable. Dasani had three fragrances to sample, each with two variations. She even had a chemist explaining the notes in the perfumes. I'd never seen anything like it, and was excited to learn something new. Once we picked our favorite fragrance between the perfumes labeled A and B, it was logged into a system—no, a real system on an iPad—for Dasani to consider later. She put so much thought into her brand, and the quality of the scents was unmatched. I had a hard time choosing but ultimately went with bottle A. I'd already planned to stock my growing perfume collection with every single fragrance on launch day, and was happy she had little samples for us to take to tide us over until the full bottles released. They were that good.

The Sniff-and-Sip was perfect content for me, and as much as I wanted to complain about missing out, I held back. I always felt uneasy about filming in their home, even though the other women did it. I didn't want to do anything that might risk my welcome or get me barred from their houses, so the most I did was ask the hired photographer to take a picture of me solo at one of the balloon arches with my untouched beverage in hand. Once we finished with my impromptu photoshoot, I offered her a tip, but she declined. I was sure Dasani or her husband had given explicit instructions for the hired vendors to not accept any money from guests. Before I could stuff the fifty-dollar bill in her black slacks, she had sent me my photos via Bluetooth and blended into the party. Looking through the pictures, I was so excited to post them because of how good they looked. The pictures she'd taken of the wives and me were magazine-worthy. Those were without a doubt going on my social media platforms.

The drinks were flowing, marijuana was lingering in the air somewhere, and the DJ had the party pumping while I was on cloud nine, enjoying my girls. The summer was ours for the taking, and this party had been the perfect kick-off. These ladies lived the dream life, and I was just happy to be included, even if only partially.

Dasani had gone off to tend to the rest of the guests, leaving Pia, Jisei, Scarlett, Mocha, and me in our destinated section of the party. Discover had come through briefly, but was escorted out by Vello as soon as she sniffed the fragrances and gave her gift.

"I be seeing these bow parties all over the internet but never thought I'd be at one. It's so cute and girly." Mocha held up her flute. "Even got a little satin bow on the leg of the glass. Period!"

"Yes, you know this is right up my alley," Jisei agreed. Anything pink, with a bow, or feminine, my old neighbor was obsessed with. She'd even been a tad bit disappointed that baby Ezio was a boy.

"I love the whole aesthetic of this party. It's executed perfectly," I added, admiring the monogrammed napkins.

"So, Glow..." Pia's ponytail, which had been flipped at the ends, bounced as she spoke. Red was always her choice of color, so I wasn't surprised to see her in a black jumpsuit that cut off right above the knees with red bows resting on the shoulders. She, too, was in red lipstick with her belly bump on full display. "I heard your little sister is here from college."

I smiled, thinking of Glee. "Not yet. My mom wanted her to

go home first. She'll be coming to stay with me soon, though. Her and her best friend, Blayke."

"I want Pearla to meet them. She's doing better these days, but maybe more girls in their *clique* can snap them back to their normal selves. Pearla also needs to talk to someone her age about college because I think Blake would be perfect for her. The further away from Jagoda Bay she is, the better. She'll be a senior this year, and I don't want her thinking her heartbreak is the reason she gotta stay here. Too fucking much done happened. She needs to go on and see more of the world."

My heart went out to Pearla. I didn't know Grind, but I'd caught a glimpse of him at Pia and Nel's engagement. I could see why she was bedridden after hearing the news that he was married. Add in him getting shot, and I'd also shut off from the world. I still didn't know the details of the shooting because, again, I wasn't integrated into the circle beyond girly meet-ups and celebratory events, but the entire family had been concerned about Pearla.

"That should work. Glee needs some new friends, and she doesn't know anyone in Jagoda Bay besides me. I'm sure she'd be happy to meet Pearla and tell her all about Blake U. It's a nice school in a cute small town. I was nervous about her going all the way to Georgia, but when we got to the campus to get her settled in, it almost made me jealous that I hadn't gone to school. They even have condos for dorm rooms. I think Pearla will like it."

With the way my sister had shut my ass out as soon as she got to that damn school, I didn't think that would've been the move for Pearla, but the brightness my little spill put on Pia's face had me feeling good.

"Yeah, we need to link them ASAP. Text me as soon as she touches down."

"Will do."

I turned to ask Jisei about coming over soon to play with baby Ezio when Dasani reappeared. Her dazzling attire screamed, "This is my party," and with the way her body was slightly swaying, I could tell she was feeling the overpriced champagne. She smiled before saying, "Forgive us, Glow. I need to snatch the ladies away real quick. Have something else to drink since you haven't touched that glass. We will be right back."

I nodded, refusing to let them see my crushed feelings. The rest of the ladies gave me what felt like sympathetic smiles as they followed Dasani out of the room, leaving me with the fragrances, DJ, and the elders who were on the dance floor, getting it. Just that fast, I'd gone from indulging in conversation to being ostracized. The chemist had done their job and was now packed up and gone, so the party had officially kicked off. The men had come up, picked out their fragrances, and disappeared, so I was assuming that's where the women went.

Leaning against the wall to relieve my foot of pain, I took a tiny sip of champagne to ease my nerves.

"Who got you over here looking all sad, Greedy?"

Jumping, I placed my hand on my chest as my woeful thoughts were interrupted. His eyes drifted from mine to my shoulders and then to my breasts, which the bow did a poor job of concealing. I was tastefully dressed, mindful of the many married men in the room, but being sexy had slowly become an intricate part of my brand. He licked his slightly darkened lips and set off fireworks in my panties.

Shit.

"See, you not living right. Scary ass," he stated in a chuckle.

Tunan.

The store runner.

My impromptu date.

It was pitiful how the sight of him made my panties cream.

157

I'd tried hard to forget that shameful night, but anytime I came in contact with my vagina, whether I was relieving my bladder or cleaning myself in the shower, I'd set my honey pot on fire with yearning. How can one night—one fucking man—leave an impression that showed no signs of dispersing? Just like that night, he looked and smelled delicious next to me, and just like that night, he was out of dress code. I'd quickly learned that Tunan wasn't a rule follower.

When he showed up instead of Shio for dinner, he made my followers fall in love with him. I would have never believed he'd be the one to break my celibacy. All it took was half-eaten food and a riding through the city, while I gawked at him like a smitten girl, for him to fuck me on the worn, back seat of his ancient-ass car like I was a groupie. You'd think he was the one with the millions of followers, the way I let him bust my ass wide open. Just thinking about it had my cheeks on fire.

I knew he had some ties to Shio, since he sent him as a replacement, but the last place I thought I'd see him again was here at the Rinaldi estates. Honestly, I was hoping to never see him again. I told myself I was going to forget that night. Hell, I'd even told *him* that. As for the video of us at the restaurant, I'd yet to edit and upload. I didn't want to deal with all the think pieces in the comments or be reminded of that night. I was shocked my sister hadn't mentioned the live, or that no one had screen recorded it. The next day, when I came to my senses, I nearly had a panic attack waiting for someone to tag me in some clips taken from the live. It had been weeks, though, and so far, so good.

Mocha was chronically online, and even she hadn't said anything. That was nobody but God. Tunan was fine, and the dick was immaculate, but that night should have never happened. I was supposed to end my night with Shio and be one step closer to the "in crowd," but no, I had to open my legs for the nigga under him.

I cleared my throat and placed the flute on the stand beside me before responding. "I just wasn't expecting you, is all."

The smoldering flame I saw in his eyes startled me. He was so damn attractive. I was hoping I'd imagined his good looks the other night, or that the alcohol had adjusted my eyesight, but nope. This man was fine as hell. The best way to forget a fuck was to be embarrassed by it. Looking at this man in the daylight made me quickly realize I wasn't forgetting shit. His smooth, dark coffee skin didn't have a single blemish. His lips were the perfect shape for his face, well moisturized from either his wet tongue or some lip balm. His brows were unruly but shaped up just like his haircut, and both fit the hardness of him seamlessly. I fought hard not to come right on the spot from checking him out. And although he wasn't dressed for the occasion, the simple jean shorts, fitted T-shirt, and all-white Air Force Ones looked damn good on him.

When he leaned back with a slightly amused look on his face, the soft gust of his cologne rushed me, and damn, the man smelled heavenly.

"Oh." He placed his fist to his mouth, while I attempted to compose myself. "The store runner don't belong in the Don's mansion, huh?"

My eyes bucked, and I nearly tripped over my own feet rushing to place my hand over his mouth. Looking around, I was inspecting the nearby crowd to see if anyone had heard his loudmouth ass. He hadn't made a move to remove my hand, but when I felt his lips smile against my palm, I dropped it. That fast, I could smell him on me from being so close to him. The last thing I needed was to be carrying the scent of a man who'd made me come harder than I ever had. However, something told me that the scent wasn't on my clothing, but instead, in my mind. This nigga was doing something to me without doing anything at all.

"Don't say that," I told him as I rubbed my hands down my pants.

"Don't say what?"

"Don. Call him *Demise* around me."

"For what? That nigga the Don."

"Tunan..." I warned as I tilted my head.

He grinned, sending electrical currents all through my body. "Your hand tastes good, Greedy."

"Boy! You licked me?"

He licked his lips again. "Shit, my tongue was halfway outta my mouth when you cuffed it. It was inevitable, Greedy."

"Ugh, that nickname is atrocious. I hate it."

"You'll be aite. You haven't answered my question, my baby. What got you to drinking, and why I can't call him *Don* around *you?*"

"I wasn't drinking... I only had a sip to attempt to calm my anxiety. And I'm not supposed to know certain *things*, so I turn a blind eye. As long as I don't know what I'm not supposed to know, I won't be kicked out the friend group."

"Friend group?"

"Yes. The wives' friend group. I'm the only one single and the only... Never mind. Let's just change the subject, okay?" I looked around on the sly, trying to spot the cameras I knew were in every nook and cranny of this mansion.

"Hold up... That's why you over here looking like you lost your best friend? They off doing wifely shit and left the single friend to hang with the aunties?"

His taunting expressions added to my already embarrassment. It was pitiful the way I'd turned into a desperate loser over wanting to be accepted by Jisei and the other wives. I had my own motion, so I couldn't understand for the life of me why it was so important that these ladies be my friends.

Rolling my eyes, I squared my shoulders. "Tunan! Let it go, please. I'm fine. I'm just happy to be here."

Even that sounded desperate, Glow.

I stared straight ahead, but could feel him burning a hole in the side of my face with his piercing eyes. The aunties were definitely cutting up on the floor, and the way I was embarrassing myself in front of Tunan, I may as well join them.

Thinking back to the fact that Tunan was present, I turned and asked, "Wait, what *are* you doing here? Where is Shio?"

Tunan leaned his back on the wall next to me, his arm brushing mine. He folded his right foot back on the wall, and even that was sexy. His scent was drowning me at this point. After he answered my question, I needed to get away from this man.

"You don't give a fuck about that nigga, Greedy."

"More like he don't give a fuck about *me*. I haven't heard from him since he stood me up."

"Glow?"

"Yeah?"

I faced Tunan when he didn't immediately respond. It was the wrong move because his eyes were dangerously low, and my panties instantly became a sloppy mess. Fuck washing; I'd have to toss these out when I got home.

Licking his lips, he sighed. "He stood you up, or he sent the realest nigga you ever encountered to get you right?"

If I had a mirror, I was sure my reflection would resemble a tomato. I'd never been more ashamed in my life. I was so turned on by this man saying nothing but regular shit. Trying my best to get right, I chuckled.

"Real nigga. Store runner. Comedian. Driver. The list keeps getting longer..."

Throwing his head back, he laughed, and it shook my core. "You funny as fuck." He leaned in. "But don't forget pussy beater. Add that to the fucking list too."

Oh, God. Please be a fan.

At this point, I could smell my own arousal, so I was sure he could. The ladies walked back in, laughter following them, but they stayed on the other side of the room. Jisei spotted me, winked, and mouthed "one second."

With a smile that didn't quite reach my eyes, I blew her a kiss and waited patiently.

Tunan chortled, which annoyed and reminded me that he was still next to me as he observed the interaction.

"Greedy?"

"Whaaaat, Tunan?"

"When your next food review, and where is it?"

I had six new restaurants to try before I started on my seafood series. With the way Jagoda Bay was growing, I'd never run out of places to review. If I ever did, I could hop on a flight and explore other cities nearby. I'll even consider trying different countries too. Food was essential—I'd always have somewhere to review.

I sighed and kissed my teeth. "Needs to be tomorrow, but that won't be happening."

My eyes were still on the women as they laughed and whispered. They all looked so happy. Like my name, they were all glowing.

"Why not tomorrow then?"

"Because I'm tired of eating," I admitted.

"Hunh? You serious?"

"Yeap. I love my job, but since I eat so much, I get sick of the smells."

"Glow?"

"Hmm?"

"What do you desire, my baby?"

Breaking my gaze from the women, I faced him again.

"What do you mean?"

He stepped forward, towering over me even in my heels. My breathing heightened as I looked up at him.

Shit. My panties aren't going to be able to hold much more of this mess he's causing.

"I mean... What do you want? Right now... If it's one thing you could have, what would it be?"

Getting lost in his syrupy brown eyes wasn't the plan. Tunan may visually be what I want, but he has no way to help me get what I desire. He couldn't give me the status I wanted, even though my body said he could give me what *it* wanted. I was at his mercy as I stared at his sculpted face, and even though the girls hadn't seen my live video, all they had to do was look across the room and they'd see the passion. We'd fucked like horny dogs in the back seat of a car that probably had expired tags.

At least we used protection. I thought, smirking as he grinned and waited for my answer.

They say "condom dick" isn't real dick, but all I've ever had was condom dick, and I was lightyears away from being a virgin. And after being fucked in that car, I for damn sure wasn't a virgin. Tunan was the star in that car, and I'd happily be his co-star if it allowed me to feel him on top of me again.

Easy, Glow. We said never again.

Feeling his hand on my lower back, a tingle sprouted in the pit of my stomach. He radiated a vitality that drew me in like a magnet. He was eager for my answer, but at the same time, something in his manner soothed me. Was it the dick? The good looks? The chalice he possessed? Or was I just so deprived of affection that his simple actions had me in a tizzy? I didn't know what it was about Tunan that had me wide open, but I was two seconds away from spilling all my hopes, wants, and dreams to this man, and I didn't even know what he'd just gotten out of jail for. He could have been a murderer or a molester, and I'd been smiling like my name was Chester.

Pitiful.

"You ain't gotta tell me, but I know." He took his place back on the wall, cool as a cucumber, like he hadn't just semi-hemmed my ass up.

My breathing staggered, and my chest rose and fell. "I... I don't know what you talking about," I mumbled. And I truly did not. I was just counting down the seconds until the ladies called me over. I wanted to laugh too.

"You know... You know a lot of shit, Glow. Just like I know a lot of shit."

"Okay, enlighten me. Inform me about some of the shit you know, even though I have the faintest idea of the context you're speaking about."

"I know your panties are wet." He tossed that out like an erratic, summer storm, as if he were discussing the weather.

He was right, but I refused to confirm his statement. Instead, I inhaled as heat rushed to my neck.

"I know you want to be a part of the 'wives club,' and it's hurting your pretty little feelings that you're not."

I swallowed down a thick pool of saliva, still refusing to confirm.

He then leaned over and pressed his lips to my ear. "I also know you know I'm not no fucking store runner, my baby."

"Tunnnaaan." I stomped my foot, clicking the high heel harshly on the marble floors.

"Aite, aite. I'm through," He held his hands up in surrender with a mischievous grin. "I got a proposition, though, Greedy."

"God, no. The answer is no."

"Marry me."

I whipped my head around so hard that it snapped, cracked, and popped. "Nigga, what? Are you high?"

With this being a Sniff-and-Sip, Tunan must have taken it literally because his being high on cocaine was the only explanation for him to ask me some shit like that. I didn't know this man at all. Did I think he was the store runner for real? No... Yes... Maybe. But, still, I didn't know shit outside of him having a way with words *and a skillful dick.*

"High as a muhfucka. But I'm in my right mind, fasho."

"You in your right mind by asking a complete stranger to marry you? Not only that, you didn't even try to dress it up. You standing here in Forces, leaning against the wall, asking for my hand in marriage. Boy, if you don't get on somewhere." I was in utter disbelief. This further proved I, too, had lost my damn mind by giving this man the nookie.

"So if I got on my knees, would you say yes?" His eyes burned through mine with that question, and I knew he wasn't talking about getting on his knees to propose. We hadn't kissed that night, let alone him going down on me, and with the dick being grade A, I knew that mouth was lethal.

Shaking that image from my head, because we'd never go down that hole again, I tried to steady my breathing. He couldn't be serious. I mean, he was joking, right? He had to be because no sane person would ask a one-night stand for their hand in marriage.

"Tunan. You can't be for real. You realize who you talking to, right?"

"Yeah, good pussy..." He flashed that smile again.

Closing my eyes, I counted down while biting my molars. He was stressing me the fuck out. "Yeah, no. My answer is no."

"That's your final answer, my baby?" He cocked his head.

"Nigga, yes! The fuck!" I scream-whispered.

"Even if it meant that shit would only be on paper? Even if it meant you could get accepted into your beloved "wives' club," or circle, or whatever the fuck you call it? Even if it meant you wouldn't be left out of top-secret mob shit? Ooop! My bad, I'm not supposed to say dat 'round you." He smirked.

Now, he had my attention. "What are you saying, Tunan?"

"I'm saying... If you married me, you in. All-access pass. Unless you still trying to run with that store runner narrative."

I mentally ran down the list of single men in the mob, and Tunan wasn't one. Hell, his name had never even come up in the conversations I was privy to. I did know that Demise had brought in men who weren't family, like Lorenzo, Big Zan, Rut, and the other young guys I saw around, but they were all married or on their way down the aisle. I didn't know if Tunan was pulling my strings, or what? Hell, I wanted to be part of the pact, but I didn't even know if I wanted to be married, for real. It wasn't anything a husband could do for me that I wasn't already doing for myself—except disturb my peace.

Unless he had mob money.

I took another look at Tunan. He was just as handsome as any of the mob men, if not more, even in his modest clothing and jewelry. He had just as much aura as the other men at this event, but he'd come from nowhere. However, the other men at this party wouldn't be caught dead sitting in a car that was barely better than a hooptie. And Shio being connected to Tunan somehow further confused me unless...

"You need a wife."

He held my gaze and said, "I do."

"You need a wife to *get in*," I repeated.

"I told you, you know shit."

"You don't want to marry me, Tunan. Get somebody else to do it."

"You don't want me to do that, my baby."

"I do."

"So..." His voice dropped. "You cool with a new bitch joining the pact before you? Not only a newbie, but one that's gonna be fucking me and sucking me?"

His words were an immediate turn-on, but I felt an eerie and unfamiliar feeling settle in my gut.

Envy? No, Glow. Can't be from just one session, no matter how good it was.

"You don't. But you cool, Greedy. No pressure. Ion even got the time to convince you."

"How much time you have?" I squinted.

He looked down at his invisible watch. "'Bout five days."

"Five days!" I screeched so loud that Jisei looked over at me with a raised brow. Her gaze shifted from me to Tunan, and her brow lifted even higher into her hairline.

"I'm good," I said slowly so she could read my lips rather than hear me.

Turning my back to them, I stood directly in front of this crazy-ass man. "Five days, Tunan?"

"Yeap. Apparently, he, who must not be called Don in front of you, gets a kick out of fucking with my kind."

"Your kind?"

"Forget it, my baby. Just say yes."

"To being your wife?"

"To being my wife."

"But, why, though?"

"I just told you why. We both can get what we want."

"Seems like you get more out of the deal than me..." I sassed my words, hoping they weren't shaky due to my nerves.

I was trying to process this while calming my body down. Tunan was too handsome for his own good. Throw the elephant dick in there, and he was a fucking problem. He had the potential to be my downfall, and I didn't need that. I didn't even need a fucking husband, to be clear; I just wanted to be included. A few unlimited shopping sprees, a mansion, and a big rock on my finger wouldn't hurt either. That's it. Some would say I wanted the impossible, but anything was possible, especially in the world my friends had been married into.

"You don't want to marry me because there would be no sex, no love, no living together, no communication—unless we absolutely had to talk, and you wouldn't be able to have other women out in public. I would be an intolerable wife. An impossible one. Find somebody else."

"No sex from a woman I already fucked the shit out of?" His thick brow rose, and I wanted to slap that sexy-ass smirk off of his face. Laughing, he held his hands up. "Aite. No *more* sex. No love, no living together, no communication unless it's business, no flaunting these bitches, so that my greedy, *impossible wife* that won't give me no more coochie won't get mad. Got it." He said the words tentatively, as if me not letting him screw me again was merely an idea instead of a fact.

"Could you stop bringing that up? It was just one time, and I was drunk. I barely remember anything," I lied, my voice drifting into a hushed tone.

I remembered everything.

Every inch. Every pound. Every which way he dug me out.

How could I forget the time when a man was able to knock my period on in a mildew-smelling-ass car?

"I need it in writing too... Drawn up by a lawyer and notarized, please. Stamped and sealed." I couldn't believe my own words.

"Anything else, my baby?"

"And don't call me that."

"Don't call my impossible wife *my baby* because it makes her pussy moist. What else?"

"And you'll pay my mortgage. It's no way I'm going to be paying bills when I'm married, on nobody's earth. I'll handle my car note and other bills."

"Pay the mortgage, even though I can't step foot in that

muhfucka. Noted. Anything else, Greedy?"

"No wedding—it's not real. A judge and that paper drawn up is good enough. Demise would be okay with that, right? Being that it's not real?"

"That nigga don't give a fuck what we got going. He just want us married."

"Okay, that's it... No, wait. If we argue, for any reason, you have to walk away. That's non-negotiable, " I stated, being sure to look him directly in the eyes. My parents used to argue as if it were just the two of them in the house, instead of the four of us, with two being their adolescent daughters. I refuse to ever have a screaming match with the man whose last name I took. That was dead.

He grew serious. "I'll never put my hands on you, Glow. I was raised by women," he assured.

"Well... good."

"Aye?"

"Hum?"

"You gone tell your followers we married and shit?" He grinned sexily.

Rolling my eyes, I turned as I heard Jisei calling my name.

As I stomped away, I looked back, and he was still in the same spot, his eyes on my backside. All the while, I questioned my sanity. I had to be the most grouped-out bitch on the planet to agree to that shit. But as long as he followed my demands, nothing on my end would change, except I would finally be added to the other group chats. I didn't know about five days, though. I still needed time to process this shit.

CHAPTER 9
SHIO CUPPACIO

G rass crunched beneath my boots as I trudged across the yard. I hadn't done any work on the cabin's landscaping or exterior, but the grass had grown lush and green. The spring rain, as well as the mist from the neighboring lake, had done wonders for the nearby plants and turf. The trees curving over the cabin didn't allow much sun to get through, so I didn't have to worry about the greenery growing too tall. In the instance that it did, I was getting Nel over here to handle it. That nigga lived for yard work. If he could take his nose out of Pia's ass for five minutes and think, a landscaping company would be a good way to invest his money. But when a nigga is making dough by the boatloads, small investments are the least of their concerns.

The coolness from the central air dried the sweat that formed during my short walk from the truck to the front door. Walking past the covered furniture that had become the resting place for dust, I noticed the thermostat's setting was way too low for my liking. The central air was one of the few upgrades I'd made to the cabin. When I bought it, I didn't initially know what I would do with it. But something compelled me to add a state-of-the-art security system that included soundproofing and a non-penetrable door for the basement. I could hide the fucking president in here, and no one would know unless I gave them insight. When the temperature was set, I made my way down the stairs into the basement.

The smell of Dove soap hit my nostrils as soon as my foot hit the last step. Not much had changed since I was last here, but there was a cot in the corner, a dresser, and the bathroom had been stocked with toiletries. Besides that, it was just concrete walls.

Tossing the bag of food in the middle of the floor, I crossed my arms at my crotch. "Aye, whatever it is you trying to pull, just know... it's only one outcome and that shit ain't gone work in your favor. Not now and damn sho' not later."

A grunt, followed by the scraping of feet, sounded to my left, but instead of turning my eyes toward the noise, I kept looking straight ahead.

"Nigga, I could kill you in here."

Reaching behind my back, I held out the Glock for Hobo to take. He stood a few feet away from me in the joggers and white T-shirt I'd provided him. Steam was still emitting from the small bathroom, letting me know he'd just handled his hygiene. The last time I was here, the nigga smelled like he'd shitted himself, so I made it a point to bring some sanitation products down here along with soap and clothes so he could handle his fucking business. He was too fucking grown to be smelling like something had crawled up in his ass, died, and clawed back out.

In his hand was a metal pole that he must've pulled from the iron bed nestled against the wall. With a snarl on his face, he eyed the gun, contemplating his next move. If he decided to take it, he would have not only one but two weapons, and if he knew what the fuck he was doing, he could overpower me. That was a big-ass *if*, though.

"You got me in this bitch, locked away like a fucking animal, nigga!" He spat on the ground, releasing a nasty, thick yellow glob.

Keeping the gun held out, I looked around the space, doing a one-eighty with my head. "I don't see no fucking chains or cuffs. You're free to roam this bitch just like you're free to take this gun and blow my head off. Or... you can use that pole to slap the gun out of my hand and beat me to a pulp."

His expression hardened, and he tightened his grip on the black pole. His knuckles were bruised and cut, and the faint blood marks above his bed provided evidence that he'd been in here punching the walls. If he broke his gotdamn bones, his ass was just going to have crooked fingers. I wasn't dragging a doctor down here unless he was facing a life-or-death type illness.

"What the fuck you on? You'n think I'll take your gun and kill you, nigga? I'm a real killa! A real fucking gangsta! You not really 'bout it because you would have killed me. You don't have the heart. What type of kidnapper gives clothing and food to the nigga he kidnapped? A bed? I would have been in this bitch torturing you!" He snarled like he had all the answers.

I'd never been the type of person to point out what another person looked like, but Hobo was the bottom of the barrel. Shit —the nigga was the barrel. His dark skin didn't shine; it was dull and textured, and that was before I tossed him down here. Even the huge veneers in his mouth did nothing to improve his features. Honestly, it made him look more like an animal than anything else. I didn't know if he was part horse, gorilla, alien, or all three. I have no idea what Pia was thinking when she hooked up with this nigga. He and Nel were in two different leagues. Luckily, her beauty overshadowed everything because if it hadn't, my nephew would have come out looking all types of crazy.

Taking six steps in his direction, he flinched but tried to play the shit off. "I've been holding the toolie out for six minutes now, but all you've done is talk about what you *would've* done. You're alive, yes... but only because I'm a man of my fucking word. I told your jit I'll keep you alive until he's ready to take your ass out himself. Plus, I'm not into caging and starving grown-ass men. My rap sheet is extensive, but kidnapping isn't my usually choice of crime until I snatched yo' big ass up. It would have brought me great pleasure to take yo' hoe ass out like I'd done that bitch you'd been laying up with."

His eyes expanded as he stumbled upon my revelation.

"Oh, you think just because I wear this fucking Jesus piece that I have compassion?" I took another step in his direction. By now, he was damn near in the bathroom. "When it comes to my family, matter of fact, it can't come to them. And that's why yo' bitch somewhere stankin'.'"

"You... You killed a woman? I thought... I thought mobsters don't kill women and children?"

Flapping the gun in the air, still waiting for him to take it, I laughed. "Ion know why you thought that dumbass shit. And when the fuck you become the moral police? I mean... I knew yo' ass was the police since you and Detective Davis had a good rapport with one another, but... morals? Nigga, you tried to take yo' baby mama out but shot your son instead. Then you ran, like a bitch. Hobo, you in this bitch without shit binding you. If you was really 'bout it, you would have been gone. So, last chance—take the gun."

We stared one another down, and even though this shit was a complete waste of my fucking time, I wanted to give him a fair chance.

"I should kill you."

"Shit, what's stopping you?" I cocked my head. "Take the gun. I gave you the play. But you may want to grab that Bible from over there on the corner. You're gonna need it because, if you miss, your ass is done."

"Fuck you and that bible! You niggas playing a dangerous game."

"Stop thinking I play by any rules outside of my own, Hubert." Waving the gun at the bag of food before tucking it inside my waistband, I crossed my wrists in front of me. "Pick the fucking food up and eat it. You need your strength."

Still with the frown on his face that made him look worse than the fucked up physical attributes he was born with, his ungrateful ass kicked the bag. A salad, fruit, three turkey sandwiches, and six bottles of water rolled out.

"Ion want this shit! I need a burger! Some wings! Steak or some shit! Fuck I look like? A rabbit?"

"With those big-ass teeth in your mouth? Yeah, you can pass for a rabbit, but not the furry, cute ones. Eat the fucking food, Hobo. I don't have to feed yo' ass. Don't take my kindness for weakness. Besides... the fucking cholesterol and blood pressure you have, you need healthy choices."

"Nigga, you looked at my MyChart?"

"Yeah. I had to make sure I'm not housing a sickly-ass nigga. Eat the fucking food, Hobo."

Instead of waiting for his reply, I walked backward. This nigga didn't pump any fear into my heart—not even by a long shot—but weak niggas like him did coward shit like sneak hits. If he did some shit like that, nephew was going to have to understand my reasoning for ending his sperm donor.

"This mob shit can't save y'all forever! I got people that's gone come see about me! Watch! You gone be begging for my mercy, and it's gone be *you* that need the Bible."

I smiled. "I'm looking forward to it."

That shit made him even more mad, and he started yelling. "My son will let me go! He will never hurt me! I took care of him and his dusty-ass mammy their whole lives. Where was you mob niggas? Hunh? That lil' nigga came from my nutsack!" Hobo was foaming at the mouth, but he hadn't moved from his spot.

"You a talker. I'm a doer. Remember that shit, Hobo."

Closing the basement door, I left the house the same way I came. Hobo had been my last stop of the day before I took it in. Hopping in the truck, I picked up the blunt that was still lit and inhaled. I'd put the lean and the pills down, and I didn't drink as much as I used to, so my daily blunt was one I hadn't been able to let go. Outside of working out and prayer, it was my calming mechanism, and if I didn't have the potency in my lungs, a whole bunch of motherfuckers would be in the dirt.

Pooh Shiesty rumbled through the speakers as I drove in the direction of my home. Rolling my left arm as I came to a red light, I held the blunt in between my lips as I attempted to relieve the ache in my shoulder. I'd gone a little too hard in my home gym this morning and was starting to feel the burn after taking the long-ass drive to the cabin. I didn't know if Hobo's words were true when it came to Neltz not being able to kill him, but it had been lingering in the back of my mind. I had to keep him alive for the next eight years. That shit was nearly a fucking decade. If Lil' Nel Jr. let his sperm donor go, that was going to pose a problem for me and the mob as a whole. The gorilla-looking nigga knew too much and was a known rat. I had eight years to handle this shit, though, so I tried to calm my overactive mind. I'd worry about it when the time came.

My phone ringing paused the music. It was my personal phone, and the number on it was one I'd learned by heart in the last few months.

"Wassup?" I pushed out a thick wad of smoke with my greeting.

"Mr. Cuppacio. You have a guest. A female companion here at the front gate."

"Shit." I'd forgotten I'd scheduled with ole girl today. The thought of her soft body underneath mine made my dick throb. "I thought I already added her to the list temporarily," I said more to myself than to the guard.

I live in a gated HOA community that costs me way too much money, but I prefer being out in plain sight rather than in the middle of nowhere, on some secluded land. My neighbors are mostly high-powered investors, politicians, and even a few athletes. Everyone minds their own fucking business, and I fucked with that. Besides, minding their business was the safest thing for them to do.

"Let her in. I'll be there soon." I disconnected the line before the guard could get another word in. I fucked with Samuel, but right now, I needed to take this exotic to the head and release all the fucking negative thoughts that had surfaced while dealing with Hobo.

I didn't like to bring any weird vibes across my threshold. Energy lingered—it was the reason why I rarely had my people over. People's spirits had to be checked at the front door. Right now, shit was good in the family, so I didn't mind them stopping by. However, back when Renello and Metavello were plotting against Rio and didn't want anybody telling them shit, I had barred their asses from my oasis.

By the time I made it through the gates and drove the eight minutes it took to get from the front gate to my home, I'd finished my blunt, thought of nineteen different ways I was about to slang my dick, and said a long prayer.

The three-story house, built of warm-hued brick and

sitting atop a basement, was one of my few joys, and it cost me a ticket. Besides the million-dollar price tag, I was still paying out of pocket annually for pool access, the country club membership, monthly activities, and other amenities I never planned to use. I was a simple man who didn't need much to feel fulfilled except security. Living in Majestic Creek provided just that, but it also involved a financial sacrifice that would have shame little boys. There were hardly any rentals here, and I managed to buy my property for nearly thirty percent off the asking price because I lucked up with the former owner. He was an investor who freaked out when the stock market dipped. Instead of selling the property of one of his side chicks, he decided to abandon his wife and kids and put this place on the market. Tough luck for them, but great timing for me.

I loved everything about this place. My home was tucked in a cove and often admired by my neighbors because of the landscaping. Neatly trimmed bushes lined the windows, and the lushest grass—rivaling both the Dons' estates—formed the foundation. I put just as much love into the inside as I did the outside. My space—all eighty-six hundred square feet—had been well planned and carefully thought out. If there was no sign of that on the outside, once you crossed the front doors, it became obvious. Every inch of my house was decorated in warm tones, with brown hues as the primary color. It was masculine but not so much that a woman couldn't live comfortably here. I also wasn't tied to the choices I'd made. If I found a wife today, and she told me the inside decor had to go, the shit would be on the street faster than a New York minute, no matter how much I loved it. Luckily for me, the woman sitting behind the tint in my driveway wouldn't be making those demands because she didn't have that kind of pull and never would.

Pulling into the garage next to my Porsche, I killed the

engine of the truck. I shook my head, looking at the candy red vehicle. I purchased the car solely because I liked the way the Cuppacio Twins looked in theirs. I had only driven it twice: once from the lot and again to the tint man. Whenever I drove it for the third time, it'd probably be to sell the shit. I had a handful of cars, but the truck was what I considered my everyday car. The shit was a gas guzzler with how much I milled her up on the daily, but she was the most low-key vehicle out of my lineup.

Instead of hitting the electrical button to let the garage down, I kept it up and let my hard dick lead the way into the house. I'd barely made it out of the mudroom before I heard her heels echoing on my freshly waxed floors. I wasn't anal about shoes being kicked off at the door, namely because I rarely had company. Even if I didn't allow outside shoes inside my space, I would demand that she keep hers on. There was something so sensual about a woman getting fucked right out of her heels. Instead of taking her down right in the living room, I continued walking into the first guest room to the right. I always use one of my spare bedrooms, and never my personal one, to handle my dick's business. That space was for me, and hopefully, the woman I would be spending the rest of my life with. It was bad enough that I let the siren inside my most sacred cave, but since she'd been vetted, I allowed it.

I eyed the cream decorative pillow on the queen-sized bed that sat in the middle of the bedroom. It was crooked by an inch, but to the untrained eye, it looked just fine. It wasn't how it should have been, and I noted such in my mind. Before I could investigate the room further, the woman of the hour sauntered her way in while untying her trench coat. Standing at the foot of the bed and facing the door, my dick grew even harder at the sight of her. I was a man of patience. A man of discipline. At the end of the day, though, I was still a fucking

Cuppacio. I needed my dick wet, and while I didn't have to fuck every night, I needed mine at least once a week. I could even go two weeks depending on my work schedule, and since I'd been busier than usual, it had been thirteen days since I'd sunken into something warm and wet.

The flawless beauty before me was one of two that I kept on call in case I needed a nut. Ever since I'd had to get rid of Bahati's ass, I made it my mission to not stick my dick in just one woman. Exclusivity meant commitment in most people's eyes. I'd learned that, and all it took was for me to see some shit once for me to never repeat the fuck up again. When I became a one-woman man, it would be because that one had the potential to be my wife. I didn't entertain a slew of women because any smart man knew multiple women meant multiple problems. Two was the magic number for me, and this week, the sculpted frame in front of me held the number one spot.

"How do you want me?" A small smile tugged at her glossed pink lips while she waited for me to give her instructions.

Her yellow manicured nails moved slowly as she toyed with the belt of her jacket, waiting for a command. To any other man, a woman arriving to get fucked in a trench was something like a fantasy. Fuck a fantasy. I was trying to figure out how she hadn't passed out in that Jagoda Bay heat with the heavy overgarment on. It didn't matter; my dick was still hard.

With the coat now pooled around her black heels, I was staring at what could only be described as a work of fucking art. Her breasts, which were a D cup, were shielded by a black lace bra. The matching thong on her lower half covered a waxed pussy, and her dark skin had an irresistible glow to it. I didn't know if she'd rolled in cocoa butter before she arrived, but every part of her looked smooth. She was in the gym just as much as I was, so her taut stomach was flat, but since her hips and ass were colossal, there was no way her body fat would ever get down low enough for her to have abs. All the fucking fat was stored in the curves of her hips and the plumpness of her ass. It was an ass that I'd grown fond of feeling bounce on me as I drilled her from behind.

"I want you on your knees, Uriah."

Without hesitation, her heels carried her to my front, and she plopped down in a squat. I wasn't a fan of her perfume; the scent was too strong, in my opinion, and better suited for evening wear, but I wasn't here to smell her. I'd already done enough smelling at Dasani's Sniff-and-Sip to last me a month. I was here to bust a nut, and Uriah was one of the best to make sure that happened.

As she undid my zipper with precision, I reached into my pocket to remove my two phones, money, and wallet. By the time I had it all resting on the dresser, my dick had been spit on and was now being jerked.

"Stop playing with it, Uriah. Let that muthafucka meet your tonsils."

Her sleek eyes were lined in black, giving them a more catlike effect than they naturally were, and her face had been made up as if a professional makeup artist had done it. She didn't know it yet, but she would be riding dick till her knees were sore. The last time she came over, I had her face in the mattress as I beat her shit in from the back. My housekeeper couldn't get all of the Fenty and Maybelline products out of my fucking sheets. To anyone else, that wouldn't have been an issue, but I invested my coins in quality bedding. I wasn't willing to risk her fucking up anymore of my good linen, especially since the set on this guest bed didn't ship here anymore because of those damn tariffs.

Opening her mouth, I bit down on my bottom lip as her

warm tongue lapped up the precum as if it were icing on a cake. I felt her relax her throat as she tried her best to get my dick as far down her throat as she could. I appreciated her attempt to do as I asked. It was one of the reasons she was on call. The other reason: Uriah's mouth was a fucking vacuum. The pussy? I'd had better, but it was wet and warm enough. That throat, though? Her throat was the reason why she was my one call. I'd never been interested in having a slew of women. I didn't have time for the shit. Only bedding one woman often gave her the inkling that she was the end game. Luckily for Uriah, she knew what it was. I didn't have a potential wife as of now, but I did have a fucking eater at my disposal, and at this moment, I was feeling good about that.

Her makeup was still in place even though she was making a sloppy mess on my shit. I liked it that way, and she was proving how well she'd learned me. The hairs on the back of my neck stood as I watched her swallow me up like her favorite popsicle. Sucking and slurping sounds filled the room, and I was sure that if one had good enough hearing, they would be able to hear the sound of my toes cracking in these hot-ass Timberland boots. The only reason I'd even worn them today was in case I had to put my foot upside Hobo's head. Luckily for him, he was a bitch-made nigga that chose the safer route.

Normally, I watched Uriah do her thing, but in order not to nut, I looked straight ahead at the closed door of the en suite bathroom. Depending on how I felt, I would take Uriah down in the shower. I hadn't done it yet because I didn't want to cross any lines that would confuse her on what this shit was. I wasn't one to play any games, and my intent was always forefront. I told women exactly what I could offer them, and to most, it wasn't much. I didn't disrespect women, nor did I use them. They provided a service, and I provided compensation. I didn't hold conversations over the phone because, again, my life wasn't set up to be sociable right now. Even if I could, Uriah wouldn't even be in the lineup of potential companions. Yes, she was fine as fuck and the sex was decent, but nah. I was cool on her outside of her making my dick throw up.

Popping my dick out of her mouth, she kissed the tip, making chills cover my body before putting it back to its temporary home—her deep ass throat. If I had to call it, her dick sucking skills were the reason why she'd gotten a ring out of her ex-husband. I didn't fuck married women, nor did I fuck taken women. The only reason Uriah had been able to even get a glimpse of the dick was because the day we met, she'd just finalized her divorce. Unfortunately for her, that was also the reason she couldn't be anything more than my bedmate. To the mob, she wasn't worth enough to be a wife. In my eyes, though, I'd marry any fucking body I felt like it and dared the mob to speak on it. But Uriah wasn't someone I saw myself being tied to, so regardless of the circumstance, the only vow she was getting from me was the vow to pay her for her time.

With my hand planted on the wooden dresser, I looked down at Uriah, whose lashes were now resting on her cheeks. When she closed her eyes, that meant she was really locked in, and I knew it wouldn't be long before she was making my dick spit up. I never gave her the chance to swallow, though. I didn't want a woman consuming my DNA on any level if she wasn't to be tied to me indefinitely.

Reaching behind the mirror mounted to the dresser, I removed the gun that was taped there and pointed it at the bathroom door as it was opening. A gasp filled the air as the unwanted guest threw their hands up. Steam surrounded the silhouette, but I couldn't see through the fog clearly. Once I could, my dick betrayed me and grew longer. Perfectly crafted curves were revealed as the towel fell from shielding the body that had to belong to a woman. Uriah wasn't expecting my growth and began choking. Only then did she open her eyes, and seeing the gun pointing toward the bathroom caused her to stop.

"Aht, aht. Keep sucking. I'm almost there," I informed her without looking down.

Like the obedient little housewife she'd been portraying for the last ten years, she closed her eyes and kept doing what the fuck she was called here to do. Getting my dick gobbled while catching someone breaking and entering wasn't on my list of things to do today, but here we were. Instead of focusing on the hardened nipples of the body of the woman I'd identified, I locked eyes with her.

"What the fuck are you doing here?"

When Samuel called about the female companion, I should have known I was right about already adding Uriah to the guest list. There were so many other questions I had, like how she even got inside, but even a badass kid could pick a lock. Still, something told me she didn't do it herself. She had help getting inside my crib. Granted, I was the one who gave her access, but she was not on my list of tasks for today. The final task was currently on her knees, so I was puzzled as I stared at the naked intruder.

The scent from the Olay soap and eucalyptus oils I kept in all the bathrooms lingered in the air. Uriah must've caught the scent, too, because she started bobbing her head faster. Tucking my bottom lip in between my teeth, I held my nut. I needed answers more than I needed to come.

"Mi padre me envió aquí—"

"Aht, aht." I waved the gun, making her stumble back with wide eyes.

Her breast dribbled, making my dick expand further down Uriah's throat. Not many could handle him when he reached his full potential, and the way she was gagging and smearing all of her makeup now was proof she was struggling.

"Me no speak no Espanol today. English... before I send you back across the water with a hole in your head and in a pine box." My voice was strained from me fighting a nut, but I know she heard me because her round, brown eyes looked down at Uriah doing her thing.

"Eyes up here!"

She shifted her eyes back to my face, her wet lashes long and full. "Mi padre—"

"Fuck! Turn around," I shouted out.

Uriah had tightened her jaws as if to pull my attention away from our visitor. I couldn't do that as I watched her spin, doing a one-eighty. Her dimpled ass didn't make shit no better, and I swallowed the moisture that had accumulated in my mouth.

"Pick! Pick up the fucking towel!"

Without bending her knees, she snatched the towel from the floor, and the gap in between her thighs gave me a peek of her fat pussy lips. I kept my gun pointed toward the woman while looking down at Uriah. Her eyes were glossy from all the deep throating she was doing. Pulling my dick from her throat, I sat it on her left cheek and watched as it erupted all over her eyelash and forehead. My chest was pounding hard as fuck as I released. I'd had a lot of nuts, but this one was going down in the history books.

"Here."

I picked up the money from the dresser, not caring how much it was, and handed it to Uriah. She stood to her full height while I opened the dresser with my free hand, pulled out a T-shirt, and pressed it against Uriah's face. Once I was sure I'd gotten all of my DNA off of her, while taking half of her foundation too, I jutted my chin toward the door. I could see little Miss Break-in shaking in her towel, face forward, while the big-ass pink shower cap sagged on the back of her head.

"Um, would you like me to wait in the other room?"

Focusing back on Uriah, I watched as she pulled the trench coat back over her shoulders and stuffed the money into the pocket of her coat. I'd probably given her more than I should have, but I needed her to leave.

"Nah. You can leave. I'll hit you up." I left it at that.

Uriah smiled, nodded, and made her exit without looking at the toweled woman again.

"Mi—"

"Aye... Shut up," I instructed. I needed to hear Uriah actually exit my home. When the alarm sounded, alerting me of her departure, only then did I give her my attention.

Pulling my jeans up around my waist, I tucked my dick back inside, zipped my jeans, and walked in her direction. The closer I got, the more the oils and soap she'd used made my head dizzy. Water droplets were on her shoulder, and the light bra strap that ran vertically on her skin let me know that she spent way too much time outside in little to nothing.

"Turn around."

Instead of following my command, she tensed and stayed with her back to me. "Mi padre—"

"Aye!"

She jumped, but didn't do as I asked.

Leaning in, with my lips near the back of her ear, I inhaled her scent, and it was even more tantalizing. "Didn't I fucking say speak English? I ain't with language hopping today. Now... either you gone use my native language or your preacher gone be standing over your casket speaking yours. Turn the fuck around!"

She spun in a huff with glistening eyes. Instead of raising her hands, she pulled the towel tighter around her frame. Her lips trembled as she began to speak. "Mi... Mi padre—"

Completely depleted of patience, I grabbed her by the neck, placed the gun to her dome, and slammed her up against the wall. I'd only used enough force to let her know I wasn't playing with her ass.

"See... Ion think you know whose house you done pranced into. I may look inviting, love, but I'm far from it. You up in here where I lay my head; nobody comes to my fucking house outside of the people I love. If you in here, that means I trust you deeply, and last I checked, I don't fucking know you. I don't know what the fuck you Hispanics got going on, but I'll make like ICE and snatch you up, except I ain't dumping you at the border *alive*. Now, why the fuck are you here?"

Her chest swelled as she pushed out a deep breath. I was so close to her that I could not only feel the pulse in her neck, but I could hear it too. She was just as pretty as the last time I saw her, which was a little over four weeks ago. At the time, she had a problem with her evil stepmother cutting off her credit cards. Now, she'd stumbled into the lion's den, and a simple phone call to Chase wouldn't be the quick fix she needed. Fucking around and being in my home without my permission had put her in some real danger.

"Mi padre—"

Squeezing her neck, her lips quivered as I gave her one final warning. "Solana..."

"So, *she's* someone you love?"

"What?" I shook my head.

She'd finally complied and spoken in English, but not to clear her name so that she could possibly return to her family Earthside. No—she was questioning me about Uriah as if she had the right. These women were unbelievable. I was choking this girl out, and instead of answering my question, she'd pivoted to ask about another woman. The confusion had to be written all over my face, but that didn't stop her from doubling down.

"You...You said no one comes to your house outside of those that you love?" She scoffed, and the sound shouldn't have been attractive, but she was just that damn pretty, so it was. "What can you teach me? She'd received your ejaculation from a two-dollar whore and drastically overpaid for it?" Rolling her eyes, she shifted them since her neck was still in my grasp. "My father sent me here to shack up with you and your lover. How pathetic of him and you."

Giving her neck another squeeze, I leaned further into her ear and spoke. "You worried about the wrong shit. Dipping off into lanes that have nothing to do with you. You broke in *my* shit. You don't get to question me about a muthafuckin' thing."

Letting her neck go, I took a step back and grabbed my jeans before they could fall. Even as I stood back—removing myself from her space—I still smelled her scent just from that brief encounter.

"I was just saying..." She rolled her eyes as she used one hand to rub her neck while the other one held the towel, even though it was tucked tightly in a roll at her chest.

Ines had asked me to groom his damn daughter like I was some kind of instructor. That nigga had to be hard of hearing and seeing, and the shit must've been hereditary because it took four times of asking her before she finally spoke English.

"You told my father you would get me in line for my future husband."

"No, the fuck I didn't, Solana."

"Well... I'm here, and I'm not leaving." She shrugged. "Rinaldi Mob needs us. And in order for us to bend, you'll get me in shape."

"I'm not discussing what the mob needs or doesn't with you. As a matter of fact, who the fuck is the mob?"

"Really?"

"Yeah, really. Y'all got the Feds on your trail."

"Does it look like I'm wearing a wire?" Her free hand flapped at her side, and I sneered at the fact that I wanted the towel to drop again.

Her Hispanic accent wasn't as thick as her father's, and she spoke perfect English. Still, her heritage ran deep within her pores. She looked like my people, but when she opened her mouth, it gave way that she wasn't from around here. Ethnicities came in all different shades, though, which was why people saw me as a Black man and her as a Mexican woman.

"Fuck all that. Why you break in my shit?"

"I didn't break in! You let me in!"

"I let you in the gate because I thought you were Uriah."

"Right. Cumface..." She snickered.

"My cameras didn't trigger you, and you don't have a key to my shit. Your people went out of their way to sneak you in, and that poses a problem for me. That actually means war, which is some shit y'all can't afford right now, being as though your father is already beefing with the cartel. The same cartel he's swapping you out for. You're a fucking peace treaty, and I'm not the nigga to *prep* you up so that you don't get yourself killed. That's your mama's job."

Solana rolled her eyes and snapped her neck. "Well, she's dead, so..."

"Well, ion know what to tell you." Looking her over again, I frowned. "Where the fuck your clothes at? Put that shit on." Tossing my head for her to move, I nearly popped a vein when she didn't budge. "Yeah, your ass not gone last a day with the Rodríguez Cartel." I chuckled, but it wasn't shit funny.

Not only had my night of nuts been interrupted, but my safety had been compromised. I wasn't fucking with it. Turning, I made the short walk to the dresser and snatched up my phone.

"Who are you calling? Your Don? It's no use…"

Blocking her out, I dialed the number and waited very fucking impatiently for him to pick up. The voicemail came on, but his voice interrupted the greeting as he intercepted the call.

"Shio!"

"Aye, what the fuck going on?"

"Whatever do you mean, Cuppacio?" This nigga had jokes. He knew what the fuck I was talking about. There was no way Solana was here, and he didn't know.

"This girl. Ines daughter. She in my crib."

Solana was picking at her nails as if I hadn't just had a gun pressed to her head. When she started biting down on her cuticles, I had to look away. Shorty was pretty, and her lips looked like they longed to be kissed, but her ass was trouble. And I needed her out of my shit, like yesterday.

"You told him you would get her right."

"I ain't tell him no shit like that!"

"Well, she here now. Handle that."

The phone line went dead, and it took everything in me not to toss that bitch across the room. I felt like I was being set up. I didn't know what the fuck Don had going on, but I wasn't with his obstacles, games, and nonsense-ass riddles he liked to dash out. I didn't have time for this shit—not when my plate was already full.

"I could have told you that your Don already knew," she stated matter-of-factly.

Pulling my pants up on my waist, I swiped my wallet from the dresser. Even though my eyes were on the Afro-Mexican beauty, I was mentally running down my list in my head.

God first.
Make sure the family good.

Eye them Cuppacio boys, the little and the big ones.
Build a relationship with my brother.
Get my brother rich. Health and Wellness.
Stay on top of my mob shit.
Keep Hobo alive.
~~Get through this fucking meeting~~.
House a random.
Find a wife.

I was pissed, but I'd never been the type of nigga to purposely put a woman in harm's way. If she found herself on the wrong side of my wrath, then that was between her and God. This toweled damsel was just a fucking chess piece on the board. Pushing past Solana, I slammed the door behind me. I didn't know this girl from a can of fucking paint, and Don thought it was safe to bring her to me. I didn't know what the fuck that nigga was on, but Ines had one agenda while Don had a whole other one. I felt like I was stuck in the middle of some shit that I had no knowledge about. Fuck I looked like... the babysitter?

Nah. These niggas thought they were playing monkey in the middle, and I was the gotdamn monkey. Little did they know, if they kept fucking with me, they'd be in an all-out war because I wasn't scared to throw the first cannon. Unlike my cousins, nothing I did was predictable, so they'd never see it coming.

CHAPTER 10
SOLANA DAMITA LEDESMA

I never imagined my first trip to America would be under my father's wishes. I had been begging to come to the States long before I found out about my siblings and my dual citizenship. It felt as if I'd been craving to escape Mexico City since I could form a sentence to ask for it. Now here I was —twenty-five and finally given the chance to see the land of the free. Yet, all I wanted now was to go back to Mexico and lock myself in my bedroom, barricading the door.

Ines Ledesma. Mi padre. My papa. Not only was he my everything, but at one point, I would do whatever it was he asked without blinking. As the years progressed, so did his empire, and while the man I loved was still somewhere buried deep inside of him, he'd changed. Long gone was the loving father who used to make tres leches to ease my sweet tooth and take me fishing to help calm me. That papa was a distant memory. He'd turned into someone I didn't recognize most days. The man who would have stood in the line of fire for his family had turned around and deemed his loved ones as expendable. Our entire lineage had either been traded, killed, or jailed for the sake of his freedom, and after a while, it became our norm. Today, all that is left of the Ledesmas are my brothers and I, and now we are collateral.

While I was ecstatic to be away from Maura, my father's wife, I felt like a fish out of the water. I'd been out partying like always, and when I pulled up to my condo to end my night with a shower, my father was there with two of his guards. Funny enough, the guards were the same two who'd flipped on my papa when the man, whose home I was currently in, snapped his fingers. I thought they would be dead the moment our American guest left, but my father had been moving strangely and frantically, so I shouldn't have been surprised to see they still had their jobs and their lives.

Intoxicated and all, my father forced me onto a plane. I was so distraught that all I could do was cry myself to sleep. By the time I woke up, I was shoved into the back of a car. The driver didn't speak to me the entire drive through the foreign city until we approached this neighborhood. Only then did he instruct me to tell the guard at the gate that I was here for Shio. I was even given a key to enter the house, and although the mini-mansion wasn't as big as any of our properties in Mexico, it was still nice. Walking from the back of the truck through the front door, the first thing I noticed was the smell of the air. It was different. It smelled cleaner and lighter, but there was a heaviness present. I couldn't explain it, but anytime I got those types of feelings, nothing good came from it.

Now here I was in a country I yearned for, for so long, not knowing what my father's agenda entailed. I'd been promised to the eldest son of the Rodríguez Family for a year now, but I'd known the possibility of an arranged marriage my entire life so the idea wasn't repulsive. It was how men, like my father, did business. Somewhere in my mind, I'd hoped it wouldn't happen to me, but arranged marriage was normal in my culture. Did I want to be sold off like livestock? No. But I wasn't going to cry about it. It was our way of life, and I respected it. I just didn't think my father would ever match me with a Rodríguez of all the option available.

The Rodríguez Family was one of Mexico's most feared and idolized familias. They were ruthless, and for a long time, the Ledesmas couldn't be touched. When my father began making faulty business decisions that cost us our family, and ultimately his empire, it became easy for the Rodríguezes to step in and take control. The Rodríguez Family was the leading cause of Mexico's rising crime rates, including kidnapping, homicide, trafficking—both human and drug-related—and everything in between. There was a saying that when a Rodríguez had their claws in you, you were as good as dead —*muerto*.

Being in the United States was a way for me to get away from the Rodríguezes, even if only for a little while. It was no secret that they despised Americans, which made me uneasy. I am half African American, with my mother being the most beautiful Black woman I've ever seen, according to the only picture I had of her. I'd be lying if I said I wasn't afraid of what my life would look like after being married off to the son who was set to inherit his family's empire. Just the thought alone made me want to vomit. I'd been primed and prepped to be the wife of a crime boss, and if preparation meant being able to party and spend freely for years, then I'd be the best wife on the planet. I knew better than that, though. My papa had locked me into a deal with the devil. All the years of my papa trying to get me etiquette training and me acting out in response have now come back to bite me. I'd grown fond of doing what I wanted and saying what I wanted, and now that it was time to pay the piper, I didn't know what to do.

My papa was forcing me on this American now, as if he'd

given up, which wasn't a surprise because he'd given up on almost everyone for his own comfort. Then again, Shio had been the first one to give me a command, and I actually listened to it. It wasn't because I feared him either, which is probably what my father assumed. Shio had caught me off guard with his fluent Spanish and good looks. Had I been better prepared, then he would have never sat me down so easily with just his words. There was no taming Solana Ledesma. But for some reason, my father thought shipping me off to another man was the answer to his "me" problem. But, again, his assumption was wrong.

From the moment I was put on the plane, I knew this was where I would end up. Well, I didn't know I would end up sitting in the middle of a bed in Shio's modest-sized home with a growling belly, but I did know that I was going with the American. My papa had outlandish and impulsive ideas that he never methodically thought through. How ridiculous was it to send me off to someone he knew nothing about, to train me to be a "good" wife? What the fuck was a single American man going to teach me? How was an American going to teach me how to be a wife to a Mexican ruler? From the looks of it, the only thing he could teach me was how to receive his ejaculation on my face.

Was there an attraction to the man whose skin tone mirrored mine? Yes, but that didn't mean I wanted to see his penis. I only wanted to shower because I still smelled like hookah smoke. When I saw that the first bedroom I stumbled across was equipped with everything I needed to clean myself, I got lost in the shower. I had no idea I would walk into him getting pleasured, nor did I expect him to place a gun to my head or choke me. My life was in danger; I could see it in his eyes. If I hadn't done what he said and told him why I was here, he was going to harm me. He meant everything he said about sending me back to my family in a body bag; I could feel the truth in his tone. Yet, I was turned on like never before. If I wasn't scared, I would've showered again, but as soon as he left the room, I curled up on the bed in the towel. My brain was in such an overload that I passed out. I must've needed the sleep because I was just now waking up, and it was late in the afternoon.

Still wrapped in the towel, my eyes adjusted to the sunlight streaming through the window. I could feel the heat radiating through the blinds. I'd read about how hot it could get in the States. It was usually the rainy season in Mexico around this time, so the heat came and went quickly, leaving cooler days. Standing up from the bed, I popped my back, adjusted my towel, and let the cold floor beneath my feet guide me to the bathroom. I had a headache, and since there was already enough sun coming through the window, I left the lights off. My clothes from the night before were still damp and scattered across the floor. Stepping right on top of the skimpy dress, I sat down on the toilet and nearly moaned at how good it felt to relieve my bladder.

I was hoping my menstrual cycle wouldn't show up early. I didn't have any sanitary napkins with me, and the only thing I'd found in the vanity drawers when I first showered here were tampons. Tampon use wasn't common in Mexico. Many women were taught that foreign objects did not belong inside of you, and some women even believed that a tampon could get lost once it was in you. I didn't believe anything like that could happen, but I still didn't use them because my father said not to. I'd have to figure out how to get something soon because, according to my Flo app, the bleeding was due to start in a few days. I was crossing my fingers that something would be available in a store here because I didn't want to disobey my father or figure out how to get the cotton inside of me.

Once I wiped and flushed, I stood in front of the mirror. Tightening the towel around my frame, I stared at my reflection.

Estoy hecha un desastre (I'm a mess).

I'd gone to sleep without my eye pads, and it showed. My eyes were swollen and starting to darken around the perimeter. I'd been dumped here with nothing. Well, I had my purse on the nightstand, holding my phone—which was probably dead—my wallet, and my passport. Besides that, all I had were the clothes on my back, which were damp and dirty. I needed to go to the store, but how was I going to do that when my credit card was still cut off? I didn't know anyone in this God-forsaken country who could assist me either. Why would my father dump me here, knowing I had nothing without him and his money? Pretty privilege, that's why. My father thought that because I was pretty and he was who he was—a Mexican crime boss—people would bend to my needs. But this isn't Mexico, and even if it was, he's no longer the most feared in our country; my future in-laws have taken that role.

Pulling the drawer open on the vanity, I found a pack of toothbrushes, toothpaste, and floss. Either this American was as organized as he appeared, or he entertained guests often. After getting myself together as best as I could and finger-combing my thick, straight hair, I went into the bedroom. Instead of making the bed or slipping back inside, I went to the dresser—the same dresser he'd been getting his dick sucked in front of. Snatching a drawer open, I found neatly folded white T-shirts. Since the shirt wouldn't be enough to conceal my entire frame, I pulled a second drawer open. A variety of plaid colored pajama pants stared back at me, and I smiled. Picking up the first pattern I saw, I slid the cotton pants over my bottom and looked at the door as if it would fly open before pulling the shirt over my head. The door was locked, and the chair that was once sitting in the corner of the room was now propped up against it. I didn't know what my homemade barricade would do against a man with a gun, but I couldn't comfortably lie in the home of a stranger without trying to protect myself.

Now, I was fully dressed in his clothing, biting down on my cuticles, and debating going out to find food. My stomach had growled once or twice, but I didn't feel hungry. However, it had been a full day since I consumed solids. If I didn't want to be over a toilet, I needed to get something in my stomach.

"Get it together, Solana." I sighed as I moved the chair out of the way.

With my hand on the knob, I took a deep breath before pushing the door open. The smell of food hit my nose instantly, making my belly rumble loudly. Laughter could be heard from where I stood, which put me on alert. I didn't know if he was entertaining the one he loved again, but I knew I didn't want to walk in on it for a second time. She was on her knees in the most degrading way possible, and then he went and messed all over her face. My body oddly heated from it, and I was still ashamed of that. I tried not to look, but he was so long and thick, and the veins in it made it look as if it were muscled, as if it were his arm instead of his penis. Shuddering, I fake-gagged and shook the image from my mind.

"*Sí, finge que te da asco, Solana,*" ("Yes, pretend he disgusts you, Solana,") I stated my thoughts out loud.

Letting my stomach guide me, I found myself walking to the opposite side of the laughter and into the kitchen. This was the first home I'd been inside in the Americas, and I was trying hard not to fall in love with it. I'm not usually a fan of wooden floors; I tend to prefer other options because I associate wood with a cottage vibe. But the way he had the dark mahogany wood flowing throughout the house, combined with his impeccable taste, was enough to make you swoon. The expensive art lining the walls looked to have cost a small fortune. His home smelled and felt so much like him, which was crazy because I didn't even know the American boy.

Three pizza boxes and four aluminum-covered trays lined the counter. Glancing behind me to ensure the coast was clear, I grabbed a plastic plate and lifted the foil from the first pan.

¡Sí! Pollo.

An assortment of deep-fried chicken wings that had been dipped and tossed in sauces and seasonings stared back at me. This wouldn't be my first time having hot wings. In Mexico City, there were plenty of Americanized restaurants, especially at the malls. Since I practically lived in Centro Santa Fe and Polanco, I'd indulged more than a few times in American cuisine. Picking up the plastic tongs, I added two hot wings, three lemon pepper wings, and what I assumed was a barbecue wing on my plate. In the next pan were French fries with seasoning on top, so I grabbed a few of those too.

"Uncle Shio didn't tell us he had company."

"Ahhh!" Clutching my chest, I jumped back from the counter upon hearing the boyish voice.

My racing heart pained in my chest, and it felt as if every piece of hair on my body had been lifted. My breathing was caught in my throat, and the feeling of something sticky on my feet had me looking down rather than looking back at who had startled me. Sauce decorated my toes, letting me know what I already did—I'd dropped my whole plate.

"Damn, you scary."

Footsteps could be heard behind me, and then the ripping of paper towels. I was still trying to get my bearings together and steady my breathing, so I didn't notice the boyish voice squat down beside me until I could feel the paper towels on my feet.

Looking down, I visibly relaxed, even though my internal organs hadn't gotten the memo just yet. The first thing I noticed was a big ball of silk hair fitted into a bun, and then a tapered fade along the side of his cranium.

"Aye. You good?" he asked.

I nodded my head in response to his question as I stared at him. The boyish voice belonged to a dark-skinned little boy whose skin tone was similar to mine. As he wiped the food from the floor, his eyes met mine, and he smiled. He was so handsome with his perfect white teeth shining against his rich, toned skin. This was the fourth person I'd seen in less than twenty-four hours with skin as dark as mine. The driver, Shio, the one he loved, and now this child. People with darker skin weren't ordinary in Mexico unless they were tourists. That is why my father let me party as much as I wanted. I blended in with many visitors, but amongst my people, I stood out like a decorated sombrero.

"I'm good," I replied, finding my voice as I squatted to help clean up the dropped food.

I'd lied. I wasn't good. I was in a foreign place, unsure of what was coming next or what my papa's endgame was by bringing me here. I didn't have any money or clothes. I felt as if I was in danger, but had no urge to call anyone. Who would I call anyway? My papa? He was the reason I was in this circumstance to begin with. No, thanks. I'd rather be a sitting duck than beg my father to be the father I once knew.

Looking back at the boy, who was dressed more like a grown man in his streetwear, I found him looking back at me. I'd spotted at least three different designer brands on him. Like this house, he was well put-together and looked expensive. I could see the wheels turning in his mind as he tried to figure me out, but instead of asking who I was, he took the plate from me.

"Aite. Go have a seat. Let me clean this shit up," he instructed.

Choosing not to question him either, I stood and walked to one of the barstools connected to the bar top counter nearby. I didn't know what to do or say after I sat, so I gazed around the kitchen. There wasn't much décor in here, but the granite counters, ivory-colored cabinets that didn't clash with the floors, and top-of-the-line appliances were enough to fill the space. The American had done a great job with his home. Even the room I'd slept in was tastefully put together. I'd been begging my father to upgrade our home, but he was old-school and preferred his casita just as it was when he purchased it. His wife didn't give a shit what it looked like as long as she could shop and spend money in peace. She was one of the reasons I'd rented my own apartment in the city. I couldn't stand that bruja.

Even though I had no idea what was next for me as I skated my eyes around the kitchen, I was pleased my second encounter in the States didn't involve a gun being pulled on me. The little boy had been kind enough to clean up my mess, but I cringed at the thought of children. I didn't see myself with any for a long time, if ever. Considering who my future husband was, I was going to find a way to secretly get on birth control. There was no way I was going to have children with a kidnapper, killer, and trafficker rolled into one. I did love children, though, and seeing the handsome boy made me wish for my own little dark chocolate babies. My father and Maura had a house full of kids, and even though I couldn't stand the older ones now, the small ones were my *nenes*. There was just something about the innocence of a child that put me at ease. This one was no exception.

"You my Uncle Shio's bitch?"

The smile on my face fell no sooner than the words left his

mouth. Here I was basking in his innocence, and this little boy was cursing like he was an adult. I'd heard the small one earlier, but thought I'd imagined it since my nerves were coming down from his scaring me. Now I know I wasn't confused. With his legs slightly gapped now that he was standing, his hands were crossed at his waistband as he looked me up and down. My little brothers were always plainly dressed when they weren't in their school clothes. However, this kid was wearing shorts with rips at the knee, Bottega sneakers, a Bottega T-shirt, a diamond necklace and diamonds in both ears, along with a Rolex on his wrist. This was an adult male in a child's body.

Blinking away my concern, I scrunched up my face. "Excuse me?"

He cocked his head and squinted his eyes at me. "I said, 'Are you my Uncle Shio's—'"

"No!" I rushed out before he could curse again. I didn't know if his parents were near and didn't want him to get in trouble if they heard the vile language spewing from his mouth.

"Oh," he replied dismissively.

"Oh?" I found myself questioning.

"Yeah." He shrugged. "I thought he'd finally found his wife."

The kid looked me up and down again, and it was only then that I realized how much of a hot mess I must've looked. I had rolled out of bed and come into the kitchen like I lived here.

"If he did, it isn't me," I assured him, chuckling to ease the tension I was feeling in my chest.

He and I engaged in a stare-off, where it appeared that he was trying to read me while I was only trying to figure out what the hell had become of my life. Just yesterday, I was living carefree, doing what I wanted, and moving as I pleased, following my father's one and only rule that he had set for me.

"Nah..." He shook his head. "If it ain't you, then he *definitely* hasn't found nobody. Nigga ain't gonna *ever* get solidified."

I didn't know what he meant by that, so I replied with, "Oh."

I watched as he tossed the dirty paper towels and plate of floor food, washed his hands, and then grabbed another plate. He stood gapped-legged in front of the foiled pans, and I had to place my attention elsewhere so that I didn't go over and lift his shorts on his waist. He was too handsome to be sagging his pants. I'd seen visitors in Mexico City wear their clothes this way, and it looked silly to me.

"Remind me what you had again. I know hot wings and fries."

"Uh, the lemon pepper one and a barbecue."

He grabbed the tongs and piled my plate, adding more than I originally had, which I appreciated. I was only being modest when I fixed my plate, but I was starving. When he was done with the plate, he opened the fridge, grabbed a bottle of water, and then set the plate down in front of me.

Is he wearing Baccarat? Who the hell is this kid?

"This ain't barbecue. We don't eat barbecue-flavored hot wings 'round here. Here. I'm sure you want some ranch."

He slid a small sauce cup in front of me, which I frowned at. I didn't eat ranch on my chicken wings, but I wasn't going to tell him that, so I just let it sit while picking up a fry. He took a seat next to me and watched as I bit into a hot wing.

"You Black, but you not a nigga..."

I nearly choked on the wing and had to take a swig of water. When I was able to inhale appropriately, and the chicken made its way down my esophagus instead of down my windpipe, I wiped my fingers with the paper towel he'd given me.

"You're a child, but you speak like an adult."

Rubbing his hand down his hairless face, proving he was indeed a child, he looked off. "Yeah, well... life will make you grow up faster than you need to."

I could wholeheartedly relate to his statement that held weight. Growing up, my father allowed me to be a child until he didn't. The switch-up was quick, and I had to grow up and adapt to our way of life fast. Mexico was as brutal as it was beautiful. There was no time for dolls and dance recitals once it was evident that I was no longer a young girl, but a budding young lady.

"I get it..."

His eyes widened before softening as he looked back at me and said, "I've seen a lot, heard a lot, and been through *a lot*. I'm trying to work on my cursing, though. It's hard, but my mama been appreciating me trying."

"Your mother..." I trailed off, not sure what I wanted to say. I was trying to imagine what I thought the woman he'd come from looked like. He was a handsome little boy despite his potty mouth, so I knew he had to be the product of at least one good-looking parent, if not two. With his facial structure that was nearly perfect, I put my pesos on his mother. She was pretty—had to be.

"Yeah. She's pregnant. I been trying not to stress her out. She's happy these days. Got everything she ever wanted."

"And you?" I found myself asking.

Using his teeth to scrape his bottom lip, he looked off into the distance. "After I handle this business I got when I turn eighteen, I'll have everything I ever wanted then."

"And how long is that?"

He held up eight fingers. "This long. I can't fucking wait either."

This little boy was ten years old and rushing the next eight, while I was wishing I could rewind my life back eight years. I had Maura to deal with back then, but I hadn't been kidnapped by my own father to prepare me to be auctioned off to save his ass. Back then, my worries were finding excuses to skip etiquette classes and dodging our chef, who'd been tasked with teaching me the basic cooking skills. All of that seemed so far away.

"My father is Mexican, and my mother was Black," I answered his question from earlier.

"So you half-nigga and half-wetback?" he asked with a straight face.

My hand covered my heart in fake disappointment, and before I could respond to his insult, he burst out laughing.

"I'm just messing with you. You do look Black, though. The only way I know you got some Mexican in you is from your accent. It's thick as fuck. You sound like you straight out a telenovela."

"What do you know about telenovelas?" I grinned. I hadn't watched them since I was a little girl. It was comical hearing him refer to them.

"I watched a few of 'em." He shrugged like it was no big deal. I didn't know much about this country, but I didn't think they watched telenovelas.

"What's your name?"

"Neltz."

Neltz.

To me, it was an odd name for an interesting little boy. It fit him, though.

Smiling at him, I asked, "You're not going to ask me my name?"

He shook his head and stood. "In this family, you learn not to ask too many questions. Besides, I already got a name for you."

"Family?"

"Yeah. We deep as fuck too."

"Well, I would say, 'I can't wait to meet them,' but I'm not sure that I will. I'm just temporary. Just passing through."

Neltz gave me another once over. "Nah. If you're here, you ain't temporary. Everybody got a job to do 'round here... You'll figure yours out soon. Eat up. Yo' stomach keeps on growling. I'ma see you later. Mexi-mami."

Mexi-mami?

Before I could question the child, he was gone. I was shocked he could tell I was Mexican because most Americans tossed me into the "Latina" box, which technically wasn't wrong. But Latina could mean a million different things depending on where you from. Other countries might've mixed in Portuguese or French over the centuries, but Mexico? We've always been Español first. Being from Mexico made me Mexican before anything else. Not every Latino feels connected to that, and not every Mexican fits neatly under the "Latino" label. It's messy, especially for Americans, who never really cared to understand the difference. For that reason, I made it a habit to specify my Afro-Mexican ethnicity in conversation. The fact that Neltz saw me so *easily* made me even more curious about the grown-acting ten-year-old.

Looking down the hall, I assumed he was going back into the area where the laughter had been. Grabbing my plate and water, I made my way back to where I'd come from, closing the door to shut me inside. I was going to eat, fall back into a sleep coma, and pray that my time here was kind to me, and if it was, that it crept by as slow as a snail. I wasn't ready to fulfill my mail-order bride duties. America couldn't be as bad as what the Rodríguezes had up their sleeves for me. At least, I hoped it wasn't.

"Aye... Get up."

My body curled up in a fetal position as the thick duvet was snatched from my lower half. Chill bumps appeared instantaneously. It wasn't that the house was cold, because I hadn't needed to turn the ceiling fan on. It was that I couldn't sleep without covers. My body preferred warmth over coolness.

"Aye," his deep voice sounded, carrying a warning that I could understand even with the sleep fog occupying my mind.

My body wanted sleep, but apparently, the person who was housing me had other plans. I couldn't feel the sun peeking in, even from behind my eyelids, and it felt as if I'd only been asleep for an hour, so I knew it was way too early for me to be awake. Still, I peeled my eyes open to see what it was I was being summoned for.

Shio.

Standing over me, even at this ungodly hour, he was looking just as good as he had every other time I'd seen him. This time, instead of him being in his suit and tie, he was in shorts that stopped high up his thighs and a matching long-sleeved shirt. The room was dark, so I couldn't tell the color of his attire. Whether it was black, brown, or blue, or whatever the hue, he looked *asombroso* (amazing).

I blinked more than a few times awkwardly while reaching for the duvet that was rolled at the end of the bed. Shio quickly grabbed it off the bed, tucking it under his left arm while holding something out to me with his right hand.

"Put this on and come on."

"*Es demasiado temprano para vestirse,* (It's too early to get dressed)" I groaned.

"It's actually *too* late." He dropped the clothes on the bed. "Solana—"

His voice carried a hint of caution. I wasn't sure how many times he'd said my name from his lips before I woke, so instead of waiting to see if he would call my name again, I sat up in bed. My body was still covered in the spare clothing he kept in the drawers.

The same drawer he had been receiving pleasure in front of.

I shook my head, trying to erase the image heating up my body. It was too early to be turned on, especially by someone I had zero intentions of doing anything with. I was only here to be taught whatever my father thought he could teach me. I shook my head again. My father and his ridiculous decisions were starting to cloud my mind again. The math was off. For someone who was considered a crime boss, his logic never made sense to me. The one time a man runs his mouth to me, and I actually listen, is the one time my father decides that same man should train me how to be a wife. A wife! Shio didn't even have a wife of his own to teach me anything.

Dragging my heavy eyelids upward, I blinked a few times to signal that I was now awake. Even in the gloomy room, I could see his dark skin had a slight shine, and I could smell the toothpaste on his breath.

"What time is it?"

Shio, looking down at me with his intense glare, made me reach up and smooth my hair down. I knew it was a mess. Not only had I not tied it back, but I hadn't done anything to it since the night I went partying. I hadn't washed my face or brushed my teeth since yesterday, and with the way I'd been comatose, I knew there was dried saliva somewhere on my face. Here he was looking like he was ready to tackle the day, while I barely knew what day it was.

"It's time to get dressed. Handle your hygiene and meet me downstairs."

Deciding not to give him any trouble, I sat up on the bed.

My body begged to sink back into another sleeping slumber, but the way he was glaring at me made it clear my beauty rest had come to a halt for today. Without waiting for me to reply, he walked out of the room, closing the door behind him.

Mira nomás, one decent man in the world. Miracles do happen.

Opening my eyes widely and then closing them again to allow more moisture to saturate my eyes, I exhaled. After taking a beat, I shifted them to the digital clock on the nightstand.

"Five in the morning? ¡Ay, ya, ya! What is wrong with this man?"

Instead of dwelling on how I had never in my life gotten up this early, I swung my legs over the side of the bed. I wasn't sure if I'd properly handled my hygiene because I had one eye open and one eye closed, but by the time I was dressed, I knew I wouldn't be stepping back into the bathroom, so what I did would have to do. The clothes he dropped on the bed were a deep hunter green ALO set. The leggings, bra, and matching jacket, which I left unzipped with thumb inserts, felt good against my skin, and they fit perfectly, as if he'd filtered through my laundry to guess my size. As I rubbed my hands down the lightweight fabric, I thought about how nice it would be to get back in the sheets before me. I didn't do anything with my hair, letting it hang loosely down my shoulders. I didn't have the energy to pull it into a top knot, and the strands looked like a mix between a bird's nest and a rat's nest. It was a mess. My mind shifted to the bed again. Slipping back onto the cozy, queen-sized mattress wouldn't alter my current state. Knowing I didn't want a gun back in my face, I turned away from the bed in a huff.

Walking down the hall until I reached the stairs that descended, I held onto the wooden rail, careful not to slip in these brand-new socks. By the time I reached the bottom stair and saw what type of situation I'd been summoned into, I turned right back around.

"Aye!"

That one-word syllable froze me in my tracks. With one knee bent, I had a foot on the stair, ready to crawl back to the bed I was already calling my own. Shio's tone—deep, gritty, and *mandón* (bossy)—hit harder than I expected. My papa used to think he could put me in my place by raising his voice too. Shio wasn't my father, though. His voice wasn't just commanding; it sent shockwaves through my brain. When he spoke, my body chose to listen.

"Shio..." I sighed. "I spend my days sleeping until at least noon, shopping, and partying. *Solana no hace ejercicio nunca* (Solana does not exercise, ever.)"

I wasn't the smallest person, and at one hundred sixty-nine pounds and five feet seven, I could stand to hit the gym. Still, even with my reckless eating and weekly drinking, I looked good naked. I hadn't gone up a dress size in two years, and men still tripped over their tongues when I walked into the room. Turning to face him so he could see I was serious, I zipped my jacket because I was starting to feel a cool breeze. Now that I was able to see him in the light, I'd done a double-take of the man before me. With his arms crossed at his crotch and shoulders squared, his black workout attire fit his body and his mood from head to toe. The Nikes on his feet reminded me of my brothers, which reminded me of home. If I were there, I'd still be sleeping in bed.

"Shio! It's too early," I whined, hoping he'd change his mind about whatever was on his agenda today that included me.

Shio wore an expression, though, that said he wasn't buying what I was selling. "Actually, it's late. Thirty minutes, to be exact. I'm usually done with my cardio and finishing up my first rep by now."

"Who works out at five in the morning?"

"Shio Cuppacio."

"Well, *Solana Ledesma* does not." I was bantering with him, but hadn't made a move to go back up the stairs. "My papa sent me here because... I really don't even know why. But whatever he thinks you can fix, trust me, amigo... the gym isn't it."

There were at least eight different machines in the room I'd yet to enter, including a StairMaster. I didn't work out, but I'd seen enough online to know that even though that machine gave you the best butt, it was intense. There was no way in hell I was getting on that contraption.

"To be honest... I don't know what the fuck your father thinks I can do with you either. But you here now, and under my roof, you do as I do. I work out six days a week, but for you, we'll start with two and build from there."

He scanned my body in a non-seductive way. I could see his eyes evaluating me, which was good because I didn't want to die from heavy weightlifting. Still, his gaze made me shift my weight.

"Everyone can benefit from working out," he said as he turned and walked toward the dumbbell rack. "You should want to be the best version of yourself. Working out makes you live better, sleep better, breathe better, *fuck better*." His voice dropped an octave on the last two words he stated, or at least my mind imagined it did. My neck heated, and if there was a mirror, I was almost certain my cheeks would reflect a flushed face.

"You can work out in socks, or you can slide those gym shoes on next to you," he said, snapping me from my internal thoughts.

Looking down, there were a pair of shoes, exactly like his,

but in my size. I wanted to ask where all this had come from, but I had no right to question anything. I had no money, no friends here, and no clue how to navigate this foreign land. I was at his mercy.

Once I had the shoes on, I dragged my feet until I was standing within arm's length of him.

"Working out and eating better are among the hardest things you could do as a human. Consistency produces results and builds healthy habits. There is no man of substance walking the earth who wants a wife without some kind of routine to ensure she's taking care of herself."

The Rodríguezes didn't have any substance. They were *animales*—pigs, to be exact. They had no regard for anyone outside of one another. The only "routine" they'd ever want from me was one that involved me on my back or on my knees, with one of my holes readily available. Just the thought of me being my fiancé's personal sex slave for the rest of my life made me want to vomit. Of all the men my father could have chosen for me, I had to end up with the worst of the *malditos* (bastards).

"Aye."

Blinking away my crude thoughts, I focused on Shio.

"We gone start off on the treadmill. Light day for the newbie."

Nodding, I walked over to the treadmill, looking at the machine like I'd never seen one before. Stepping on the belt, I looked at the screen, wondering how to start it. Shio reached in between and began pressing buttons, close enough for me to feel his authoritative aura. Trailing my eyes from his face to the flexed veins in his arm, I swallowed a moan creeping up my trachea. The tattoos on his dark flesh were tastefully done, the ink telling a story far more interesting than my own life. *Chicago*—the only word I could read, permanently drawn on his skin, stood out the most. Picasso himself must have been the lucky artist responsible for the art on him. They were too well done. My older brothers also had tattoos, and since they were fair-skinned, the details were visible. Looking at Shio's arms, it proved their ink to be cheap, uneven, and *culeros* (ugly). There was no comparison; Shio's ink was perfect. Everything about him was, down to the crisp sheets in the guest room and the natural oils placed at every sink I'd encountered in my three days here. Too clean. Too controlled. Meticulously cautious.

Extremely attractive.

As he continued tinkering with the settings, an alluring scent wafted up my nose. It was masculine, rich, and strong. I leaned in slightly, trying to catch hints of his aroma as if it were my oxygen source. The moment I inhaled deeply, I felt a calming sensation. Lavender—as if a warm blanket had been wrapped around me, followed by praline—a sweet and nutty sensation, like my favorite ice cream. It was the only reason I could identify it. Oud and bergamot couldn't be missed either, dark and heavy. Before I could delve deeper into the scents radiating off this fine specimen, the machine hummed to life, forcing my feet to move.

"*¡Dios mío!* (Oh goodness!)," I screeched out.

No warm-up. No warning.

The belt was moving too fast for walking, but too slow for running. A manageable jog was forced out of me, but I was maintaining for now. Just as my body had grown accustomed to the pace after a few minutes, Shio reached in again, the delightful scent overpowering me, and increased the speed.

"Wait. Wait! This is too fast."

My heart rate tripled, and my lungs became desperate for reprise. My forehead was now drenched in sweat as the belt roared at an alarming speed. I felt at any moment I'd trip over my feet and topple into the elliptical behind me.

"I don't know what the fuck your father is cooking up over there across the water, but I'm not the nigga to plot on," he spoke in an even tone like I wasn't fighting for my life millimeters away from him.

Shio looked calm, but his eyes weren't. I could see the seriousness—the deadliness. I'd seen what he could do when he had my papa's own men turn on him, and then again when he pulled the gun on me without a second thought. I didn't need a treadmill scare to know what kind of man he was. The proof was in the car being angled at the bedroom door. I had no plans to piss this man off in any way, shape, or form.

Crossing his hands in front of him, he licked his lips and tilted his head back. My legs struggled to keep up with the belt, but I knew if I missed a step, I'd seriously injure myself, or worse.

With his eyes still locked on my frantic ones, he kissed his teeth before stating, "I'm bringing you around my family. You're staying where the fuck I lay my head at. If *your people* are on anything other than whatever the fuck they think I can do for you..."

He gripped the railing and leaned in, bringing his sensual scent with him. The gold Jesus piece around his neck dangled as he watched me try to keep the pace. I wasn't breathing; I don't even think I was actually running. I was just trying not to fall because if I did, I'd be on my way to a hospital, if this scary man would even take me. With him so close in my personal space, keeping up with the speed was becoming more and more difficult. My lungs burned, and his watching me as if I were prey had me scared and aroused.

"The Rodríguez Cartel will be *the least* of your worries. If you can't keep up with a five-speed on a treadmill, there ain't shit you can do with me, Solana. *Anda con cuidado, joder. No*

213

estoy bien conectado. (Tread fucking lightly. I ain't wired right.) That's lesson number one."

He hit the emergency stop button just as I was about to go flying backward. He grabbed my forearm to hold me in place, and once I was steady, he let me go. It felt like my heart was trying to escape through my throat. To try and ease some of the pain, I bent over to catch my breath. I shook uncontrollably as my body pumped adrenaline through my glands.

I felt his hand in my hair, and I didn't know whether to cry or beg. If this man thought I'd be able to do anything else after that, he really was *loco* (crazy). When I felt the slight tug on my tresses, I knew then that he was French braiding my matted strands. The touch was unexpected, but I didn't flinch because I didn't want him to stop. I knew who I belonged to, and I had long ago accepted it. Still, whatever braiding technique he was doing felt so good that I had to hold back a moan.

As frightening as Shio was, I wasn't afraid of him. I knew he could hurt me without trying, but he had an aura that made me feel safe. I hadn't realized how comfortable I was in his home until this very moment. I'd been doing nothing at all, but hadn't felt the urge to go out and party as I would've back home. Shio felt like a protector, so even though I haven't made it a priority to hang around him, I knew I was safe under his roof. I had no plans to try him, physically, mentally, or sexually, even though he may assume otherwise.

"I'd hate to have to do you dirty, Solana. Don't fuckin' test me. I'd always been the nigga to ace them shits. Stand up."

On command, I stood, still feeling as if my chest might cave in at any moment. The weight of my hair shifted my head backward, and now that I had a clear view of the mirror in front of me. I pulled my gathered hair over the right side of my shoulder. My tangled hair was now in a neat, thick braid.

Glancing to my side, Shio was no longer there. Hearing the

weights clang together, I found him at the bench, lifting nearly double his own body mass.

"Turn the machine on and press beginner." He lifted the bar with ease. "Like I said, light day."

My heart was pounding as if it wanted to jump out of my chest, run up the stairs, and out of this house without me. I bent over for the twentieth time this morning, trying to catch my breath as my palms rested on my knees, moist from perspiration. My arms felt like flan, my stomach was queasy, and every muscle in my body was on fire. If this was his idea of "taking it easy," I would hate to see what a tough day looked like.

I felt like I was going to throw up, but it had been days since I ate solids, so all I could do was spit. The braid had given up halfway through the workout, stray hairs sticking to my face like glue. I looked like a slob while Shio had barely broken a sweat and looked like he was ready for his closeup for a fitness magazine. The only reason I could think of for his lack of exhaustion was that he wasn't human. He pushed through his workout without a moment's hesitation while I cried, complained, and cursed for the entire two hours of torture. Yes, we'd been down in this hellish zone for one hundred thirty-five minutes. I'd been counting every miserable second, hoping it would end soon.

Dios, envió el rapto. (God, send the rapture.)

"You good?" he sounded from doing pull-ups on the huge machine he'd made me try. While I had to use the stool to help me do the two I did, he had removed it and was solely lifting his whole body over the bars with no help.

Dropping my head back down from staring at his back, I gave a thumbs up even though I wanted to tilt my hand one hundred and eighty degrees. Hell no, I wasn't feeling good. I wasn't "feeling" at all, being that my whole body was on the verge of collapsing. I'd never worked out, and he had just put me through Army recruitment training at the crack of dawn without a single ounce of water or a bite of food.

"Here..."

Looking up, he had a bar in his hand along with a bottle of water. Grabbing the water first, I twisted the top off frantically and chugged it down. The room temperature water felt great going down my throat, even though I preferred my water ice cold.

"You'll cramp up if you drink cold water after a work-out," he said as if he knew what I'd been thinking. Once the water was nearly gone, I took the wrapped snack and noticed it was a cookies and cream protein bar.

"Come on." He turned on his heels before I could reply.

¡Jesús! How does he still smell so good?

I swallowed down my thoughts and made the painful trek behind him. Climbing the stairs was harder than the actual workout. My body felt both weightless and heavy, and my mind hadn't decided if it wanted to float away or give up as we ascended the staircase. I wasn't a bath type of girl; I preferred showers because they were faster, but I would need to soak my limbs if I was going to do another one of these "light" sessions.

By the time I reached the top, he was nowhere to be found, so I followed my nose. His aroma left a trail that led me right to the bedroom I'd been occupying. The bed was made with fresh linen and a candle flickering on the nightstand. My phone was even on the charger next to the candle. I would have preferred it to stay dead because I had nothing to say to the man who helped give me life. Unfortunately, I knew if he couldn't communicate with me, he would show his face, and I didn't want that. Ines Ledesmas showing up here would more than likely end this—whatever this was—and ship me on to Rodríguezes. I wanted to hate my father for selling me off; I'd even tried to will myself to no longer care for his approval. However, the little girl in me held onto the beautiful memories we'd created, and that alone kept me from wishing him harm.

At least he cared enough to send me here to get some kind of help, even though I didn't think Shio could help me in any way. One thing that would come out of my time in America is that I'd leave in the best shape of my life. I didn't know how I felt about that, considering I was set to become Mrs. Rodríguez. The sexier I was, the more that horrible man would want to hump me like a stray dog.

Shio's scent filled the entire room even though he couldn't be seen. I slowly moved into the bathroom, past the open closet door, and found him with his back resting against the dresser in the middle of the walk-in. Despite being a guest bedroom, it was modest in size, and the closet was larger than the one I had in my father's house and my apartment. Shio was texting on his phone as if the closet hadn't changed since earlier this morning.

There wasn't a piece of clothing on the racks, and now one side of the closet had been filled. Threads in a variety of colors hung from the hangers, and shoe boxes were stacked on the shelves above the clothes.

"Shio. You didn't have to do this for me."

"I didn't..."

I gasped at his reply.

"But I did. Your workout days are every Monday, Wednesday, and Thursday. I go to church on Sundays and prefer to do my work outs alone. I've laid out the schedule, so drill that, along with everything I showed you today, into your mind. I hate tardiness, Solana. Find a way to be up and ready without me having to wake you." His eyes drifted from the phone to

217

me, even though his head was still facing his phone. "Listen... You can enjoy your time here, Solana. As long as you don't cross me, we're good. And know that *hiding* shit from me is the same as crossing me. As long as you don't do that, you're good. I'll teach you what I know, and you'll go on to your fiancé."

Licking my dry lips because that one bottle of water wasn't enough, I cocked my head. "You're going to teach me how to be a good wife?"

Shio pushed off the dresser and walked the three paces it took to stand in front of me. He was much taller than me, so to speak directly into my ear, he bent slightly. "I'm going to teach you how to survive. Lesson two. Preparedness. Be aware enough and alert always, so nothing catches you by surprise. Start with waking yourself up and being ready for workouts. Once I see you can do that on your own, we'll discuss heavier tasks like knowing when someone is conning you and how to act with your right hand while your left stays still."

I dropped my head and picked at my nails. He was literally teaching me how to be a woman, and I felt shame for the first time in a long time. My papa didn't speak to me the way Shio did. My papa didn't think it was necessary for me to know much beyond knowing I was meant for another man. I felt small, and for the first time in a long time, I wished for a mother.

Straightening to his full height again, he stared into my eyes. "You'll need to know how to stand on your own two feet. You're going to need that knowledge when dealing with the cartel. Breakfast will be ready in twenty. Get cleaned up."

With that, he exited, and I took a moment to look at the new clothing. Wondering how the hell he managed to get these clothes in here within just two hours, I found the perfect lounge dress to go eat in. I turned and grabbed my purse, pulling out everything I needed after my shower. My papa truly made a mistake by sending me here. Shio sensed my fears and my weakness, and, in short, he was planning to make me strong. I had no idea how effective his methods would be, but since I had no other plans or obligations here in America, I decided to try his way. Once I leave here, I'd be handed over on a golden platter to the Rodríguez Cartel. Hopefully, I'll be a new woman by then. While I didn't know how long I'd be here in the States, I planned to enjoy the time away from my current family and my future one. Being here was about Solana the woman, not Solana the daughter of a cartel boss.

CHAPTER II

TUNAN "TUNE" PAYNE

"Not you got a whole fuckin' brother out here. I just knew your introverted ass was an only child. You ain't never gave *I got a sibling* vibe." Vello hit the blunt before passing it to his twin.

Seeing him and his brother standing next to each other threw me for a loop. I didn't know motherfuckers still walked around sharing the same face. I saw maybe two sets of twins growing up and hadn't seen their asses since. These niggas were identical, and the only thing telling them apart was the big-ass Pia tattoo in the middle of Nel's neck and the way they wore their hair.

Shio kissed his teeth. "Vello, we all grew up like brothers, so the fuck is you saying?"

I glanced at my brother. He had his head in his phone but would bob to the beat every so often. Shio hadn't hit the blunt once while the twins had one in rotation. We were at the studio where Essex was in the booth. He was recording a hard-ass song, and the lyrics were real nigga shit. When Shio told me he was part of the mob, he forgot to mention that Essex was like a brother to him. I'd known about Essex—the tattoo artist—and even tried to book him a few times, but he stayed busy and booked solid. You almost had to show your bank statement just to get a session with that man when he was in his shop. Then, his mixtape dropped a few months back. I was blown away when my cellie told me that his tattoo artist was *the* Essex and that his ass was rapping now.

"I was wondering who the fuck this nigga was at the sniff and dip." Nel tossed his head my way, referencing me.

I'd seen all these niggas at Don's big-ass, mega mansion, but introductions hadn't been made since I wasn't officially in the mob yet, so I played the background. Growing up with a house full of kids, I'd always known how to fade in into the crowd and scope the scene, so that's exactly what I did. Outside of the niggas having some top-of-the-line bad bitches for wives, and everybody rocking limited edition time pieces and pulling up in six-figure cars, it wasn't much to scope out. The scope was that these niggas were living extra fucking large, and I wanted in.

"What the fuck you call that shit?" the light-skinned one, Ezio, asked.

In the short amount of time I had been formally introduced to the Cuppacios, I was able to decipher everyone's personality. Ezio was the leader of the group, but, somehow, I felt like it was by default. I didn't take him as no slaw-ass nigga, but with the way his knee was bouncing, I could tell there was some unspoken shit with him. If he had a choice, he wouldn't lead anything, but he had his family's backs—I could tell that from the way he gripped his toolie while his colored eyes looked to the door every time it opened. Something had happened, and I knew it wasn't my place to know their past business, but I figured if I stuck around long enough, I'd find out what it was. He was the only one wearing a wedding band, and even though he was a man, the ring was icy. It made me wonder what kind of band I was going to get for myself once I locked some junt down. I still couldn't believe I was actually going to get married. Hell, I hadn't even said a word to anyone about it because, technically, Shio wanted to wife Glow for himself.

I'd officially passed the deadline Don had set for me, but that nigga hadn't said shit, so I wasn't either. Two weeks was impossible, especially since I hadn't given women a second glance outside of Glow. I was going to ride this shit out until one of these niggas verbally told me I had no choice. I'd get married eventually, and that Don nigga wouldn't be able to say shit. Until then, I was thuggin'.

"The sniff and dip," Nel repeated as he handed his twin the blunt back. Since Shio and Ezio wasn't smoking, I faced my own, letting the twins have at theirs. It was some killer weed too; had me relaxed as fuck.

"Sniff and sip," I corrected with a chuckle, nearly choking on a cloud of smoke.

Nel raised up in his seat. "Well, excuse the fuck out of me Mr. Corrector. Dip, chip, a fucking bag of zip. All that shit sound dumb as fuck. I thought they was inviting a nigga to sniff some fucking powda. I was about to be like, 'What the fuck Don's ass is on?' It wouldn't be too far-fetched, though, with the way he have us tumbling with the lions. He gotta be on some shit higher than Preston's giraffe's pussies with the bullshit he be coming up with."

"On foe 'nem," Vello affirmed his brother.

Hearing my brother clear his throat, we all shifted our eyes to Shio who spoke with his eyes. The silent communication would have gone unnoticed if I had been slightly higher. It was cool, though; they could have their secrets. I had one of my own.

Shio hadn't spoke to me about Glow since the date night

rescue, and I didn't know if that was his way of giving me the green light or what. Either way, I had zero regrets about fucking her. She had good pussy, was fine as fuck, and wasn't studying my ass. She'd be the perfect wife because that meant she wouldn't be on my back, and since she had more fucking motion than me, she wouldn't be after my money. I didn't have much of it anyway, which is why I was here strictly to get my bread up. Anything outside of that, I didn't give a fuck about. I mean, if I were included, that would be cool. If I wasn't, that was cool too. I had enough family with all of my mama's kids.

"You said you just got outta jail?"

"Yeah," I hesitated to answer Ezio.

"Well, I hope yo' ass learned some finesse in that mutha-fucka. We ain't going to jail. We got too many fucking mouths to feed and too many fucking kids on the way. Matta of fact, I'm glad we got another adult Cuppacio joining the pack. You can take up some of these bills, make it lighter on my pockets. I got a whole baby on the way," Nel fussed, but something told me he didn't mind holding the weight of his family. It could be the brightness in his eyes, or it could have been the grin on his face once he blurted out he was expecting.

I braced myself, expecting them to ask what I'd been involved in, but since it never came, I relaxed. I wasn't the type of guy who walked around, putting his hands on women, and even though Stella deserved for me to break my foot off in her ass, I wasn't happy about what I'd done to her. People hear "domestic violence" and automatically label me as an Ike Turner motherfucker. I wasn't cut from that kind of cloth. Where I'm from, we protect women and children. Unless she did something foul as fuck that warranted repercussions, we didn't lay hands on women unless it was to bring them pleasure.

"So, what do you remember about the Cuppacios?" Nel sat

up a bit in his seat. "The old, sick dead ones; not us new generation of 'em."

Essex spoke into the mic, asking the engineer to restart the track, which I appreciated. He was spitting to a Marvin Gaye classic. I didn't know how the fuck that nigga got the shit cleared, but I was fucking with it, and the streets would too as soon as he dropped it.

"Not shit. Ion recall nun' at all," I spoke truthfully.

I didn't remember much and didn't care to. All I remembered was what the hell my mama and sister went through trying to raise us all. My mama had six different baby daddies, and most of them were either dead or in jail. A daddy was like a foreign language in our house, and we'd learned to operate without them.

"Them niggas weren't shit to remember no way. Ion know how you grew up, and I don't want to downplay your childhood, but just know... you was better off without any of them niggas," Ezio stated through gritted teeth.

"On foe 'nem," Vello added as if that was the only thing he could say.

"No cap," Nel nodded. "We done made them niggas graves fucking porta-potties"

All of their heads whipped in Shio's direction, who was still looking at his phone. He must have sensed us staring at him because his head shot up and he frowned. "What?"

"Nigga, we bonding over our hate for ghosts, and you in la-la land. Can we get a hell yeah, Amen, or something?" Nel blew out a cloud of smoke. He tried to hand the blunt back to Vello, but he declined.

"Shit starting to taste funny," he said as his mouth twisted in disgust. "You done with your cup, Tune?"

I handed him the empty Styrofoam cup at my foot. It had been full of Hennessy until I downed it a minute ago. When the nigga spit in it, I glared at him as if he'd grown a second head.

"I thought you was done with all that fuckin' spitting?" his brother asked him as Ezio and Shio started chuckling.

"Shit be coming and going." He spit again.

"Yeah, just keep yo' lips off my weed until Discover push out them lil' gremlins. Yo' mouth be too fucking wet anyways. Got the blunt soggy as fuck." Nel flicked the lighter and ran it down the length of the blunt.

Vello huffed before spitting again. "Nigga, we got the same fucking DNA!"

"And! We not munching on the same bitch, though. Ion wanna be tasting Discover. She used to be married to a nigga that slurps dicks for dinner!"

"Hunh?" I was caught off guard like a motherfucker with that one. The confusion was evident on my face. "Mane, what the hell you just say?"

"We got a newcomer to the circle. Let me lay shit out for you..." Nel scooted to the edge of his seat. "Ezio is married to Don's long-lost sister. Crazy-ass nigga almost killed the girl too. She overdosed and everything."

"Mane what now?" I asked, making sure I wasn't too high to the point that I was hearing shit.

"Yeah, mayne, he was—"

I held my hand out. "Take that ye out mane, or don't say that shit again."

They all looked at me before Ezio burst out laughing. "Yeah, Nel. Tryna mock this nigga."

"Shut up before I crush a perk and put it in your cup," Nel said while Vello laughed and Shio shook his head. "Like I was saying... this nigga was full of the perky erkys, and Jisei fucked 'round and popped a bad batch. Shit was all bad. Thought they was gonna kill this nigga. Anyway, they married now." Nel shrugged like he hadn't just told me a whole-ass urban fiction storyline in less than three seconds.

Ezio, with his mug on, looked like he wanted to knock Nel's ass out. He'd just been laughing, but I guess the memory of what went down had him in his feelings.

"And my brother here, fell in love with orphan Annie. Come to find out, she was married to the other mobster, who so happens to be our ally, and the nigga takes it in the ass. They got a divorce, though, and now... my brother expecting twins by a bitch he really slick can't afford. It's cool. I can lend you loan or sum'n, Twin." Nel laughed before coughing—an indication that he'd swallowed too much smoke.

Vello didn't take his identical twin's words to heart. Instead, he smirked and flipped him the middle finger. "I can afford my bitch *and* yours, too, nigga. Better ask about yo' big brother."

"Oh, and his pregnant girlfriend is also Essex's baby mama. First baby mama, that is. You know what they say about the BMs and BDs..." Nel kept stirring the pot, and at this point, I had chuckled a few times.

"Shut the fuck up, Nel! Yo' messy ass telling everybody business but yo' own. Tell Tune how you fuckin' on yo' cousin."

"Oh, hell nawl! On God?" I blurted in disbelief. My head was whipping back and forward between all four of these niggas. I didn't know what the fuck Shio had dragged me into, but this shit was entertaining as fuck.

"And that same gay mobster, who is a Don that he's talking about, is about to be his father-in-law. The nigga lived in his house for like six months straight." Vello grinned, knowing he'd poked a bear.

"Nigga! You got me fucked up! I lived in his house on the *other side* of the compound while fuckin' his daughter every gotdamn night. Get that shit right."

"So... you do fuck with yo' cousin?" I asked, and the room went silent.

I tried to remember if I saw him interact with anybody at the Sniff-and-Sip, but came up short. I wasn't watching niggas love connections; I was trying to put faces with names and feel the mob out. Plus, Glow may have caught my eye a time or two. She was just too fucking pretty. How could she not?

"Don't listen to these niggas. She is *not* my cousin!" Nel yelled out.

"Well, why her last name Cuppacio and y'all ain't got married yet?" Ezio challenged.

"And why she on *all* our baby pictures?" Vello was cracking up while Nel was pissed.

"Ezio, you a crack smokin' shit starter—you fuckin' zombie." Nel faced me. "Okay... so we thought she was our cousin—"

"All hell nawl! What da fuck?" I shrieked.

"Nigga, listen to the full story before you judge! We grew up as cousins, but her Cuppacio daddy used to pimp her mama's twat out. So, Pia turned out to be fathered by a different man."

"So, her mama had sex with the gay Don?" I was trying to make sense of all this shit, but I was too damn high and it all was too damn much.

"Yeah. It's a long story, but come to find out, none of Niccoli's children were actually his. One is by the gay Don, and the other is by our Don's uncle, Reuchie. That Matteo nigga is Pia's little sister's big brother. You gotta keep up with this shit nigga... we deep as fuck with a shit load of trauma and problems. But... I ain't fucking my cousin." Nel waved dismissively.

"Nah. You fucking yo' *used to be* cousin," I added.

Everyone roared in laughter, even Shio.

"Aye, let's take it from the top," Essex's voice boomed over the loudspeaker. The engineer pressed a series of buttons, and the beat started over.

This rap shit too close to cap shit
I fuck with killas that will wipe you off the map and shit
I know niggas that's really 'bout that trap shit
Movin' bricks by the boats and stay strapped and shit
Yo' main bitch? Real whack shit
Pussy dry, gotta spit and slap the shit
Follower-ass nigga always trying shit
I'm the nigga that do the crime and the time and shit.

"WE REALLY GIVE that nigga some shit to rap about!" Nel boasted, eyes now red

as fuck from getting too fucking high.

"He be spitting our lives on the track. Just know, if we get a Rico from him telling our fuckin' business over instrumentals, I'm turning into Woody. I'ma be on the phone with Pia like I'm Thug. You *niggers* going down alone."

"Fall back up off my nigga. You act like he wasn't in the field right with our asses," Ezio defended Essex.

"I believe yo' snitching ass too. You be on the phone with Pia telling her all our business, and you ain't even locked the fuck up. Y'all be on the phone in the same fuckin' house, just gossiping."

Nel held up a middle finger in response. These niggas were worse than my brothers and me. I had half a mind to tell Shio fuck no when he told me he was introducing me to the Cuppacios. I'd been in Jagoda Bay for a hot minute and hadn't officially met these niggas, so I didn't see the need. I had too much shit I needed to do before I made a trip back home to the M. But I tagged along after realizing that this meet-and-greet shit was a part of joining the mob. I couldn't lie and say I'd made the wrong decision. I'd been laughing nonstop since I walked in this bitch. These niggas were fools, and I mean, completely ignorant as hell. Nel played too fucking much, but that nigga was someone who made the fucking day. You either wanted to knock his ass out or laugh with him until your fucking face hurt. More than a few times, all the fucking teeth in my mouth had been showing like I was a bitch.

"You been mighty fucking quiet, bible boy," Nel said, setting his sights on Shio.

Without looking up from his phone, he huffed. "Nel. I ain't in the mood for your shit today. Ain't you supposed to be coordinating your pending nuptials?"

"*Ain't you supposed to be coordinating*—shut that shit up! That's what the fuck I hired the wedding planner for."

Vello moved fast, snatching Shio's phone out of his hand. Shio's face hardened as Vello held his phone between him and his brother. Both of them nosy-ass niggas were hovering over the screen.

"And who the fuck is you spying on? I knew yo' quiet ass was crazy, but damn! You stalking now?" Nel asked, his eyes not leaving the screen as his twin held it with a smirk on his face. Now they had me interested in what the fuck it was they were viewing on Shio's phone. "Stalking? What the fuck going on, big bro?"

Ezio stood and hovered over the couch where the twins were sitting so that he could get a view. The studio was dimly lit, so the glow of the screen was on all of their faces. "Who the fuck you spying on, bruh?" Ezio asked with a tilted head as he rounded the couch to get back to his seat.

Shio plucked his phone from the twins' hands, locked the

screen, and stuck it back in his pocket. While Essex continued to rap, we all waited on Shio. I hadn't seen the screen, but from everyone's verbal observation, he was watching a woman.

"I got a house guest."

Nel grinned. "Neltz said you had some fine shit in the kitchen, eating all the chicken. I thought my young nigga was cappin'."

"Hold up! What the fuck you mean you got a *house guest*?" Ezio probed, and I'm happy he did because I was curious too.

Shio rubbed his hand down his chin. "Long story short, Don set me up with a business acquaintance. This *acquaintance* thinks I can teach his daughter how to be a wife. She's promised to one of the members of the Rodríguez Cartel."

"Talkin' 'bout the ruthless Rodríguez Cartel? The mutha-fuckas they say the Mexican version of our dead-ass daddies?" Vello asked for clarification.

I didn't know who the fuck the Rodríguez Cartel was, but with the look of disgust on everyone's faces, I take it that the Cuppacios weren't a fan.

"Yeah. Them. I have one of their fiancées in my crib. Her daddy wants her to get prepared before he hands her over to them."

Confusion plagued everyone's faces, including mine.

"Wait a damn minute..." Nel chuckled. "Ion follow. So the nigga who have yet to secure a wife is teaching a hoe how to be a wife? You better off teaching her how to swallow."

I shook my head, holding back my laugh. This nigga had no home-training.

"Nel, this ain't even that type of party." Shio sighed, and for the first time today, I could see how the quiet shit was Shio's way of thinking through his current predicament. "The most I can do is help her not get herself killed on the honeymoon."

Vello whistled. "Shit, what 'bout after the honeymoon?

Those crazy-ass Mexicans just might sell her ass off to some unheard-of country if it means they can get something out of it. At least that's what I heard. I never seen none of 'em before."

Nel kissed his teeth and leaned away from his brother. "That's cuz you ain't got no fuckin' passport. You barely seen Jagoda Bay."

"I do got a fuckin' passport, nigga. My bitch well-traveled. Soon as she drop them loads, we on the jet. And if I didn't have one, I could just use yours, Twin. We identical, remember?"

Nel held up a middle finger before looking back at Shio. "So. You got a broad that you gotta take care of now? What the fuck kind of shit do they have you tied to? Shit, you may as well say that's yo' hoe."

"I don't know what the fuck going on, to be honest. But she not mine," Shio declared in a sharp tone.

"You got a bitch that you can't give no dick?"

Shio squared his shoulders. "I ain't trying to fuck that girl, Nel."

"You got a dime that you 'bout to give all yo' time."

Shio sighed while Ezio and I pressed our lips together. I was trying to match my brother's serious stance, but Nel was stupid. How could we not laugh at his ass?

"You got a girl that you gotta let in your world?" he continued.

"Shit's crazy." Shio grunted and locked his hands behind his head.

"You got sum'n thick that can't hop on yo' pogo stick?"

I cocked my head at Nel. "Okay, now, Dr. Seuss." Shio looked indifferent, and I knew the Cuppacios weren't helping his brainstorming.

Ezio laughed. "Nel stupid as fuck."

"Being in this studio listening to this nigga rhyme got me inspired and on that type of time."

"Twin... you serious, ain't cha?" Vello asked, and Ezio laughed harder.

"This nigga needs to shut up," Ezio said, and I was happy he did because I didn't know these niggas well enough to have said it myself.

Nel tossed his dreads back. "Shut don't go up, shut go down. All you niggas some Cuppacio clowns."

This mane don't got no sense.

"Aye, G. You good, though?" I gave Shio my attention. Despite being quiet and refusing to give in to the banter, he didn't look stressed. I let it go because I would like to think that if he needed help with whatever the fuck was happening at his crib, he'd let me know.

Vello shrugged. "While you're trying to teach the next nigga's hoe, you need to track the lo' on one of the singles out here. On foe 'nem."

"Aye, Tunan. You got a bitch? You know you gotta get hitched?" Nel asked.

"Getting married ain't gon' be a problem," was all I gave his Cat in the Hat ass.

I had essentially taken my brother's bitch, and before I told these niggas, I had to tell him. He couldn't have cared much about Glow because he sent me to entertain her for the evening. As much as I told myself I wasn't looking for a girl, Glow came to mind every time I thought about one. I kept telling myself our union would be one of convenience, so I would do best to keep the shit about my gwap.

I noticed how she looked when the wives were talking amongst themselves. Outside of Don's fine-ass wife, I didn't know which woman belonged to whom. Don made it a point to let the party know who the queen of their massive castle was, but the remaining men played it cool. All of the women were fucking finer than a fresh stack of blue faces, and everyone had big-ass rocks on their left hand.

I didn't know if it was the marriage, the lifestyle, or just the sisterhood she wanted. Maybe it was all three, and I didn't judge. She'd given a nigga a whole list of shit that proved she wasn't trying to be committed, so my guess was that she just wanted to belong. My hope was that it was because, outside of paying her bills, this marriage was strictly business for me. I fucked with Glow, but this wasn't going to be anything but a role for her. This was not about to be another Stella situation. Tunan would be no one's doctor or nurse ever again. Glow had her own bag and was healthy to the naked eye. I had half a mind to ask her for her MyChart. I was deadass serious about not nursing anybody back to health.

"Aye, let me see that phone again. All I could see was the silhouette of a woman in bed sleeping. What she look like? Neltz mind still a lil' foggy from the shooting. The other day, he claimed something fine, and she looked like she was straight out of the Bricks."

"What's wrong with something out of the Bricks?" Ezio spoke up.

"Nigga... just because Jisei's poor ass lived in the hood for a bit and her crack-headed-ass step daddy still roaming the dirt, that don't mean you got a ghetto princess. You know what I meant. Not the fine ones from the Bricks, the busted buttaface ones," Nel stated matter-of-factly. The weed was gone with nothing but the smoke lingering in the air.

Jisei was Ezio's wife.

She must have been the brown-skinned one that Don couldn't seem to stay away from. Judging by her clothing and jewelry, she was the mafia princess indeed. I'd seen her hold a baby briefly, and now that I think about it, the baby had the same eyes as Ezio.

"Nigga, you talkin' shit when Pia lived just a block away

from the Bricks. Plus, she ghetto as fuck. Newsflash, all ghetto girls aren't busted."

Pia. Pia. Which one was Pia?

I thought back to that night. There were two dark-skinned pregnant women standing next to each other most of the night. One looked like she was about to pop, and I remember thinking she had to have been pregnant with more than one. Discover was what I'd heard someone call her. She was wearing a ring, except it wasn't on her ring finger. Yeah, that had to be Vello's bitch. He'd left early, and I didn't see her anymore either. They'd said she was married once before, and since Vello had yet to marry her, the ring finger being empty connected the two. The other girl had a boulder on her finger. I'd gotten a good look at her ring, and it was carved with the image of a rose. Nel's tattoo had roses surrounding the name. That had to be Pia.

These niggas had done damn good. Exceptional, actually. All the women looked good, and in a way, matched these niggas to a T, even from the small glimpses I was able to catch. I was certain that an unspoken requirement to join the mob was that your wife had to be a walking sin. I hadn't seen an ugly woman the whole party, Glow included.

"Fuck all that! Y'all playing dumb, but y'all know not all the bitches from the Bricks ugly. Any-fucking-way, Shio let me see that phone again, my boy."

"I'm not letting you see shit. Fuck is you so worried about what I got going on for anyway?" Shio spoke casually.

"Because I need to see if you really gonna be schoolin' the bitch, or if you gonna be over there breakin' the man's wife in. The way she looks is going to tell me *everything* I need to know."

Shio stood, pulling his jeans up on his waist which immediately fell right back to the prior position due to the weight of his phones and money. "She straight. But, again, I ain't on that."

Nel twisted his mouth, and when his brother did the same, I nearly barked out a laugh.

"If she straight let us see..." Vello egged the exchange on.

"If my brodie said she straight, that mean she straight. If the broad was decent, he'd say she was. Get off his dick, Double Mint twins!" Ezio stood, slapping hands with Shio.

"I'm not you niggas. I can practice self-control. I don't know what the fuck Don got going on, but I'ma teach her how to protect herself, and that's all I can do. I'm sending her right back to Mexico the same way she came."

"What do you mean, the same way she came? As a Mexican? That's how you're sending her back?"

Shio looked Nel square in the eyes, unblinking. "Unfucked by me. That's what I mean."

Nel squinted his eyes, and their stare off seemed to go on for minutes until Nel stood. "Aite. I know you not gone fuck her. You always liked Black girls. I've never known you to go to Taco Bell, ever."

I'd fucked a few times outside of my race, and that shit was a zero out of ten. I did not fucking recommend it.

"Well, Tune, welcome to the fucking family. You straight?" Ezio asked as he slapped hands with me.

I knew he was asking if my pockets were good, and even though I wasn't in a position to turn down any help, I did just that. If I wasn't taking any chunks of change from my cellie, I definitely wasn't taking any from Ezio. I had about a hundred and twelve thousand, mostly from Shio and the rest from my brothers. I wasn't rich, but I wasn't as fucked up as I was when I found out Stella and her scammer had run off with my shit. Still, I didn't like handouts. I worked for mine—always had.

I appreciated Ezio, but I was good. I was still driving the

old Infinity and living with my sister. I didn't have any bills, not even a phone bill, since Shio blessed me with two brand new iPhones. I took that as a sign to use one for any business I handled, and the other for my personal usage. I hadn't bought any clothes outside of the suit we wore to see Don when he canceled on our asses. My brothers had gifted me a new wardrobe, so I looked the part. I was blessed, and once I made this nuptial move, I'd be even more blessed. I never saw myself in the mob, but if it meant fattening my pockets, then I was all in.

I stood with my hand still clasped in Ezio's. He embraced me in a brotherly hug.

"We Cuppacios are all fucked up, but we go to war for our own. You're one of us, so that means the same way I feel about these niggas, I feel about you. Time don't mean shit when we share the same blood."

"I appreciate that, bruh." I shook hands with the rest of the clan, including Shio. He was still spaced out, but if the nigga said he was good, I wasn't going to pry.

"Now that we got the meet and greets out the way... Aye, Essex!" Nel swaggered to the door of the booth with Vello shaking his head, but hot on his tail. "Let me spit some shit on the track. I'll waive my feature fee."

Nel pulled the door open without permission, alarming Essex who probably didn't hear his ass through the walls of the booth. Still, he pulled the earphones from his ear and handed them to Nel with a grin, knowing what type of time Nel was on.

"Twin, you can't even rap—" was all we heard from Vello before the door closed, shutting them in the soundproof booth.

"Aye..." Ezio diverted his attention to Shio.

"Yeah?"

"You sure you got that under control?"

My eyes shifted to Shio. He licked his lips and rubbed his hand down his wavy head. "Yeah. You know me... I'm not gone fuck her, Ezee."

"Yeah. I know *you*, not her. No temptation has overtaken you that is not common to man. God is faithful, and he will not let you be tempted beyond your ability, but with the temptation he will also provide a way of escape, that you may be able to endure it," Ezio quoted.

Shio's eyes lit up. "Corinthians 10:13. You been reading your bible."

"Nigga, I been reading that book of daily devotions you gave me."

Shio beamed in approval. "You may as well come to church."

"I may as well not. I tithe to your crooked-ass stepdaddy every Sunday, read my devotions, and I pray. That's all I got for ya."

Shio nodded.

"I'll take that. But I'm good, Ezee. I promise. You know ion make those without the intention of keeping them."

They both looked at each other, communicating with their eyes, and even though I didn't know what was being said, I knew. Shio was a man of his word. Ezio knew it too. There were a whole lot of gaps in the story of this woman, whom he was now housing, but if he didn't tell me, I wouldn't ask. It wasn't my problem one way or another. I couldn't afford those any fucking way. These niggas could.

"Good. You always been the better Cuppacio. If it was me or Dumb and Dumber over there before we met our women, we would have started a whole war."

"How so?" I butted in.

Ezio swiped his nose with his thumb. "We would have fucked."

"Even though y'all don't know what she looks like?"

Ezio eyed Shio again. "With the way this nigga all tense, I know she decent. He just better hope his faith in his restraint is bigger than his desires. Ion feel like shooting shit out with Mexicans. I'll call Trump on them muthafuckas."

We all laughed. I was all for making my bread, but a war? Nah, I ain't sign up for that shit. I'd hoped my daddy's son kept his dick in his pants. Temptation was a motherfucker.

CHAPTER 12

GLOW

As I watched myself scarf down a large bite of a cheeseburger, I had to swallow back the bile that rose up my throat. On the plate in front of me were three double cheeseburgers and a platter full of French fries. I would never eat that much food, but I needed it for my thumbnail on the video I was editing. This review would not only go on my personal social sites, but also on my YouTube channel.

Greasy Meats was a brand-new burger spot not far from the Bricks, but not too close to the nearest suburb. The owner, a middle-aged Black guy with a bodybuilder physique, who looked like he'd never consumed a burger in his life, had been in my inbox and email for months. He was trying to get me to film at his new place of business to attract a crowd. Finally deciding to give it a try, I went in yesterday. While the food was delicious, seeing myself consume that much food in the playback had me full already, and I hadn't even eaten anything today yet.

"Whatcha doin'?"

Diverting my gaze from the laptop resting on my lap to a

younger face that was uncannily similar to mine, my heart skipped a few beats as I admired my sister. Glee was finally home. Well, she'd been home in Sparkling City with our mother for a couple of days, but now, she was at my townhouse, where she would remain until she had to be back to Blake U come August. I knew I missed my baby sister, but as soon as her car pulled into my driveway last night, I was able to relish in how much I actually missed her.

"I'm editing this video, so I can post it today," I replied before turning back to the MacBook.

I tried to post a food vlog at least twice a week, even though sometimes it only happened once. Posting consistently meant sometimes I had to get in the kitchen and whip something together. I wasn't the best cook, but I followed directions well, and with all the recipes floating online, my food could give Gordan Ramsey a run for his money. I rarely cooked, though, because with it being just me in my townhouse, leftover food almost always went to waste.

Glee, wearing her oversized school shirt and a pair of biker shorts, flopped down next to me. She'd gotten the Dominicans to straighten her hair, and the smell of the products mixed with whatever fruity-scented body wash and lotions she used sat down with her. Her hair had grown longer, now flowing past her bra line, and the countless hours she spent walking around campus under that Georgia sun seemed to have lightened her hair. It was now a lighter brown and looked great against her light complexion. I made sure she didn't come up here until she was no longer sick, and while her golden color hadn't fully returned, she didn't look as pale as before. She could only get a few more shades darker anyway. Both of our parents are light-skinned, so we didn't stand a chance. We had just enough melanin in our skin for people to know what we were: beautiful Black American women, and proud of it.

"Ugh, you could have waited for me to get here. Those burgers look too good."

Glee looked as if she was about to salivate all over my computer, so I playfully nudged her back. It felt good to have my sister here; I thought I was going to have to pop up at that school and snatch her up when she was ignoring my calls. She spent last summer on campus, able to start school earlier than most because of her scholarship. I was glad she decided to come home this summer and start her sophomore year with everyone else. I was planning to have the best time with her over the next few weeks. My hope was that she and Blayke would focus on being young, single women. I didn't want them to get caught up in the glamour that niggas had in Jagoda Bay, thinking they needed boyfriends, or even "play" friends. She would be going to school for the next ten years, so I wanted her to have fun. But it was equally important to me as her big sister to encourage her to remain responsibility-free—that included other people and their needs and feelings.

"For what it's worth, there are plenty of leftovers in the fridge. I don't know how you feel about microwaving them, though. Burgers may be soggy." I gave a one-armed shrug.

"I'm a broke college student. I've had many days eating leftovers of far less desirable things. I'ma tear them burgers up."

Snapping my neck to my sister just as I was cutting down some of the video, she held in her laughter. Glee was many things, but being broke wasn't one of them. Since she'd gone to school on a full scholarship, that helped my mother out tremendously. She deposited a hundred dollars a week into Glee's account, and each month when my social media payments came in, I transferred funds into her account as well. Her scholarship also included a meal plan that allowed her to eat at any of the restaurants on campus, plus I randomly sent groceries to their student apartment. If she was eating cheap leftovers, it was because she had her head so far in the books that she chose to eat whatever she could grab to get back to her studies. I'd rolled my eyes, but just that quick, I'd smiled. I remembered being her age, not knowing what the fuck I wanted to do. Social media had come through and changed my life, giving me not only a career but a purpose.

Had it not been for that, I don't know what I would have done. My baby sister, though, was a bright soul. She'd been sure of herself from the moment she entered this world. When we used to play dolls, she would always be the one giving our Barbies full check-ups, with a pink stethoscope in her ear and one of our mothers' white T-shirts that mimicked her white coat, until she was gifted one at seven for Christmas. Calista Glee had been put on this earth to do the right thing, and I was going to support all of her efforts on her current path.

"You know I'm so fucking proud of you, right?" A wave of emotion hit me out of nowhere while eyeing my beautiful sister. She was so driven, so focused, so innocent. The thought of anyone touching a hair on her head made me tear up.

Glee tossed her arms around my neck and placed her bony chin on my shoulder. She was so close that her nose tickled the side of my face.

"I'm proud of you, too, sister. You tend to downplay your achievements, but in reality... you're in the twentieth percentile, and you're not number twenty!" We giggled as she snapped her fingers. "You have a dedicated fan base that adores you. The Eaters are like a cult with how fiercely they support you. All it takes is for Glow the Pretty Eater to show up at a restaurant, and here come your minions... selling them out. You're totally the female Keith Lee!"

We both laughed as I blinked away my tears.

"For real, you made something out of nothing, and now

you're living it up. You like to boast on me, but you make a doctor's salary without all the hard schooling and dreadful hours of studying. You inspire me, Glow. I love you, sister."

I still had another two weeks before I was on my period, so I didn't know why I was so emotional. It had to have been my approaching ovulation. The tears fell, but I used my shoulder to swipe them away.

"Mama did good with us, hunh?" I boasted.

Glee rolled her eyes, making me laugh. "She swears that."

"That's because it's true."

Our mama really did do her big one with us two. A divorced mom raising two daughters in a new city wasn't easy. But both of her girls had made it out of high school without a baby, and one was in college on a full ride, while the other had made a name for herself in the online communities. She had done damn good.

Ping

The alert of a new message appeared on the screen, and I, not thinking much of it, clicked on it. I hadn't heard from the girls in a few days, and as much as I wanted to reach out, I held back. Jisei was my best friend, but she was also a new mom and a new wife. I didn't want to come off as the "worried single friend" and have Ezio side-eyeing me, so I let her have her time. With the other women, I usually sent them a quick "hey" text, but I kept those to a minimum too. The group chat had been quiet since the day after the Sniff-and-Sip. I couldn't even pretend that didn't bother me, especially since I knew they'd been communicating in their other group chats that didn't include me.

901-428-6632

Pull up on a nigga.

"Oh, so The Eater been holding out. Who is *a nigga?*"

I didn't know if it was from amusement or confusion, but my heart was racing as I stared at those five words on my computer screen. The number wasn't saved, but somehow I knew exactly who it was. I could even hear the message in his deep, southern voice, which was more southern than mine. I hadn't heard from Tunan since the party, yet his image and scent had appeared in my mind more than once over the past week. Tunan was a walking red flag. He wasn't the flashiest, didn't drive a six-figure car, and didn't have the wealth and stature of the men my girls usually date, but just the thought of him made my girl below tingle.

Probably because he knocked the dust off my coochie.

"Are you going to text Mr. Nigga back, orrr...?" Glee snapped me out of thoughts I shouldn't be having, and instead of replying, I closed my computer and placed it on the ottoman in front of us. "Uggh! You're no fun."

Standing, I snatched up my phone from the couch and headed to the kitchen with Glee on my heels. Stopping at the sink, I washed my hands, dried them with paper towels from the stainless steel holder that matched my appliances, and opened my fridge. Pulling out the carryout container, I made a note to go grocery shopping. With two college students, who would be living with me this summer, I had to make sure everything was stocked. Glee could go without, but that Blayke could eat.

"Where Blayke at? Her people making her stay home to attend Bible camp?"

Assembling the burgers on a plate, I placed them in the microwave to heat them up.

"Oh, her flight comes in soon. I'm picking her up from the

airport."

Unlike my sister, Blayke didn't have a car yet. They weren't allowed on campus during their freshman year anyhow, but Glee planned to take it back to school with her for their sophomore year. I guess since Blayke didn't ride with my sister here for whatever reason, she decided to fly in from Sparkling City. I assumed a flight to such a nearby city cost her nothing, but to get away from the Deacons, I was sure Blayke would empty her account. They would be straight here, though. I even planned to take them shopping for a few summer outfits. I also planned to pay them to help me sort through my PR packages; anything I didn't want or had too much of, they could have. Sometimes a brand would send me one of everything in every color. I loved clothes just as much as the next woman, but I didn't need that much.

Instead of responding to Glee, I handed her the hot food and gestured toward the stool at the island. "Eat."

A toothless grin spread across her face as she sauntered to sit down.

I grabbed her a bottle of water from the fridge and slid it across the granite. Once I was sure she was busy with her burger, I finally pulled my phone out of the pocket of my athletic leggings and unlocked the screen. Swiping past hundreds of notifications from various apps, I went to the messaging icon. His message was right at the top. My thumb hovered over it.

What should I say? Do I want to see him? Was he serious about the marriage? Was I even serious about agreeing to a marriage?

I wanted to belong, to be fully a part of my only friends' circle, but at what cost? I didn't know what the hell my friends' men were involved in—I mean, not really. I knew it was a mob, even though I pretended not to notice. I kept telling myself I'd just been hearing things over the last two years when someone let a comment slip in my presence. Tunan, however, had cleared up any doubts I might've had about what was going on, and while I didn't know the intimate details, I knew enough to still want to be included.

I hadn't been hearing things, and those slipped-up comments were real life. My girls were mob wives, and the men they married were a part of the mob—a mob I was sure was run by Demise since he was titled Don. Now, this man, whom I didn't know at all, had offered me a way in. His offer would give me the one thing I'd been craving, and all I had to do was take his last name.

Pull up on a nigga, hunh?

He wanted to see me. A small part of me wanted to see him too. But I wasn't going there with Tunan. Not now. Not ever. I'd see what he was talking about with our arrangement, though.

> Where are you, Tunan?

IT TOOK him less than a minute to send me his location. He was almost seven hours away, in a completely different city—one I had no interest in visiting, especially given how the city stayed in the news with the rising homicide rate. Memphis was worse than Chicago these days. Their artists were killing the music scene right now, but their YNs had the streets in a chokehold.

Looking up from my phone, I found my sister watching me as she ate her second burger, with only juice left from the first. Ignoring her teasing looks, I typed out a reply.

> Absolutely not.

901-428-6632

Why not?

> Because you're in Memphis. Y'all too ignorant down there for me. 🏚️

901-428-6632

Stop watching the news. We ain't that bad.
Come fuck with ya boy.

> I'm good. A nigga has never had me that "in like" for me to take a road trip for him. 🙄

901-428-6632

Who said some shit about driving? 😏

BEFORE I COULD REPLY, the Apple Pay notification bubbles popped up on the screen. I held my breath in anticipation. The last person who sent me money was Shio, and even though it was always unexpected, I really appreciated it. I hadn't heard from Shio since he stood me up for our date. I'd officially been disqualified by him, and even though rejection stung, I wasn't too upset about it. I knew that man wasn't feeling me like that. His actions, or lack thereof, proved it.

Twelve hundred dollars was now sitting in my Apple Pay wallet, and the smile on my face was an indication of it. He'd paid the tab at dinner, which wasn't cheap, agreed to pay my bills in the wake that I did take his last name, and had now sent me a little over a stack. If his intentions were to impress me, he was off to a good start.

Glow, you not looking for a man, nor do you want one.

247

901-428-6632

Attachment There is a flight that leaves out
in two hours and it can take you back home
tomorrow morning. You ain't gotta be scared,
I ain't gone let shit happen to you, pretty
eater.

PRETTY EATER.

It was something one of my followers called me years ago,
and it then turned into my brand and a whole fan base. Nowa-
days, "eater" has a whole new meaning, but it was too late for
me to change it. For some reason, Tunan calling me the nickname, I felt like he didn't mean it in the context of my brand.

901-428-6632

I got that paperwork you wanted drawn up.
Come on. Plus, I can take you to a spot that
will for sure have your views going up. Best
food you'd ever eat. 😊

"MY VIEWS ARE ALREADY UP," I mumbled.

"What was that, sister?" Glee said, trying to get any bit of
information out of me.

Sticking my tongue out at Glee, I exited the text thread and
went to Delta's website. It only took three taps for me to find
that flight he'd sent. For the round trip, it was only a little over
four hundred dollars. He'd sent three times that amount. I
didn't know if it was desperation that had me checking out the
flight or pure curiosity.

My God, am I really that desperate to be in the friend group that

I'm considering this stupid shit?

I'd just been bragging about how my mama had done a good job raising us, but that statement may have been flawed. I was stupid as hell, especially since my ticket was secured. I was acting a whole damn fool out here for a man that I hardly knew, all because he was a path for me to no longer be the outcast of my friends. It was too late to beat myself up, so I pushed off the counter and gave my attention to my sister.

"Glee."

"Hmm?" She held back a grin as if she already knew what I was going to ask her.

"What time does Blayke's flight get in?"

She placed her last half-eaten burger down. I didn't know where Glee's food went. As of late she ate what she wanted and didn't gain a pound. Well, she'd gained the freshman fifteen, but if she kept walking around campus for the next few years, she'd lose it.

"So you getting flewed out?"

I stomped. "Girl! What time is her flight coming?"

Glee's smile didn't vanish; she simply picked her phone up to check the time. "In a little under three hours. She had a layover in Kentucky."

I shook my head. That was wild considering the flight from here to Sparkling City was about thirty-eight minutes, depending on the pilot.

"Don't have no boys in my house." I pointed at her as I walked out of the kitchen to pack a bag.

I'd be back here by noon tomorrow, but I still couldn't travel without my necessities. I had TSA PreCheck, so I didn't have to worry about getting to the airport more than thirty minutes before my flight. I usually traveled in something comfortable, but since Tunan would be picking me up once the plane landed, I was about to beat my face and get fly.

By the time I had my carry-on from the hall closet unzipped but packed on my bed, my sister was in the door-frame of my room. "I'm serious about the boys, Glee."

I knew my sister and her bestie were adults by law, but I didn't want anyone in my house while I was in another city. Niggas were grimy. I wasn't worried about them taking shit except of advantage of my sister. Blayke could hold her own, and materials could be replaced, but stealing my baby sister's innocence was irreplaceable and would grant me a first-class flight to jail. I wasn't playing behind Calista Glee, ever. She was too fucking good for these niggas.

Glee folded her arms. "Boys are the last thing on either of our minds." Her words were laced with hurt, and it made me snap my head up.

"Did something happen at the school, Calista?" I stopped tossing underwear into the bag, ready to burn Blake University to the ground behind mine.

Glee waved her hand. "No, Glow. I'm just not worried about men."

"Men, hunh?" I squinted my eyes.

"Boys... men... same thing. I'm not focused on them. Now, where you flying to?"

Opening another drawer, I grabbed a pair of pajamas. I didn't fully believe my sister, but I would let it go for now. When I got back, I was going to figure out what had gone down all those months she hadn't been taking my calls. My initial intuition was proving to be correct.

"Memphis."

Her eyes expanded, but her smile widened. "Oh, baby... you got yourself a certified YN. How the hell you get caught up with a Memphis nigga?"

I didn't have an answer for Glee because, at this point, I was asking myself the same thing.

"Aye mayne! Say mayne. Whole lotta Memphis ish going on," Glee mimicked, causing me to roar in laughter.

"Please... *never* do that again. You sound like Terrance Howard in Hustle and Flow."

I hadn't really known many people from Memphis, but I knew enough to realize that her impression of the accent was terrible. Memphians are country, and they have that twang in their speech because I could hear it every time Tunan opened his mouth, but they weren't that damn country.

"I'm just saying, that's how they sound. Now, where you meet him, and is it serious?"

Plopping down on the bed beside my half-packed suitcase, I shrugged. I didn't know what the hell I was doing. As a big sister, who wanted my little sister to be the complete opposite of me and do everything the right way, I wasn't about to talk to her about the arrangement Tunan had proposed to me. No way. I'd have a heart attack if I knew my sister was getting fucked, let alone marrying a stranger just because she wanted to "belong."

"Glee..." I used my strict voice.

Rolling her eyes, she made her way into my closet. "I know, I know. No boys. You can say that until you're green in the face, and my answer will remain the same." I could hear her shifting clothing on the rack. "Blayke and I aren't worried about boys. I'm telling you..."

Once she graced me with her pretty face again, I smiled at the outfit she had held out. Taking it off the hanger, she shook it and handed it over while looking at me. "Let us live vicariously through you, though. Wear this. I hid it in hopes you'd forget about it so I could wear it myself."

I chuckled at her candid personality. It was about to be a long summer with Calista and Blayke, but the grin on my face said it would be a fun one. I just had to get through this mess

251

with Tunan first. Hopefully, it was all a bluff because hiding my marriage from my sister and mother was something I didn't want to do.

But I would.

It wasn't like it would be real if we did get hitched. It would only be for the plot.

SHIELDING my hand over my eyes to block out the sun, I squinted while looking among the row of cars. I didn't know what I was looking for; I just knew he was coming to pick me up. I'd been off my flight for about ten minutes, and in that short time, I'd relieved my bladder, touched up my makeup, and gotten through the airport. I knew Memphis was small, but their airport? It was almost laughable how tiny it was. Jagoda Bay's was huge; not as big as Atlanta's, but at least three times the size of Memphis. Even Sparkling City had Memphis beat, and before now, theirs had been the smallest to me.

I could feel my edges curling up, which meant the heat was melting the edge control, and if sweat poured from my hair-line, my makeup would be ruined. I wasn't trying to look like a melted candle, but didn't have a solution since I'd packed light. I'd already talked to my sister, who was now at home with Blayke and waiting for the pizza I'd just ordered for them. I'd even texted Tunan before I had gotten off the plane, since we were on the landing strip for a few minutes. He hadn't replied. That was twenty-five minutes ago, and I was trying my hardest not to let my anger get the best of me. Just as I was about to bite the bullet and call Tunan, a loud voice boomed beside me.

"Ain't that my fucking luggage?" A man, who was so slim that he had to use one of his hands to hold his black sweatpants up his waist, approached another guy with an accusatory glance, who was hauling a navy suitcase. "On God, I'm 'bout to lay yo' thieving ass out if you stole my shit!"

Black sweatpants pulled up his pants one last time before getting into a fighting stance, holding his fist up while the person with the suitcase just stood there as if he wasn't about to fight.

As I scanned the area, I tried to see if I was imagining this or if it was really happening. Two people stood with their cameras out, snickering, while everyone else walked past them, either shaking their heads or ignoring them completely.

"Is anyone going to stop this?" I asked myself, since I was alone in a city I'd never frequented.

I had no ride, I couldn't take a Uber because I didn't know where to go, and I had no desire to stick around in the murder capital of the South. I was about to use the remainder of the money Tunan sent and book a flight back home after blocking his number.

"Girl, that nigga shouldn't have stole his shit. Times too fucking hard for niggas to be snatching up muhfuckas' suitcases. I hope he dog walk his ass," a cute brown-skinned girl with a round face and a laid gray frontal that looked like it was grown from her scalp said.

Before I could reply to her, black sweatpants threw the first punch, but didn't stop there. He rained blows on the guy who still hadn't let the luggage go, even while getting his head pounded.

"Period! This ain't that, beat that nigga ass!" The girl held her phone up so that she could capture the fight.

My phone was still in my hand, but I was in disbelief that these people were fighting at the airport. There was no way I could ever. Who was trying to get put on the No Fly List? Not me.

The girl with the gray weave glanced from the fight to her phone and then to me. She kept recording, her phone positioned toward the fight, but her eyes lingered. "You look cute, boo. I love that Lactose set."

I'd put navy biker shorts underneath my white outfit to make it more practical for travel, and the entire time I prayed I hadn't gotten it dirty. My look was simple but cute: a white Lacoste polo with the collar lined in navy. I had the shirt tucked into the matching double-pleated skirt. At the hem of the skirt, there was also a navy line. The brand's logo, which was an alligator, sat on the upper left side of the shirt. I finished my look with navy Bottega sneakers that had been a gift from Jisei; she'd been in the store buying herself a few pairs and bought me some. It was my first time wearing them, and they were more comfortable than I assumed they'd be. I'd also added a silver anklet and some minor silver accessories to top off the look.

"I had my eye on that set, but the booster got caught up with all my shit in the trunk. I told that hoe not to play in Tex-Ar county!"

"Thank you..." I was trying to engage in the conversation while also making sure I kept my eyes on the fight.

I didn't know if I was watching for enjoyment or terror. Nonetheless, I was stuck. Black sweatpants were still winning, but the luggage thief had now begun lifting the suitcase and attempting to hit his opponent with it.

"You must be here to see you a lil' junt or sum'n?"

"Hunh?" I'd looked back at the girl, and even though I was clearly alarmed, she continued to check out my attire.

"I said, 'You must be 'bout to get up with a nigga?' Don't get me wrong, we got us some bad bitches out here, but you stick out like a sore thumb. Plus, I know you not vacationin' out here. Memphis in May ain't until next week, and it ain't shit else going on in the city. Unless you one of them TikTok people that travel to test out different cities. You do look familiar…" She squinted and tilted her head, all while still holding the phone and recording the fight.

I couldn't fathom how this girl was having a whole conversation with me, like there wasn't a fight going on, only a few short feet away. "I hope you not out here by yo'self. Cuz unless you stickin' to the Collierville, Germantown, and Cordova areas… Shit, Cordova even getting outta hand." She shook her head, looked toward the fight through her phone, and then back at me. "Yeah, you either out here for a nigga or for the net."

Gray Wig looked at her phone again. This time, she stared at the screen while moving her lips slowly. Shifting to get a closer look, I realized she wasn't recording the fight, but actually live-streaming it on one of the social media platforms. From the icons flying on the screen, I assumed it was Facebook.

"Whoo… you talking… to," she read. "Oh, D-Baby, you nosey as hell. Tell Mel I'm coming by soon as I leave this airport to get me a three-point-five. I done had to leave them hoes in Miami. They was too cheap for me!"

Black sweatpants had now snatched the suitcase and hauled it across the concrete, which was baffling to me, considering he claimed it to be his.

"Ohh! Y'all nosey. Everybody wanna see who I'm talkin' to." She pointed the camera at me. "Turn straight, boo! The people wanna see my new friend. Look at her, y'all. Ain't she pressure? I told her she better watch out for dem YNs. They don't give a fuck 'bout no bad bitches. Dem niggas will put dey own mama on her asses for a come up."

My heart was racing, pores sweating, fingers twitching, and face tight. I was overstimulated like hell, but I still waved at her camera.

"Ohhh, they sayin' you fine, boo."

Clearing my throat, I rubbed the back of my neck.

"Peebo! Don't nobody want yo' twelve-baby-mama-havin' ass. Ain't you got dat lil' young hoe pregnant? Yeap! You do; that's twelve." She read more words from the screen, while I stood there not knowing whether to laugh or walk away. "Coulda! Shoulda! Woulda! But I ain't. Don't get blocked! I could've been the thirteenth but that abortion was a blessing, baby. Stop bringin' up old shit, po'-ass nigga. Dis girl don't want cha. You can tell she fuck with ballers! She 'bout here for Ja Morant. She don't want no nigga dat's a professional baby mama player when she got a pro baller. Da fuck!"

Security had finally come out, and just when I sighed in relief, I clutched my pearls seeing that he, too, stood back and watched the two men claw at each other. This was a mess—a mess I wasn't use to in no shape or fashion.

"She is The Pretty Eater... The girl on TikTok with the seafood boils." Wig looked from reading her phone to me again.

Beep! Beep!

A horn not only paused the fight but halted ole girl's next words. Turning to see who had pulled up, we all took in the black Mercedes-Benz on to the curb. There was a pretty lady leaning over the passenger seat, scanning the small crowd. Her skin was light brown and reminded me of a honey cake recipe I'd saved on TikTok. The beat on her face was clean and should have been on the cover of a cosmetic magazine.

"Hey, boo. Tunan sent me," she stated, pulling me from the trance I was in, looking at her.

Eager to escape the chaos, I tugged my luggage behind me and nearly tripped over my own feet while heading to the car. The trunk popped open, and even though I wasn't sure if the pretty girl was driving me to my doom, I tossed my carry-on inside, careful not to hit the folded Burberry stroller.

When I closed the trunk, the fight was finally being broken up by a different security guard, who was an older White guy. The young Black one was still standing idle.

"Heyyy, Tuscany, boo!"

Gray Wig was now bent, with her whole head sticking inside the vehicle. I had no choice but to stand idle while she finished her conversation. This Memphis heat was proving to be no match for my edges and makeup, but I waited patiently for Gray Wig to finish talking to Tuscany through the passenger-side window. Since I wasn't in my element and hadn't heard from Tunan, it was best I now make a fuss over anything minor. For a fake pre-husband, he was already fucking up. He'd been adamant that I come see him; the least he could have done was wait outside the airport for me to arrive.

"So, the Pretty Eater done took my boo." Gray Wig's face was twisted up, but the amusement in her expression gave away that she was joking.

Good; I wasn't up for tussling with anyone over a man that wasn't mine in real life—or in fake life either, since we hadn't made the agreement official.

She pulled the door open for me and took a step aside so that I could get in. Giving the driver, whom Gray Wig had acknowledged as Tuscany, a small wave, I placed my purse between my legs and got comfortable in the E-Class vehicle. Gray Wig pushed the door closed gently, and I turned to her before she could walk off. "Thank you for keeping me company."

"Girl, boo. You don't gotta thank me. Just shout ya girl out on TikTok. I'm tryna get the fuck up outta that messy-ass warehouse I call work. I'ma have to dog walk a hoe clean off the assembly line! They need to quit playin' and accept me in the creator fund." She huffed and pulled the phone up to my face.

If I had a dollar for every time a person asked me to help them grow their following, I would be rich. Social media seemed like it was easy money, but it was far from it. Was I able to live a lucrative life from it? Yes, but she probably worked fewer hours in the warehouse than I did by as an entrepreneur. Still, I winked at her live-stream and said, "I got you."

Leather, the tangerine-like notes from her Chanel perfume, and the faint smell of something fried lingered as my ride navigated through the nearly nonexistent traffic. This is probably the first time I'd ever seen an airport without an influx of traffic.

Not wanting to be rude, I turned slightly in my seat to at least thank her.

To my surprise, she was already eyeing me as we came to a stop sign. Now that we were inches away from each other, the resemblance to Tunan was uncanny. They shared the same thick brows, except hers were perfectly groomed. From the small nose, high cheekbones, and semi-round chin, I could tell they were related.

Tuscany. That was his sister. She'd birthed two sons—his nephews. The conversation from our meetup at the restaurant came back full force. That wasn't the only thing that had come back, and since I didn't want my pheromones floating around the car, I squeezed my legs shut and cleared my throat.

"Glow Eats," she said before I could say anything. "Pretty in person, just as you are on those seafood boils." Tuscany smiled, nearly blinding me with her stark white teeth.

I didn't think women outside of the mob actually walked around with teeth that white, but Tuscany had proved my theory wrong. She was gorgeous, looking like the female version of her brother.

"You're pretty too. And you watch me? Thank you for the views."

No matter how many views I got, it was still baffling to me when people recognized me. I wasn't a celebrity. I was just a girl who ate on camera and got brand deals for it.

"Girl," Tuscany tsked. "Who doesn't watch you?"

She turned the steering wheel to the left while her right tires careened down the incline. The airport was now in our rear-view mirror, and the bubbles had now settled in my belly.

"Lots of people don't watch me." I chuckled. "But I appreciate your support. I know you're his sister. Can you tell me your name again? I want to make sure I pronounce it right."

Tunan didn't do much talking that night, mostly listening, but he'd spoken about his sister a few times. It was clear that he loved and respected her to no end.

"Tuscany Payne... Cherman, I mean. My husband hears me use my maiden name, and he will appear out of thin air, looking ugly in the face!" She beamed at the mention of her spouse.

Her smile was infectious, causing me to produce a grin of my own.

She shot me another quick glance as she veered through traffic. "I'm fan girling over here, and that's something I usually do not do. My daughter, Athena, put me on to you. Thanks to you, her daddy done made more than a few seafood places rich 'round the city. I'd appreciate it if you ate some peanut butter jelly sandwiches or some shit the next few videos. Go easy on my nigga."

Tossing my head back, laughter escaped from my chest, and just as Gray Wig had done, Tuscany made me feel at ease.

"I am not a fan of peanut butter, but I got you. Don't have Athena spamming my comments, going off on me when I switch up, though." We laughed together, knowing how girls and women can be.

The semi-smooth tar of the expressway was now long gone and had been replaced with crater-sized potholes that Tuscany dodged with ease. Buildings that had seen better days, some with air conditioning units hanging from them, appeared alongside children playing on the sidewalks and riding bikes in the streets. There was a man with a towel covering his head while pushing a shopping cart and a green old-school car on tall rims, doing donuts in an empty parking lot. We were in the hood. I wasn't a stranger to the hood at all, but I'd never visited the areas since I grew up lower-middle-class. I wasn't green to the ghettos. I'd gone to the Bricks on a few occasions with Jisei and Mocha, and each time I'd gone, I had a time. But this wasn't Jagoda Bay. This was Memphis, Tennessee, the fucking murder capital.

"Ion know what you and Tunan got goin' on, and even though my brother is cute or whatever..." She rolled her eyes. "I can't *believe* he knows you. But I am glad you came to visit here with him."

There was a red light, and instead of the car slowing, Tuscany looked both ways and ran it. My heart accelerated as I searched the area for the police, expecting flashing blue lights. When they didn't come, I relaxed. I opened my mouth to say that Tunan and I weren't together, but that wouldn't be entirely true. I'd fucked that man like I was on camera, getting paid for it. I'd drenched his dick with my juices, and the mere thought of it had me saturating my panties. So, I just gave his sister a tight-lipped smile.

"He's been through a lot when it comes to these bitches. Tunan is one of six, but he's one of one, for real. He's always been his own man—always figured his own way out. Right now, he needs someone real; someone who has too much to lose. Never will I ever encourage a woman to build a nigga up, even if that nigga is my brother. I will say, though, I'm glad he's not giving these nothing-ass hoes his time. You a great look, Glow."

I'd been ten seconds from saying I wasn't with her brother, but here I was, smiling like a crazy woman in the front seat of this vehicle. Hearing that I was a good catch didn't have the same effect as being recognized by someone. I knew I was a catch. My knowing I was a catch was one of the main reasons why I was single. I'd built myself up, brick by brick, and refused to let a man come around trying to tear it down or control what I'd done myself. The men who had the pleasure of fucking me hadn't been worth ten dead dogs. Being single was easy. It was stress-free. And before I linked with my girls, it had been the best choice I'd made.

Being single wouldn't get me the inclusion I want with my girls, though. If I truly wanted to belong, I had to change the status of my relationship, and Tunan seemed willing to help with that.

The car rolled to a stop in front of the last house on a dead-end street. Even though we were in the hood, all of the houses were new. They couldn't have been more than fifteen hundred square feet, but the different exterior colors made them look bigger. The home we stopped in front of had white siding, dark green shutters that almost looked black, and a small, lush lawn. It was the biggest on the block, and even though it was just as slim as the other houses, it went up two stories.

There was a group of men hunched down in the middle of the yard, fussing and pointing at each other, while others stood, scanning the area.

"These niggas gone burn the fuck up, gamblin' in the hot-ass sun." Parking the car, Tuscany's phone rang, and the name Aphrodite flashed across the display. "Bestie boo," she sang as I attempted to scan the yard for Tunan.

"Un hunh! Don't *bestie boo* me, hoe! Where my baby daddy?"

My eyes nearly flew out of their sockets as the voice blared through the speakers. Still, Tuscany smiled while looking past me at the yard of men.

"I can't *wait* to tell Goal you called my husband your baby daddy."

"Oh God! Please don't get him started."

"Right. But he shootin' dice. You'll have to wait till he takes these niggas money, and then call back."

"Is Tunan playing?" the voice asked.

It was as if he sensed his name because he stood up from the ground with a stack of money in his hands, his hat sitting atop his head in a cocked manner, and a lazy grin on his face. I couldn't tear my gaze from his profile while his grin remained in place. His eyes were on the car, but he hadn't moved. I wasn't even standing, and I could already feel my knees threatening to give out. My lips parted, but nothing came out except a slight breath. My hands moistened as I gripped the seat belt diagonally across my body. Someone said something to him, causing him to look away from the car, and only then did I snap back to reality.

He's so damn fine.

My inner voice sounded, not helping my current state. It didn't take long for the other side of my brain to speak up.

But, you know that, Glow. He's just a man—one of many.

Pulling me out of my head, Tuscany sounded beside me. "Girl, bye! I'ma call you back!"

"Yeah, Exhilarate crybaby self about to wake up anyway."

"Give my baby a kiss for me," Tuscany cooed.

"Nope! Y'all shouldn't have left my daughter. She like Memphis too!"

"No the fuck she don't," a deep voice boomed, making both

of the ladies laugh.

The line disconnected while Tuscany continued to giggle and shake her head as she gathered her purse from the back seat. She was in the middle of the hood with a Kelly Birkin, reminding me of Jisei and Dasani.

"I can tell we gone be sisters, even if my bigheaded-ass brother don't make it off the bench."

I chuckled, and she reached over and grabbed my hand.

"I mean that, Glow. I know Tunan is a little... hardened, but life be like that. I'm not tellin' you to be with my brother, whatsoever, but I'm a walkin' testament that sometimes the complex things do work out. Take my best friend, Aphrodite, that was on the phone just now. She used to be with my husband before I even knew that nigga existed. They share a daughter, Athena, and she's all our baby girl. Her husband, Goal, is my son's biological brother. Crazy... yes. I had a damn child by my *best friend's husband's daddy*, and she got a baby by my husband."

Tuscan shrugged like she hadn't just given me a whole novel's worth of drama.

"It's complicated, but it works for us, Glow. That's all I'm sayin'... complicated can work. Come on... I know Mama 'nem done with the food."

Before Tuscany could open her door, a fine-ass man, whose skin tone reminded me of a worn penny, was at the driver's door with a blunt hanging from his lips.

Damn, he's fine. All these niggas are fine.

If this is the husband, I understand why both her and Aphrodite had babies by him and were now best friends. He pulled her from the driver's seat, and she giggled like a schoolgirl as he wrapped his arms around her waist while blowing smoke in her face. That was the sexiest thing I'd ever witnessed. The trunk opened, and then closed, and before I could turn to investigate, my door was being opened too.

"I thought you was gone flake on a nigga."

How dare the fucking sun sit behind him just right?

Tunan's smile wasn't full, but it gleamed just as the biggest star behind him did. I was starting to make his style, which was streetwear. While some of the other men I'd been in the presence of opted to mix and match designers and have a perfect balance of street, casual, and business, Tunan didn't balance shit. He was all street. A white graphic boxy tee, cut right above his belt loop, matched the yellow and blue Travis Scott Nikes on his feet. His shorts were also white, fitted, and sat an inch above his knee. There was a chain belt hanging from the left side of his belt loops. He couldn't have been in the sun long because he smelled like soap and Tonka Beans. His hair had been freshly cut, and if his barber was in the yard, I was giving him not only a tip but a shout-out on my socials. He'd outdone himself.

"Hi, Tunan..." I simpered.

Tucking his bottom lip in his mouth, his teeth were on display as he held out his hand. Placing mine in his, I flinched at the shock and wondered if he noticed since he hadn't reacted. My luggage was at his side in his left hand, confirming he was the one at the trunk a few seconds ago. I'd overpacked and nearly had to swap suitcases, but I didn't want to risk checking my bag with the airline. Glee had been the one to remove a few items and zip the suitcase closed before she shooed me out the door.

As I stood to my full height, which was still many inches shorter than his, he took a step back with my hand still in his.

"You on dat straight from the airport, hunh?"

I didn't know the context of his lingo, so I just shyly grinned.

Tunan often used words I hadn't heard before, even though

I was heavy in these social media streets. Memphis just had its own language that I wasn't sure I'd learn before I was back in the air in twenty-four hours.

"You look good, my baby. That's all a nigga sayin'," he said, reading my mind.

"Thanks. You look nice too. I love the shoes. I get jealous when I see people in them because I had too many raffles to count and still came up short."

I remember when the shoes first dropped. I had my fits picked out and all. But I didn't get them, and I wasn't about to ask any of the girls to help me secure them. I refused to wear replicas since those were the only brands that had reached out to sponsor that particular shoe, and I wouldn't dare pay five hundred for a pair of Nikes. I'd just continued to admire them from afar.

"That ain't shit. I'ma cop 'em for you."

"Who dat in da whiteeee?" A face identical to Tunan's stood from the gamblers' circle while shaking his fist.

"None of yo' business. Just roll dem fuckin' dice so I can get dat bread up outcha."

The men looked like twins. They even smiled alike; it was scary.

"Baguette, this is Glow," Tunan said as she came up to us with her man's arms still around her waist as he walked behind her. He hit me with a quick head nod, and I gave a small wave.

"That's my brother, Turo. Tulen is bent down in the red hat, Tuden got the twist in his head. Tulscan on the way with his wife, Kassie."

Turo was still shaking his fist as Tunan led us past the group of men. Tulen and Tuden looked up at the same time, and they had faces identical to their other siblings. Their mama literally said copy and paste. I'd never seen anything like it.

"Damn, Tune. How long you been home again?" The one in the red hat, Tulen, licked his lips while pulling money from his pocket.

The whole yard roared in laughter, including Tuscany's husband. She even laughed with her eyes now red and low from the smoke she'd ingested.

"Long enough, young nigga," Tunan replied as he pulled me up the four steps that led to the porch. It was massive, stretching across the front of the house with much depth. Four oversized rocking chairs sat empty, and three different children's bikes leaned against the railing.

My face was warm as the men complimented me from behind. Even though I had on shorts, I still held my skirt against my butt as we ascended the stairs. Once we crossed the threshold, ice-cold air dried the sweat beads along my hairline while chill bumps formed on my arms. The inside was just as nice as the outside. As we stood in the empty living room, large enough to accommodate all the siblings and a few grandkids, the homey feel was a nice blend of modern and traditional. A brown leather sectional wrapped around the room, while the snowy white walls were covered in family pictures and paintings. A large rug sat atop light wood floors; more toys were lined along the back wall, and a TV, which had to be at least eighty inches, was on YouTube. Essex was on the screen rapping to Missy in his latest video. Not even caring that Tunan was watching, I pulled out my phone and recorded a quick video.

attachment You look so good Missy! I didn't know the video was out! 🔥

SHE'D TOLD the group that she had flown to Chicago last month for Essex's video shoot and hadn't said much else. Pia, Discover, and she rarely texted in the group. I knew that was because they had been the recent additions to the clique, but I liked all three of them. A part of me also figured they'd been added to the other group chats since they were officially with men in the friend group now.

Before I could get into my head too much, my phone sounded with incoming text messages.

JISEI

Period! Too bad Missy boo! I seen it this morning! I love itttt!😋

MOCHA

I haven't seen shit! Let me go look. 😌

MOCHA

Hold up biiitch! 😅 Where you at? Who is them niggas in the pictures on the wall?

AZURE

Language Mocha! 🤐

Memphis

DASANI

😶I loved the video. And Memphis? Uhhh… Did you forget about tomorrow? 😬

I STILL DIDN'T KNOW what it was that I'd been invited to, but I hadn't forgotten and planned to be there. All I knew was that I'd been included and sent a black invite resembling a wedding invitation with a black dress code.

☺ I'll be back on time. Promise.

NOT WANTING to be any more rude than I already was, I locked my phone screen. I knew the ladies would have questions, but they could wait; I didn't have answers for them anyway. Well, I did, but not ones I wanted to answer.

Looking up, Tunan was no longer beside me but coming from out of a bedroom down the hall from the living room. I saw my luggage sitting on a made-up king-sized bed just as he closed the door.

His eyes raked my body, and his tongue licked his lips. It was a sign that he liked what he saw. Tunan had five other people outside with the same genetic makeup, yet he was still one of a kind. He radiated sex appeal and didn't need designer clothes or hundreds of thousands of dollars in diamonds to look good. Like now, a twenty-four-inch Cuban link chain that was maybe ten inches thick sat around his neck, and even though it wasn't encrusted with diamonds, it complemented his outfit. He was that classic handsome who looked good in a raggedy T-shirt and dirty sneakers. He'd taken me in a raggedy car on the first night—that's how good he looked—and not once did I regret being fucked on those old-ass seats.

"You pulled up on a nigga for real..." He shook his head while removing his hat, setting it on the coffee table.

"You sent me twelve hundred dollars, Tunan. What'd you think I do? Run off with your money? If I had no intention of coming, I would have sent it back." I shrugged.

I should have been at home trying on my clothes for

tomorrow, but here I was, hundreds of miles away, squeezing my legs together, trying to talk myself out of not fucking the best dick I'd ever had again.

One foot in front of the other, chain on his pants clinking, he was now towering over me after four strides. He licked his lips, peering directly into my eyes. "Nah. I sent it, so that mean it's yours. I'm glad you showed up, though. But had you not, the money woulda still been yours. To be honest, I didn't think you would."

"I... I shouldn't have. I still need to take my hair out. I have an appointment tomorrow afternoon. But... here I am." I play-fully rolled my eyes to break up some of the sexual tension. I'd booked my flight to leave out first thing in the morning and I hoped Tunan was an early morning person. This was an in-and-out visit. I had to make my flight if I wanted to get my braids out, make my hair and makeup appointments, and be on time to the event. If Tunan isn't an early riser, I'd call an Uber or a Chauffeur to get me back to the airport on time. It was best that he take me, though, since he didn't pick me up today, which was low-key rude. I should've mentioned that, but it was clear I'd lost all sense of logic when it came to Tunan. Further evidence of my lack was that I'd even agreed to come here.

My braids still looked good, but I'd had too much content in them already, especially since I'd gotten them done twice, so it was time to switch it up. Plus, the dress I had picked out for the event on tomorrow night wouldn't go well with it.

Tunan tugged at one of the two braids that were cascading down my face. I had it styled in a high bun with two pieces hanging on each side. These braids had been convenient, and I was definitely going to patronize the salon again for a third time when I was ready for more. I would more than likely take the girls to get their braids done, too, so that would be one less thing we would have to worry about this summer.

"I appreciate you." The sincerity in his words was nearly too much to bear. "Come on."

This time, he didn't grab my hand, which I was fine with. We needed to keep our physical contact down to a minimum. If not, I'd find myself spread out on one of these tricycles floating around.

There was a formal dining room next to the living room, and it also followed the same modern traditional scheme as the front of the house. I'd smelled food since the moment we walked through the door, but I was trying to ignore it so my stomach wouldn't growl. However, as we got closer to the kitchen, my mouth couldn't help but water. White cabinets, gray granite counters, and an enormous island lined with aluminum trays of food resting on burners greeted me. A curvy lady pulling a cake out of the oven took up residence in the kitchen. I didn't know what was underneath those pan lids, but if she'd done all this by herself, I knew it had to have taken her all day and probably most of the previous night.

"Tunan, I know you bet not have that hat on in my kitchen," she fussed.

She hadn't faced us once before calling out to her son. Her back was turned completely, but she'd known Tunan was the one in the kitchen.

He rubbed his hand down his waves and guffawed. "Mama, I ain't Tunan."

I nearly gave him away by laughing at his failed attempt to change his voice. He sounded ridiculous.

Keeping her face forward, she added the cake to a glass dome. It reminded me of one my mama had. Without looking our way still, she replied, "I went through seventeen hours of labor witcha. I know when you enter the room, boy."

"I swear... ion know how you do that."

"Yeap. You used to say that back then too." Grabbing a dish rag, she wiped her hands, and only then did she face us.

Wow. No wonder they all look alike.

Tuscany was the spitting image of her mother, but the slender version. Mama Payne looked damn good and had dangerous curves that would have any woman green with envy. No wonder she had all her kids back to back; she was gorgeous in the face with a body to match.

"Hey! I'm—"

"Glow! I watch you on YouTube with my grandbabies. Didn't think you'd be at my birthday dinner, though." Her head tilted while she fixed her gaze on her son.

Using my elbow, I rammed Tunan's side as he laughed while blocking my jabs. "Really, Tunan? I could have brought her a gift!" I rolled my eyes at him. Giving Mama Payne my attention again, who was now sporting a smile, I shook mt head. "I'm *so* sorry. He only asked me to pull up. I didn't mean to intrude, especially empty-handed. My mama taught me better than that."

Waving her towel, she motioned for me to enter the kitchen. "Girl, please. I was only teasin'. He'd already told me you was comin' on a last-minute flight." She held her hands out for a hug, which I accepted.

Hugging her made me miss my own mother, who worked way too much. I was going to have to vlog more frequently so I could try to get my mom to cut her hours back some. I knew she wouldn't take a retirement proposal, but I needed to try to convince her to free up more time so we could see each other more often.

"It's so good to meetcha. And you're just so gorgeous! My grandbaby gonna be maaaad at y'all!" She cut her eyes at Tunan.

He was leaning against the doorframe with his eyes still on

me. "Athena know her uncle got her. Might have to hit The Pretty Eater's manager and book a one-on-one with my baby girl." He winked, and I melted like butter all over this lady's kitchen.

"Well.. let me double my price real quick."

"Ha! I know dat's right!" Mama Payne laughed.

"You chargin' me like dat? Shidddd. I'ma have to fuck 'round and start vloggin' to be able to afford you."

"You'll think of something," I voiced with a shy grin.

"Mamaaaaaa!"

"Un hunh, Tulscan! My grandbabies are sleep! Come in here with all dat hollerin'!"

"That ain't even him, Mama," Tunan said and looked behind him with a smirk.

Mama Payne sighed and threw a dish towel his way. "Boy, hush. I know my kids!"

Tulscan, the last brother, appeared. Tunan turned and hugged him, whispering something in his ear. Behind them was another full-figured woman. She was pretty as fuck and stylish as ever. I loved her ripped jorts and button-down top that she had tied underneath her breasts. She finished her look with some Retro Jordans and plenty of jewelry. Her being iced out reminded me of Mocha and Scarlett. Lorenzo and Matteo kept them in nothing but the heaviest, brightest jewelry.

Both men turned their eyes to me, and when a slow grin spread across Tulscan's face—who, like the rest of his siblings, was a clone—he slapped his brother's hand again. "Don't play with dat boy! He not one of dem. I see ya, baby!"

"Y'all do too much." The woman walked past them, but not before giving Tunan a hug. "Glowwww! It's nice to meet you, girl! I'm Kassie, Tulscan's wife."

We hugged, and she smelled as good as she looked. "You pretty online, but you pretty pretty in person, Miss Glow. You look cute, too, in this fit."

"Don't she?" Mama Payne orated.

The two ladies hugged, and Kassie handed her a jewelry box, making me roll my eyes again at Tunan. I didn't like showing up at places empty-handed if it was a special occasion for the gathering. It was tacky, and under normal circumstances, I would never do that. I was going to see if I could order something and have it delivered today, even if it was only flowers from Publix.

Wait, do Memphis even have a Publix?

"You good in here?" Tunan had the nerve to ask, like I would say if I weren't.

"Boy, bye! We not gonna hurt her. Y'all got five minutes on dem dice before I break dat shit up anyway," Mama Payne expressed.

"Aite! Come yo' slick ass on, Tune. Happy birthday, Mama!" Tulscan winked at his wife and then tossed me a head nod.

"Sooo. You and Tunan? I'ma be honest... I been hounding him since I saw him on your live some weeks ago. He was acting stingy with you. I recorded the whole thing and sent it around the family," Kassie revealed.

"Sure did. We been telling him to bring you around, but Tunan is Tunan. I was beginning to think he crashed your live!" Mama Payne revealed, and we all chuckled.

If she only knew how close to the truth she was. Tunan hadn't crashed my life or my live, but he'd crashed my date, being sent as a replacement for Shio. That counted as the same thing as crashing to me.

Wails had all of us halting in conversation. Mama Payne began removing her apron, but Kassie placed her hand on her forearm. "I got it. I haven't seen my babies in forever." She then faced me. "I'll be back. I'm for sure about to get on your nerves all weekend, I hope?" Her brow rose.

"Not the weekend. All night and a little bit tomorrow; I fly back home in the afternoon."

"Good enough for me!" She cheesed and excused herself from the kitchen, leaving me with Tunan's mother.

I'd never met a man's family before. Either I had been the side bitch in my last situationships, unbeknownst to me, or men didn't deem me worthy to meet their mothers. So being in the room alone with the woman who gave Tunan life had the back of my neck heating. I was in uncharted waters. I watched as Mama Payne began removing foil from the pans. Decided to offer some help, I went to the farmhouse sink, used the hand soap that smelled like lemon pound cake, and washed my hands.

Once they were dry, I turned to her and asked, "What can I help you with?"

Most women didn't like others in their kitchen, but since Mama Payne hadn't shooed anyone away, I figured I'd help out in any way that I could. I also wanted to see the food before it was touched. It smelled so good, so I could only assume it looked good as well.

"Now, I've watched enough of your videos to piece together dat you don't cook. Am I right?"

"I don't cook, but that doesn't mean I *can't*. I can cook enough to survive, but I'm eating out most of the time, so not much time to practice."

Mama Payne lowered her head as if she were looking over invisible glasses. "And you still keep that little figure with da way you eat? You must have God and genetics on your side because even a solid fitness routine wouldn't have you lookin' that pretty with all that processed food you consume."

Gathering all of the saliva that seemed to flood my mouth, I swallowed hard. I could feel myself wringing my fingers as I looked away from Mama Payne.

"I didn't mean to—"

"No, it's fine. Sometimes I just feel a bit insecure with all of the food I eat," I admitted.

"Oh, girl! You're good. I love a woman who can eat, and so do my sons. You see me and Kassie. The rest of dem are always sniffin' after something thick too. But ain't nuttin' wrong with being slim either. One day, I'm gonna get my life together and stick to a meal plan or somethin'."

"You look good. You don't need a meal plan."

"Tell dat to my doctor." She chuckled. "Everything is done. If you could help me take the foil and stir up the sides so dat they don't stick, dat would be appreciated. Grab an apron, though. I don't want you gettin' dirty."

I almost opted out of wearing an apron, but remembered I was in white, so I tied one around my waist and got to work. By the time I had the third foil covering removed, I'd surmised that Mama Payne should have been a chef. Her food looked amazing, and I'd only gotten to the sides.

"My mama taught me how to cook greens when I was no more than eight, and I've been making dem the same way ever since," Mama Payne boasted as I stirred the greens with the pronged spoon.

The steam slapped me in the face, and the extra meat tangled in between had my mouth watering. I wasn't going to stuff my face, but I was definitely adding some to my plate. Smiling her way, I spoke the truth. "They look and smell good."

She'd begun icing the cake since it had cooled down. With her eyes on the glass platter that housed the cake in front of her, I watched as she spread the white butter cream evenly across the top layer.

"I started havin' children young. I don't know why, but I did. I guess it was out of boredom or curiosity. Either way, when I started, I didn't stop. Every man dat blinked at me, I was spreadin' my legs. Nine months later, I was poppin' out a baby for him just for him to pop outta the way." She shook her head, black curls bouncing.

"I have six children, Glow, and all six of dem have different fathers. I used to be so ashamed. Then, when the fathers didn't want anything to do with dem, I zoned out. Workin' and havin' six mouths to feed, six personalities to deal with, and a small two-bedroom house to raise them in... Girl, it nearly drove me crazy. It *did* drive me crazy."

Mama Payne dipped the spatula back into the Betty Crocker container, scraped it, and continued icing the cake.

"My boys take good care of me. They had this house, the one I raised them in, torn down and rebuilt. They even bought many of the homes on the block, doin' the same thing. They make sure I have everything I need and some, but I know they resent me for how things happened."

My eyes felt like sand had been poured into them, and I needed eyedrops to lubricate them again. I didn't know what type of conversation Tunan's mother and I would have when I realized I was meeting her today, but this one wasn't it. I didn't know we were going heavy with our first chat, and while I wasn't uncomfortable, I wasn't sure how much to say regarding Tunan and me. I expected her to ask about my intentions regarding her son, and I knew I couldn't say I was thinking about marrying him just to be included more in my friend group. Thinking it alone sounded extremely immature, and I scolded myself because no mother wanted to hear that her son was being used. Although Tunan was the one who offered the marriage to me, I knew our reasons for possibly getting married were not solid. I flipped the greens over in the pan, moved on to the next pan that was cabbage, and waited for her to continue.

"My daughter... I owe her everything, and I still don't know how to repay her. She gave up her life, her youth, to raise her brothers. She sacrificed more than I ever have. They have been tryna move me out of the hood, and each time, I give dem an excuse. I don't deserve their gratitude. I was a horrible mother. I let my daughter raise kids dat I laid on my back and made, and I have to live with dat forever." She put the spatula down and faced me.

"I'm not the kind of mother who hands out demands and expectations when it comes to my children. Tulscan got it right with Kassie. Tuscany got it right with Baguette. The others, I don't really know what to say 'bout dem, but I'm praying for 'em. Tunan, though... he thought he had it right with his last woman. I met her once and didn't say more than hello 'cause I knew. I wanted to tell him she wasn't right, but I felt I didn't have the right. I hadn't even raised him. I let men change me, Glow. I fell for one man after another, thinkin' a baby would be the reason dey ran off into the sunset with me. But when the baby arrived, they left, and in a way... I detached myself from the baby too.

"I like you. But I'm gonna tell you sum'n I wish a woman had told me... Don't let him have his way with you. Sexually, mentally, and emotionally. Don't let him have his way unless he sees a real future with you.

"Some people come into our lives for reasons and seasons. Don't let dat man do anything permanent to you if he's not prioritizin' you. You're too young and pretty to let a man use you up and toss you aside. You ain't got no kids... keep it dat way until he proves to you he can be the man you need. We got to stop lettin' these niggas 'baby mama' us while we stuck with the babies and dey 'round here living their lives to the fullest. I love my sons, but I'm a woman first. The first time you spot bullshit, block his ass and run for the hills. You hear me?"

I had never had a woman put me up on game when it came

to boys. The only thing my mother told us was to go to her when we needed birth control, not to let a man put their hands on us, and to keep them out of her house. I knew Mama Payne's words came from not only experience but from wisdom. The error of her ways and pain were the driving force of how she operated with her kids, and now me.

"I'm here to tell you what I'm sure you already know. You made a life for yourself—a damn good one. You're the first woman he's been with dat has her own. That much I can guarantee you. Make sure he meets you where *you* are. If he can't give you something you can't give yourself, leave his ass at his sister's house. Ain't no nigga, no handsome face, or no dick worth your mental."

Nodding, I picked the spoon back up. "Yes, ma'am."

"AM I HURTING YOU?"

Using the pointed end of the rat tail comb on the braid, I shook my head. As soon as we uncovered all of the foil, Mama Payne remembered she hadn't made her spaghetti, so I was forced out of the kitchen. I ran into Kassie and mentioned I was ready to take my braids down. Next thing I knew, she, Tuscany, and I were on the porch taking my braids out. The only reason I agreed to porch sitting was because the sun had begun to go down. If it had still been blazing, we would have stayed inside.

"All this hair you got, I know the Africans charge you extra," Tuscany said as she slid the weave out of my head and dumped the crinkled piece into the plastic Walmart bag sitting in my lap.

"Nope. They did it for free in exchange for a promo. Oh, and it wasn't an African salon. They're Black owned."

"Ohhh! I wouldn't know how to act. How do you not get

overwhelmed with all the free shit that is offered?" Kassie asked.

She and Tulscan's one-year-old son were in the middle of the yard pushing a toy, while Tuscany's son played with blocks at the far end of the porch. The kids could go for siblings instead of cousins, rocking that signature Payne look everyone seemed to have. I hadn't even known Tulscan and Kassie had a kid because they were empty-handed when they came in, so I didn't meet him until I was ushered outside with the ladies. One of his uncles had grabbed him on their way in, and the poor baby had been outside ever since, playing in the grass like he wasn't dressed in Kith. Seeing the kids made me miss my Godson, Ezio Jr. I couldn't wait to steal some snuggles from him the next time I saw him.

"It gets overwhelming sometimes, but it comes in handy."

"So you just gonna walk 'round nappy-headed?"

I was so focused on getting the braids out that I hadn't noticed Tunan walking up. He looked just as good as he did an hour ago. With everyone constantly shouting his name and the large bulge in his pockets, I could tell that the dice game, which was now winding down, had been a successful one for him.

"Ain't nothing nappy about her hair. Fall back," Tuscany noted.

"Umm-hmm," I added while looking up at Tunan as I worked on the right front side of my hair.

We'd already cut the braids as far as they could be cut without snipping my real hair, and Tuscany was doing the back left while Kassie handled the back right. Tunan tugged on the braids on the left side like he'd done earlier, but this time, he kept it in his hands and started unbraiding the hair.

Turning my head, I peered at him with squinted eyes. "Really, Tunan?"

Licking his lips, he stood gape-legged while unraveling the

braid. "I'm the best at this braid removal shit. You know how many times Tuscany had us taking hers out? I was a fuckin' pro before I hit puberty."

I sat stunned as he backed up his statement. He had just walked up and already taken the braid down while I was still working on the same one for five minutes, and I had a comb to help. He dropped the weave in the bag on my lap, ran his fingers through the freed piece of hair, and scratched the dirt from my scalp.

"Yeah, you was the coldest, no lie." I could hear the smile behind Tuscany's words.

"Who was the coldest? I know you not talkin' 'bout dis nigga?" Tulen had his red hat cocked to the back as he jogged up the steps with a snarl on his face.

"You know what it is. You can barely get through the braid without tangling it," Tunan chided.

Sucking his teeth, Tulen came to the right of me and gently grabbed the braid that I had been working on. I was still in disbelief that Tunan was taking my hair down, so I didn't even have the words for his little brother joining in.

"Yeah, Tulen... I need to see if your skills done got up to par. You used to slaw me all the way out."

"Mane! Y'all so fuckin' cap. Ain't it, sis-in-law?"

"Yeah, brother... they lying on you," Kassie answered with amusement in her tone.

"Who lyin' on who?" Tuden had joined the party, tossing his twist out of his face. He was proof that Tunan would still be handsome if he decided to grow his hair out.

"This nigga actin' like I ain't the best at this braid take down shit," Tulen stated with his chest puffed out.

Sucking his teeth just as his brother had just done, Tuden took a spot beside Tulen and grabbed a braid. "Ain't no fuckin' actin'. He tellin' the truth. You be gettin' hair tangled up and shit."

I now had five people in my head, four of them being Payne siblings. They were all clowning each other as if taking my hair down was a normal family activity.

"See, Den... you fuckin' up and talkin' 'bout me," Tulen pointed out when Tuden struggled to unravel the weave from my real hair.

"Mane, get the fuck outta my section. I'm doin' this new technique I came up with. Watch I finish more than you niggas."

"Aye! Don't be fussin' and shit over my wife's head."

Cutting my eyes at Tunan, his teeth were on display while the braid in his hands became undone.

"Wife? Ion see no ring on her finger," Tulen asserted.

Tunan and I held each other's gazes, with me shooting daggers at his ass, and him grinning like he was funny.

"Not yet." He winked at me, not breaking the stare off we were having. "But not never. Then again... you unpredictable as a muthafucka, so let me not even put shit past you."

"Y'all gone pull her fuckin' hair out!" Tulscan yelled as he and Baguette shared a blunt a good distance away from the babies while keeping their eyes on them.

I didn't know what else to do with my hands since I had a headful, so unlocked my screen to check my social media accounts. The ladies had texted me back, but I wasn't opening my texts with all these people being able to see my phone over my shoulders.

"Boy, please! Come help or shut dat shit up," Tulen yelled back.

"Y'all got it." Tulscan blew out a wad of smoke.

"Glow." Tunan's voice always went past my ears and straight to my panties. I couldn't squeeze my thighs together, so I aggressively liked a video that I wasn't sure if I liked since I hadn't watched it yet. Getting closer to my face, he asked, "Is it hurtin'?"

Those three words shouldn't have made my kitty thump, especially since he wasn't meaning them in the context that my brain processed them. Trying to shake the arousal from my voice, I answered. "N...no."

He leaned back up, dropped more weave in the bag that had begun to get full, and pulled softly at the hair he'd just freed. When his fingers grazed my scalp, I tensed as he removed the dirt from my hair.

"Aite," was all he replied, but it was still the sexiest thing ever said.

The boys went back and forth for the next half hour while the ladies cut in with snide comments, and I'd laughed so much that my stomach was hurting. I couldn't imagine growing up with as many siblings as they had, but if their banter went anything like this back then, I knew it was a chaotic household. I see why Mama Payne went crazy.

"Glow."

I tensed. Tunan had given my girl below a break by not addressing me during his family's roasting session. Now, he was staring at me again; I could feel his eyes without turning to face him.

"You okay? You comfortable? Been sittin' on this step for a hot minute." The concern laced in his voice wasn't missed by his family or me. Tuden and Tulen started mocking him under their breath, but he ignored them, never taking his eyes off me.

"Uh... yeah. I'm good. I—"

"Food done!" Mama Payne shouted as she burst through the door with a plate piled with food that had steam still coming from it.

I was happy to be cut off because conversing with Tunan in front of everyone made me sweat, and the sun was about gone.

Mama Payne stepped down the porch to face me. Cuffed under her arm was a Coke Zero, and in her left hand was a foldable table. Even though the food looked amazing, that was way too much food for me. My plan was to try a quarter scoop of my favorites once they let me up from the braid removal. I was most excited to taste the greens and mac and cheese.

"That's my plate, Mama?" Tulen asked in what I assumed was his sweet voice.

She kissed her teeth before saying, "And ain't!" causing most of us to snicker.

Mama Payne set up the medium-sized tray in front of me. When she placed the hot plate on the tray and the ice-cold drink beside it, my scalp began to prickle, and it had nothing to do with the people tugging at my scalp. She couldn't expect me to eat all this food. There was no damn way I could.

"Wanna go live while you eatin'? It will be *the best* birthday gift." She batted her lashes while her hands were propped on her hips. She'd removed the apron, revealing a flowy, navy dress that looked so good on her. She had her feet stuffed in Coach sandals, and I'd seen the matching purse sitting on her couch.

"Sure." Reaching inside my purse that was crossed around my body, I pulled out the portable phone stand that I carried everywhere I went.

Once I had the contraption set up on the tray, I placed my phone on it and hit the plus button for the live. Tunan reached over and removed the hair bag from my lap.

"You want Tuscany to put it up in a ponytail while you eat?" he asked.

"No, it's fine. Unless you all don't want to be on camera?"

As my reflection looked back at me from the camera, I wasn't looking too crazy. It wouldn't be the first time my followers had seen me looking a mess. I'd had a few videos on my page showing me taking my hair down, and they all did well. Who knew Black girls doing Black girl things would be widely romanticized all over the net these days?

Peering at the siblings and Kassie through the phone's front lens, which showed our every movement, I paused before hitting the live button. "Y'all cool with me going live?"

Tulen excused himself, saying he was ready to go inside and eat. Tuden had his phone resting against his ear with his shoulder, so he didn't hear the question. He'd been showing every tooth in his mouth for the last few minutes, so I assumed he was flirting with a woman. Tuscany nodded excitedly, and Kassie said she was cool with it. I didn't bother asking Tunan because my followers loved him. I still hadn't edited and uploaded our video, and didn't really have an explanation as to why.

Their mother was out of view and nodded for me to start while she held up her own phone. I had no doubt she was recording me to show her grandbaby later. The screen counted down as Tunan slid another braid out of my hair, dropping the weave in the bag now on the ground between his legs.

Steam rose just as the live populated, and all of a sudden, I'd become camera-shy. I felt everyone's eyes on me, and viewers hadn't joined yet. Clearing my throat, I pulled hand sanitizer from my bag and drenched my hands. By the time I had the clear bottle back in my purse, I'd had four hundred viewers. Comments from those who'd joined began to pop up, but I was too chicken to read them, so I just stared at the camera.

"Hey, guys! Y'all missed me? I missed y'all." I had to pause, having to catch my breath because it sounded shaky. Only then did I read the comments that were scrolling across the screen.

"You stay on an adventure... Hey, Glow..."

"Heyyy, boo!"

"Where you at, Glow? Who all them people behind you, Pretty Eater?"

There were too many comments to read at once, so I went back into my spill. "Today, I'm with my... friend's family. This right here," I leaned aside so they could get a glimpse of Tuscany, "Is my boo, Tuscany, and this," I leaned in the opposite direction, "This is Kassie."

"Hey, y'all!"

"Hey, Pretty Eaters!"

Both the ladies smiled in the camera. Tuscany removed another braid and let it fall to the floor in front of her. The comments continued to rush the screen, but instead of interacting, I proceeded with the purpose of the video.

"It's Mama Payne's birthday today. She's Tuscany's mommy and Kassie's mom-in-law. She threw down in the kitchen, as y'all can see."

Lifting my plate, careful not to let the juices spill over, I angled it so that the camera could catch it.

"Hey, y'all! I'm not tryna get on the camera, but heyyyy!" Mama Payne giddied.

Tunan took another braid out and removed the dirt from my scalp. When he began massaging the area, my thighs tightened, and I did a long blink to try to compose myself.

"Oh my God! They said, '*Happy birthday, mama. The food look good, but who dat in da bacccck?*'" Kassie sang the comment, and I hid my smirk.

Tuden leaned forward and smiled at the camera while keeping the phone up to his ear, while still taking out a braid.

"'*Damn he fine. Let us see the other one.*' Ughh! Y'all please... do not hype these fools up."

"Nah, don't listen to my sister. Hype ya boy all the fuckin' way up," Tuden boasted.

Tunan chuckled but stayed out of view with only his

abdomen, arms, and hands showing.

"Y'all, I know I look a hot mess right now—"

"You look good, my baby," Tunan interrupted, making my cheeks blaze.

I knew the viewers were going to eat that all the way up. I hated how Tunan's voice sent my body spiraling.

"Thanks," I gulped. "I'm getting my braids taken out, and I appreciate everyone here for helping me."

"'***They still look good***.' Thank you. They do still look good, but I already have an appointment set up for a sew-in."

"'***My baby? Is that our boy from last time?***'"

Turning, I faced Tunan. "Are you the guy from last time?"

Licking his lips, he slid another braid out, removing the dirt. "I better be," he sneered.

Not wanting to further embarrass myself by getting flustered, my eyes went to the plate in front of me. The food looked delicious and smelled heavenly. I was hungry, but at the same time, the thought of eating everything on this plate had me gagging internally.

"I'm done. I'm gonna go feed my baby. I'll be in the comments with the rest of The Eaters," Kassie announced.

"Ohh! My bestie on dis junt! Heyyyyy, Aphrodite! Hey, Athena! Cuz I know you watchin'!" Tuscany blew a kiss at the screen.

"Where my baby at?" Baguette was already making his way to the porch. Kassie grabbed the baby out of his arms and went into the house with her husband on her tail.

"Glow on live, and Ditey in the comments. Look."

Baguette went behind me, wrapping his arms around his wife's waist.

GoddessWearsBoutique: Hey daddy! OMG you know Glow!

Come get me!

BAGUETTE TOSSED his head back in laughter. "Okay, I'm on da way, baby."

"I'm done too. Come on, so I can fix our plates. Aphrodite, I'm 'bout to FaceTime you so my boo can see."

Tuscany lightly scratched my scalp before walking into the house with her husband behind her.

"Let me make sure dey not diggin' in my food. I'll be watchin' from my phone," Mama Payne assured before following behind the couples.

Tuden winked at the camera before following suit, leaving just Tunan and me outside.

"Hi, Athena! I can't wait to meet you too!" I cooed at the camera, seeing that she'd left heart comments, giddy that her daddy was on my live.

"Next time you come to the crib, I got you niece," Tunan replied.

There were a slew of comments asking Tuden to come back, with some even asking about Baguette and commenting on his looks.

GoddessWearsBoutique: Is that my uncle Tunan? I cant see him.

REACHING UP, I pulled Tunan by the sleeve of his shirt until his face was in the camera. His tall ass had to bend down in order to get in focus.

"Wassup, niece." He grinned that smile that had gotten me out of my panties faster than speeding light.

Ohhh be my uncle.

There go OUR man.

I love GoddessWearsBoutique clothing.

Damn everybody fine.

Glow if that's yo man just say that. Ready for the couple's content.

Tunan laughed out loud at the comments while I simply picked up my fork. Bowing my head, I said a silent prayer before sticking the utensil in the greens. The flavor burst in my mouth, and I had barely chewed and already deemed these the best greens I'd ever had. Putting more greens on my fork, I worked my way around the food, deciding what to pair it with for my next bite. The food tasted even more flavorful as I tried different items together. Greens, lasagna, mac and cheese, turkey legs, cornbread, cabbage, and black-eyed peas all stared at me as I tried to eat what I could. The food was so good that I nibbled on a little bit of everything while Tunan read the comments and responded to the people he knew.

When I was full, I pushed the plate aside and took a sip of my water.

"Mama Payne needs a restaurant. That food was so good! I know y'all used to me going to restaurants, but this has everything beat that I've eaten all year. The greens were well seasoned and meaty, the mac and cheese... well, I know y'all saw that cheese pull. The lasagna had a sweet taste that I can barely describe, but I loved it, and the cornbread was soft and buttery like cake. Ten out of ten, for sure."

Tunan stood and took out the last braid in my head. When the weave hit the bag, I felt the urge to pee.

That food looked so damn good.

I know a Memphis plate when I see one.

Glow you barely ate. I would have smashed that shit.
She always barely eat.

My neck tightened. Pulling at my skirt, I pushed back from the table. "I'll be right back. He's going to keep y'all company while I use the restroom."

Not waiting for Tunan's reply, I went into the house. I could hear the family eating, but couldn't see them. There was a bathroom off to the side of the kitchen, so I entered, relieved my bladder, and wiped myself. I shook my head at the amount of essence from my vagina that was between my legs. After properly cleaning myself and washing my hands, I was back outside where Tunan had taken my seat.

As I circled the chair, Tunan pulled me into his lap, turning my body so that my legs hung off the side of his thigh. "Feed me while I comb out your hair, my baby."

Not wanting to argue about my live seeing us, I scooped up the greens on my fork while he sectioned off my hair and used the wide-tooth comb that Tuscany had brought out.

I didn't dare look at the comments; I knew it was a party in them. Tunan shifted his gaze from my hair to my face while finishing the rest of the food I fed him from the same fork I'd just used. It was just the noise of the hood in the distance, the crunch of the food, chewing, and my racing heart. Somehow, we were in our own little world, not caring that hundreds— maybe thousands—of people were watching us. His steady gaze looked into mine with silent expectation. Tunan didn't have to do much; in fact, he didn't have to do anything at all. He was undoubtedly that guy. He wasn't dripping in designer clothes, nor did he have jewelry worth seven figures, yet my heart couldn't help but race while in his embrace.

"Thank you, my baby. Shit too fye. Now, turn 'round so I can comb out your hair." He nodded toward the phone.

Holding in my groan, I peered at the screen. The comments

were coming through so fast that all of the words looked like they were running together. Scrolling up, I attempted to see if I'd missed any comments from important figures, like a brand or fellow content creator. I'd had comments from my favorite female celebrities in the past, and I always tried to catch them so they'd know I appreciated their support. When I couldn't spot any in the sea of comments, I scrolled back down to the most recent ones. I laughed at the number of people going crazy about Tunan and me.

Tunan began sectioning my hair, and he hadn't lied when he said Tuscany had them taking her braids out because he was combing from the roots. His touch was so gentle that it almost felt euphoric. I had to hold my composure, though, because we weren't alone.

Okay! Y'all so fucking sexy!

That nigga so damn fine, Lord! I see what you do for others, Big G!!

Glow you deserve this!

Yasss bitch!

Oh, Glow in there. She had the whole family taking her braids down. That's having her way for real!

Oh bitch you holding the fuck out! What the helly?????! I'll blow your phone up and fuck up your live right now!

The last comment was from Mocha, and it caused me to bark out a laugh. "Mochaaaaa! I'll call you!"

I knew I had some explaining to do, but they'd have to wait until I got back home. I didn't even know how to explain what was occurring and was already trying to figure out what I was going to say, and what I wasn't. Everyone had secrets, so maybe I was being petty, but I felt compelled to hold Tunan close to my chest.

BlaykeNoU: Ohhh see you should have took us to Memphis with you! I need a YN that's in touch with his feminine side.

"I got you next time, Blayke." I winked.

Oh so she is in Memphis!

I know my people from anywhere! Glow in my cityyyy!

You gotta go to Dixie Queen. It ain't shit fancy but the best late night wings, especially on some drunk shit.

"Big tyme! You home, baby?"

Straggling up the yard was a man who couldn't be much older than my little sister. He was clearly under the influence, of something and with the way he could barely hold his eyes open, my bet was on weed.

"Yeah, yeahhh," Tunan replied.

He was done with my hair, so he tapped my thigh for me to stand. Once I let him up, I sat back in the seat that now felt cold with the absence of his body. I was toggling from the phone to the interaction in front of me. Tunan slapped hands with the guy who also gave him a welcome home speech.

"Baby on live and shit," Tunan informed him.

The guy, whose swagger reminded me much of Tunan's with his jean shorts, chain hanging from them, Jordan 1s, and a graphic tee, pulled his pants up his waist and grinned. "Okay den! What you on... Facebook live?"

Picking up the phone up, I turned it so that he could see. "No, TikTok."

"TikTok... I shol' been tryna get my shit poppin'. Damn." His brows drew together. "It's five thousand people on dis hoe. God damn! Aye, what's up with it? Aye, dis hoe live!"

He placed his fist to his mouth in excitement, and asked

me, "How da fuck you get dis bih jumpin' like dis?"

He hadn't turned away from the live, so before I could respond, he was reading the comments out loud. "'**Brick-house99 Damn Memphis just got all the fine niggas. What's yo name?**' I would tell you my name, but I'd have to cut dese bitches off first."

"Shit, last I checked… you had a lil' junt you was tryna wife up." Tunan set the comb on the windowsill before leaning against the railing.

"Aye, foo! 'Bout that. So you know yesterday was my G-day?"

"Nah, I didn't know. Happy birthday, my nigga."

"'Preciate that, foo. Anyway, I'm in da shower, you know… gettin' my shit cleaned up so I can murk dem folks ass in da Balencies. I hear dis bih on da phone with her slaw-ass sister, talmbout she 'bout to turn up cuz it's ha *nigga* birfday."

"Ain't she white?"

He held his arms out in front of him, but at an angle where his hands were facing the ground. "Ex-muhfuckin'-zactly. Bih white as my teeth and pull dat bullshit. I hopped out dat shower so fucking fast, I damn near broke my back. I pop my head ina room like, who a fuckin' *nigga*? Mane, stop playin' wit me before I make you touch 'er wall in dis bitch. She apologized and shit, but soon as I got back in da shower, I hear her call up her nigga, making plans wit' him and shit."

"On yo' b-day, G?"

"On…my…fuckin…day!" He slapped his chest with each word. Since he was the source of entertainment, I flipped the camera back around. "I wanted to knock them danglin' ass blonde hairs off her fuckin' head. I stamp dat! I let da bitch make it tho' cuz I'm still on papers. Bitch ain't 'bout ta send me back to fuckin' jail."

Tunan shook his head while I couldn't help but crack up at

the story.

"Anyway, I'm Doom, Miss Lady. I'm fuckin' up y'all vibe and shit wit' my drama."

I gave him a small wave. "Nice to meet you, Doom. I'm Glow."

"Glow. Like Glorilla?"

"Umm, yeah…" I lied.

"Cap." He twisted his lip. "But, I'ma let you rock. I'm too fuckin' high." He ran his hand down his waves.

Doom couldn't be more than twenty years old. Even though he was cursing like a sailor and could barely stand up, he was handsome in a boyish, thuggish way.

"Aye, let me see dat live again."

With my permission, he grabbed the phone. He squinted his eyes as he read the comments. "'**Dom. Yo name Dom like, Dom like Dominican?**' Nawl, baby. My name *Doom* like, any muhfucka that try to go against me is *doomed*. Fuck kinda lame-ass name is Dom?"

"You ignat, bra," Tunan sounded from beside him.

"'**BlaykeNoU How old are you? Uggh Glow for sure should have never left us.**'"

"Don't answer her, Doom. That's my little sister." I left off the part where Blayke was actually my little sister's best friend because I didn't feel like explaining all of that to him.

"I'm nineteen goin' on ninety, baby. At least dat's what my grannie say."

He handed me back the phone, where the low battery alert flashed across the screen. Instead of charging my phone with the portable charger, I ended the live. When Tunan saw me stuffing my phone and equipment back in my purse, he spoke up. "You done?"

"Yeah. I was on the live long enough."

"Dat hoe was jumpin', but I'm glad you ended it. Now,

lemme tell you what happened after I heard da bih makin' plans with her nigga."

"Doom, you talmbout her nigga? Last I checked... that girl was married."

"Married, but ona young nigga dick bad. Mane, fuck dat fake-ass marriage. Da nigga can have that slaw ass hoe. So, listen... I told her I was straight and went out wit' my niggas. She was pissed, but she thought a nigga had let her ass off da hook. WRONG!" He motioned his hand as if he was pulling a ski mask down his face. "We kicked the fuckin' doe in and made the whole house come clean. You know she got two babies, the youngest was ona bottle, and I snatched that shit up too! Fuck you talmbout. Gimme all dat shit! Her square-ass husband had all types of Rolexes and compurrters and shit."

Memphis people tended to add an "R" to the most random words. His pronunciation of computers was hilarious, and I didn't even try to hide my giggles.

"Damn, you still got da watches? I'm bare as fuck out here." Tunan held up his wrist.

"Mane, hell nawl! Me and my niggas busted that shit down. It was one for every one of us." Doom showed his wrist, and sure enough, a gold Rolex sat there.

"Yeah, y'all did good, my boy," Tunan praised the watch as he inspected it.

"I do got sum'n you can get doe." Doom reached into his pants pocket and pulled out a stack of money. A few twenties fell to the ground, but he didn't stop digging. He pulled out a blue velvet box, picked up his money, and handed the box to Tunan. "I was on my way to da HH to see what I could get for dis. But if you want it, you can give me ten bands for it. P's shiesty ass 'bout ain't gone give me nun but selm (seven), and I know for a fact dat boy a fifty ball. I can't take it to the pawn shop 'cuz I know dey white ass got insurance on it."

Flipping the box open, a built-in light shone on the ring, and Tunan looked in the box before turning to Doom, who was still going on.

"Dat bih so icy, Tune. I got da paperwork back at da crib, but it's a three carat H with VVS1. Dat's basically excellent grade."

Holding the ring out for me to see, Tunan asked, "You like it?"

A circular diamond sat in the middle of a thin silver band. The ring was simple but beautiful. I'd always thought I'd want a cluster ring, but the solitaire setting was perfect and dainty. The rock radiated under the porch lights, and I was dazzled by the size. Chuckling, I looked at Doom. This boy had really robbed his sneaky link and her husband.

Did I like the three-carat diamond ring? I loved it, but this was a stolen damn ring! I looked from the ring back to Tunan, then back to the ring before shifting my eyes back to Tunan.

He snapped the box closed, shoved the box in my hand, and reached into his pocket. "Damn, Doom! You taxin' the fuck outta a nigga."

"Nigga, you gettin' a steal. Plus, her and Snow 'bout da same size and shit. I know she can fit it."

"Try it on, my baby," Tunan encouraged as he counted out the money to pay Doom.

"Wait, her name is Snow?" I asked, genuinely curious.

Doom smiled. "Nah, dat's just what I call her."

Tunan handed him the money while I sat idle, staring at the ring.

"Yeah, dat bih got by, but she won't get away. Aye, I'm 'bout to hit up the dice at the sto'. I'll be back through here to give Ma a gift and get a plate."

They slapped hands again.

"Bye, Miss Lady. Enjoy dat ring."

Doom was gone like he'd never come, with only the ring as a reminder that he'd been here.

"You like it?" Tunan asked again, hovering over me as I opened the ring box.

"I mean... I like it, but what I'ma do with a ring, Tunan?"

"Shid! Whatchu mean? We getting married and shit, ain't it?"

"Uhh—"

"You said you needed da paperwork, and I got dat. Let's gone get dis shit outta the way."

"When, Tunan?"

"Shid..." He licked his lips. "Tonight. I know a spot."

CHAPTER 13

TUNAN "TUNE" PAYNE

"Tunan, you're serious about this?"

Glow's eyes were wide with disbelief as she held the papers I'd given her. I hadn't expected Doom to show up with his married hoe's ring, but he had perfect timing. When I reached out to Glow earlier, I just wanted to show her the papers and introduce her to the family. The marriage would be fake, but the thought of my people never meeting the woman who would carry our last name didn't sit right with me. Even if the shit was only on paper, my folks had to at least know who she was. I hadn't told any of them about the marriage, but at least when they found out, because Tuscany's nosey ass found everything out, they could say they'd met her. It made shit even better that they were familiar with her and loved her videos.

"Hell yeah, I'm serious! I got all yo' demands and shit notarized." I pointed to a section on the paper.

We were in my bedroom with the door closed since everyone was full off Mama's birthday dinner and lying out. Even though it was past nine, they'd be up again once the babies were down and the food was settled in their stomachs. My mama had invited the whole neighborhood to show up, and I knew they would be here around midnight. We have always been the family that prioritized naps, and that habit followed us into adulthood. I hadn't napped since I got locked up, and didn't see any more in my future either. I'd sleep when the fucking casket became my permanent residence. Right now, all I needed was to rest my eyes for a few hours so I could get back to the fucking paper, especially with me taking over Glow's bills soon.

Pointing to page three of the papers that were spread across my bed now, I tapped the black ink. "I even had the lawyer mention me paying ya mortgage. It's all dur."

Glow's brown eyes scanned the papers, reading over everything listed out regarding the marriage. Before she would even look at the paper, she kept talking about the ring and how wrong it was to buy a stolen ring. She wasn't talking about shit, though. I wasn't marrying her ass without at least giving her some bling; I'd bought worse shit off the streets anyhow. She lived all the way in Jagoda Bay, so Snow 'nem were not going to find that ring. Plus, it could very well be a million rings in the world like this one, being that it was simplistic. The ring was pretty as fuck, and snatching a natural grown diamond for ten bands was a good lick. She'd been worrying for shit. This shit had been the steal of a lifetime.

"You trying to do this now?" Her sculpted brow rose as she gazed into my eyes.

Her hair had been pulled into a bun at the top of her head with a few of the wavy pieces crawling from the thickness. Glow was fine as fuck in those braids, and I'd enjoyed having them wrapped around my hand when I'd been balls deep in her, but her natural hair was fitting as fuck.

Blinking, trying hard as fuck not to go back down memory

lane, I licked my lips. I wasn't trying to waste any more time. I had a nice little stash, but I was ready to get this fucking gwap with the mob. I told myself I wasn't studying no bitches, but Glow came along and proved that theory wrong. She'd been the only woman I'd been with since being out, and she wanted to be part of the mob just as much as I wanted the money that came with it. We might as well get this shit popping now rather than later.

"Where?"

Snatching the papers from the bed, I pulled my shorts up on my waist. "Come on. I'll show you."

I grabbed her soft-ass hand and led her through the dimly lit home. Tulscan and Kassie were on the couch with my nephew on my brother's chest while the TV played rain music. It had been the only way to get his little ass to sleep. We crept through, careful not to wake them up. I could feel her body shaking as I led her outside and down the steps. I'd already gotten my sister's rental keys, so once I unlocked the door, I helped Glow in before running to the driver's side. The hood was buzzing in the distance, but our street was quiet. In another two hours, it would match the cadence of the rest of the hood, and by then, we'd be back like we hadn't left at all.

"Tunan, this ain't crazy to you?" Glow asked in disbelief while I put the papers in the visor.

The street lights glowed on her light tan skin, and it was times like this that I understood why her mother had given her the name she held. I didn't know if Glow slept in a pool full of oils, but her skin was always hydrated and fucking moisturized.

Shaking my head, I replied, "This whole shit is off the wall to a nigga, but getting what the fuck we want ain't crazy."

I eyed her as I drove off the street. When I met the rest of the mob and saw how well off them niggas were living just by being a part of an organization, that shit had put fire under a nigga. It was no different than being affiliated with a gang, where most of the time you were nothing but a name.

Crossing her arms in her lap, her white skirt lifted up her thigh, making my dick stiffen. Everything about Glow was sexy. Even though she'd been skeptical as hell of my bootleg purchase, she looked damn good with the ring on her finger. Snow's husband had done well; that bitch was shining like the fucking sun.

Her phone lighting up in her hand had me concentrating back on the road. Her social media had been going fucking crazy since the live video tonight. She'd shown me at least one hundred notifications from her Pretty Eaters commenting on her old videos and asking her to go back live. They were commenting on videos that had nothing to do with my brothers or me, begging her to show them the "hood niggas". Tuden and Tulen were eating the shit up.

"We here."

Parking, I kept the engine running so that I could check her temperature. This marriage wouldn't be a traditional one, and I wouldn't impose on her life, but I did want her to be sure about this shit since it would be linking us.

Her eyes lifted from the paper to the two-story building in front of us. It was dark as fuck because the surrounding streetlights had been busted out, and the city hadn't misused its time repairing them because they'd only get busted again. The building looked spooky as fuck, especially since it was black, but wasn't shit scary about what went on inside.

"A church at nine at night, Tunan?"

"Yeah, Glow. A church."

She gawked. "Are they even open?"

The lot was full of cars, so I assumed her question was rhetorical. Still, I answered her. "This ain't no regular church, my baby."

Glow was unsure like a motherfucker. Her eyes scanned the lot, and the way she kept swallowing and making her throat move had me licking my lips and gripping my crotch. Driving my head back into the headrest, I watched as she damn near had a mental meltdown.

"Glow... This shit just on paper. I promise, I ain't gon' impose on you or no shit like that. I even showed you the prenup. Ion want shit from you, my baby. Swear to God. I'm in a church lot, so that nigga can strike me down right now if I'm bullshitin'." I held my hand up to emphasize my point.

She blinked rapidly, long lashes fluttering as her shoulders tensed. "You just said yourself this isn't a regular church. Plus, you cursed and promised in the same sentence! That disqualifies anything you've said!"

Keeping my face neutral, I looked at her until she turned her gaze to me. "Glow. You ain't gotta do this shit."

Because she didn't. I'd have to find another girl, and even though I preferred it to be her because I didn't have the time or energy to explain to a woman that I just wanted a wife on paper, I was going to do what the fuck I had to do. I was getting this bread one way or another. Don made it sound easy, but you couldn't just pick a girl off the street. I couldn't see myself finding a woman I trusted enough to bring into the mob world like that. She could be the fucking feds or on some setup shit. With what Stella had done, I wasn't putting shit past nobody.

Sucking in a wad of breath, she looked down at her ring. She was making this shit more than what it was. Glow was fine and had some of the best pussy I'd had the pleasure of entering, but this was about the money for me. I fucked with Glow, and that was why I had agreed to let her call the shots and fold into her requests. But the bread was the fucking motive. Aside from her having my last name and her bills being paid, her world wouldn't change much. She was already in the door with the women despite what her mind told her.

"All right... Let's go."

I didn't expect my heart to pound in my chest at her submission, so it caught me off guard. Instead of getting out of the car, I watched her flip down the visor to fix her hair. She tucked a few strands back into the bun before opening her crossbody bag. She pulled out an edge brush and a small bottle of edge control. Tuscany and Athena used the same kind. Once her edges looked like they were in cursive, she added lip gloss, then pulled out some type of powder that matched her skin tone and pressed it into her face.

Glow always had products. I didn't know how much she could fit in that damn bag, but when she pulled out her sweet-smelling-ass perfume and nearly sprayed me in the fucking eye with it, I knew then that shit had to have been laced with magic. Giving herself another two glances in the visor mirror, she flipped it back up and turned to me with a content expression on her face. She was legit about to do this with a nigga.

"Okay," she said, rubbing her lips together, smearing the gloss all over her lips evenly.

She's too fucking fine, yo'.

My dick was now at full attention, so I grabbed the papers and tucked them in my back pocket. I hopped out of the car before I gave in to temptation and pulled her glossy-ass lips in my mouth and leaned the seat back so that she could ride my dick.

Checking my surroundings, I opened the passenger door and helped her pretty ass out. Hand in hand, I led her scary ass through the double doors, shutting the outside out and welcoming all the bullshit that went on inside.

Glow paused, eyes roaming the entryway, confused about the whole ordeal.

"Welcome to the Haunted House."

She drew her head back. "Like... Halloween?"

Grabbing her hand again, I led her out of the entryway and down the left hallway.

"Nah. This place used to be a church. Well, it's still a church, but it doesn't operate as one anymore. Just think of it as a one-stop shop for the hood." I pointed to an open door that we walked past. There were slot machines in about six rows with ten machines on each row. "This is the gambling room."

It wasn't like Don's Dungeon. They didn't have crap tables or anything like that—just slot machines for the grannies of the hood to spend their fixed income. Even though it was late at night, nearly every seat was taken as machines sounded off.

Pulling her along, I pointed to the next door. "This is sum'n like a convenience store except... if you ain't got no bread, you can get shit on a pay-later type shit with a lil' bit of interest."

The next room was run by an Arab, who was behind the counter, serving a young girl in a bonnet and flip-flops with a baby on her hip. His shelves were stocked with everything you could need, from clothing and diapers to household products and car parts. He even had liquor in the fridges lining the room.

"Oh, wow!" Glow gasped as I pulled her along.

There were two more rooms on this side of the hall, and then there were double doors at the end of it. The next room's door was closed, but the moans could be heard, so there was no explanation needed. Her cheeks grew red, and her palm sweated in my hand, but we kept it moving.

The last room had three desks in it with women behind them, typing on the computers and shuffling through paperwork. There were people in front of each desk in a line.

"This is the business room. You can get all types of paperwork filed, renew ya license, pay tickets, get ya passport, pay ya light bill, rent, get loans, and damn near any other legal thing you need handled can be done here. There's always at least two different attorneys here. They've been getting niggas off child support for years."

"Is this where you had the paperwork done?" Her eyes went from the busy room to me.

I grinned. "Hell yeah. You had muhfuckas laughing at a nigga too. Attorney asked me ten times if I wanted to marry yo' lil' bossy ass."

A grin broke through the nervousness on her face, followed by the rolling of her eyes. "Whatever. I can't believe a place like this even exists. In a church of all buildings too... I have so many questions."

"Dey gone have to wait, my baby."

I continued pulling her behind me as we moved toward the end of the hall. I was ready to get this shit over with so I could get back to my people and smoke. Bad enough, Glow had my dick harder than arithmetic. Around my folks, I could at least relax and no longer be turned on. I was surprised they had even taken a nap. They took up her energy with someone always being in her face, so she and I wouldn't be paying each other much attention once we got back.

Taking one last look at Glow as we reached the double door, I tapped the back of her hand with my thumb as she swallowed hard. Pushing the right door open, she jumped as bass flowed from the soundproof room. We were entering the worship hall, or what used to be the worship hall. Though no praise-worthy sermons or catching the holy spirit went on in here anymore, there were still rows of pews that were empty and a choir stand at the head of the room.

"What the Hell! What the Hell! What the Helly! What the Helliyuntaaae!"

"Really, Tunan?" Glow's eyes were on the choir in front of us, even though her question was directed at me.

About ten singers were in black robes as their director stood in front of them, dressed the same except his dragged the floor. "Sopranos! Take it!" He pointed at a section of robed singers.

"What the Helly-on! What the Helly-Berry! What the Helly-'Burton! What the Helly Bron James!" they sang in perfect high-pitched voices.

Pulling Glow along, who was still fascinated by the choir rehearsal, I cleared my throat once we got to the stage. The director turned, and when his eyes landed on Glow, a sinful smile appeared, showing open-faced gold teeth. Pinky from Friday had to have been this nigga's brother because he looked exactly like him, down to the wet-ass Jheri curl. His voice was even all screechy, matching the look of his sketchy ass.

"Choir, hum it out," he instructed, and the choir began to hum and rock side to side.

This wasn't a traditional choir, just as it wasn't a traditional church. Concerts of local artists and open mic nights were held here from time to time, and sometimes, neighboring hoods brought their choirs and had a sing-off. It was a whole-ass thing. When my mama first brought Tulsaire here, the little nigga was laughing for a week straight. Her loving the Haunted House was one of the reasons why her ass was always wanting to be out here in the hood instead of being put up like we intended.

Not feeling the way he was eyeing Glow, I stepped up. "Aye, nigga! This ain't that. Go grab one of them hoes you got in the back room."

He held his arms up, robe flapping, while his grin never wavered. "Just admiring the beauty, young blood. I'm Pastor Lucifer."

Glow frowned. "Lucifer? As in... the devil?"

"Yeah, some say I'm worse, though, pretty lady." His evil grin broadened.

Pastor Lucifer was a motherfucker who never hid his true nature. The nigga used to own this church back when I was a kid, and it used to be a decent place. He got caught fucking on the neighborhood women, shaming his wife and making the whole congregation leave his ass. His wife and a few of the church's board members ended up dead, and while he was fighting the case, the city shut the church down. The nigga beat the case, and a year later, he reopened the church as the Haunted House.

He was the worst kind of fucked up, but I couldn't lie as if this place hadn't been helpful to the community. Even his ghetto choir got paid to compete. Hell, if women needed a quick come up, they could try their luck at the slot machines or sell that pussy in the back room where Pastor Lucifer would get a small fee. He was a motherfucker, but he was fair to an extent, so people fucked with him. Everybody knew the nigga killed them folks, but the hood kept that shit concealed. Wasn't shit much that could be done anyway; he'd beat the charges.

"What you need, Payne?" He shifted his attention to Glow to me.

"I need you to marry us."

"Wait! Him? The devil about to marry us?" Glow's eyes widened as she pulled her hand from mine.

"This nigga ain't no fucking devil, my baby. He's an offi-ciant, so he can get us right," I assured her.

Pulling the papers from my back pocket, I handed them to Pastor Lucifer. He took them, eyes scanning over the various pages, and the way his smile fell toward the end, I chuckled.

"Well, damn. The pussy must be *immaculate*. What the fuck

you gaining from this shit, Payne?"

Glow's face reddened, so I snatched the papers back. "None of ya fucking business, Luci. Now, let's get this shit poppin' so we can be on our way and y'all can keep singing Rob49."

"Fuck you, Payne. Y'all come on. I got another wedding in ten minutes, so we gotta make this shit snappy."

Hesitantly, Glow let me lead her onto the stage. Once we faced each other, I placed the papers on the podium and straightened my shoulders. She wiped her palms down the front of her skirt as the choir's hum became louder.

"Wait. Can they sing "Young and Beautiful" by Lana Del Ray?"

Pastor Lucifer nodded and lifted his hands. "You heard the lady. From the top!"

The choir began to harmonize a tune that was familiar to me, but I couldn't pin it. It was probably some shit I heard on TV.

"Aite. Y'all got some vows?"

I shook my head. "Nah."

"Aite, I'll use mine then. Hold hands."

Accessing Glow's face, I could tell she was feeling insecure about her appearance. One of the hairs from her bun kept falling into her face. I tucked it back in place and lifted her chin. "You look beautiful, Glow."

Taking her hands in mine again, I locked eyes with her. In a fucking tennis skirt and sneakers, Glow was the baddest fucking thing this side of Memphis. She could be in a paper bag and still kill everything within a fifty-mile radius.

"Payne, you first. Repeat after me."

"Hot summer nights, mid-July... When you and I were forever wild," the choir sang their asses off.

"I, Tunan, take thee, Glow, to be my wedded wife, to have and to hold from this day forward, for better, for worse, for richer, for poorer, in sickness and in health, to love and to cherish, till death do us part... Say it nigga," Pastor Lucifer spat when I hesitated.

Clearing my throat, I repeated his words.

"I, Tunan, take thee Glow, to be my wedded wife, to have and to hold from this day forward, for better, for worse, for richer, for poorer, in... in... health, to love and to cherish, till death do us part."

I'd loved a bitch through sickness already, and the thought of doing that shit again had my own fucking palms sweating. I couldn't do that shit again. I wouldn't do that shit again. If a woman had any type of medical shit going on, I was out of there. Stella was the last hoe I'd bring back from the dead. Glow had her own money and looked healthy enough, so I wasn't too worried about the sickness part. But still, I wasn't repeating that shit, even if this was a cursed-ass church.

"Will you still love me when I'm no longer young and beautiful! Will you still love me when I got nothing buuut my aching soul! I know you will."

No cap, if the choir didn't win their next competition, I knew something was up. They were singing like the rent was due.

"You next, pretty lady," Pastor Lucifer said, low-key fucking Glow with his eyes. If I weren't trying to give Glow some decency through this ceremony, I'd bust him in his shit.

"I, Glow, take thee, Tunan, to be my wedded husband, to have and to hold, from this day forward, for better, for worse, for richer, for poorer, in sickness and in health, to love and to cherish, till death do us part," she rushed out in one breath.

"At least somebody got the shit right. You got the band?"

Pulling the other portion of the ring out of my pocket, I slid it on her finger. It was crazy how perfect it fit—shit was almost as spooky as the souls of the pastor's wife that I knew roamed these damn halls.

"By the authority vested in me, I now pronounce you... husband and wife. You may now kiss the bride."

Swiping my thumb over her hand again, I pulled her into my chest and lifted her chin. Her eyes watered, but she didn't let anything fall. Leaning down, I pecked her lips before swiping my thumb over them. I could feel her heart drumming against my chest as she stared at me. I was ignoring my own heart as the choir serenaded us and Lucifer's creepy ass looked on. Glow was the perfect fucking wife, but this was a job—a duty. So instead of tonguing her down, I let her go. I had to remember what the fuck this was and what the fuck my ultimate goal was.

"Yeah, nigga, you a damn fool for real. Come sign these papers and give me my bread so I can get the fuck on with the next wedding."

Ignoring what looked like disappointment on Glow's face, I went to the podium to sign and then motioned for her to come and sign the documents too. I pulled out a two bands and pushed it into the pastor's chest so he could take his eyes off *my wife*. While I had no plans to treat Glow as my wife, I, for damn sure, expected everyone to treat her as such.

"Don't forget to file my shit, Luci. I'll come back for a copy later this month."

Pastor Lucifer waved me off while beckoning for the choir to stop singing. "Take five, y'all, and not a minute longer. It's gonna be a long night."

We made our way back to my sister's car in a comfortable silence. Glow didn't look nervous or anxious anymore, so I left her to her own thoughts while I succumbed to mine. I'd done what Don needed for me to become an official member of the mob. Now I had to make sure Glow stayed my wife on paper and didn't become my wife in real life because I didn't have time for the relationship shit. Glow wasn't Stella, and Stella damn sure wasn't Glow, but one bad apple had spoiled it for the whole bunch. That love shit was a no-go for me. Glow had come up with all these boundaries any fucking way, and I fully intended to abide by them. Pussy was cool, but money was so much fucking better.

Now, I had to figure out a way to tell my brother that I'd married his bitch.

CHAPTER 14
SHIO CUPPACIO

My day started like any other—early. I was up at 4:00 a.m., showered and dressed by 4:30 a.m., and had my Nikes on the pavement by 4:35 a.m. Today, instead of working out inside, I decided to do a ten-mile run. Near the end, my lungs felt like they were about to collapse inside of my chest. My mind was going haywire, and by the time I got back to my driveway, the world had woken up, but my thoughts hadn't settled.

One reason I'd been uneasy was because of my new house-guest. Don was surely going along with this quest of me "teaching" Solana how to be a wife, but I hadn't figured out why. I knew he'd researched Ines and Solana; he wouldn't dare bring chaos in his own backyard that he couldn't eliminate. I, too, have always been the type to solve any problem that comes my way, and this one was no different. The problem was that I was under Don's hand, with little control over what I could do outside of my home. While Don had the advantage of knowing everyone's secrets and plays, I had my own ways to gather intel on folks. So after my intense run, I did what I do best—research. I needed to find out everything about the Ledesmas from my home.

I already knew about her father and his business dealings, but I hadn't been told about a daughter. Why'd he hide her from the world? Ines had Solana put up in that cold-ass, castle-like home, but for what reason? Besides the Rodríguezes and his witch of a wife, no one knew about Solana's existence. Well, no one knew she was his daughter, but she hadn't done much to hide herself on the streets of Mexico City. Little Baby was out there in the clubs, bars, holes-in-the-wall, and elusive lounges. I spent most of my day talking to my sources, and considering how long it took to find out shit about her, you'd think I'd know more than just her "party girl" lifestyle.

For as much as Solana partied, I was expecting to find a long line of men who had been linked to her. She was living in my home, and although temporarily, I didn't want any fucking surprises. If any of them fucks were dumb enough to try and come and be the fucking hero by professing his love on my doorstep to stop her from marrying into the Rodríguez Cartel, I was going to send them bitches back across the water, wrapped in a Mexican flag and soiled in their own blood. Shockingly, all I found were a few associates I'd hardly call that, and some club owners who loved it when she came through and respected her because she spent mad bread in their establishments. I couldn't find a man *or* a woman who had been romantically involved with her, which would be virtuous for the nigga that was set to be her husband, but terrible for me. It meant that she had either learned the art of sneakiness or she was untouched. I knew for damn sure she was no fucking virgin. Solana was not only attractive, exotic, and desirable, but she reeked of "I've been fucked" under that shy yet sassy demeanor. With a father like Ines Ledesma, I was certain she got her shit off when she could, which meant her ass was slick. I didn't like sneaky motherfuckers, and I damn sure couldn't be easily fooled or manipulated. While my eyes saw what they could, my antennas were up higher than ever.

"Aye... Get up."

The room was dark, even though the sun had risen and been out all day. She was in this bitch, lightly snoring like the whole day hadn't passed, and it wasn't damn near three o'clock in the afternoon. Lifting the Audemars to my face, I was wrong; it was ten minutes past three-thirty, which meant I'd been standing here watching the rise and fall of her back for well over thirty minutes.

Get your shit together, Shio.

Solana grumbled inaudible words as she rose from her slumber. I hadn't known anyone who could sleep like the fucking dead all day. Especially not a fully grown adult. Most of the women in our family, if they didn't have obligations like work or school, still got up at the crack of dawn because they looked forward to spending our fucking money. It was as if this girl didn't look forward to anything outside of partying, and since there hadn't been any of that going on, sleep was her only hobby.

I watched as she moved around in the bed. Her phone lit up on the nightstand, and that was another thing I noticed in my few days of observation—she didn't check it. I was sure the battery was fucked up because it had been on the charger for days, untouched. Hell, the only notifications she got were emails. I knew because I'd zoomed the camera in to see the first few days she was here. People might think I was going to extremes, but my safety and the safety of those around me had me doing whatever was necessary. I didn't know many women who weren't glued to their phones, either gossiping or scrolling through social media nonstop. Solana didn't do any of that shit, and that had me even more puzzled.

Who in the fuck was Solana Ledesma, and why had God put her in my path?

"It's Saturday. No workout. I remember," she groggily explained, like I didn't know the days of the week.

She'd cried, thrown up twice, and cursed more than a sailor during our workouts. She was feisty once she was comfortable, or rather, uncomfortable. I half expected her to walk out, but no matter how many bodily fluids were extracted from her body, whether it be tears, spit, sweat, or vomit, she kept going.

She was still on her back, but now her head had lifted from the pillow. Her hair was still in the braid I'd done, but now it looked more like a tangled vine than a neat plait. I was surprised she even let her hair get that matted. At first glance, you'd think Solana was a rich, spoiled daddy's girl who never let a hair out of place. But if it weren't for my housekeeper, the room would reveal she wasn't the cleanest or tidiest. She kept her hygiene decent enough, washing her ass and brushing her teeth. But she hadn't bothered to care for her hair or put on clothes to explore the area outside this room.

"It's three thirty, Solana."

Sitting upright, she stretched her arms above her head. The sports bra she was wearing was twisted, and as soon as she lifted her arms, the bottom half of her breast peeked out. Turning my head, I backed up three paces to flick the light switch. Her eyes squinted to adjust as the room turned from her personal hibernation cave into the bright, airy space it was meant to be. She fixed her bra and let her legs hang over the side of the bed. One side of her hair was mashed entirely to her head, while a few strands were stuck to her face. I was almost sure she'd gotten vomit in it the other day, so it needed a good wash and conditioning. If this was how she handled her hair's upkeep, I didn't understand how it had gotten so long, or how she'd managed to keep the length and density. It should've been broken off and damaged.

Now with her feet on the wood, she started rolling her head to stretch her neck. There was sleep in her eyes and dried drool on the side of her face, yet she was sitting in bed without a care in the world. Her daddy had given her to me to groom so she could blend in with the wolves, but she just didn't know, he'd placed her in the den of a fucking lion.

"Why am I awake again?" Her heavy accent was deeper than usual due to her still being sleepy.

She should've been rested enough to last her ass a lifetime.

Standing, she pulled the matching athletic shorts out of her crotch. They were high-waisted, but she had them folded down her abdomen, showing her smooth, dark hazelnut skin. As she popped her back, I backed out, nearing the door.

"We got somewhere to be, Solana."

Her head swiftly shifted in my direction. There was a look of indifference on her face, and if she called herself reading me, she wouldn't succeed. Her eyes looked past me as three outrageously expensive motherfuckers entered her room: Lunar, Chimo, and Bruno—or Lamar, Chinko, and Bruna. I didn't know which name they were going by today, and I didn't give a fuck as long as they did what they do best. What I did know was that I'd had to shell out a ton of fucking money to have them leave Don's estate just to come fix her up.

They each carried some type of trunk and had even more shit in the hallway. They were the official glam squad for the women of the mafia, and since I'd be bringing Solana around them, I knew that matted ball of fur on the top of her head wouldn't cut it. They'd look at her like a lost puppy before looking at me like I'd lost my mind for bringing her.

The women of the mafia were always well-groomed, and most of the time, the three men barging into the room were the reasons behind the mob's hefty credit card bills. These niggas looked like some shit straight out of the movie *The Hunger Games*. With their loud hair colors and eccentric attire, even though all three were in all black, they looked like they could wreak havoc. But I'd seen their work, and as peculiar as they looked, they were the best, according to what the wives said.

Solana pulled her shorts upright and crossed her arms over her chest. She'd even tried to wipe the eye boogers from her face. Crazy how she was shying away from three gay niggas but didn't give two shits when it was just her and me.

Lunar clasped his hands while the other two gave her a silent inspection.

"This week, a hot new bombshell enters the villa." Lunar giggled.

"Ohhhh, she's pretty. Skin so flawless even with the dried-up spit," Chimo added.

"You did good, Mr. Cuppacio. The body is bodying…"

"Thank you," she dragged out, her accent now a little less heavy.

Instead of correcting Bruno on the fact that I hadn't done shit because Solana wasn't mine, I let my eyes rake over her frame. My gaze lingered over her ass for a bit longer than it should have before I dragged it back up to her face. Solana's dark eyes were on me, and her cheeks had grown flushed. She continued to eye me as I eyed her while the trio moved into her space more, now circling her and humming. I needed to break eye contact, but she had me cemented.

Hell no, Shio.

"We got us an Afro Mexicana? Yassss! I am Lunar. I'm in charge of the hair, and it looks like I have my work cut out." He frowned while holding up a string of the mangled hair.

I was thankful for the interruption because, for a second, it felt like Solana and I were eye fucking each other, and that was a no-go.

"This is Chimo, he does the nails and little piggies on your feet, and this is Bruno, he does the makeup. ¿Hay algún look específico que queramos lograr esta noche? (*Is there a certain look we are going for this evening?*)"

"No estoy seguro de cuál es la ocasión (*I'm not sure what the occasion is*)."

Solana looked at me as if to ask for help on that matter, but I avoided her eyes as I looked at the trio with a down-payment price tag.

"No hay un look definido. Simplemente haz tu magia. Si hay un tema en particular que les gusta a las otras chicas, sigue ese ejemplo. (*No certain look. Just do your magic. If there is a certain theme the other ladies are in, go with that*).

All three men's eyes bulged in amusement.

"Ohh! To be a fly on the wall when you two tangle. There is nothing like a man who can speak your native tongue. Makes a girl wonder what else he can do with that tongue." Bruno fanned before dropping his smile. "No disrespect to you, Mr. Cuppacio. We are just having girl talk."

Shaking my head, I left them to do what I'd paid them for. Hopefully, they could get the shit done in three hours because punctuality was a non-negotiable of mine.

I'D BEEN DRESSED for about an hour when Chimo poked his head out of the guest room and said Solana needed some feminine products. Looking at him as if he had two heads, I nodded and made my way to the market outside the neighborhood entrance. The guest room she was in had feminine products for Solana, so I was confused about needing to get more. It had only been about two weeks since she arrived, so I knew there was no way she'd used all the items the housekeeper had stocked in the vanity.

Making it to the market, I hopped out of my truck, being sure not to wrinkle my fit. My family loved to knit-pick about shit as if we weren't wearing bullshit just two years ago. Browsing the numerous options and not knowing which brand she preferred, I grabbed four brands of pads and three brands of tampons before I checked out and headed back to the house. Sitting it all at the guest room door, I knocked, then walked away.

Another twenty minutes had passed when I reemerged from my office. Instead of going to the guest room to see what the fuck was taking the three stooges so long, I stepped outside to take a few phone calls while toking on a blunt. For the car we were taking tonight, I had banned smoking in it. With its six-figure price tag, I wanted to keep the new car smell for as long as I could. My truck was my everyday vehicle, but occasionally, I liked to take the luxurious route. The four cars that took up space in my garage didn't get nearly enough drive time. I may have bought them on impulse just because I could, but tonight was the Maybach's turn, where her tires would become one with the streets of Jagoda Bay.

Taking one last pull from the blunt, I put it out using the chrome cigarette snuffer I kept on me when I went out. Most people who carried these were cigarette smokers, but the fancy-ass tool had only been in use for my blunts. Reaching into the pocket of my slacks, I pulled out a mint and popped it in my mouth. I didn't want to smell like outside, so I made my way to the Maybach, and before I could even open the door, the clacking of heels had me pausing in my stride.

I had to do a double-take.

The first thing I noticed was her hair. It had been a pile of kinks before I braided it, and when I first met her, it had been bone straight. Today, though, it wasn't straightened to resemble silk. I didn't know what they'd done, but thick, coarse spiral coils framed her face and ended just below her shoulders. The curls were voluptuous but complemented her face well.

Her face.

Her face had been made up flawlessly. Whatever products they used must've cost a fortune because you couldn't tell where the makeup ended or began. Even her neck blended seamlessly into the glamorous makeup. The dress she was wearing should've been reserved for her fiancé's eyes only, and had he been here, he surely would've told her to change. It was sleeveless, and judging by the way it wrapped around the base of her neck, it had to be backless. It didn't show much cleavage, but the little black dress stopped right at the bend of her hips, making her legs look endless.

The strappy tortoise heels on her petite feet were simple— red bottoms but nothing too crazy. It didn't matter, though; the red French tips on her toes didn't need much distraction for they were perfect. The clutch in her hands matched her toes and paired with the heels, giving the dress a pop of color. Her lips were glossy and painted red, and the cat-like lashes waving at me made her look like a seductress. Just from her appearance, one wouldn't know she slept all day, didn't clean up behind herself, cried from walking on the treadmill, and was a certified party girl. She cleaned up nice as fuck. She cleaned up like a fucking wife—a badass wife that made other husbands despise the one they had at home, but a wife nonetheless.

"Hola," she spoke with a grin.

Rounding the car, I caught a whiff of her perfume, which was more of a rich, evening scent than something dainty. Still, it smelled damn good coming off her skin. I opened the car door for her and waited until she took those few steps to get into the passenger seat. Because I was a gentleman, I didn't look at her ass—at least, I didn't let my eyes dawdle on her ass. She was here to be trained for the next man, and even though I didn't know why her dad thought it was a good idea for me to be her etiquette teacher, I was going to let this shit play out.

"Thank you for the sanitary napkins, Shio. I knew my womanly was due soon, but wasn't expecting it to start today," she turned and stated before sliding into the car.

"No problem. Sorry there wasn't anything in the bathroom for you to handle your business."

She shook her head. "No, there was... just nothing *I* could use."

Instead of asking more questions, I closed the door and rounded the car. I hopped into the driver's seat, and the new car smell and her perfume blending together greeted me as soon as my back hit the leather.

"You're going to just leave them—the glam guys there?" she asked as I reversed.

"Don't I just leave you there?"

I watched the side of her face as I waited for her to answer. Putting the car in drive, I glided through the neighborhood.

"Well... yes."

"Okay, then. I've known them far longer than I've known you. They'll lock up when they pack up."

Her lips turned up over her nose. "How do you have them on speed dial anyway? Do you use them for all the women you pleasure?"

"How do I use them for all the women I pleasure when I'm not pleasuring you, Solana?"

Her mouth opened, then shut. I could have given her an explanation of how I had their contact information, but she was only here temporarily. The less she knew about our lives, the better. In a short bit, she'd be back in Mexico, never to be seen or heard from again.

Thumbing the dial on the steering wheel, HER blasted through the speakers. She was one of my favorite singers. Her voice was not only smooth but soulful and emotive. I couldn't wait until she dropped some new shit, but for now, her old hits would do. She was ahead of her time and deserved all of the Grammy awards she'd racked up over the course of her career.

Solana hadn't given me a response to the question I'd asked. Instead, she sat pretty as a pansy to the right of me with her natural pouty lips puckering while gazing at the passing trees. We'd made it through the gates of my subdivision and were now on the E-Way. She was trying to fake an attitude, but it was easy to spot the delirium in her stance.

"You've really never been to America before, hunh?"

We had only passed trees, and maybe an overpass, but with the way Solana was peering out the window, you'd think I'd driven past Disney World. Mexico City was far more beautiful and most certainly had paved roads and luscious trees.

"I haven't. It's still surreal that I'm here. It's beautiful."

"It's nothing."

I could see her stiffen, so I cleared my throat to soften my tone. I wasn't trying to scare Solana. I think I'd proven my point not to fuck with me on the treadmill a few days ago, but I didn't need her to fear me.

"What I mean is *this* is nothing. There are some stunning sites, even here in Jagoda Bay, but the intersection is just the same as it is everywhere. Crowded, cracked gravel, and muthafuckas that can't drive."

She diverted her attention from the window to me. "I haven't been able to experience it... America. I don't even know if I'm going to be able to experience it fully. But from what I've seen, it's remarkable. I... I can't explain it. The air smells different, feels different, and I probably sound like a mad woman saying that because I've only been in *it* twice. But, it just feels like... I don't know what it feels like." She shrugged.

Solana had been sheltered. Her father allowed her to run amok in Mexico City, but I could guarantee that she had a guard on her heels unbeknownst to her. She was his most prized possession. One that he held near and dear to his heart until it was time to trade her for his own selfish greed. She'd had a leash put on her back in Mexico, and even though she likes to sleep the fucking day away, I only have one mother-fucker captive. That nigga was starving in the basement of the cabin, which was a drastic difference from her pretty ass being in my home. She was free to do whatever she wanted here, and I was just realizing that maybe she didn't know that.

"You can do what you want," I prattled.

Her lash extension batted. "What?"

"You can do what you want. Solana, you a grown-ass woman in a whole new country. If you want to get out and explore, do that shit."

Solana wasn't chained to my house. If she wanted to disappear until her father popped up, demanding that she return to Mexico, she could do that. She was free to explore all she wanted.

"I cannot do what I want for many reasons." She drove her back into the leather seat, making her chest poke out.

"Yeah? Name 'em."

Swiping her tongue across her shiny red bottom lip, she pondered as if she were grouping a list. "My father sent me here to *prepare* for marriage. That's a reason."

"You can still do whatever it is he feels like you should be doing, all the while living."

"And I don't know anyone out here. I don't have a car. I don't have any money. Remember... I was screaming at my father's wife because of my credit cards."

322

Rubbing my hand down my chin as I pulled into the venue lot, I waited in the valet line. The lot was full, and I'd already spotted four more Maybachs. Two of them looked like they were the same color as mine. Well, they seemed to be because my truck had been sprayed onyx, and you could see the difference when the moonlight hit it.

Sitting back in my seat, I crossed my hands in my lap. I was arriving at this event with a woman who was more trouble than a two-year-old. I would be taking Solana back home, all the while going into two different rooms. Solana was beyond gorgeous tonight, and I'd be lying if I said I didn't desire to pleasure her, as she calls it. But I wouldn't. She was off-limits, and I was a man with restraint. The most I had for her was a prayer when she went back across the border to her fiancé. While she was in my possession, she would have the same privileges as any other woman who occupied space in my world.

"Aye."

Solana had been watching a nosy-ass Pia walk into the building. I knew it was her from the Rose clutch folded in her right arm. Nel had mugged my car, but the nigga and his fiancée couldn't see inside. The most they could make out was that I had someone in the front seat.

When I caught Solana's attention, I noticed that she had a hair out of place. Reaching in, I tucked it into one of her curls before speaking. I didn't miss the way she sucked in air, but I let it roll off my back.

"I have five cars in the driveway. All the keys are inside them. Money isn't running out over this way. I'll break you off. And as far as not knowing anyone, there are about seven women who are about to be all over you as soon as we walk through the doors. All they do is spend their niggas money and get into shit. You're in mob-land, Solana. You're safe here. You can do whatever the fuck you want to do. Ain't nobody tell you to be cooped up in the room, sleeping all fucking day."

She winced at my last sentence, but it wasn't my intention to blast her. She didn't have to sit in the house all damn day like she was Rapunzel, though. I wanted to ensure she understood that no one was holding her hostage and that she was free to do whatever she wanted. It was my turn to move up in the valet line, so I did while keeping my eyes on her. When she still hadn't responded, I tried to reason with her again.

"Look, I'm not trying to clock you or anything like that. But from what I heard about them Rodríguezes, they don't fuck with the States. It's your first time here, and it might very well be your last. Make the best of this shit."

"So you are encouraging me to go out and party?"

"It's more to life than standing on couches and choking on a hookah stick. But if that's what you want to do, cool. I'm just letting you know that you're free to explore. No harm gone come your way."

I could see the wheels turning in her head. She was thinking too much. There wasn't shit to think about, though. If she wanted to get out of the house, she could.

"How do you know? That I'm safe." Her eyes rounded.

The valet stood at my door, so I opened it for him.

"Because a muthafucka not insane enough to play with anyone on the side of me. Whether that one be temporary *or* permanent."

Noticing the shiver her body gave, I didn't wait for her to reply because that was a good enough response. I bumped elbows with the valet as I got out. He was a familiar face since the mob kept the same workers for obvious reasons. The less motherfuckers knew about what we did in our downtime, the better.

"Aye, big dawg." The valet's eyes scanned the lot as he

lowered his head while speaking to me.

"Yeah?" I didn't know what he wanted, and had no interest in finding out, but I waited to see what it was he was gearing up to spit at me.

Reaching into his pocket, my arm immediately went to the back of my waist to clutch my gun. I could hear Solana gasp behind me, but I wasn't tearing my eyes away from the potential threat. I was on whatever the hell he was on, and if he was on bullshit, he'd be taken out, discarded, and made a missing person before the next hour.

"Whoa! I ain't on no shit like that," he assured.

Using the gun, I tapped his hands that were still in the pocket of his hoodie.

"Slow," I instructed. I could feel Solana's eyes on me, but I wasn't worried. She'd be dealing with much worse shit once she was released to her future husband.

The valet, moving as slowly as a snail, pulled out a folded gallon-sized bag of white powder. At a second glance, I realized that inside the bag were small baggies filled with the rich white man's drug. Scraping my bottom lip with my top teeth, I relaxed a little.

"I was just letting you know, I had some white girl for sale."

Tucking my gun back under my shirt, I kept my eyes on the young, eager dope boy. Had this been Don, he'd approach—which I knew he wasn't stupid enough to do—he'd be eating a bullet right now. But I had respect for him. Not only was he working, but he was hustling too. Working these events was the perfect lick. My people and I didn't play with our noses, even though we sold enough white to fill one of Preston's arctic simulations. Just because we didn't, didn't mean other motherfuckers inside didn't.

"I fuck with the hustle. If somebody in there looking, I'll send 'em out here."

With a grin on his face, he nodded.

As I said, I respected the hustle, but that didn't mean other niggas would. His hunger would either get him rich as fuck or dead as fuck when it came to the mob. There would be no in between.

Rounding the car, I waited until her door opened with the sensor I had installed and held my hand out for her to exit. She wasted no time placing hers in mine. Her heels were tall, but she was able to step in them with precision. Swapping from hands to arms with hers now hooked in mine, we were skin to skin since I was wearing a short-sleeved collar Versace shirt. Ignoring my thudding heart, I led her into the building.

She hadn't mentioned or questioned what she'd witnessed, which I appreciated.

Sticking my hand in my pocket, I pulled out a wad of twenties that I usually used to tip. "Open your bag."

She gave me a questioning look but complied.

"A woman shouldn't ever walk around with an empty purse. Especially one that cost three bands."

"Lesson *numbre tres* (number three)?"

Instead of replying verbally, I held up my pinky, index, and middle fingers. She nodded, and we proceeded into the building.

Upon stepping inside the space, the all-black color scheme had me giving a nod in approval. The décor was sleek yet dramatic, with touches of silver accents complementing the black. The decorations greeted us at the door—flowers, silks, and the scents of perfumes, food, and money flowed throughout the space. There was no doubt that plenty of fucking paper was in attendance. Stepping in stride on my side, the team had definitely done their job with Solana's look. She blended in well with the evening looks everyone else was sporting while also standing out due to the curious eyes glancing our way. I had yet to spot any of my blood relatives, so we kept moving into the main ballroom.

I didn't know an event coordinator who worked harder than Daylani. Servers were in little black dresses, hoisting trays stacked with the finest champagnes and hors d'oeuvers. I hadn't taken a sip, but I knew my people hadn't done it any other way. Grabbing one from a waitress who was bypassing, I handed it to Solana. I could feel how tense she was, and it wasn't from the encounter we had just moments ago from linking our arms. This felt like discomfort, and the bubbly would ensure that she relaxed.

She had no reason to be tense or uncomfortable, but I understood her position. These were my people, but they were no one to her. She was simply a stranger, passing through. That was why I wanted her to do something with her time outside of sleeping all fucking day. She'd been put in a situation where she could live it up before she bore the responsibility of carrying a man's last name and babies; she needed to take advantage of it.

Before we walked through the double doors, I took Solana in with my eyes. She had her head down as her clutch was tucked under her arm with the flute of champagne in her hand. The left arm was cuffed around my bicep.

"Aye?"

Her head was still slightly bent as her eyes traveled up my face. Once our gazes were locked on one another, I tipped her head up. "Keep it lifted. Don't bow to no muthfucka. Confidence... lesson four. Wear that shit like a badge of honor wherever you go. Muthafuckas can smell fear, and if you're scared, that means you can be controlled. You look good tonight, Solana. You need to act like you know it too."

Her eyes widened. I removed my hand from her chin and gently lifted the glass. Her full lips pressed against the rim as she took a sip. Her throat moved slightly as she swallowed the champagne. Knowing that the alcohol would loosen her up, I stepped into the ballroom, and she moved in sync with a nigga. I hadn't been in the room ten seconds, and I already felt the eyes on me. Mostly everyone in here was familiar, but the eyes I felt were ones I'd grown used to since the day I was born.

5... 4... 3... 2...

"Shio. Look at you! You look so handsome!"

Shannon smiled, and even though she was complimenting her only child, she had her sights set on Solana, who had placed her half-full glass on the empty tray of another waitress passing by.

My mother, as always, was ravishing in a long, black gown that covered the So Kate's I knew she was wearing. Shannon could give Zendaya a run for her money because that was always her shoe of choice. She had a pair in every color and stood proudly next to her husband in a pair every Sunday. She was a sanctified woman, but she cherished her designer brands and labels just as much as she did her Lord and Savior.

"You're breathtaking, Mama. But you knew that."

Letting Solana's arm go, I pulled my mother into an embrace, planting a kiss on her head. Bella and the girls must have influenced her, because her shoulder-length roller set she got every week at the salon had been replaced with what looked like a wig frontal. It looked good and age-appropriate, but I wasn't used to seeing her in such a modern hairstyle. Still, the black loose curls framed her face, and did little to hide her Somalian traits bleeding through. Her milk chocolate skin was flawless even under the light makeup. Her scent was one I loved since I was a kid, currently at war with my Xerjoff Alexandria II unisex parfum. Pulling her back, only then did she move her eyes to me, and as always, her eyes grew wet. She blinked away the emotion before showing it like she had always done.

Our moment lasted just a second before she was back on Solana. "You're gorgeous."

Solana lowered her head to hide her cheeks, but lifted them immediately, looking at me briefly as if she were remembering her newest lesson.

Good girl.

"Thank you. So are you. I love your dress."

My mother pressed a hand to her chest, broadcasting the shiny ring my stepfather had placed on her finger. "Ohh, and you're a Latina?"

"Yes, I'm Afro-Mexican. My father is Hispanic, and my mother was African American."

"Is," my mother corrected.

"Hmm?"

"Your mother *is* African American. Even if she is no longer among the living, she is still present in the presence of the Lord."

Solana nodded in understanding.

"Ahhh, hell nah!"

Renello, Metavello, and Ezio now stood before us. Nel was nursing a bottle of Ace like there weren't flutes and glasses all around this place to drink out of. As if we were in a section at the club, he drank straight from the bottle. Ezio had a smirk on his face while chewing on a toothpick, and Vello broke out in a full grin before hawking into the spit cup. I would be happy as hell when Discover had their babies.

"I know you not cursing like that in front of me!" my mama scolded Nel.

She was forever getting on everyone about their profanity usage. The weed smoke she didn't mind, and she even overlooked the dice games, but cursing in her face was where she drew the line.

"Auntie! My bad. This nig—I mean, this fool just full of cap." Nel shook his head.

All of the men had their eyes on Solana. She was all fidgety and shit, but these niggas didn't seem to care. Mocha and Scarlett walked up, arm in arm, both in black dresses that showed no signs of childbirth. They were prim and prepped as they always were. I gave a one-arm hug to Mocha and then planted a kiss on Scarlett's head. I still couldn't believe Benzino's daughter had grown into the woman she was, like we weren't near in age.

"Hey, boo. Who you?"

"Hi. I'm Solana." Her accent was heavy, and I could see the shock on the girls' faces when they heard her speak.

"You're pretty..."

"Too pretty," Mocha cosigned.

"I now see why the guys were in a rush to leave. You stealing our glam team, Shio?" Mocha dramatically blinked her thick lashes.

I shot her a grin before gazing at Solana, admiring her done up as I had been since she walked out of the house.

"Come." Scarlett held her free arm out.

Solana looked at me for a nod of approval, and when I gave it to her, she went in stride with the girls. Hopefully, they could get her to loosen up and enjoy herself. Food and liquor were plentiful, and the DJ was playing straight hits so far. As elegant as this space was, the music was straight trap. When I saw that she was being introduced to the rest of the women, I focused back on the people around me. Everyone was staring at me, including my mama.

"You dirty little liar." Vello joked, sounding like a bitch.

Sighing, I placed my hands in my pockets. "What I lie about, Vello?"

"Oh, you know *exactly* what you lied about. *I mean... she straight.* Ain't that what you said?" Nel egged on.

"Neltz had already told you what was up," I responded, dismissing their antics.

"And I told you that Neltz's mind was fu—I mean, messed up. He still learnin' to differentiate. He learnin' his type."

"What he need to be *learning* is the word. Children's church is every Sunday morning at 9 a.m. sharp," my mother butted in the conversation, making me shake my head. I already knew her mentioning Neltz going to church was going to rile these niggas up.

"I don't mean no harm, Auntie, but nephew walk through those doors and a trail of fire gone be behind him. That boy is a lil' demon. But I'ma stick beside my nephew."

"Hell yeah. Whole damn church gone be ashes trying to house his bad as— I mean, his bad self," Nel backed his twin.

Now chuckling, I opted to be quiet. The twins hadn't told a lie, though. However, Neltz did need his ass in somebody church. They at least should start him on some virtual shit so he could build his relationship with the Lord on his own terms.

"And back to you, college boy. She Spanish? And her name Solana? Nigga, you done went and got you a fuckin' black Selena! Can she sing? Wait, don't even tell me that shit. That shit ain't fair!"

My mama jumped at Nel, who raised up his hands while apologizing.

"Nel, this ain't the time or the place," I stressed. He was making a big deal out of nothing. It wasn't shit to Solana and me.

Ezio and I locked eyes before he tossed his arms around the twins, leading them away from my mother and me. I knew I would be hearing an earful from them tonight, but I didn't want it to be in front of the First Lady.

"Can I make a suggestion?" My mother didn't waste any

time prying.

"Yes, ma'am?"

"When you do find yourself a wife, I want her to look similar to her. Black and pretty."

I teased. "She's only half-black."

"She's dark, so that's good enough. You're half of something, too, so...?"

She had a point. "How do you know *she's* not a potential wife?"

My mother removed a flute from the tray of a bypassing waitress. "Because I know my son. I don't know why you have her around, but it's not for pursuit. She's gorgeous."

We watched her laugh with the ladies from across the room before my mom continued, "However, she has plenty to sort through before she's ready to belong to *any* man."

"You get all that from a brief meeting?" I questioned my mama, but it was mostly to lighten the heaviness I was feeling from the conversation.

My need for a wife had come back to the front of my mind. I hadn't put any effort into finding one. I hadn't hit Glow at all since ditching her for Don's Mexico quest. I knew by the time Don pressed me, I would have to settle for whatever I could find, and I wasn't a man who settled.

"Son..." My mama pressed her palm over my heartbeat. She listened to its rhythm like she'd always done before speaking. "I know things. Just like you know things. It's Him. The power of God is within us... Flows all through our veins. Always have, even before I met the pastor. That girl, she needs saving. And it's not from a person, it's from herself. Be careful with that one."

My mother stepped back and let her eyes travel across the room again at the wives and Solana. "Pretty little sinner. Such a shame."

With that, she sipped her bubbly while switching away. When she was tucked back at her husband's side, I tossed him a head nod and diverted my attention back to the women of the Rinaldi Mob. Dasani and Azure had joined the small crowd of stunning women, and just like the rest, they looked damn good.

"I knew she was fine," Ezio spoke from the side of me. I wasn't even surprised that he'd made his way back over.

"Yeah," was all I said in response.

"You're a disciplined man, Shio. I know that, and these other niggas know that too. But... just be careful. Don had a hand in putting her in your path, and you know that nigga—as ignorant as he is—just doesn't do shit for no reason. I'm not buying her father needing her here to *learn* how to be a wife. That's bullshit."

"So, what you thinking?" I queered. Ezio didn't tell me nothing I hadn't already been thinking myself. Solana did need some home-training, but no man on this earth is going to hand over his daughter to one man when she is meant for another. The shit made no sense no matter how many ways I sliced it in my brain.

Ezio sighed and shrugged. "I don't know... not yet, anyway. I know you not gone tell me your thoughts, but her daddy put her out the way for a reason. Shit feels like a lose-lose situation. Dumping a beautiful woman that's tied to a foreign cartel gang on a single man's doorstep could very well result in him unintentionally bringing a war to our doorstep. Then, if you fuck around and take her down—"

"Shit could still mean a war," I finished his sentence.

"Exactly, nigga."

"You know me, Ezee. I mean what I say."

Ezio slapped my hand in a brotherly embrace. "And you say what you mean." He patted my back before letting go.

We watched her a few more beats from across the room in the crowd of women, seamlessly fitting in.

Ezio chuckled. "The bitch bad, though."

As fuck, I responded internally, refusing to speak the truth out loud.

Another thing, besides her beauty that was certain, I needed to learn more about Solana's reason for being my current responsibility. It could have been a test from Don, but Don didn't fuck with us individually for trainings. It could have been a door to open hell between the various mobs and cartels here in the States and in Mexico. My worst thought was that Solana was her to force me to do some shit I didn't want to do.

Checking the time on my watch, I decided to stay until the main event before scooping Solana and heading back to the crib. I had shit to do to ensure my ass didn't fuck around and die over a girl that wasn't even mine.

God first.
Make sure the family good.
Eye them Cuppacio boys, the little and the big ones.
Build a relationship with my brother.
Get my brother rich.
Health and wellness.
Stay on top of my mob shit.
Keep Hobo alive.
~~Get through the meeting with Ines Ledesma.~~
~~House a random.~~
Find the true reason Solana is here.
Find a wife.

CHAPTER 15

SOLANA DAMITA LEDESMA

"It's the accent for me, boo." The pretty chocolate girl who had approached me while I was standing with Shio, and whom I now knew was his cousin, snickered.

"Mocha."

That's what she told me her name was. It was odd for someone to be named after a coffee beverage, but it fit her. Her skin resembled a mocha drink with coffee that had been brewing a little longer than usual.

"I've been wondering what Shio's woman would look like," the blasian one said.

I thought I'd seen her out front in a high-low dress barking orders, but now that I was up close, this wasn't her. While both women were gorgeous, this wife had an aura that made all the other women look at her before speaking. Whoever the leader was— Don, in this case—she *had* to be his woman. The other lady, who looked like her, had to be a relative. If that wasn't her sister, then the genes in their family were unmatched.

"Oh, no... I'm not Shio's. I'm engaged," I blurted out.

The last two words that had come from my mouth were enough to make me cringe. They didn't taste right, nor did they sound true. And while everyone shot me curious glances, I could see fire dance in the HBIC's eyes. All gazes fell on my bare ring finger, which made me wish I could take back my last statement. I'd been promised to wed, but my fiancé hadn't put a ring on it to seal the deal. In fact, I'd only formally met him once, and using the word "met" was a stretch. I'd gotten all primmed and prepped, and had a doctor do a complete check-up before I was presented to him. He took one longing look at me, as if I were the last person he wanted to bear his last name, before shooing me away and telling my father that I would "do."

These women, all donning rings that seemed to have been curated with the world's finest diamonds, continued to look from my face to my finger. While some appeared confused, they didn't speak about my lack of jewelry.

"I'm going to fucking kill Demise, I swear. He always got some shit going on," she grumbled.

Demise. Was that the Don?

"Well, I'm Jisei. I'm..." She paused and looked at Dasani, who shook her head no. "I'm Dasani's sister-in-law. Ezio, the light-skinned one, is my husband," she boasted, showing every tooth in her mouth.

She was also pretty. I was able to point out every label she'd been wearing, from the short Oscar de la Renta black halter dress to the Gianvito Rossi heels that wrapped around her leg. It all costed money—lots of it.

"He's lucky to have you as a wife. Nice to meet you."

Jisei's grin grew. "Yeah... I like her."

"Well, again, I'm Mocha. The chocolate nigga next to the one with the dreads is my husband."

We looked to where Mocha pointed. A handsome, dark-skinned man with deep waves stood next to an equally hand-some guy with long locs. The one with the locs had a frown on his face, like the other had been annoying him.

"Nice to meet you. Yours is lucky as well."

Mocha took a sip of her champagne. "Unh hunh! Period, pooh."

"I'm Scarlett. Jisei and Mocha are my best friends. The one that looks *oh so happy* to be here is my husband. Shio and the rest of the Cuppacio men are also my cousins."

Scarlett's face was like an upside-down heart, and in her black Tom Ford form-fitting jumpsuit, I could see that her bottom had the same shape. Her hair was similar to mine, except it was shorter.

"Is he... okay?" He looked like he was ready to blow the entire building up.

Everyone looked at each other and laughed. Clearly, it was an inside joke, but in order not to feel awkward, I chuckled too.

"Girl, no and yes." They laughed again. "He's okay. Matteo is just mean at times."

Dasani scoffed. "At times? That nigga is mean *all* the fucking time."

"Right! He is only nice to Princess, Scarlett, and now Pearla," Mocha mentioned.

"What about my sister?"

Two pregnant women sauntered over. One looked as if she was ready to go into labor at any moment, while the other sported a cute bump. I'd seen Maura pregnant multiple times and could tell she was approaching her second trimester. She had on rose heels that were to die for, with a rose pinned in her hair that had been brushed to the side, while curls cascaded down her shoulder. The one that was about to pop was wearing a baby-doll-style dress that went around her neck. Instead of heels, she was in Hermes sandals and rightfully so.

Still, she looked good.

"Pia, don't come over here with all that," Mocha shooed.

"I was just telling Solana that Matteo was mean to everyone sometimes, but Mocha says he's nice to his *sister*, Pearla," Scarlett spoke in a teasing manner.

Pia rolled her eyes so hard I knew they had traveled through the back of her skull. "Ugh, that nigga is not her brother."

"DNA says he is, boo. Sharing is caring." Dasani clucked.

"Leave my man alone!" Scarlett said in a high-pitched tone. "He's so happy he has a sister now. He's been nicer to everyone since finding out."

There was so much love in Scarlett's eyes as she spoke about her husband. It stirred something in my belly, but at the same time made me feel sad. I'd never know what that feels like. Anytime my future husband comes to mind, I want to barf.

"Ughhh. Patty knows she wrong for that one. Pearla and I don't do brothers."

The ladies continued to laugh and tease.

"You're pretty. Hey, I'm Discover." She held her hand out and I took it. Discover looked so familiar, but I couldn't place where I'd seen her before.

"Hi, I'm—"

"Mexi-Mami," the one they called Pia said. "My son is Neltz. He told me he met you at his Uncle Shio's house. Couldn't stop talking about you." Pia's perfectly filled-in brow rose in a questioning manner, but the grin on her face had me offering her a tight smile as well.

Pia looked no older than me. There was no way she had a son around Neltz's age. But then again, I could see the resemblance. She was beautiful. Neltz was handsome. I'd been right with my assumption that he'd come from a set of attractive parents, or at least an attractive mom.

"It's nice to meet you both. Neltz is *hermano*. He was nice too. Very well-mannered little boy."

Everyone paused before laughs erupted.

"Girl, boo... You ain't gotta lie. Neltz is bad as fuck!" Dasani cackled, and I didn't know if I was being jested on an American TV show.

"Facts. Lil' negro gone have all of us getting grey hair before our time. I'm too young and fly for that shit!" Mocha waved her hands, and Jisei and Scarlett were falling on each other, laughing.

Pia smiled while rubbing her belly. "Not too much on my firstborn."

Everyone was tossing jokes back and forth, but I just looked on in bewilderment. To make sure Pia wasn't offended, I offered more words. "Oh! Neltz is your son? Forgive my shock, but you look so young."

"That's because I am young, girl. Pushed his big-headed ass out when I was just a baby myself."

I couldn't imagine having a child not only out of wedlock but also young. My father would have never stood for that, and I enjoyed my freedom seeing firsthand how my brothers wore Maura down even with nanny help. Being responsible for anything other than myself sounded repulsive. That's why I was going to figure out a way to get on birth control before I was handed off to my new family. I was going to stall extending the Rodríguez lineage for as long as possible.

As if she could read my mind, Dasani asked, "Do you have any children?"

I shook my head probably harder than I needed to. "I do not."

"Good. Don't fucking have none. This pregnancy is tearing my back up." Pia's hand went to her lower back while Discover rubbed her stomach.

"Yes, then it's two in here, so imagine how mine feel. I told Metavello this is it! I'm so done after this. I'm having a mommy makeover and getting my damn tubes tied. Three children is too close to ten."

"Renello know to not even play with me on that level. Last I checked, it was only one in here. Hopefully it's a girl. If not, tough fucking titty."

"You two are married to the twins?" I asked for clarity.

Pia held her hand up, showing off her unique stone. "Engaged."

"I'm pregnant by the other," Discover emitted through some heavy breaths.

"Nah, for real. Demise thinks he can put a son in me. That nigga gotta be snorting that good shit if he thinks I'm carrying another one of his big-headed-ass babies. Delicate is bad as fuck. Pie face ass barely fucks with me like that!" Dasani was rolling her eyes, but the grin hadn't left her face.

"Snorting?" I questioned as my hands tightened around the flute.

"Yeap! Gotta be snorting some good shit for sure."

The ladies laughed again, but I was trying to stop myself from asking more questions. Clearing my throat, I looked around the ballroom. Everything was as elegante y precioso (elegant and precious). It felt as if I'd stepped inside a dream. I hadn't been to an event more breathtaking.

"I don't mean to pry, but what's the occasion?" I asked to no one in particular.

"Oh." Discover grinned. "It's my surprise engagement."

I drew back without intention. My puzzlement must've been funny to the ladies because they continued laughing in ongoing giggles.

"Listen, Metavello can't hide shit to save his life. With the way Essex canceled his shows and insisted I had the nanny in town to get Discovery for the weekend, and how my man has been on edge all week, I already knew what was up," Discover revealed, while Pia shook her head with a smirk on her face.

"Yeah, hood niggas can't do shit right," Mocha added.

Jisei raised her glass in the air. "Right. I'm still shook up that Ezio did mine right and without me knowing."

"Same," Pia chimed in. "I didn't have a clue what Renello had going on. I just thought we were going to dinner for my birthday."

"Well, mine tricked the fuck outta me. I'm still mad that nigga forced me to marry him," Dasani said in a spat.

My limbs tensed. Before I could fully process what she said, a deep voice boomed, breaking up our girl chatter. "Fuck y'all over here gossiping 'bout? What I tell you about this clicking up shit? Making all the other wives feel like outsiders."

Either this city was swarming *hombres guapos* (handsome men), or the organization had a requirement that you be very good-looking to join. A very attractive man wrapped his arm around Dasani's slim waist, planted her rear to his front, and stared at her side profile. She didn't turn to face him as she said in the sassiest tone, "Nigga, fuck them hoes. You ain't tell me shit, and if you did, I damn sure didn't listen. They can come over here if they want to. We ain't kissing no ass." For extra flair, she rolled her neck.

Holding my breath, I waited until he struck her down. He was the Don, or so I assumed from all my observations tonight. Like all men in charge, no one spoke to the leader of an organization with disrespect, especially a woman. My father wasn't abusive, but there had been times when he'd struck Maura for going too far with her tongue. He'd even roughed me up a time or two when I was way out of line in the way I'd spoken or when he felt I'd been disobedient. I began to feel lightheaded from how I was restricting my air flow, and since his hand remained at her waist while a lazy smile sat on his face, I exhaled.

"Stop fucking playing with me, Mrs. Rinaldi, before I turn this bitch out," he stated not so discreetly in her ear.

I'd begun breathing again, but was still on edge. No one else seemed to be worried as they all started engaging in side conversations amongst each other. When he kissed the side of her face, I accepted this was their normal banter. This wasn't an abusive man; this was one who loved his wife. I was still lost on him allowing her to lash at him, especially in public. Maybe this was the American way or the Rinaldi way? Either way, I was just relieved that this hadn't gone left as I'd seen time and time again in Mexico.

A big, burly man, who almost looked like the driver who had taken me to Shio's house, came over and whispered in Demise's ear. He planted a kiss on his wife's cheek, slapped her ass as she cursed at him about it stinging, and then he was gone. Things were a lot different here. My father had never shown any public affection toward Maura, and my husband-to-be wouldn't be doing it to me either. In fact, I probably wouldn't be seen with him in public at all unless I was summoned for some reason, such as a public engagement or some type of trade-off.

"I thought you weren't coming! Look at youuuu! Not yo' new in-laws took ya braids out. I love it!"

"Ohh! You looking fine!"

"Pretty as fuuuuck."

The women dished out compliments and smiles to a woman who walked up. The compliments weren't exaggerated; she was *hermosa (beautiful)*. Just as the men were, the women were all extremely attractive. Sticking to what seemed to be a black dress code, a short silk number clung to her petite frame, while highlighted curls framed her slender face, and a heavenly scent invaded my space from her walk-up air. I wasn't familiar with the designer of her dress, and while it was pretty and fit her perfectly, the material was not expensive. Looking from her light-skinned complexion to the women who praised her appearance in different shades of brown and black, I felt a sliver of peace. I'd never been around this many women who looked like me. Mexico had very different feelings regarding people who had our skin color, but here, no one had batted an eyelash at my deep-colored skin.

A wide grin stretched across the newcomer's face at the latest compliment from Jisei. When her orbs landed on me, her smile stayed in place. Everyone saw that she was looking at me, so the smiles fell and chatter ceased. I didn't know what was going on, but I held my hand out.

"Hola. I'm Solana," I greeted.

She took my hand in hers, and I didn't miss her dazzling ring. "Solana? That's pretty. Fitting too. I'm Glow."

One of the ladies cleared their throat, and I saw Mocha nudging Jisei. My hand fell back to my side as she cleared her throat. "Friend... Solana... She came with Shio."

All of the ladies seemed to hold their breath, as I had when I thought their Don was going to hit Dasani. As they waited for Glow's reaction, I waited for them to speak. I'd been around long enough to know what this was. Cultural differences or not, I knew when a woman had held the interest of a man. Still, I kept my head high. I'd come with Shio and would be leaving with him, but as I explained earlier, I was engaged, and it wasn't to him. She had no reason to feel threatened by me. Plus, she was wearing a rock on her finger, and last I checked, Shio was a single man.

Glow's smile didn't falter. Either she was a hell of an actress, or she simply wasn't bothered. Either way, I kept my eyes on her.

"Oh, okay."

We all stood around in silence after Glow's and my exchange. The women were communicating with their eyes when Scarlett grabbed Glow's hand.

"Wait, bitch!"

The rest of the ladies looked on in astonishment as they noticed her ring for the first time. They must have been too familiar because I'd seen it as soon as she presented herself.

"What the fuck is this?" Mocha screamed in excitement.

Glow's entire face had flushed red, yet she said nothing.

"More than braids done went down in the M. What the fuck you got going on?" Jisei squealed.

I could feel my heart accelerating in my chest. I didn't know if it was because I was starting to feel anxious about being in the mix of people I didn't know, or because it was finally hitting me that I was really in America, all alone, with no word yet from my father. Talking to these ladies had been a nice distraction, and even to the glam team earlier this evening. But the fact remained that I had no idea what I was doing. Being sent here to be "trained" was a load of bullshit. I knew it. Shio knew it. My papa knew it, but he was the only one who could reveal what my true reason for being here was.

While all the women were balancing nervously on their tippy toes, waiting for Glow to reveal what she was going to tell them, I felt myself fighting sweat that was threatening to erupt from my hairline and the mucus attempting to slide out of my nose. I wasn't trying to ruin my hair, my makeup, or my composure in front of these ladies.

Pia yelled, "Spill it bitch, damn!"

I scanned the room to see if I could spot the man I'd come with. I needed a reprieve. To my dismay, he was nowhere to be found.

"Okay, so I may or may not have gotten... married?"

A tight knot within me begged for release as my breath was trapped inside my lungs. My head was deprived of oxygen as I didn't know how to stop the oncoming panic attack brewing.

"To Shio?" Scarlett asked.

"I—"

"Excuse me, ladies!" I said, interrupting Glow. "I have to make a call."

That was the weakest excuse I could have formulated, but it was all I had as I dashed through the doors of the ballroom. Nearly toppling over a waitress, I apologized but didn't stop until I made it outside. I inhaled the night air deeply as I bent over to relieve the pressure in my chest.

Married?

"Ma'am. You straight?"

Black sneakers were now obstructing my view of the concrete. I sucked in more air that was so much cleaner tasting than what I was used to back home.

Standing, I straighten my hair.

"You need some help?" he asked with questionable, kind eyes.

The person offering help was the one who had parked Shio's car, and in the distance, was indeed the man who had driven me to Shio's home.

"As a matter of fact, I do need some help."

I didn't know where Shio had ventured off to, but my night here was over. Then again, depending on how it is viewed, it was only the beginning with what I had planned next.

CHAPTER 16
TUNAN "TUNE" PAYNE

A nigga been married less than twenty-four hours, and even though the shit was ghetto and spontaneous as fuck, it had been one of the best days I've had since I've been out. Hell, since before I got out when Stella had fucked me over. My stomach was still aching from all the fucking laughing Glow and I did in Memphis. When we left the Haunted House, we sat in the parking lot so long laughing about all she'd seen. Hearing Glow's narration of our wedding venue had me in tears. Glow, who was well put together and had her shit on point, fit right in with the ignorance of my city. I hadn't lived in Memphis in years, but every time I was home, it felt exactly like that, *home*.

Glow had made it clear to me that our marriage was nothing more than contractual, and I let her know that I wasn't looking for anything outside my role in the mob and stacking my cheese. But after signing our names on the dotted line, it didn't feel right getting on the plane and going our separate ways. We hadn't even consummated the marriage outside of the kiss we shared. It had been less than twelve hours since Glow was in my presence, being that she'd flown out this morning. My own flight hadn't been scheduled to leave until later on in the day, but I felt like I should've been with her. As soon as the wheels were up on the plane a nigga felt empty or some shit. I almost felt like I was doing this husband shit wrong or something. I'd been taught not to play with marriage, and here I was double dutching that shit.

The papers had been signed, and despite how it had been acquired, she had a ring on her finger and was officially my wife. I had yet to tell Don, because I owed my brother an explanation first. Well, it wasn't much to explain, but I owed him the *news* first. Shio sent me in his place for their date, so that let me know he had some level of interest in Glow. He didn't want to leave her hanging, and while I was learning that my brother was an upstanding guy, Shio did everything with reason. I hadn't heard the nigga mention her name since sending me to that fancy-ass restaurant, though. It was probably because he'd been caught up with the girl who got dumped on his porch. I wouldn't be surprised if his ass had been in his house stressed the fuck out over that girl, but I know he wasn't going to say shit about it. Shio was a self-solver, like me, and because I was realizing we had more in common than our faces, I knew if I were in his shoes, I'd want to know if my brother had married my potential girl. I'd planned on chopping it up with him before I even married Glow, but the shit just happened so fast. Even though I felt indifferent about the nigga we came from, Shio was still my brother, and I didn't want to come off as backdooring that nigga. Not only had he broken bread with me, he'd brought me into his world with nothing to gain. I was letting him know what it was first, and then I'd tell the mob.

Opting out of valet parking, I whipped the Infinity into a vacant parking space. My whip stood out like a sore thumb, and even though I could have easily snatched my sister's keys,

I wasn't worried about what the fuck I was driving right now. As long as I had a set of wheels to get me to and from, that was all that mattered. Soon enough, when I secured this bread, I could get whatever the fuck I wanted. I'd lost it all and was eager to get it back and some, but losing everything often made you not give a fuck about much shit else.

Stepping out of the car, I pulled my chino pants up and smoothed my hands down my collared shirt. Shio had invited me to what he called a "surprise engagement," and I nearly forgot about the whole thing until he sent me a reminder this morning. Even with Glow constantly stressing that she had an event to attend, I hadn't made the connection that it was the engagement. Two hours ago, I found myself at Bayside Shops trying to put some shit together. I'd copped a black Versace shirt with the brand's signature design embroidered on the collar. Black bottoms and low-top Rick Owens completed my look. This was the most I'd spent on a fit since I'd been out, and that was just on the shirt and bottoms. My sister bought me these shoes as one of my coming-home gifts, part of what she called her "mini haul." I didn't plan on being out late because my nephew had come home, as well as Athena, and I owed one a game night and one a spa night. I'd just hoped Tuscany had nail remover because my little step-niece had asked to paint my nails.

Walking up, one of the valet workers was walking away from a good-looking chick with thick, curly hair that had begun to switch into the parking lot toward a car. I was fake married, so I turned to watch her backside as she climbed to the back of the car with the driver closing the door behind her.

"She's thick as fuck, but she came in with Shio. Off limits, big dawg," the valet informed.

Shio. His ass was over dur fucked up, fo' sho'.

A string quartet played as I walked through the doors of

the luxurious-ass building. I'd never seen so many drapes all over the walls and shit before in my life. If nothing else, those motherfuckers knew how to throw a party. I couldn't even phantom how many bands had been dropped on this shit here. I wasn't pocket watching the next nigga, but if this was the engagement, that nigga was going to come out the ass for the wedding. Mine had only cost me what I'd won in the dice game, and that made me consider the fact that maybe this was what Glow wanted an elaborate-ass celebration with identically dressed servers and candlelit corners.

Oh, well, it's done now.

Plus, these niggas were in love, for real. Glow and I were two people using each other to get what we wanted, who just so happened to know what each other's private parts looked and felt like.

No sooner than I had walked inside the crowded-ass room, I spotted Glow. The women all had their eyes on her ring, and that had my stomach clenching. I hadn't considered the fact that she would tell the ladies before I could tell Shio, but Glow didn't know shit about what I had going on.

"Excuse me, ladies and gentlemen! Baby! Where you at?"

Metavello was at the front of the room, dressed in an all-black tuxedo, speaking into a microphone. His pregnant girl-friend smiled as the women's attention shifted from Glow's hand to her. The crowd parted like the Red Sea as she made her way to the front. The women were already fanning their perfectly made-up faces, but I couldn't take my eyes off Glow. Her hair was pressed down her back, and the dress she was rocking did her body good as fuck. The way she looked had my eyes twitching, but the fact that *my* ring was on her hand had me ready to take her down. It was as if my mind understood she was just my fucking wife on paper, but my heart didn't give a fuck about my mind.

"I didn't think you was gonna make it." Shio appeared by my side, eyes still on the couple that had everyone's attention. Discover looked like she was ready to deliver those damn twins at any moment.

"I damn near forgot about the shit," I honestly spoke.

I'd been so fucking consumed with Glow and marriage that I was forgetting the fucking days of the week and shit. I was aware of what was going on in front of me, but I couldn't stop looking to the right of me, where my bride was standing with her phone out, recording.

"You straight?"

Breaking my gaze, I turned to Shio's brow rising as he waited for my response. "Yeah. Nigga, is you straight? I saw ole girl outside. You ain't tell us she looked good." I grinned.

Shio chuckled. "I ain't tell you niggas she was ugly either."

"True."

He had a point, but damn, I didn't see how he was housing her ass without fucking. And that was coming from a nigga who wasn't worried about fucking. Well, I wasn't worried about fucking a few months ago.

"Discover, stumbling up on you in Walmart... I didn't think we'd come to this."

"Nigga, you didn't think her ass was married to a gay nigga either!" Nel yelled from the crowd, making everyone laugh, including me. That nigga couldn't be serious for shit.

"I told myself I was going to wait to propose to you when you felt your best. But I couldn't wait no longer."

"Nah, nigga! I put that pressure on yo' ass," Don added, causing more erupting laughter from the crowd.

"Y'all, stop it. Let my man get off," Discover encouraged while rubbing her belly.

"Ion know, Big Mama... you just make a nigga feel good. You make a nigga feel good, look good, and live good. You was bossed the fuck up when you met me, and knowing that you have already experienced the finer things in life makes a nigga want to be a better man just so that I can get you the things you haven't had yet. You're so fuckin' loving and caring and understanding. I have never met a more classy and graceful woman in my fuckin' life. You just do it for me, baby. You can have it all. You can have whatever it is your pretty-ass heart desires, baby. I couldn't go another day without asking you the one question I'd never ask another person."

Metavello dropped to one knee, causing the crowd to gasp as if they didn't know why the fuck we were even here. Pulling a box out of his jacket, he opened it to reveal a ring that I knew had to have cost a grip. I could see that bitch shining across the fucking room.

Discover gasped and covered her mouth with her hands.

"Big Mama… Discover, will you marry a nigga?"

Her hands dropped from her face to her stomach. When her face contorted and she shook her head no, even I was thrown off by the shit.

"Will you marry me?" he asked again, this time with a shaky voice.

"No… No!" she screamed, shocking the fuck out of all of us.

"Did this pot belly bitch just tell my brother no? But she told the dick gobbler yes?" Nel asked.

"No! No, it's too early! My water just broke!"

The crowd gasped again. Dasani pushed her way through the crowd, not stopping until she got to Discover's side.

"Yes, yes, I'll marry you, Metavello. Slide the ring on, but these babies are coming."

He did what his now fiancée said and then stood by her side. Dasani had her hand on Discover's belly, asking her hushed questions.

"Shit." Shio rubbed his hand down his face. "You drove? Or

you riding with me to the hospital?"

I shifted my eyes to Glow, who was now walking behind Metavello as he carried Discover out of the room along with the rest of the ladies. I didn't know how much more hectic the night would get, so I opted to ride with Shio so I could tell him what it was. I was sure she'd already told the ladies, and it wouldn't be long before it got back to him.

Looking at Shio, I replied. "Yeah, I drove, but I'ma still slide with you."

We all filed out of the building. Renello had pulled his Maybach to the front door, and Metavello was putting Discover in the back seat as Pia sat in the front.

"Y'all good?" Shio asked.

When Metavello nodded, the valet attendant tossed Shio his keys. Most of the cars were lined up in the front, so I hopped in the driver's seat of Shio's, knowing his from the color. I was forever driving this nigga's shit like I was the hired help. It often gave me a chance to test the whips and see what the fuck I wanted once I was ready to buy. It would be a while before I dropped a ticket on some shit like this, but it was nasty. These niggas were riding in Maybachs like the dealership had given them out two-for-one.

Before Shio could plant himself in the passenger seat, heels clacking on the pavement had me looking out the passenger-side window.

"Um, I took a chauffeur here. Do you mind if I catch a ride?" She was asking Shio but looking at me.

Shio held the door open for Glow, letting her step inside. Her perfume wafted up my nose and straight to my dick. Once Shio was in the back seat, I peeled off. I'd never been in a more awkward setup in my life. I couldn't tell Shio shit in front of Glow because I didn't know how the conversation would go, and I would never put her on blast. Hell, she didn't care about

Shio when I propositioned her and had even insinuated that he didn't want her.

I damn sho' ain't beating the store runner obligations, I thought as Shio's phone rang, breaking up the silence.

"She made it in?" he asked the caller.

I assumed he was talking about ole girl with the big booty. I didn't know what the hell he had going on, and I had my own shit to worry about, so until he was ready to talk, I'd leave the subject be.

Glow was looking out the window while I was shifting my eyes from the road to her side profile.

"You look pretty," I complimented.

Shio was still on the call, and even if he weren't, I wouldn't have hesitated to compliment her. I respected that nigga because of who he was and what he'd done, but when it came to what I wanted to do, I was forever doing it.

"Thank you," she replied shyly, like she hadn't put the pussy on me or was carrying my last name. Women were a fucking trip.

"Jagoda One," Shio said out loud as he lifted his head from the phone call.

I could see Nel and the others ahead of us, but it was good to know where I was going in case I lost them. Behind me, though, was a long line of expensive, foreign cars, all heading to the same place. One thing I noticed about the mob was how close-knit they were and how they all showed up for each other. I had only dealt with people who shared my blood in that manner. It was rare as hell to see the dynamic of the Rinaldi Mob, and right now, I wasn't sure how I felt about it.

I liked it for Glow, though; even from across the room, I could see how radiant she was, with the ladies staring at her wedding ring. The glare from her ring caught my eye as I pulled into the lot of the hospital. I could see the twins at the emergency entrance helping Discover out of the car.

Shio tapped the back of my seat, so I stopped and let him out. He still had his phone pressed to his ear. Turning the wheel, I drove into the hospital parking lot, passing rows of cars to find a spot. The rest of the mob was doing the same.

Glow sat up in her seat, making her dress ride up her thighs. She'd put some type of glitter on her skin, and not only did it smell good as fuck, but it looked good too against her complexion. From the top of her head to the soles of her feet, she was pretty as hell. Not only was Glow fine, she was bossed the hell up. It was almost an insult to her to be married to a man who had just gotten out of jail with only a grill to his name, but we were here now.

"I only asked for a ride because I didn't want to be a third wheel," she said as I pulled into a spot.

"Glow, you ain't gotta explain shit. You good."

Looking down, I tried to see where the shut-off button to the car was. There were so many damn dials and shit that I was confused. Her manicured hand, that was rocking my diamond, reached over and pressed a button, shutting off the engine.

"I've ridden in Ezio's with Jisei a few times," she explained.

I was embarrassed like a motherfucker, I couldn't lie. Still, I hopped out and jogged over to open her door like this was my shit. When her hand was in mine, I couldn't help myself. Wrapping my arms around her slim waist, I bent down and stuck my nose in her neck and took a long whiff.

She felt so fucking good. She smelled even better. The dress was practically painted on her body. She fit within my arms as if she was sculpted for a nigga. I knew what she'd said, but her in my arms felt right.

"Tunan," she moaned.

I knew her pussy was soaked. It made no sense how wet she had gotten the night we met. She was damn near drowning a nigga the way she was soaking my shit. Gripping her ass, I kissed the side of her neck before letting her up.

"My bad. I had to. You look too fuckin' good," I admitted.

Tucking her hair behind her ear, she grinned, showing those white-ass teeth. "So do you."

"How it feel to be a wife?"

She looked off briefly and shrugged. "Sneaky. I haven't told my mom or my sister. I was about to tell the women, but the proposal happened. My sister is staying at my house with her best friend, and neither one of them has said anything about it. So... either they haven't noticed it, or have noticed it and know I'd never get married without telling them. I don't know what I'm doing, Tunan."

She looked stressed in the face, and it low-key mirrored her face when she was coming on my dick. Lifting her chin, I licked my lips. "Ion know what I'm doing either, my baby. I haven't told anyone either."

"But you gotta tell Don, though, right? That's the whole point, isn't it?"

That was the whole point: to be married on paper and get to the paper. But every time I was around Glow, I had to tell myself that she wasn't what I wanted. I was consistently reminding myself of "the rules" she'd set when she crossed my mind. The type of aura she possessed was detrimental to a nigga's health. I was the same nigga that had fallen for a bitch like Stella, though. My judgment was cloudy, and I ain't trust shit. The way I was feeling was more than likely lust-infused due to how she felt around my dick.

"I'ma tell him tonight. I wasn't sho' if I should even tell my people. I mean, if dey find out, cool. If not, that's cool too. At least dey can say dey met you."

She nodded. "Yeah. I get it. We should go in... I don't want to miss the birth of the babies."

I almost reached for her hand like I'd done the night at the Haunted House, but refrained. We walked side by side into the hospital with her heels echoing on the gravel. Everyone else seemed to be already inside because the cars that were trailing me were all parked and empty. Walking through the doors, the antiseptic smell that only hospitals hold turned my stomach. The last time I'd been at a hospital was when Stella rang the remission bell when her doctors announced the cancer had left her body. Shit had me wishing I could find her and beat her ass again. Life had gone on, and I'd done my time, so revenge should've been the last thing on my mind. That hoe had done me dirty, though.

"Oh my God! It hurrrrts!" Discover yelled as the women tried their best to calm her.

Metavello was still carrying her bridal style, and from the expression on his face, a doctor needed to come quick. Glow had run to her side like there was something she could do to stop the labor pains.

Slap!

Nel had hit the receptionist's desk, gaining everyone's attention but Discover's. "Where the fuck the doctor at? As much money we give y'all asses every month to keep fluids pumping in that vegetable we got upstairs, y'all should be running when we enter this hoe."

The receptionist either was used to Nel's antics, or she didn't scare easily because she was sitting there unbothered like a motherfucker.

"Renello, calm down and let the lady do her job." A lady, who had to be their mother, tried to calm him.

"Ma, fuck allat! Ain't nobody tryna hear shit she sayin'! She needs to get the fuck up and do sum'n. My nephews not comin' into the world on this nasty-ass waitin' room floor. Fuck that!"

I felt eyes on me, so I followed them and saw a woman

whom I immediately knew.

Shio looked just like his mother. There was something familiar about her. I'd never met her before, but I couldn't help but feel like I had. I didn't know the dynamics of her marriage with the man who had a hand in bringing me into the world, but I knew I was a side baby. I couldn't read her expression to determine whether I should keep my distance out of respect for Shio or not, so I simply looked away.

"Ma'am, I'm not worried about Nel. He always causing hell. Now, I'll tell you what I told him. She's expecting twins, so they have to deliver them in the operating room. It's being prepped, and someone is already on the way to bring her up. Y'all will have to stay down here until the 'okay' is given for the rest of you to go up. *If* all of you can go up."

"Nawl, ain't no fuckin' *if*. We all going up. We ain't on Medicaid!" Nel reached in his pocket and pulled out a bankroll, slapping it on the desk.

"Pia! Come get your man, please," the receptionist said as she rolled her neck.

Pia pulled Nel from the counter, who was still talking shit, and I shook my head, watching their mama slide the money off the counter into her purse.

The elevator doors opened, and a nurse pushing a wheel-chair came out.

Ezio clapped his hands. "'Bout fuckin' time!"

Metavello placed her in the chair while the women assured her everything was going to be okay. It was too damn much going on with Don and them in the corner, chopping it up instead of getting their wives the fuck out of the way. I knew Discover was overstimulated like a motherfucker. Some of these wives already had children; what was happening wasn't new.

The nurse let everyone know that someone would be back

to get the rest of us, and the three of them got on the elevator.

"Pia, dis is going to be you in a couple of months," the twins' mom said, grinning, and I could hear a strong Jamaican accent.

"Yeah... I think I'm gonna do a home birth at my dad's house, though. Pearla is still not feeling the hospital, and this is the only private one."

"Pia baby... I'll give you whatever you want, but that ain't it. No way in hell my baby being born in the Mansion of Dicks." Nel shook his head.

"Shush, Nel boi. She had de baby where de gyal wants."

"Hellllp! Help! We need a doctor! We need a fuckin' doctor!"

All of our heads snapped to the entrance where two girls were running inside barefoot. All of the men's hands went to their waistbands, including mine. Blood was dripping from one of the girls, and both their eyes were flooded with tears. The receptionist ran from behind the counter to the girls as the rest of the guests stayed on edge, watching.

"My best friend... She's bleeding. She says she may be pregnant. I didn't know. I had no idea," the darker of the two said through heavy tears.

Hearing that the one bleeding was pregnant took me back to my own sister. When she was pregnant with Tulsaire, her water broke on her graduation day, and she was so scared. Shit still fucked me up that I was too young to rescue her from that pedophile-ass nigga that knocked her up.

"We need a doctor!" the receptionist screamed.

"What the fuck? *Glee*?" Glow moved through the women and stood a few feet away, almost as if she couldn't believe her eyes.

The one leaking blood eyes ballooned, and she continued to hold her stomach while being toppled over. "Glow... I... I don't know what's happening," she cried.

"What the fuck do you mean *you don't know what's happening*! You're fucking pregnant? Is that what the fuck you were doing at that school!" Glow nearly ran in her direction, but with one arm, I scooped her petite ass up. "Let me the fuck go! She's fucking pregnant! Are you fucking serious? Pregnant, Glee?" Glow screamed loud as fuck.

I held my grip because if Glow thought she was about to touch a pregnant girl, she was mistaken. I knew she was pissed, but she had to think logically.

"Let me the fuck go!"

"Nah, I can't do that, my baby. You gotta calm down. You mad, and clearly something's wrong, Glow. This ain't the time for hows and whats. She needs you right now."

Her head snaked around like her ass was the exorcist as she shot me a nasty glare. "This bitch was pregnant the whole time!"

"Glow..." I warned.

"Who the fuck are you to tell me what the fuck I need to do with *my* sister?"

Chuckling at the scene Glow was causing, I kept her mad ass suspended off the ground. "Your husband. That's who the fuck I am. Now, pipe the fuck down!" I stated through gritted teeth.

The women gasped.

"Oh, fuckin' wow. Nigga, I thought Glow was your hoe? You handed her to ya brother?" Nel's messy-ass asked Shio.

Forgetting where the fuck I was and slipping up with my last statement, I still held Glow while she glared angrily at me. If she put her hands on her laboring little sister, she would never forgive herself. The heat of the moment had me doing twelve months in jail. I knew how quickly shit could flip when you were pissed.

"Glow... so you a *brother* fucker? Ain't that 'bout a mother-fucker. I never would have thought."

Pia hit Nel's arm to shut his stupid ass up. Looking over at Shio, who just stared in silence while standing next to his mother, I sighed.

"Bro..." I started.

"All good." He nodded as we communicated with our eyes.

A doctor ran out with two nurses to the screaming girl we now knew was Glow's sister, Glee. The mob women were at the friend's side, trying to calm her as they wheeled Glee back. Their eyes were still on us, though, as I tightened my arms around Glow.

"Brother?" Glow asked me in disbelief.

I assumed that Glow didn't know we were brothers because she never asked or mentioned it before we got married. I didn't bring it up either because it wasn't important. We had established our wants, and it was what it was. I was here to get paid, and she was trying to get accepted.

"Are you calm now? Your sister needs you, Glow. You'n need to be on no dumb shit."

"Fuck you, Tunan." She spat the words with such fury that I knew she needed another reminder.

Leaning in, I pressed my lip to her ear. "Careful. You know you can barely take dick, talkin' 'bout *fuck* me. Now. Pipe. The fuck. Down. Aite?"

Stiffening, she relaxed and then nodded hesitantly.

I let her down but stopped her before she could walk off. "Give me your slippers."

She told me the night we went on a date that she kept disposable slippers in her purse for when she needed a break from her heels. Fucking Glow always kept a bag full of products. I'd seen it myself, but my sister had also talked my head off about all things Glow since she came to Memphis. I'd learned more about my wife from my family than I had from Glow.

With attitude, she unzipped her bag, took out her slippers, and pushed them into my hand. Kneeling, I lifted her right leg, smelling her arousal as I squatted and removed her heel. I slid her slipper on and did the same with the other leg and foot. Once I stood up, I jutted my chin, signaling her to follow her sister.

"Yeah, dat dere a man right dere." The twins' mama fanned herself.

Nel shook his head. "Mama, eww. He young enough to be your son."

"And I was young enough to be your daddy's daughter. Age ain't notin' but a number."

Don walked to the receptionist's desk as my phone vibrated in my pocket. Pulling it from my pants pocket, I saw it was my cellie. Looking at Shio, who was still waiting for me, I headed to the exit to answer the phone.

"What it do?" I answered as soon as I got outside. I still had Glow's heels in hand, and they smelled just like her.

"You good, nigga? How the real world been treatin' you?"

With all the chaos behind me, I slightly turned, seeing everyone now getting on the elevators, and chuckled. "If you only knew, homie. I'm married, for starters."

Leader and I had confided in each other plenty of times behind bars. I hadn't planned on telling him, but shit, he caught me in the heat of the moment.

"Married! Shit, congratulations, nigga! I haven't talked to your ass in two weeks and already missed a few chapters. Gotdamn, you move fast."

"Yeah, shit has been movin' fast as fuck in my world. You good, though?"

I knew Leader was more than straight, especially since his

brother was still holding him down in the streets.

"Yeah, I'm good. I'm just tryna process the fact that yo' ass is married."

I laughed. "Shit, me too!"

"Aye, I need a favor. My... The girl I was dealing with... My people can't get in contact with her. She's not responding back. I know you're living in Jagoda Bay now and shit. She has family that live out there. My brother can't get out of Cove City right now, so I wanted to see if he could Zelle you some bread, and you can get it to her. I want lil' baby to live her life, but I promised that I would have her set always, and I meant that shit. You think you could do that for me?"

Leader had been trying to give me some money since I got out, and as much as I wasn't in a position to turn shit down, I still declined. Bad enough, my brothers, Shio included, had come through for me when I was released. I didn't want any more handouts. I was ready to put in the work to get my own bread.

"Aye, Tune..." Shio stuck his head out the door.

"Yeah?"

"We up on the private maternity wing." Shio paused. "Don had her sister brought up there too. Come up when you done."

I nodded. He didn't seem fucked up about Glow, but still, we had to have a conversation.

Once Shio was gone, I made sure Leader was still on the line. "I got you, bruh. You know her people's address?"

"Nah... I can get it, though. She got a big sister. Her name Glow."

Choking on my spit, I pulled the phone from my face and looked at it. When I processed his words, I put the phone back to my ear, ignoring my racing heart. "Whose name is Glow?"

"My girl... Well, her name ain't Glow, her big sister's is. I think she like a food blogger or some shit. I need you to get some bread to Glee and tell her I love and miss her. I don't want her going ghost on my people. I'll keep my distance, but if she keeps running, I'ma go back on my word and reach out to her myself, and I ain't tryna do that. I just want you to give her the bread and tell me she good. That's all. A nigga ain't been feelin' right. I feel like... like some shit is wrong. Just give her the bread and let me know she's good. That's all I ask."

The fuck! This nigga had to be shittin' me.

Jagoda Bay was too big to be so fucking small.

CHAPTER 17
CALISTA GLEE

The scent of stainless steel equipment and sanitized surfaces created a metallic tang in the air. Although the room had been chaotic less than twenty hours ago, it was now eerily quiet and dimly lit, with only the light behind the bed powered on. The sharp cramps in my lower belly, rawness on my skin from the oversized pad, and thudding from the twelve stitches I'd received didn't outweigh the pain of my broken heart.

To add salt to the wound, the screams and tears of my sister replayed in my mind like a broken record. When I thought I couldn't feel any worse, my mother came hours later and looked at me with enough disappointment to fill the entire floor of labor and delivery here at Jagoda One. I didn't know how Blayke's parents had gotten wind that I had given birth, but they made the drive without even coming inside and forced my bestie to leave. She was all I had in this moment, and I needed her more than anything. But she was gone, along with everyone else in my life.

Nine months ago, I was an excited freshman at Blake

University in Cove City, Georgia. I had the opportunity of a lifetime to attend my dream school on a full-ride scholarship that
included amazing perks like a brand-new condo for student
housing. The problems I faced then were what my bestie and I
wanted to eat and finishing my homework before the 11:59
p.m. deadline. I had my life planned out since elementary
school: attend BSU, go to medical school, complete my resi-
dency, where I would probably meet the man of my dreams,
land my dream job as an attending doctor, get married, and
have beautiful children who would more than likely follow in
their parents' footsteps and become doctors as well. That was
my plan, and up until nine months ago, I'd been on track
with it.

Resting my head against the pillow, my lashes brushed my
cheek as I sighed. My body wasn't prepared for childbirth. I felt
like a fish out of water. I didn't know the first thing about
caring for a baby, let alone a newborn. I'd wanted to be a
physician, not an obstetrician, gynecologist, or pediatrician. I
had no idea what was next when it came to post-baby care,
how to care for my body while it was healing, or how to keep
this baby alive. I hadn't even known I was pregnant. Sure, I'd
been sick off and on since Halloween, but I thought it was
stress and seasonal illness. Georgia's weather was weird as
hell; I was always walking around sneezing and had some kind
of cold. My period had been spotty, but I chalked that up to
stress too. My life changed the moment I fell in love with a boy,
only to be heartbroken weeks later. I couldn't eat or sleep, and
all I did was cry, so of course, I didn't expect my period to be
normal. I hadn't gained any weight to signal something was
happening, so walking around bump-less was the biggest indicator of me not knowing I was with child. I'd carried this child
for a full thirty-eight weeks and didn't feel a kick or anything. I
was upset about my predicament, but I was also in shock that

this had happened to me.

Leader and I's meeting wasn't normal. I'd been added to a group chat with his family when they thought they'd been adding him. His sister, brother, mother, and I exchanged banter before he was added to the chat. Upon seeing that I was defending him regarding his family's criticism of his choice in baby mama, he began to call my number. I'd been bored when I sent those responses, but that didn't stop Leader from calling me. I didn't answer, and God must have been playing some sick game with me because later that night, my best friend brought her boyfriend over, who had his brother with him. They turned out to be the very people I'd been texting in the group chat. From then on, it was love at first sight with Leader.

My mother and sister sent me to college to get an education. I had been set up, not wanting for anything. Thanks to my mother's weekly deposits and my sister paying me whenever she received a check from being a social media influencer, along with the random groceries and packages she sent, all I had to do was go to class and study. Leader was everything a girl like me shouldn't have been interested in. He was involved with the mother of his son, who, I might add, wasn't trying to let up off him. He also sold drugs—not just small bags, but large quantities. He'd never made it official with me, no matter how much I wanted it. He didn't think he had a life outside of the streets. In Leader's mind, his future was either death or jail. He believed he'd more than likely fall in his father's footsteps, who had been killed when he was a boy, forcing Leader and his brother, Emperor, to grow up too fast. I had no business getting involved with Leader, yet here I was—a patient at Jagoda One hospital who had just pushed out his second child.

The first man who spoiled me, the first boy who spent the night, my first date, my first kiss, my first love—Leader had been my everything. Still, he didn't fight for me. He let me walk out of his life, just like his brother let Blayke walk out of his. My best friend and I knew we were in too deep when our lives went from being college freshmen to two girls who were in love with grown-ass men. The day everything fell apart was the day Leader's baby's mother confronted me, showing proof that she was still romantically involved with him and that her best friend had been with Emperor. She literally showed us our men lying in their beds. To make things worse, Blayke found out she was pregnant the same night. My friend knew she couldn't bring a baby around her Christian parents, so we rented a car and drove to the nearest state for an abortion. That day, we made a vow to swear off boys and focus on our studies. I was supposed to be a doctor, and Blayke dreamed of being a nurse. We were back on track by the end of September, when, in reality, I should have been getting an abortion too.

Knock knock knock

Before I faced the door, I peered at the digital clock next to the TV.

5:59 a.m.

I'd been awake for the last three hours and hadn't gone back to sleep since the previous nurse checked my vitals.

"Good morning," the nurse, who was introduced as the pediatric nurse, made her way inside but the dark-skinned beauty wasn't alone. My chest tightened as she pushed in a transparent hospital bassinet.

When the nurse saw my body tense, she stopped. "If you're not ready, I can take the baby back to the nursery to chill with me. I don't mind..."

She smiled warmly at me. She looked to be no older than my sister, and although she was at work, her bundles were flowing down her back gracefully, and her makeup was done flawlessly. The pink scrub set she was wearing featured bows all over the top

"Um, no. It's... It's okay."

She checked my face for reassurance before continuing to push the bassinet in. Once the enclosure was to the right of the bed, my face tightened.

"Baby ate an hour ago, has been changed, and is doing *so* good with sleeping."

Keeping my eyes on the nurse, I licked my chapped lips. My sister had dropped off a bag full of everything I needed around midnight, including nursing pads, a nursing bra, and gowns. I took a shower as soon as she left, where I wept loudly. Glow had been my everything since I was a child; she was the best big sister I could ask for and hadn't even looked my way when she came in. That hurt. She dropped my bags off, set my food on the tray, and left as soon as she came. Just thinking about it had me emotional. Blinking away the tears, I focused on the embarrassing question I needed to ask the nurse.

"Can you come back later, or have someone come later to show me how to feed and change? Maybe even have the lactation specialist come... I know breast milk is the best milk. I want to try, it's just that I don't... I'm a college student, and I know breastfed babies are more attached to their mother and"

"Hey..." The nurse placed her hand on my shoulder, and the weight allowed me to take a breath. "I'll show you everything you need to know," she said. "And you're right, breast milk is nutrient-packed for your baby, but formula-feeding is fine too. Because you want to try, we can start with breastfeeding. I can help baby latch, then I'll show you how to use a pump tomorrow before you leave. You can pump milk and allow your family to feed the baby while you rest."

She must've felt me tense at the mention of family because she paused, then sighed. "Listen, I know this is a lot, but you've got this. From what I saw, you have a support system. Your family will come around. They are just shocked."

A scoff left my mouth quicker than I could stop it, making the nurse giggle.

"Trust me... I've seen people fight in these rooms and leave the next day as if nothing had happened the day before. And that's with people getting the full ten months to process a baby coming. That's technically a year. Your family got none of that you got none of that too, boo.. It's been barely a day since you gave birth. Everyone is dealing with their emotions, and they are allowed that, but I know they love you. Your sister bringing you all those things..." She tossed her head at the duffel bags in the corner. "And your mother calling the nursery every hour on the hour lets me know you'll be just fine."

I lit up at that revelation. I thought my mom had gone back home and was crying just as I had been. She'd always talked about becoming a grandmother, but I knew she didn't expect me to give her one for at least another fifteen years.

"Let your people process. You can't dwell on it. You just gave birth to a healthy baby. You did it. It may not seem like it now, but this will be the best thing that ever happened to you." The nurse looked behind her before taking a seat at the foot of my bed and continuing, "I had my son when I was sixteen. My mama didn't give a *damn* about my six-month belly; she beat my ass all through the bathroom after busting in and finding me getting out of the shower."

She laughed, but I was sitting in shock.

"Girl, I deserved it. I'd been screwing in her house anytime she was at work, like I was the one paying the bills. But it worked out. My mother turned into a full-on award-winning grandma, barely letting me change a damn diaper. I went on to finish high school, graduating in the top thirty of my class, and went to college, making the dean's list three times. It wasn't easy, but I did it. I did it because I wanted to show my baby that he wasn't a burden; he was motivation. "

She grabbed my hand in hers. "I say all this to say that I know a girl who will still go on to do great things when I see one. You're going to be fine, Calista. And your family? They're going to be so smitten with this baby that it will make you sick."

My laughter erupted through the tears that fell.

"What are you in school for?"

With a baby at my side, I was almost too embarrassed to tell her. "Pre-med. I'm on a full scholarship. Well... was on one."

"Pre-med. Wow. You look like a doctor." She grinned, causing me to smile too. "And you're going to *keep* your scholarship. Study hard and use this baby as motivation. I'm rooting for you, black girl. We need more representation out here. You've got this, okay? You've given birth to one of the most beautiful babies, and I see *a lot* of babies. You were destined to do beautiful things. A baby does not end your life." She stood. "It gives it more purpose."

Giving my hand one more squeeze, she looked at the bassinet again. "I have to go now. My colleagues are already saying I've been playing *favorites*."

"Thank you so much. I really needed to hear all of that."

She smiled and made her exit.

Using the back of my hand that hadn't been poked and prodded, I dried my tears. The baby was here now, and there wasn't much I could do besides try my best. I just didn't like not knowing what was next; I liked plans. I didn't know what I would do in terms of childcare, merging our schedules, or handling doctors' appointments. I didn't even know how to strap a baby into the car seat. I was probably the most unqualified person to have a child, even at nineteen years old.

Soft grunts interrupted my daydreaming. Heat rushed to my neck, my stomach turned over, and my breathing grew laborious. Still, I looked over into the bassinet. A blue and pink striped hat covered a head that looked as if it could fit in the palm of my hand. The baby's little button nose was red, and pink lips pursed. Not wanting the baby to cry, I reached inside the bassinet, letting my instincts guide my actions. The baby was lightnot feather light, not baby-doll light, but light. This had been my first time holding my own child. My first time even looking the baby in the face, and when I thought I'd feel nothing but disappointment, my heart burst.

Pushing the hat back, silky curls framed the baby's smooth skin like vanilla ice cream. Running my finger across the forehead, the baby's lips turned up in a nearly smile-like way. I wanted to inspect all fingers and toes, but I knew had no idea how to wrap the baby back like the nurse had. I knew being swaddled brought new babies comfort, which was maybe one of five things I knew.

Vbbb vbbb vbbb

My phone was vibrating on the bedside table to my left. A white Styrofoam cup and a pink pitcher of ice water sat beside it. I should've been drinking more because the nurse last night said between the delivery and my milk coming in, I'd get dehydrated if I didn't keep my water intake higher than normal. I had made a mental note to make a list on my phone of topics to research so that I and this baby would be okay once we left the comfort of twenty-four seven care.

I picked my phone up while carefully placing the baby in between my legs. Shifting my gaze, I unlocked the phone while the baby continued to make cute noises.

MA IN LAW

> Hey babyyyyy! I haven't heard from you! I went by that empty ass campus last week to take you to lunch and forgot you were going home for the summer. Ain't nobody told me nothing! I hope you're having an amazing summer! Sending you some funds for you to enjoy yourself with. I know my son would have wanted you to have it. We love you, and I'm forever rooting for my future doctor!

THE TEXT WAS FOLLOWED by an Apple payment of three thousand dollars. Tears pooled in my eyes again as I exited from the text thread. I had half a mind to tell her I'd given birth to her second grandchild, but that was just one more person to be disappointed in me. I hadn't spoken to Leader's family in a few weeks because I'd been trying to finish exams, move out of the condo, and get over the flu, which I now knew were early labor signs. My goal was to catch up with them once I'd settle in Jagoda Bay at my sister's townhouse. I'd more than settled in the few days I'd been here.

Nonetheless, this was my mess. It was bad enough that she still hadn't been able to see her first grandchild due to Leader's baby mother playing baby games. She'd been the reason Leader was spending the next almost decade of his life locked away. Had she not gotten in his car with his drugs that she'd stolen and started a fight, prompting the police to pull him over, he'd still be here. And if he were here, he, too, would be disappointed. I couldn't bear the thought of one more person being upset with me, so I locked my phone screen without responding.

What could Leader do anyway? He couldn't raise a child from jail.

Knock knock knock

"Come in," I whispered loud enough so that the person on the other side of the door could hear me, but soft enough to not disturb the baby.

Three large yellow, pink, and blue balloons greeted me before the guest could. There was a matching gift bag that was big enough for a toddler to fit inside. Once the person entered, my curiosity turned into discontent. I wasn't sad because of who had entered, but because she hadn't meant to enter my room.

Black biker shorts sat on her thick legs, and she wore an oversized graphic T-shirt with Selena on it, along with matching black and red Jordans. Her fresh braids were pulled up in a half-up, half-down style, with two pieces hanging on the sides of her face. Had I known I was gearing up to have a baby, I, too, would have gotten braids minus the boho strands.

Who was I kidding? Had I known I was having a baby, it wouldn't have been born. I would have been right at the chop shop just like Blayke had.

"Hey, girl! Happy first Mother's Day!" She paused. "Opp, I'm sorry! Did I wake the baby?" she whispered.

Looking down, I shook my head no.

Placing the balloons and gift bag on the couch where the father of the child should have been spending his nights, she turned to the sink and washed her hands. "I'm Pearla."

"I know who you are. I'm Glee."

Pearla twisted, eyes on the baby. She wasn't cheery, but she wasn't as sad as I was. She seemed somewhere right in the middle.

"Um... I think the other lady, the one who's friends with my sister? I think she's down the hall."

I was still shocked that I'd been transported to the private wing with the lady. Before Blayke's parents had come, she had given me an earful about the fine-ass, dangerous-looking men on the floor. She'd even told me the other lady had given birth to twins—a lady I now knew as one of my sister's friends. Glow kept her friends secluded. I only knew a few things about them due to my lurking on their social media accounts from when they posted my sister or she posted them. I'd seen Pearla on one of their profiles and came across her social media accounts. I'd liked her posts anytime I saw them because she was always fly. She hadn't posted much lately, though, and I wondered if the reason was the same reason her eyes held weight like mine.

Pearla's brow rose. "You talking about my sister's stepmama?"

"Uhh..."

"Discover. She was married to my sister's gay daddy. Now she's engaged with Metavello."

"Metavello?"

"Yeah, my sister's fiancé's twin brother."

"Oh..."

Pearla squinted her eyes. "You lost about everything around here, hunh?"

I nodded.

I was still trying to process the fact that my sister seemed to have a whole man now that called himself her husband. I was in pain, but I knew what I'd heard before they wheeled me up here. I'd nearly died when I went into labor, but I still remember the shock on everyone's faces when Blayke and I walked through the hospital doors.

Pearla took a seat where the nurse had just been, keeping her eyes on the baby before looking back at me. "It's a lot going on, but we're all here for each other. That's how it is in the mo- this family," she stated, stumbling over her words. "But we protect our own. Everybody has a job to do, and one day, you'll learn yours. For now, I'd like it if we were friends. I could use another one, and I'm sure you can too."

I licked my lips again, and my need must've been evident because Pearla reached into the Louis Vuitton crossbody bag and pulled out a Carmex. I took it, smeared some on my finger, and gave it back to her. The medicated balm felt amazing as it left a greasy film over my parched lips.

"Thank you. And I'd like that. I don't know how good a friend I can be right now, though. I'm sure I'm about to be pretty occupied." I chuckled, glancing down at the bundle.

"Can I?" Pearled motioned for the baby.

"Sure."

She took the baby in her arms and smiled. "So, so, so beautiful. Hi, you! Hi, beautiful," she cooed. Pearla looked up from rocking the baby. "Girl, you made a beautiful-ass baby. OhemG!" she squealed, making me laugh.

"Thank you."

"Hey babyyyy. You are everything, for real."

Watching Pearla rock and speak to the baby had me feeling relieved in a sense. Since I'd walked through the hospital doors, I felt like my life was over, and I'd committed the ultimate act. Blayke and I had been sitting around, and I felt like I had to pee. As soon as I stood, water gushed from my leggings and then blood. I didn't know what to do because I didn't know what was happening. Once the cramps tore through my body, I screamed for her to take me to the hospital.

The nurse had poured life into me, and now Pearla had come in bearing gifts and offering friendship. I needed this, and I hadn't even known I did.

"Did it hurt?" Pearla asked with wide eyes.

I winced, remembering the labor pains, the confusion, and the baby ripping through my vaginal walls. I even felt them stitching me up. I was in and out of it, but I felt and heard everything.

"Hell yes!" I imparted.

"Oh my God! Yeah, issa no for meeee!"

We both laughed.

"I'll just love on this cutie and my sister's baby and all the other babies being born in the family."

"Yes, do that."

Pearla's smile dropped. "You know your life isn't over, Glee. Right?"

"I hope it isn't."

"I know it isn't. My sister had a baby younger than you, and while I'm not trying to shit on your situation, we had *nothing*. Everyone is going to help you. I know I am, and I know your sister is too. My girls, Bella and Mahzeyah, will help too. The three of us do everything together. They even wanted to come up with me today, but I didn't want to overwhelm you. You got us—all of us."

"Thank you, Pearla. I need y'all." I held back my tears. I was so tired of crying.

Taking Pearla in, I couldn't believe the girl I'd seen on TikTok with famous people was sitting on my bed. My sister was famous in a sense, too, but Pearla and her friends had been seen with rappers. She was as pretty in person as she was online; all of the women were, and it was embarrassing as hell that my first time meeting them had been when I was in labor.

"I told myself... I was never stepping foot back in this hospital. And yet, I did today. I'm so glad I had."

"Why, what happened?"

Pearla sighed. "My ex is here. He's in a coma, a few floors up. Long story short, I fell for a man who was constantly telling me to wait on us and to focus on my future. I fell anyway against his warnings and ended up hurt. Found out he's married."

Her story sounded exactly like mine, except Leader wasn't married. However, he wasn't exactly single when I fell for him, and against his warnings, I fell hard.

"My baby's father, gosh, that sounds weird to say." I blinked back tears. I never thought I'd put him and baby daddy in the same sentence. At least, not right now. "He told me to focus on school, but that didn't stop me from handing him my virginity like it was a two-for-one coupon. He's in jail now. He was riding with his first baby mama, and she had drugs on her. He took the charge."

"He did what now? Oh no, that bitch would have had to take her own charge."

"Right. But that's not who Leader is. He would never fuck over someone he cares about."

Besides him being in jail and us breaking up, what hurt the most about the whole situation was Leader really stepping up. That showed he loved his baby mama to some extent. I didn't fit into their world, and that's why I made my exit. Now, here I was with a whole baby.

"That sounds like Grind..." Pearla's face fell, and many tears rolled down her face. I couldn't stop mine either. We were two young girls in the room crying together.

"Life... It's fucked up, ain't it?" she asked.

I nodded, not being able to verbally answer her.

"But it's okay. We're going to get through it, Glee. Together. This cutie won't hurt like us. Never."

I nodded again.

Using her shoulder, Pearla swiped at her tears. "Let me stop crying. I done made you cry, and next the baby will be crying. Can't have that."

Pearl's phone began to ring. Using her free hand, she pulled it from her pants and rolled her eyes at the screen. Using her pinky finger, she swiped the button, connecting to a FaceTime.

"Damn, bitch! Let us see the baby! You already got us up early as hell waiting on an update." I heard a voice ring out before the black box connected to show a face.

Someone kissed their teeth. "Right! Let us see!"

"First, y'all need to speak to the mama."

Pearla held the phone up and flipped it so I could see. Tucking my messy hair behind my ears, I waved at two pretty girls. One was lighter than me but had a bonnet on her head, while the other was chocolate, pressing out her hair in the mirror. I could see a cheer uniform on her body and wondered which school she went to.

"Hey, girl!" the darker one spoke first.

"Oh, you're pretty. Hey, boo!" the other said before Pearla turned the phone back around.

"Y'all so rude. The one in the cheer fit is Mahzeyah, and the other is Bella."

"I'm big mad I gotta do cheer camp on the weekends and all summer," Mahzeyah fussed. "Now, let us see our baby before I have to go."

Pearla looked at me for confirmation. When I nodded, she held the phone over the baby.

Squeals erupted from the phone as the baby still slept peacefully.

"Y'all too loud!"

"My bad, my bad! That baby is so damn pretty! The niggas really gonna be on us with a baby riding shotgun. You know they love playing stepdaddy to bad bitches."

"Bella, please!" Pearla rolled her eyes with a grin.

I loved their dynamic, and it made me miss my own best friend. I hadn't heard from Blayke, which meant her parents had taken her phone.

"What's the baby's name?" Pearla asked.

Licking my lips, I inhaled and exhaled, repelling all the

negative thoughts and feelings.

I didn't know how he'd feel about it, but only one name came to mind. "Her name is Leader."

CHAPTER 18

SOLANA DAMITA LEDESMA

Since the engagement party, I'd been on a cloud of funk. I'd missed the not-so-surprise engagement and the surprised laboring start, but I received messages from the ladies with videos and pictures. I hadn't given out my contact information, but since they were affiliated with the mob, I'm sure my number wasn't hard to acquire. I was added to a group chat that had been quiet since the night of the engagement. That night, I went back to Shio's home solo. I felt too beautiful to change, so I got in my zone while lying in bed fully clothed. I didn't want Shio disturbing me, so I locked and barricaded the door as I had many times before. He hadn't bothered me, though, which was his usual memo as well.

The pretty lady who was about to pop had a beautiful engagement, according to the group chat, and I almost felt bad about missing it. Seeing everyone rally around her when her water broke on the stage had my stomach in knots. It was hard to witness any kind of happiness when I knew I'd never have that. A man would never get down on one knee and ask me to be his bride. I had been negotiated and handed over on a 24-

karat golden platter. Discover —*sí, ese es su nombre (yes, that's her name)* —seemed like a nice lady who deserved happiness, and she also deserved to have those who were genuinely enthusiastic about her in attendance.

Yo era simplemente una extranjera (I was simply a foreigner).

For the past week, I had been sulking. My daily activities were working out with Shio because he wouldn't let me skip out, eating the healthy stuff he kept in his fridge so I wouldn't starve, and staying up all night, lost in my thoughts, just to sleep the next day away. Before the engagement, I'd been sleeping, but I'd also been looking forward to the time I spent around the American boy. We'd work out and eat together, and that was enough because my coño (pussy) would quake the whole time. Now, I did my workouts and ran right back to my room. I felt disgusting for lusting after Shio when he had dealings with the beautiful woman, Glow. However, I told myself today that I was bringing myself out of my coma. I was leaving this room and seeing what the king of the castle was prioritizing. I'd keep my thoughts respectful.

Like always, I woke up well past noon. By the time I showered, fingered my curls since they still looked good despite the sweating and sleeping I'd been doing this week, and got dressed in a Skims tank dress that hugged my body down to the ankles, it was almost five in the evening. I'd gone braless since the dress had thin straps, but it was so form-fitting that it held everything in place. Staring back at myself in the floor-length mirror, I could see the effects of the workouts and the healthy eating. My curves were more defined, my stomach flatter, and even though my limbs were stiff and sore most days, I looked amazing. I'd asked Shio multiple times if he was trying to condition me for war, and each time he ignored me and continued to dish out instructions in his underground gym.

Shio was the calmest, most stern personal trainer I'd ever seen. I mean, I'd never had one myself, but I did see them in action online and on television. He'd show me the workout, instruct me to do it, and then go on about his business, doing his own version of the exercise. The first three workouts were brutal; I could barely get through a set without feeling like I had to throw up, but it had gotten better. All this week, you would have thought I was Superman with the way I was zipping through the sets like I'd been doing it my entire life instead of just a couple of weeks. Shio was even impressed. He hadn't voiced it, but the look on his face said it all.

Spraying Ummo all over my body until the honey fresh tobacco scent was nearly too much to bear, I took one last look in the mirror. Seeing snot dripping from my nostrils, I snatched a piece of tissue and wiped my nose before washing my hands, grabbing my phone, and prancing out of the bedroom. The warm notes of my perfume trailed behind me. After our workout on Wednesday, I got back to my room to find more items in the closet. One of my favorite addictions, aside from Skims lounge wear, was the Mexican brand fragrances I loved. Even though I looked darker than my Hispanic lineage, I had been born and raised in Mexico City, and it was pretty much all I knew. Among my favorites stored in the closet was XINU, a Mexican brand founded by a husband and wife based in my hometown, Mexico City.

Shio had been quiet since the engagement party too. He would knock on the door to let me know when he was leaving, or ask me after breakfast what I wanted the next day, but that was it. I hadn't yet joined him at church, mainly because I wasn't up for it, but he had been going without me. Seeing his mother at the engagement dinner made me feel nervous because I was not one of them. She was nice and pretty, but I only imagined the things she said about me after I walked away. Elders in Mexico had never been kind to me, so I expected nothing different in the States. It shouldn't matter either way because I wasn't here for long. I was simply going to enjoy my time in their world because, like Shio said on the drive to the engagement party, there's no telling when I might be this *gratis (free)* again.

I had yet to go into Shio's bedroom, even though I knew where it was. Both of our rooms were on the first floor, but his was at the end of the hall in the opposite direction from mine. I knew because that's where he would retreat to after our workouts. I hadn't even stuck my head in because he kept the door closed. I'd only seen the rooms I had bypassed on the walk to the gym, and one of them was his office. Shio wasn't the type to sleep in. He went to bed late but woke up early; that much I did know because, on the days I didn't wake up to meet him for workouts, I could hear him past my room.

Inhaling slowly, I rounded the corner and stuck my head inside his office. Bumps formed all over my arms, and a light gasp escaped my lips. I knew there was a chance he was in his office, but I was still caught off guard by his presence. Sitting behind a large oak desk that held only a big Apple computer, a worn leather notebook about the size of his hands, a high-tech printer, and piles of money. Shio looked majestic.

His chocolate skin gleamed as his muscles flexed while he removed money from its pile and placed it on the machine. Pausing in his action, he looked up at me, and I stumbled back a bit. He'd seen me, so it was silly to try to run away. Instead, I stepped into the doorframe fully and kept my eyes on him as he kept his on mine, not stopping his hand movements. I couldn't read his expression, but I was regretting coming in and intruding on him. I was already here against his wishes, and although he'd been extremely generous with the gifts, shelter, and clothing, I didn't want to test my luck. The sooner he sent me back to Mexico City, the sooner I would be Mrs. Rodríguez, and I wasn't ready for that just yet.

"Solana," he called out in a raspy tone.

I had the simplest name a girl of my culture could have, yet the way it rolled off his tongue easily made me feel way more important than I was. Shio and I didn't interact much, but when I was around him, I almost felt like a person. My father loved me that much I knew—but I knew what I was to him. I was a woman, so that made me a pawn, a chess piece, for only his benefit. Still, I loved the man who gave me life. He was only doing what every other cartel and mob boss did in Mexico. I'd learned that my duty was to my father and what he said, went. Here in Jagoda Bay, though, I had started to feel like a human being. Seeing these American mob women enjoy their riches in a way I never had had me wondering if all I've learned in my culture was *falso* (false). My father let me party around Mexico City with watchful eyes following my every move, but he never attempted to better me. Instead of pushing me to cultivate myself, he preferred that I remain out of sight. Shio had given me free rein, but still, I'd been confined to these walls because I didn't know what to make of this situation.

¿Qué haces cuando nadie te ve? (What do you do when no one is watching?)

Seeing that Shio had yet to move his eyes from me, I acknowledged the reason for my presence. "I... I just wanted to see what it is that you were doing."

Clearing my throat because my words came out hoarse, I swallowed the other words I'd already forgotten.

Shio continued to stare at me, letting his eyes dance from my wild curls to the bodycon lounge dress, to my manicured toes. His face gave no indication of emotion, and yet, I felt naked. I was happy when his eyes landed on my face again. This felt intimate, but I was sure I was imagining it. The most he'd looked at me in a desirable way was the night of the engagement party. Other than that, Shio kept everything platonic. And although I appreciated the fact that I wasn't placed in a house with a man who creeped me out by lusting over me, a part of me wished he'd show some sort of interest. I had been desired by men all my life, but being wanted by a man of substance was esteemed. The American boy had discipline. His body, his lifestyle, and the relationships he had with the people he loved demonstrated that.

"I'm working. You good?"

He intertwined his fingers and placed them on the desk in front of him while waiting for me to answer his question. Another thing he always did that I hadn't seen the men back home do was maintain eye contact when speaking. I didn't think I'd ever master the skill because it often felt awkward. With him, I had no choice but to match his energy because if I didn't, he would call me out on it.

"Just wanted to check in with you..."

I didn't know what I really wanted. I just knew I wanted to get out of the room and thought that since it was the weekend, he'd let me join him when he left today. The mounds of green in front of him were something I had never seen before. My first time holding American money was when he gave me the rolls of cash before walking into the engagement party. I hadn't even known how to count it and needed some help when I made a small purchase that night. I knew pesos, but the American dollar was strange to me. It was the color of lush trees and fresh turf, and each bill shared the same hue, but the faces were different.

Using his thumb to flick his nose, he pushed away from his desk. "Solana, ven aquí (come here)", he stated instead of asking.

My bare feet moved on their own accord and didn't stop

385

until I was standing behind his desk, next to the black leather chair he was sitting in. Holding his hand out for me to place mine in his, I concentrated on trying to steady my breathing from us touching. I could feel my nipples poking through my dress, and if he'd noticed them, I wouldn't know because he hadn't taken his eyes off my face.

Shio tugged me to his side, and I got the shock of my life when he lowered me into his lap. My entire body was rigid. I was as still as a *maniquí* (mannequin) as I sat on his muscular thigh. This was not a respectful action, and my thoughts matched the ambiance. I did not want to be the reason for Glow to lose her happiness. I needed to find the courage to ask Shio if she and he were a thing.

"Have you ever done this before?" he asked, breaking me from the many inner questions I had.

Pushing my thoughts aside, I melted as a delicious shudder heated my body as his sultry voice spoke directly into my ear. I couldn't clench my legs closed to relieve the pressure because then, he'd feel it. He'd know that he had me wired up with just one sentence.

"Done... what?" I asked through bated breath. I needed clarity so that I could answer his question as truthfully as possible.

Leaning in, his solid chest pushed against my back. Our fragrances blended like the chords of a musical masterpiece composed by Manuel de Sumaya himself. A delightful shiver of wanting ran through me as I felt his steady heartbeat through my back. I allowed the abundance of saliva to slowly descend my throat as I waited for what was next. Shio and I had never been this close, not since the first night when he put the gun to my head, and just like that night, I was intrigued and frightened but not scared enough to get up off his fucking lap.

"I gave you some bread without realizing you probably

don't know how to count money. Have you done it before?"

Oh, that was what he was talking about: dólares americanos American dollars).

Inspecting the neat stacks of money assembled in front of us, trying to get my mind off anything other than the closeness of our bodies, I looked from pile to pile and shook my head. "No."

"Aite..."

He scooted the chair closer to the desk so that my abdomen was lightly pressing against it. I was sandwiched between him and the wood, and hanging by a thread internally. Reaching around me, he picked up a stack of money. He must have visited his barber sometime this morning; I could smell the fumes that only a barbershop holds, whether it be Mexican or American. I had six brothers and a father. That was very much part of my upbringingI knew it all too well.

Using only one hand, he spread the green bills across the wood so that I had a clear view of each piece of green paper.

"This..." He placed his index finger on the desk just below the first bill. "This is a dollar. It equals one." He reached for a few more of the same paper that displayed an ugly man in a white wig and spread them just below the original one. "How many dollars are right here?"

Pausing, I tapped into the American vocabulary side of my brain. "*Cinco...* I mean, five."

"Yeah. This is five dollars." He slid his finger over to the next bill that had the number five etched in the corner. "Five one-dollar bills are the same as one five-dollar bill." He placed another five-dollar bill below that one. "How much is this?"

"Um... Ten?"

"Yeah. This is ten dollars, which is the same as this bill."

He went on with his lesson until we reached the one-hundred-dollar bill, and I was able to understand how to add and subtract the money. It wasn't as simple as pesos, but I got the concept.

"Each one of these bills features a picture of a dead president. I'm not going to run through who these muthafuckas are because that shit ain't important. All you really need to know is how to count it and who this one is." He pointed to the hundred-dollar bill, which was more of a blueish color but looked green when I first entered the office. "Ever heard the phrase 'all about the benjamins?'"

I nodded.

"They talkin' about this nigga right here. A blue face. C-note. Hundred-dollar bill."

Nodding, my body still not cooling down. I made him explain a few things more than once because my mind had wandered to the gutter every thirty seconds. Feeling confident to take a pop quiz if given one, I said, "I understand now."

"Aite. Now grab one of those stacks of hunnids in the corner over there."

"Hunnids?"

"My bad, *hundreds,* baby. Hunnids is just some lingo type shit."

Baby.

I knew he'd used it as a term of endearment and that he didn't actually see me as *his* baby, but that didn't stop the hairs on the back of my neck from spiking.

At the end of his desk, I saw a tall stack of blue benjamin's that was bundled in rubber bands next to the worn leather book. I lifted off his lap, because that was the only way I could reach it, and found myself with my ass in his face. I expected him to lean back, but he stayed in place, and all I could think about was how happy I was to have showered before switching to his side of the house.

With as many *hunnids* as I could hold, I took my seat back

in Shio's lap.

Bringing his face back to mine, Shio licked his lips, and I practically moaned. "This a money counter... Remove the rubber band and place the money on the tray right there."

Shio was instructing me on what to do, but he was also taking my hands in his and guiding my fingers. I was almost scared to get up because I knew I'd ruined the back of my dress. This American Boy wasn't doing anything but giving me a counting lesson, and I was turned on to the *máxima* (maximum).

Brushing his calloused hands against mine, he used my hands to place the money on the tray. The bills held a manufactured scent of fresh ink and clean cotton fibers. There was also a metallic scent that I caught a whiff of. Just like pesos, I'd not only been turned on by the man but also by being surrounded by so much money. I used cards back home because Papa didn't trust me with physical bills.

The money went inside the top portion of the machine and was spit out of the lower half with a beep. "That's twenty bands right there. A band is a..."

I perked up, and the slight movement caused me to brush against his manhood. My cheeks warmed, but I quickly said, "A thousand *dolares* (dollars)."

"Entonces, ¿cuánto dinero es? (So, this how much money?)"

"Veinte mil (Twenty thousand)." I was shocked I'd answered because I felt myself making a mess in the Skim's thong.

Shio reached around me, rubber-banded the money, and set it aside. When he leaned back in the chair, I caught on to his silent instruction. Grabbing another pile of money, I did as he'd shown me and waited for the machine to beep. I banded the money, equaling another twenty thousand dollars. I never knew counting money could be so sensual, but it was, and I was having the time of my life besides my body being on fire.

Thirty piles of money later, my phone began to vibrate on the desk. Seeing my father's name flash at the top of the screen snapped me out of my money-counting delusion and back into reality. I knew it wouldn't be long before he was calling me. I knew what time of the month it was, and just like a woman's menstrual cycle, my father was on time. Instead of answering, I left it to ring until my voicemail cued. Grabbing another stack of money, I kept the routine going as Shio remained silent, watching me.

The voicemail icon lit up on the screen of my phone, and just when I was about to grab another pile of money, two text message notifications popped up.

Shio squeezed my hip, and I froze momentarily. His grip felt right as if I was meant to be in his grasp. "That's enough for today, Solana. Get your phone."

I didn't want to stop. I didn't want to grab my phone. I didn't want to see what he had texted me because I already knew what it was. I didn't comprehend why he felt the need to remind me of the recurring procedure. The only thing I was surprised about was that he kept the shenanigans up even though I was thousands of miles away. I loved my father with all my heart, but it was shit like this that made it hard for me to respect him. I may have shown the proper regard outwardly, but my feelings were often indifferent toward my papa.

Wanting desperately to ignore Ines Ledesma, I obeyed Shio instead. Standing up, because even though it was just a text, I didn't feel right opening the thread while sitting in a man's lap who wasn't my fiancée's, I took a few paces to the front of the desk. I'd never even seen my stepmother sit in my father's lap. Leaning against the desk, I swiped past the voicemail and went right to my text messages. The one between my father and me was at the very bottom, and surprisingly, no new messages were there. I did, however, have two new texts from the group chat the women had added me to when they sent the beautiful engagement pictures.

I didn't have any of the numbers saved, but Apple was so smart that it had already used its iCloud information to help me identify was texting me.

MAYBE DASANI RINALDI

Hola Solana! Lol. Let me stop. What you doing?

I WANTED the full American experience, so I had long ago swapped all of my settings to English, even though I had no one to text with daily. Telling Apple to save all the incoming contacts, I laughed at Dasani's contact number icon of her and their Don in Halloween outfits. It looked like he was not happy with the decision to have him hold a bag of sugar and wads of money, while Dasani was in a fitted, white dress labeled "milk," holding designer luxury bags. She cheesed for whoever was taking the picture as he frowned. I understood their Don being a sugar daddy, but I didn't know why Dasani was milk with Gucci bags. It had to be some type of American joke.

My eyes scanned over to Shio, who had resumed counting the money, his eyes fixated on the task. Forgetting all about my anger generated toward my father that quickly, I replied.

Nothing much. Just relaxing.

MAYBE MOCHA

Girl it's just chilling. Not relaxing. Lol.

MY CHEEKS BURNED. I was fluent in English, but the American slang, lingo, and jokes was still foreign to me.

MAYBE SCARLETT RINALDI

Hey girlie. Mocha leave her alone. I think her English is adorable. 😊

> Gracias ☺

MAYBE MISSY DABADDEST BITCH

Get dressed hoessss. Meet me at the yo. 🎤

> The who?

PIA

Hey Solana. She means the studio.

> 😄 Oh. Got it. What time?

MISSY DABADDEST BITCH

Now. I'm about to send the address, and I don't have to say this because you bitches are always fly, but get fine. Never know where the night may take us 😜😼

JISEI

Okay let me get my baby situated and I'm game. Hey Solana boo. 👋

> Hi! 😀

> Okay. I'll get dressed

MAYBE DAYLANI

Rut made plans. 😌 Keep me in the loop of where y'all gone be in case I can pop out later.

DISCOVER

Ughhh, y'all have fun. 😒 I got these two occupying my time. I'm down for another seven weeks, but then it's uppppp

SHE'D ATTACHED a picture of two adorable infant boys who looked identical in every way. They both wore baby blue jumpers that covered their hands, with little green pacifiers in their mouths. Their covered hands were balled up at the side of their faces. It was so cute that it was almost sickening. My ovaries screamed at the photo. I still couldn't believe she'd gone into labor that night, shortly after I'd left. Her sons were so handsome. I couldn't imagine seeing two adorable bundles every day and having to decide who to pick up and love on first.

I noticed that the ladies had only spoken to me and not to each other, which meant they had communication was most likely already happening before they included me. I also noticed that the only person who hadn't replied in the chat was Glow. She hadn't replied the night I was sent the pictures as well. I'd hoped she wasn't upset with me because of Shio. I was uncertain about the connection still and hadn't worked up the nerve to ask Shio myself. Shio hadn't brought Glow home, nor was he wearing a ring, so maybe I was overreacting, and maybe she had married another man. If they were married, the act of practically creaming on his lap just a few moments ago would bring me nothing but shame. To save my conscience, I was going to assume they had not eloped. There's no way a woman would allow her husband to house another woman without being present.

My only hope was that Glow and I could at least be cordial when in the same quarters. I would be nothing but a memory as soon as my father snatched me out of here. I didn't have the time or the energy to hold a feud. I'd be doing enough fighting when I was married. I just hoped it wasn't physical because I knew being married into the Rodríguez family would bring many days of mental battles.

> ¡Hijos guapo! You have handsome sons Discover🖤🖤

THE WOMEN all oohed and ahhed over Discover's identical twins, and Missy gave the location of the studio. Excited to have an excuse to leave the house, I locked my screen.

Shio was still counting money, but was now returning the gaze I had upon him. It was almost sinful how handsome this man was. With his clean-cut and neatly trimmed beard, lounge clothes that could be worn outside the house and still cause women to double-take after, broad shoulders, full lips, and a perfectly structured face—Shio walked around as if he wasn't God's gift to women, but he was.

"Wassup, Solana?"

Folding my arms, I licked my suddenly chapped lips. "The ladies invited me for a night out..."

My phone vibrated again, and I opened the notification quickly, hoping it wasn't my father. I didn't need my mood soured before the fun began. Sighing with relief that it was Scarlett, I read the message.

SCARLETT

I can come and get you if you'd like.

"That's good. You need a ride, you takin' a whip, or you callin' the driver?" Shio asked with a raised brow as he neatly piled another rubber-banded stack. He hadn't missed a beat as he continued to glare at me while grabbing another stack, popping the band, and placing it on the money counter. The money filtered through and then stopped with a beep. My girl below thudded at the sound.

"Solana..."

"Uhh, no. Scarlett is coming to get me. Wait, that's okay, right?"

"Yes. Scarlett is my blood, Solana. If any of the women want to come by, you don't have to run that by me. Matta fact, ain't too much shit you gotta run by me. I told you... You can do whatever. You be the one barricaded in the fuckin' room like you hiding from the fuckin' boogie man."

He'd called me out, and I could only stand there in shame because he wasn't lying.

Shio held my gaze, eyes searching mine for whatever it was he always seemed to be after. Every time he did that, I held my breath and nearly passed out once. I had to get myself under control when it came to this man, which is another reason I stayed in that room. There was no point in letting myself get aroused by a man who I knew would never be mine, although the arousal had already occurred multiple times.

Shio. An American boy. An intelligent, attractive man, actually. A *rico buen hombre* (rich fine man) if he were in México.

"Aite. Call me if you need me," he said, pulling me from my thoughts.

Nodding, I rounded the desk. Before I could take another step, I was halted by the booming of his voice.

"Solana…"

Turning, I faced Shio once again.

He held out one of the stacks of money we'd been counting. Twenty thousand dollars. "Have fun."

Grabbing the money, I thanked him and hurried out of the room before I caught myself doing something my father would never forgive me for. Shio was a dangerous man, and it had nothing to do with his reputation or affiliation. And me—I was poison swathed in a flower. It was best that we kept this strictly about the lessons, which meant I needed to stay out of his face and his lap.

"Bitch, I cannot sing!"

Mocha tossed her long, straight hair over her shoulder, and it flowed freely behind her back. We were all at the studio but dressed like we were headed to the club. I had poor Scarlett waiting an extra thirty minutes because I couldn't decide on an outfit. The first two were jeans, and I was glad that I'd put in the extra effort to change. Everyone was in something short or tight, and I was no exception.

Huddled in a circle, we were all sipping from red cups while another American guy sat behind a table full of dials, lights, and buttons. The studio was modern, wood grained, and smelled good. As soon as Scarlett and I walked through the doors, the ladies shoved drinks into our hands. With one sip, my nerves were immediately settled. I'd never been inside a studio, but if I imagined one, this would come to mind.

"You don't have to know how to sing, girl! Big T going to use the autotune," Missy assured while running her hands through Mocha's hair.

"Okay... Now tell me again what we doing?" Dasani asked as she took a sip from her drink. The matte nude lipstick on her lips hadn't moved, and it looked so good against her almond skin.

"Okay, you know the trend on TikTok, where they use the "Chopped and Screwed" instrumental? They're freestyling, talking shit basically. I want to do that, but in the studio. Essex weak-ass baby mama been talking shit online, but the bitch can't pop up and get her fuckin' kids. It's cool because they're my little babies now, but I'm over this hoe. So, we hitting the booth!"

I had no idea what she was talking about. I hadn't been on the internet much, but the rest of the ladies all agreed, so I would just follow their lead. If I was going to make a fool of myself in the booth, I needed more courage.

"Are we consuming anything other than liquor?" As soon as the words left my mouth, I regretted them. I tried to think fast about whether I'd interpreted the words right because the questioning looks staring at me had me clearing my throat. "Weed... Do any of you smoke?" I clarified.

"I don't want to drink more liquor if we are smoking," Dasani spoke first.

Mocha's face finally dropped into a laugh. "Oh, girl. I thought you was talking about crack or some shit. I was about to salsa walk your ass outta here!"

Pia nearly choked on her apple juice from laughing at Mocha.

Pulling my silver skirt down as much as it would go, I took another sip of my drink, chuckling with the ladies.

"But yeah, some of us smoke. We drinking tonight, though,

but feel free to indulge," Dasani spoke up again. It was clear she had settled into her role, and while the ladies all seemed to move on their own accord, I could tell from the first time I'd encountered them that Dasani was the gate between being in and out of their crew. I wasn't offended. Keeping mob business sacred required boundaries for the men and women.

Missy ran her hand through her long, wavy frontal hair-style. It was a blondish color and looked like it had grown naturally from her scalp, flowing down to her knees. She was wearing a tan halter dress that she had to pull each time she walked, paired with platform heels that wrapped around her ankles. I wasn't familiar with the dress brand, but the shoes were Gucci, and she was gliding in them with ease. A thick diamond chain that read "Essex's Bitch" sat on her chest, which must have cost way more than the twenty thousand dollars that Shio had given me for the night.

My eyes went right to her ass as she switched to the booth, and I couldn't stop my eyes from bulging at the roundness. Women in Mexico were voluptuous, but it was usually after a visit to an operating room. Missy's body looked natural. She had one of the best bodies I'd ever seen, and when she mentioned she was a retired exotic dancer, I could see why. Placing the black oversized earphones on her head, she signaled for the man to start the beat.

Jisei snickered. "This shit about to be so funny!"

A tune I was sure I had heard some time before blared through the surround-sound speakers, but Missy missed her cue.

"Run it back! Run it back! I'm ready now." The beat restarted over as we all looked on eagerly, but Missy waved her hands. "Hold up! Stop the beat."

The guy did as he was told.

"Bring y'all ass in here. It's enough space and earphones

for us all. That way, when I say mine, y'all can jump on with yours."

"Loooord. What y'all done dragged me in?" Pia shook her head, tossed back her apple juice, and headed to the booth.

The rest of us followed suit, keeping our cups in hand. Missy was right. The room was huge, and when the door shut behind Dasani, since she was the last to enter, the sound from the outside was locked out, proving the room was indeed soundproof.

We all grabbed headphones and placed them on our heads. Missy signaled for the beat while they split up on the two microphones between us. Missy, Pia, and Dasani were on one, while Scarlett, Mocha, Jisei, and I were on the other.

The beat started, and my stomach bubbled. I'd never done anything like this and had no clue what I was doing. Hopefully, everyone would go before me so I could figure out the expectation.

"I let him give me head, then he pulled out that monster dick toooo. Ewed-ewed. But I'ma big girl, boooo. Unlike your baby mama, I can take dick, duuuuuude. Dude, Dude. That bitch smells like doo, doo! You've officially been chopped and screwed! Screwed, screwed!"

Missy sounded terrible, and all of our laughs were an indication.

"Run it back, so they can hear it!" she spoke into the microphone.

The guy behind the board did as told, and when her voice flowed through my ears, I was impressed. Seconds ago, she sounded like a wounded cat, but now, she sounded like a recording artist. Now, hearing the cadence, I kind of understood what we were doing.

"I'ma go again. Keep that, but start it over." Missy grabbed her earphones and leaned into the microphone. "I beat your ass once, but next time I'm gone dog walk youuuu. Ewed-ewed. Beat that ass, booo. You not gone know what the fuck to dooo. Ewed-ewed. When I get ahold of youuuu. I'm gone turn you every way but loose... Loose loooooose. Yes, you are screwed!"

The guy replayed the two-part track back, and by the time it was over, we were all doubled over in laughter.

"That hoe got me fucked up! I got more to say, but one of y'all can go next. I'll circle back."

"You crazy as fuck, best friend. But I'll go next."

Missy stepped back a bit so that a pregnant Pia could sing into the microphone. "My daddy loves my mama, but deep down he still wants to fuck dudesssss. Dude, dudes. But if she likes it, then I love it tooooo! Ewed-ewed. Patty boo... You've officially been chopped and screeewed."

Everyone was screaming with laughter, but I must have missed the joke. It took minutes for everyone to regroup behind Pia, and Dasani said she was up next.

"I was living my best life, but a Don hit me with some voodoo. Ewed-ewed. With some demon dick tooooo. It's okay cuz now I run shit tooooo. Ooo Ooo. He's been chopped and screwedddd. Cuz he can't sit me down if he wanted to. Ooo Ooo!"

"I know that's the fuck right, Mrs. Rinaldi!" Missy slapped hands with her while cackling.

Our side had the floor, and Scarlett was up first.

"I'm married to a nigga who gone always act a gotdamn fool. Ewed-ewed. And he strict as fuck tooooo. That nigga missing all types of screwssss! Screw Screw. But that's my lil' big booo! I've officially been chopped and screwedddd!"

"Yeah, Matteo so fuckin' mean. That nigga is the definition of *my program*. Ion see how you do it, friend!" Mocha shook her head.

"Bitch, fuck youuuu! That dick got me coo cooo. What do you know about that, boooo?"

Mocha smiled and held up a middle finger, and I giggled at their banter.

Jisei moved up to the microphone. She was the only one in shorts, but they were tastefully short and made her brown legs look extra-long.

"My nigga was on perks and was stubborn as a fucking fool. Ewed-ewed. I nearly overdosed tooooo. I had to beg my brother not to off my duuuude. Ooo Ooo. Cuz Demise is the king of loose screwssss. Ezio was almost chopped and screeeewed!"

Again, the ladies were cackling all over the microphones. I didn't get the joke again, but laughed along with them because clearly, they all had been through some stuff with the men in their lives.

I was next, and even though I had liquor courage, I didn't know how to rhyme, especially in English. However, I was going to try.

Closing my eyes, I let the words out. "I'm promised to a man who sells women, and he sells kids toooo... Ooo Ooo. I don't know what to doooo! He might fuck around and sell my ass toooo. Too, too. He's a ruthless duuuude. I can't believe my father set this up. Ooo. Ewed-ewed. Pray for me, boossss. I've officially been chopped and screwedddd!"

Pulling the earphones back, I opened my eyes and turned to the women who all had their mouths open.

"Okay, so maybe we don't add that part in there." Dasani nodded to the man through the window.

"Shit, even if we did, she doesn't need autotune. This putha can saaaang! Let me find out," Mocha added.

Scarlett and Jisei exchanged questioning looks, but I remained silent. I'd revealed too much, but so had the rest of the ladies. It just so happened that my reality was sadder than theirs.

"Okay! You need some ass shakin' after that. I'm 'bout to order a black truck to take us to the club," Missy said, shifting the mood and conversation.

The ladies exited the booth, leaving Dasani and me behind.

"You good, boo?" she asked with a sincere look on her pretty face.

Lifting my head, I nodded, slightly embarrassed.

"All right. Come on. Let's turn up!"

CHAPTER 19
SHIO CUPPACIO

I heard the front door slam shut, indicating that Solana had left to hang out with the wives. She hadn't come back to the office to say goodbye, and that was probably the smartest thing she'd done since she landed her pretty feet on American soil.

Shit had gotten extra thick in here, and I was cringing at how close my ass was to folding and taking Solana down on my desk. I'd made the first physical mistake by sitting her on my lap, but she made the first unintentional mistake by bringing her ass on my side of the house in that tight-ass dress. I knew better, though. I'd preached to all that would listen how important it was to move with reason. Logic. And my ass was in here moving like a boy who'd just hit puberty.

Solana was pushing buttons I didn't think I'd possessed. She was quiet but sassy, which kept my interest piqued. She was a natural learner, and that surprised me because I didn't meet many people who desired to be better. She looked like a plate of enchiladas straight out of the oven—immaculate and ready to be devoured at any second. I'd been around pretty women all my life, but Solana was an exotic Black beauty. She smelled perfect, even when she was sweating like a racehorse during our workouts. I had gone from dreading sharing my gym with her to looking forward to the days we exercised and ate breakfast together.

I had been keeping my feelings at bay, or whatever the fuck this was that was happening, because it'd only been a couple of weeks since she walked out of the guest room bathroom with my gun pointed at her dome. I thought I was doing a good job by doing two-a-day workouts, needing to do one by myself just to release whatever the fuck had come inside of me and placed images of Solana there. I'd even double up my workload with Don and Matteo to keep busy and out of the house, but reality had checked my ass this evening. I'd heard every voice from every person in my life telling me "no" clear as day, and I'd been listening up until two hours ago. I had to get my shit together before my dick started a war.

My dick.

That's what the problem was. I didn't like Solana. My ass just hadn't released in days. I wanted to be respectful and not bring Uriah to the crib while it was Solana's temporary residence, so I'd ignored my human need. I needed to bust two nuts, and the sooner the better. I'm sure afterward, I'd be straight to continue this roommate situation.

Going to the lounge chair, I twisted one of the buttons in opposite directions until I heard a click. The chair seat opened and displayed rows of rubber-banded money. I'd asked Preston to help me with this custom safe, and he'd significantly delivered. Putting all the money Solana and I had just counted inside the chair base, I updated my logs, closed the chair back on its base, and stood.

Seeing my personal phone vibrating on my desk, I walked over to see that Vello was FaceTiming me. I hadn't heard much from him outside of business, and I knew it was because those twins were occupying his time. I was happy for him and Discover. Between the engagement and the twins' arrival, I'd say Vello was on track to be an official member of the Rinaldi Mob. Pia was deep in wedding planning, so Nel was close too. It was now on me to ensure I fulfilled my obligation and got myself a fucking wife. Shaking my head, I thought about Glow and Tunan. Not having the mental space to even think about that shit, I shook my head again to clear the two from my frontal.

Chuckling, I answer the phone. "Yes?"

"Yo'! You going to the Dungeon later tonight? Nel said they gettin' together since the wives went out."

"I ain't heard shit, but I'll slide through."

"You probably ain't heard shit cuz you over there reading the Bible and looking at that Hispanic girl's ass!" Vello roared into the phone. "At the same time too!"

I ain't have time for this nigga's antics tonight. I had one destination in mind, and if time permitted, I'd swing by the Dungeon after.

When I didn't reply, Vello kept jesting me. "Oh, you on mute now? It's all good. I know your ass over there, fuckin' her in your mind and shit." Before he could say anything else, I heard Discover saying something in the background. "Aite, Big Mama. Text me pictures so ion get the wrong shit. Aye, Shio... I'll catch up with y'all later. I gotta go to the store for *my wife*."

I could hear the smirk on his face when he said, "my wife." Niggas were clowns. Just months ago, they were in my house crying and bitching about the Don's, their women, and our duties that had to be fulfilled to become authentic mobsters.

"Yeah. Later." I hung up the phone and headed to my room to shower and change.

Everyone had jokes about my current predicament, but if

any of those fools had been in my shoes, Don would be sending out SOS signals to allies to help him with the Ledesma Cartel's declaration of war.

I wonder if that's why that slick-ass nigga gave Ines the okay to send Solana to my house? Did his ass want a war or was he trying to prevent one that was already brewing in Mexico. Whatever the fuck Demise had up his sleeve was costing me my fucking peace, and I ain't like the shit.

A conversation would need to happen soon if he expected me to keep this shit going. Today was only the first strike, and I had a plan to cease any further attraction between Solana and me. But the problem was that my plan was weak as shit. I was relying on my dick when I'd always relied on my mind and intuition. The problem there was that my mind was consistently showing me signs that Solana needed to get took. Still, I was going to try my shitty plan if it meant I could continue sharing space with the Mexican princess without wanting to beat her shit in. At this point, I was no better than my clown-ass cousins.

"Shio? You heard me?"

The gentleness and softness of Uriah's voice made me shift my gaze from the late-night traffic below. Horns, headlights, and engine exhaust could be heard, smelled, and seen from up here on the thirteenth floor. Pulling from the blunt that was perched between my lips, I took a long drag. Tomorrow was Sunday, so I needed to get my herbal fix now. Leaning back in the chair that I was relaxed in, I blew out the fumes once my lungs could no longer hold onto the marijuana.

"I said, 'When are you coming in?' I've been out of the shower for over an hour."

With lowered eyes, I peered at Uriah's black toenails. I wasn't a fan of the color choice against her skin tone, but the clear six-inch pumps she was standing in made up for it. Balancing her weight, she pressed a hand to her hip, showing the gap between her thighs. We were on the thirteenth floor, but she was standing outside in a red lace bra and panty set like there wasn't a building of condos across the street. Uriah looked fucking good. Her hips and ass were swallowing the panties, and unlike the black polish, this did look good on her chocolate skin. Her breasts were spilling out of the bra, and she must've used some quality body oil because her flat stomach, legs, and all the other exposed parts of her body were glistening. Uriah was fine as fuck—so fine that my dick should have been standing at full attention, especially since it had been a minute and my reason for chopping it up with her was to bust some much-needed nuts.

Taking another hit from the weed, I repeated the notion of holding it in before releasing it; this time, I blew the smoke in her direction, the cloud temporarily blocking her. Her hair was in some drooping curls that hung down her back, and I could tell she had just gotten it done.

"Shio, no. Please put the weed out. I just got this done. Come to the bedroom." She was begging. She'd actually been begging me to come inside for over an hour. This had been her fifth attempt to get me inside. While I was enjoying the view, I was also low-key stalling. I wanted to run up in Uriah; I just wasn't sure if my body would cooperate since I'd had no urge since getting here over an hour ago.

"I'll get it fixed again," I stated lowly, and I would. I never left Uriah without hitting her off with some bread.

With one hand on her hip, she ran the finger on her other hand across her glossed lips as she looked at me as if it were dinner time. Uriah had the sexual appetite of a man; or at least when it came to me, she did. I never had to do too much; she always looked good, smelled good, was wet and willing to do whatever the fuck I wanted. I didn't have to work for it. I'd never put my mouth on her, and she hadn't even fucking asked me to. It wasn't like I would if she had worked up the courage to ask. She was just willing to go along with whatever, and I was sure she got what she needed from my dick.

"Come on, Shio. Please..." She poked her lip.

"Don't beg no nigga for shit, Uriah," I spoke in an octave higher than my own due to the smoke still infiltrating my system.

She groaned. "But I'm horny."

And I'm not.

But I didn't tell her that, though. I was the one who had hit her up after my realization earlier. I caught her out with her friends, and she was so used to me calling at sporadic times that she already had a bag in her trunk and was ready to meet me at whatever location I sent her.

I was starting to feel like the twins with the way my mind was stirring shit up. I low-key needed to get my shit off to prove to myself that ole girl wasn't as great as my inner being was telling me she was. Now that it was time for me to do my part in telling my mind to shut the fuck up, I was chilling like I was at a Fourth of July barbecue. Uriah was here and ready to get the job done. I should have been standing at attention from the moment I saw her in the hotel lobby, and if not then, at least now, since she'd changed into the red getup. But all I'd been able to think about was Solana's red toes, and telling my cousins we had to go to war because I needed to stick my dick in the Mexican princess.

"Don't matter. Lesson number five: ask always but beg never."

Uriah's cute face drew back in confusion. "*Lesson?*"

Reaching my arm down beside me, I put the blunt out on the concrete. "Come on."

I forgot who I was talking to for a moment. That was the reason I'd come out here to smoke in the first place. Solana Ledesma had entered my thoughts and hadn't left yet since early today. I had no good reason to be thinking about her ass all day like I had been, but I couldn't fucking help it, and tonight had done nothing but make me admit to myself what was happening. That's why I needed to fuck Uriah. She was my last hope in pushing Solana back into the safe zone.

Standing tall and looming over Uriah despite her heels, her breasts pressed against my chest as I looked down at her. Her body trembled against mine, and lust flickered across her face. She'd washed her body clean but kept her makeup on. It didn't matter to me, though, because she wouldn't be messing up my sheets tonight.

Moving past her, I removed my Dior T-shirt as I walked into the suite, tossing it on the chair nearby. Next were my Jordan 1s Retro Dior sneakers, and then my Audemars watch, which I placed on the dresser.

"Want me to keep my heels on?" Uriah moaned as she snaked her body inside from the balcony. Each step she took, I could see her ass wobble from the front.

Instead of answering her, I watched as she came to the side of the bed where I was standing and dropped to her knees.

I'd told my people that I wasn't fucking with Solana. I stayed on my side of the house while she stayed confined to her room. When she first got there, I'd watched her like a hawk on the cameras and laughed seeing how she'd jam the accent chair against the door as she slept, bathed, and dressed in the closet. She spent equal amounts of time in the bathroom and closet as she did in bed. I wasn't no freaked-out nigga, so I didn't have cameras in the bathroom and closet to see what she was doing, but knowing how the mob wives, my mom, and aunts acted, I wasn't concerned about her behaviors of wanting to be alone. She also was traumatized from being dumped here, so if she found some solace in the ten-by-ten closet, I wasn't going to question it.

The more comfortable she got, the more she showed her feisty personality. Solana had snapped at a nigga plenty of times, especially during her workouts. I would catch the wrath of her frustration, but the work was proving foolproof today in the lounge dress. She'd fucking thrown up every damn workout session the first few times. Her hair was usually a mess and had only been tamed since the engagement party. She was untidy. She slept too fucking much. She was timid as hell. Yet, I couldn't get her out of my fucking head.

"I've been missing the fuck out of this big-ass dick." Uriah was fumbling with my belt and jeans, and without even lowering my boxer briefs, she began licking up and down the material of my underwear. That alone should have had my fucking toes curling, but I was standing here mentally battling myself like my name was Kanye. The weed had my body feeling lighter and more relaxed, but I was still fucking tense. I was still fucking thinking about the forbidden Afro Mexicana.

Uriah reached her soft hand inside my briefs, pulled my dick out, and placed it on her tongue. Taking it further inside her mouth, she let me feel her tonsils, leaving my dick glistening with her saliva when she pulled back from it. Her brows furrowed, more than likely wondering why the hell my dick was still flaccid, so I closed my eyes and tried to concentrate. No sooner than I saw the black of my lids, long, thick black hair, smooth dark skin, wide hips, and a birthmark on the left side of her chin came into view. None of the physical attributes belonged to Uriah.

Solana.

My dick bricked in an instant, catching Uriah by surprise and causing her to gag. Her reflex felt good as fuck, squeezing the tip of my dick. I began pumping in and out of her mouth ferociously. I had a point to prove. I needed to fuck the shit out of Uriah to take my mind out of uncharted waters. Yet, the only thing that was making my toes curl was the Mexican beauty that left my house in a dress so short and tight, I wanted to yell out of one of the front house cameras' speakers and tell her to bring her ass back in the house tonight.

My pelvis slapped up against Uriah's face as I used her throat as if it were her pussy, and when she couldn't keep up, I snatched out of her, stating, "Bend over."

Keeping my eyes closed, I could hear Uriah assuming the position. Grabbing my dick, I placed it to her opening, picturing Solana's wide ass bent over.

Popping my eyes open just as I touched the opening of her pussy, I stopped myself. I was about to go inside of Uriah raw —some shit I'd never done. Shaking my head, I grabbed a condom from the nightstand and slid it on.

"My tubes are tied. You could have went in bare," Uriah mumbled.

Slapping her ass, I felt my dick growing soft, so I closed my eyes again. As soon as Solana came back into view, I slid inside of Uriah. Her pussy muscles hugged me, driving me further inside. Lifting my white beater, I pounded the pussy, feeling my body tingle all over.

"Ohhh, Shio! This dick is the best!"

I shushed her, not wanting to lose focus on the visual that was keeping my dick hard.

Waves of pleasure rocked through me as I felt the force of my dick being pushed out. She'd come. Feeling blood rush to the tip, I snatched out of her, removed the rubber, and she was on her knees, taking me down her throat without me asking.

"Fuck…"

Her throat tensed, but she swallowed all of my fucking kids as I released in her mouth. Sweat formed at my hairline as I came down from my orgasmic high. It had been a short fuck, but she got hers, and I got mine. I was so in my head that I wasn't even tripping about my DNA going down her throat. Usually, that shit was a no-go.

Opening my eyes, I stepped back, removing my dick from her jaws, and pulled my boxers back up. I couldn't even look at Uriah. My conscience was calling me a fuck nigga because I'd used her body as if she were a hired escort.

"Why didn't we do this at your house like always?" she asked, breaking the uncomfortable silence.

I heard Uriah climbing into bed as I continued to dress, avoiding her face. Once my pants were on, I stepped back into my Js. I hadn't nutted in the condom, but still, I went and flushed it down the toilet. The bathroom was still warm from Uriah's shower, and if it hadn't been for the smell of her body wash and the fog on the mirror, I wouldn't have known she'd taken one. The bathroom was as neat as the housekeepers had it when we first entered. Walking back into the room, Uriah had removed her heels and was under the covers, pointing the remote at the TV.

"You didn't answer my question, Shio."

"I know, Uriah." I sighed as I scooped my watch from the dresser table and clasped it on my wrist. Grabbing my unwrinkled shirt, I pulled it over my head and skimmed the room one last time to make sure I hadn't left anything.

She sat up in bed. Uriah usually didn't question me about shit, so it was blowing me that she was doing it now, especially when I was already frustrated. She didn't deserve a nigga's bad energy, though, which was why I was about to take my ass home. Fuck the Dungeon; my ass needed to think. That nut I'd wanted hadn't done shit but told me what I already knew: I'd fucked up.

"I can't go to your house because *Solana* is there. Right?"

Before I could blink, I had my gun resting on Uriah's forehead. Her hands shot straight up, dropping the remote on the white duvet. Her eyes watered while I mugged her.

"What the fuck you just say?" My body shook as I barked out the question.

Her lips trembled, but I wasn't for that shit. Tapping her forehead with the gun, I grazed my bottom lip with my top teeth. "Run that shit back, Uriah."

"I... I said... that, that Solana must be at your house."

"And how the fuck do you know about *Solana*?"

Uriah and I fucked occasionally, but she didn't know shit about me at all, outside of what my dick tasted like. Her bringing up Solana would be the very reason she wouldn't see her kids again.

"B... Because! When you were coming... You said, '*Solana.*'" She cried immediately after shouting her response.

Staggering back with the gun still pointed at her, I ran back to seconds ago. "Nah... I said, 'Uriah.'" I was trying to convince my damn self.

Snot was coming from Uriah's nose as her face was now drenched with tears. "No! No! You said, 'Fuck... *Solana!*' That's what you said, Shio!"

Had I called her Solana?

Thinking back to the only time Uriah had the opportunity to know Solana's name, I realized her name hadn't been said. I was careful always, but even more meticulous that day Uriah was topping me off, and Solana had come out of the guest bathroom in that fucking towel.

I hadn't said her name. She hadn't said her name. That meant I was tweaking like a motherfucker tonight, and as I'd assumed earlier, my shitty-ass plan was indeed shitty. I should've never hit Uriah up on this type of time.

"Is... Is that the girl who was at your house? Is that *Solana*?"

"Aye, shut up." I needed silence for two seconds.

My gun was still lifted, and I had my finger on the trigger. This whole fucking situation had a nigga out of body. I didn't like that shit. I didn't like not knowing what the end result of all of this would be. I didn't like the fact that I knew there would be bloodshed. And I didn't like the fact that when I thought of the wife that I had to have, Solana's lazy, moody ass came to mind.

A woman who was already promised to another man.

"So, you... You were thinking about her while you were fucking me? Why, Shio?"

Uriah looked fucking pitiful. Here she was on the other side of my gun, and instead of asking me to lower the shit, she was asking me about another woman. Women were a trip.

"Why not just go to Solana, Shio?"

Hearing her name raised the hairs on the back of my neck, and my dick stiffened again.

"Aye, don't say her name again, yo'." I didn't like the way my body reacted to hearing it. Why was this shit happening? I was king of self-disciplined. How the fuck had this shit happened in less than a calendar month?

"I'm just saying! Why would you call me *her* name? Why would you put a gun to my head? I haven't done anything! I thought you were a man of God! You wear that chain, but here you are about to kill me! That's a sin."

Tucking my gun into my waist, I fastened my jeans, then my belt. Giving a hysterical Uriah one look over, I licked my lips. "And fuckin' you outta wedlock is a sin too. Yet, you fall all over this dick anytime I call. Bye, Uriah."

Leaving the room, I shook my head all the way down to the

lobby. I nearly caught a body without a silencer in a busy hotel, all because she mentioned Solana.

God first.
Make sure the family good.
Eye them Cuppacio boys, the little and the big ones.
Build a relationship with my brother.
Get my brother rich.
Health and wellness.
Stay on top of my mob shit.
Keep Hobo alive.
~~Get through the meeting with Ines Ledesma.~~
~~House a random.~~
Find the true reason Solana is here.
Figure out if Solana is supposed to be my wife.

I HAD to get my head back in the game. The list was becoming longer with hardly anything accomplished. It was time to stop churning my thoughts and figure some shit out. I guess I was headed to the Dungeon after all. But first, I had to go to the crib and wash Uriah's juices off a nigga.

CHAPTER 20

SOLANA DAMITA LEDESMA

It had been over a month since I'd been in the club, and I had to admit that partying with these ladies felt different. I usually partied with tourists or strangers at the clubs back home because I had no friends. But here, these women made me feel more at ease than I ever had around the women in Mexico. My own stepmother acted like I was the worst thing to ever come into her life, which made me question if all women were like that. These women proved me wrong. We were at a strip club called Passion. We sat in a section with three stunning women, who were dancing for us. Their bodies were like a work of art, and seeing their naked bodies pop, lock, and gyrate had my body rising a few degrees. The DJ announced Missy's name several times throughout the night. The bright lights, sparkles, dollars, and endless bottles made me feel like I was on top of the world.

From the moment we walked in the doors, and I spotted a familiar face, I knew my night had just gotten an upgrade. I'd excused myself from the women, paid my new friend a visit, went to the bathroom to freshen up, and had been on a high

416

ever since. The booth we were in was elevated, with a metal railing lining the section. Glorilla blasted through the speakers, and every fiber in my body stood to attention. Running past the strippers, I gripped the railing and bent over, not caring that my entire ass was out as I shook to the beat. The skirt I was wearing had shorts attached, but still, I felt nothing but cool air as I clapped my cheeks to the beat.

"Ahhh shit! Mexicana can get the fuck down!" Mocha yelled.

"Fuck 'em up, boo!" Missy egged on.

Everything around me was enhanced. The blue and red lights lining the ceiling were the most vibrant I'd ever seen in a strip club. The sound of the DJ wasn't just noise; it was a texture that I could almost reach out and touch. The base was so crispy as if I was inside the speakers, bumping along. I felt a hand slap on my ass and it had me bending over further, grabbing my ankles, and moaning at the same time.

Soft arms wrapped around my waist, and when I looked back and saw Missy, I grinned and kept dancing. Mocha moved behind Missy, then Jisei and Scarlett, and then Dasani followed. Pia stood to the side, sipping from a water bottle, her chocolate skin glowing as she recorded us. The seven of us ground against each other while the bass pulsed through our veins. I could feel sweat dripping from my pores, but I was having too much fun to care. The night was still young, and so were we. The more I danced, the more vibrant the colors seemed, and everything began to blur together. My head was spinning, but clear at the same time. I'd tossed out five thousand of the dollars I'd gotten from Shio and planned to rain plenty more. Why not? There was more where it came from. He told me to enjoy my time here, so that's exactly what I was going to do.

This was life, and even though it would be short-lived, I

was making the most of it. Right here, dancing in a train of stunning women, I made a vow that I was done moping. My life was my own. Yes, I would follow my father's orders, but I wouldn't lose myself in the process. I was going to live my life without fear, worry, or doubt. Whatever happened, happened. All I could do was show up as myself and pray that my future husband had even an ounce of compassion that these Americans had shown me in the last couple of weeks. I wouldn't know a life of torment and misery once I made it back to Mexico, or at least, that was my hope. I knew every day couldn't and wouldn't feel like this one, and I knew there was more to life than partying, but partying was when I felt the most free. I was able to dance without worry, drink until I vomited, and ride the high of the tallest cloud. I loved this moment.

Horns blaring jolted me from my movements, and all the ladies removed their arms from our makeshift train, but when I realized it was just the sound effects the DJ was making, I fanned myself and kept swaying my hips.

"Here, boo! Cool off some. You sweatin' real bad." Mocha twisted the top off a bottle of water while Pia used a napkin to dab at my face, careful not to smear my makeup.

Jisei had even brought a portable fan and was blowing it all over my body until I looked like I was at a comfortable temperature. The way these ladies were looking out for me had me overwhelmed with emotion, so I pulled them all into a hug. "Thank you so much, chicas. ¡Gracias! ¡Gracias!" My voice cracked on the last thank you, but I exhaled to keep myself together.

"We take care of our own, boo. No thanks needed. Plus, I like your little Spanish ass!" Dasani teased.

Letting them go, I turned around with a smile so big that it lit up the already bright room. The ladies all took spots beside me, placing Dasani in the middle, with me on her right. We all were rocking to the beat of a rapper I didn't recognize, but the ladies knew him because they'd been rapping word for word.

"You know that lil' nigga came by my daddy's house?" Pia voiced loudly so that we could all hear her.

"Who?" Mocha inquired.

"Him—the one rapping this song, Flexer. I guess Mahzeyah calls herself talkin' to him. I watched their asses *all* night. His ass had on more jewelry than a light show."

"Yeah, he's getting to it," Jisei added.

"Don't let it get back to Matteo. He will be down Pearla's throat like the boy was there for her." Scarlett shook her head, and some of the ladies chuckled.

"Girl, right. I hate that Grind is in a coma, but that's probably the best thing for now. My sister hasn't quite gotten back to herself, but at least she's sworn off love. I had to tell her, Bella, and Mahzeyah that the last thing they want is a baby. Not until they have lived their lives at least and found a man worthy to procreate with," Pia preached as she rubbed her belly.

I didn't know anything about the business they were referencing, so I kept my mouth closed and sipped my water. I was still smiling at the affection they'd shown me. I was having a ball, and their company was proving to me that I'd been missing true feminine friendship back home.

"I hate like hell she's gotten with a rapper! But all I could do was give her some game. Essex don't play those games with me, but he's also older than Flexer. Flexer is young, and there will be a *plethora* of bitches. My words went in one ear and out the other, but they all gon' have to learn like we had to." Missy shrugged.

"True..." Dasani added, and that ended the conversation.

Scanning the club, I kept dancing while I stayed seated.

Just as the DJ changed songs again, a shiver swept through me. I felt eyes watching me, but hadn't yet located them. There had to be at least three hundred people in the club, not including the naked dancers. As I was about to head to the side table to grab the bottle for a shot, anxiety spurted through me. My stomach felt as if someone was holding me upside down, saliva pooled in my mouth, and my world began to spin. I had to grip the rail to avoid falling backward.

Eyes so cold that they should have been blue instead of brown burned through me; it physically felt like I was being engraved with a laser. His goatee was short, and the mustache above his top lip wasn't much fuller. His hair was tapered on the sides, while the top fell loosely in lazy curls. His skin resembled wafers and was marked up with tattoos running from his neck to his wrists. He was dressed in all black—a fitted V-cut T-shirt on the upper half and black jeans on the lower half. A thick diamond necklace hung from his neck, and even though his outfit wasn't much, I knew it was all designer, and the diamonds spoke what the plain clothing didn't. I couldn't see his sneakers, but I knew they were black as well. There were four other men beside him, and three of them I knew were his brothers. My heart dropped into the soles of my shoes when I realized that the fourth man wasn't one of his siblings, but mine.

"I know I'm married as fuck, and I love Lorenzo down. I don't fuck outside of my race, but damn, those dudes are fine as fuck over there," Mocha complimented.

"Where? What dudes?" Pia asked out of curiosity.

"Right there. I don't know if they're white or Italian or whatever, but they got the swag of a black nigga."

"They're Mexican. The one in the middle has a Mexico chain." Scarlett hit the nail on the hammer.

Or was it hammer on nail?

"Solana..." Dasani called out, but I was too stuck to look away, lost in my mind of swirling thoughts. "Solana, boo! How do you say, 'YN...' well... 'young nigga' in Spanish?"

"Negro joven," I spoke loud enough for her to hear me, but I didn't know if I had even given her the correct translation. My heart was racing with the power of an F1 car.

"Well, them some fine ass joven negros!" she yelled out, and the ladies fell into a fit of giggles and laughs.

I felt a hand on my shoulder pull me away from the stare off. Scarlett's face appeared, and she had her phone in her hand with a concerned look etched on her face.

"Solana... Do you know them?"

Nodding, I pulled away from her and looked back at him.

He hadn't taken his eyes off me in that brief moment.

"Si. That's my fiancé. Excuse me, ladies."

I didn't want him coming into the section, causing problems with the nicest women I'd ever encountered. So, I was going to him. Two bulky security guys had been guarding the booth, but that meant nothing to the man I was set to marry. He'd not only kill the men in a club full of people, but he'd also hurt the ladies.

"Gotdamn her fiancé fine as a muthafucka! If that nigga kidnapping women and shit, I don't really think it's kidnapping, y'all. Them hoes going with him willingly," I heard Mocha yell.

Moving through the crowd with my heart drumming so hard that it made my head rattle, I didn't stop until I was in front of him. I should have known when I didn't answer for my father, someone would show up. I didn't think it would be the Rodríguezes and Esteban, my eldest brother, born two years after me. We had never been close because his mother had drilled into all my siblings' heads that I was nothing more than the daughter of a dead whore.

"*¿Sabe papá que estás en el club bailando como una puta?* (Does father know that you are in the club dancing like a whore?)" My brother was the first to speak.

The ringleader held his hand up, silencing my brother, who zipped his lips like the puppet he was. Not even acknowledging Esteban, I kept my eyes on the man I was set to marry.

"*¿Por qué estás en el club en lugar de en mi cama, esposa?* (Why are you in the club instead of in my bed, wife?) He reached up as if he was going to touch my face, but paused.

Felipe Rodríguez was easy on the eyes. All the Rodríguezes were attractive, but their reputation preceded them. Despite his good looks, there was nothing about him that was desirable. He was a ruthless, cold-hearted individual, and the day his father gave him the kingdom would be a sad day in Mexico City. Things hadn't gotten nearly as bad until Felipe came of age. It was said that he would be ten times worse than his father, and his joy came from causing everyone else pain.

Taking a step back, I squinted my eyes. "*Todavía no soy tu esposa. Soy libre de ir a donde quiera.* (I am not your wife yet. I'm free to go where I want.)"

He took two steps forward and grabbed my arm, digging his nails into my skin and pulling me toward him. I bumped into a girl, who spilled her drink, but didn't get a chance to apologize.

Felipe gritted his teeth as he pressed his nails further into my flesh. "*¿Con quién carajo te crees que estás hablando? ¿Crees que solo porque tu padre te envió a América te liberas de mí? ¡Me perteneces, perra! ¡Me respetarás o me casaré contigo hoy y acabaré con la pequeña libertad que crees tener!* (Who the fuck do you think you are talking to? Do you think just because your father sent you to America that you are free of me? I own you, bitch! You will respect me, or I'll marry you today and end the little piece of freedom you think you have!)"

A blinding red light had Felipe's men reaching for their guns, but they came up short. The club must've denied them entry with their weapons, so they had to come in without them. Following the red dot, Felipe released me and took a step back.

"Nah... Back the fuck back a few more paces, my nigga."

I'd never been so happy to hear Shio's voice. The club immediately began to clear out in an orderly fashion, as if seeing Shio with a big gun was a normal sighting. He was no longer in the lounge clothes I'd seen him wearing at the house. Unlike Felipe, he was dressed all in white. His white Dolce & Gabbana jeans fit perfectly, cuffed right at the top of his pure white Dolce & Gabbana sneakers. The matching Dolce & Gabbana T-shirt hugged his six-pack, showing he put in work in both the gym and the kitchen. The Jesus piece he once wore had been replaced with a thick diamond chain, I'd never seen him wear, with a cross hanging from it.

Felipe didn't move another inch but kept his eyes on Shio.

"*Esteban, pregúntale a este americano por qué juega con su vida interrumpiendo los asuntos de marido y mujer.* (Esteban, ask this American why is he playing with his life by interrupting the affairs of husband and wife?)

Felipe didn't speak English, so he was asking my brother to translate. Esteban swallowed, looking every inch like his mother, then looked at Shio and me before clearing his throat.

"He wants to know..." He started, trying to keep his voice steady. "Why are you interrupting the conversation he is having with his wife, and says that you are playing with your life by doing so."

My brother knew Shio was fluent in Spanish. He witnessed it at our dinner table just as I had. I didn't know why he hadn't informed Felipe instead of translating, but I kept my mouth shut.

Shio cocked his head. "Wife? Nigga, what wife?"

The color drained from my face as my brother translated, and Felipe turned a shade of red. Shio wasn't done, though.

"Solana... Hold your left hand up for me, back side showing."

Without hesitation, I did as Shio said. I could see steam rising from Felipe.

"I don't see no fucking ring. You ain't got no wife up in here."

Esteban translated, and I could have sworn Felipe grew horns.

"*Te equivocas, estadounidense. Solana está dispuesta a casarse conmigo. ¡Es mía y llevará mi apellido y mi linaje!* (You are mistaken, American. Solana is arranged to be wed to me. She is mine and will bear my last name and carry my lineage!)

I had to hold in my throw up as my brother delivered the message to Shio, who already knew what Felipe had said. My nerves were shot, and I wanted to look back to make sure the ladies were safe, but my head was ringing too loudly to move an inch.

Shio, who was standing alone against five men, tossed his head back in laughter. I could see his muscled abdomen tighten as he chuckled. This was my third time seeing him with a gun in his hand, and even though it wasn't pointed at me, it still made my panties damp. Felipe's rage and the thought of the punishment I'd face someday didn't even cross my mind.

With his free hand, Shio used his thumb to flick his nose. Holding his hand in front of the sexy smirk that graced his face, he flicked the ring on his middle finger with the same thumb.

"I tell you what..." He looked Felipe square in the eyes and lowered his gun. "If you can call her name and she comes to you, I'll get out of your business, and she's free to go with you, *ese* (man)."

My brother's face dropped as he repeated Shio's words to Felipe. Felipe nodded once and shifted his attention to me. A menacing grin covered his face and made my skin feel as if needles were pricking me all over.

"*Solana, ya sabes dónde estás. ¡Vamos o si no!* (Solana, you know your place. Let's go or else.)"

My spirits were out of tempo with the tense drawn face that greeted me. I'd been having the time of my life until Felipe and his *grupo* (posse) showed up. I couldn't control the spasmodic trembling within me. I'd felt like I was about to pass out until Shio's words came.

"Solana, baby... Let's go home."

Not even looking at Felipe any longer, I turned on my heels and walked into Shio. Wrapping his hand around the back of my neck, but this time much more gently than the day he found me at his home, he pulled me into his chest and stared down at me. I couldn't control my breath as we engaged in a stare-off. He was so fucking handsome, smelled so good, and made me feel so safe. Letting my neck go, he reached behind me and pulled my skirt down.

With my chest still pressed against Shio's, he broke our gaze and shifted his attention back to Felipe. "Like I said, you ain't got no wife up in here. I suggest y'all go back to CDMX because being out here not gon' do nuttin' but speed up ya death date."

My brother didn't translate, the men understanding the threat within the foreign language. I heard them retreating until Shio's body relaxed, indicating they had exited. He grabbed my neck again, but this time more of my collar. His eyes searched mine until he lifted my chin and tilted my head back.

"You good?"

I nodded, still too rattled to speak.

"Not my nigga goin' toe to toe with Joker, Lil' Joker, and Baby Joker. Mexi-Mami, what type of shit you got goin' on?" Renello was chewing on a piece of chicken from the platter Jisei had ordered, while the rest of the men stood behind their women. Even their Don was here, holding onto Dasani as if someone was going to steal her. Metavello was also present, even though Discover was at home with their newborn children.

"You good, Shio? Them niggas gon' be a problem?" Essex asked as he wrapped his arms around Missy's waist, who was slowly moving her hips against him as if music was playing.

"Yeah, are they gone be a problem?" their Don probed. He was the only one in a three-piece suit while the rest of the men were in casual clothes.

Shio grabbed my hand. "Ion know. You tell me, Don."

Their Don chuckled. "Yeah, nigga... Aite."

"Aye, we know you just had a baby, so when are you cutting them fuck-ass hospital bands off? Ma told you that shit country as fuck!" Renello scolded his brother, while Shio escorted me out of the club.

His gun was still at his side as I carefully held my balance in my high heels. My legs were starting to feel wobbly as the adrenaline fought like hell to lower itself within me. Even as we made it outside, the cool night air wasn't enough to calm me. I'd disrespected the man I was to spend the rest of my life with for one I knew I had no chance with. Shio and I were from two different worlds, and I knew as much as my father loved me, he would kill me before he allowed me to go against his word. Our family had been minimized because of my papa getting rid of those who defied his word or didn't agree with his plans. I knew the consequences of my actions, yet I felt no ounce of regret. If I could do it all over again, I'd go to Shio whenever he called my name. I'd never felt more protected, more seen, and more respected than I had when I was around this American boy and his American people.

Shio's Maybach was parked on the curve in front of the club. Behind him was a mini line of exotic cars. He held me inside his right arm and took his time getting to the passenger seat. I wanted to crawl into this skin with how comforted I felt in the moment. When we got to the car, he helped me inside before circling the car and dropping inside. He placed his gun on the back seat and slouched in the driver's seat. I expected him to drive off with rubber burning, but he sat there, calm, cool, and collected like he hadn't just opened a can of snakes. Or fucking worms with the way he'd handled them.

"Shio, are you going to drive?"

"Nah, not yet. I'm waiting on my people."

I began to shift in my seat, looking around to see if I could spot Felipe.

"Solana, baby..." His words were like silk against skin after a long, hot shower. "They not gone fuck with you. You hear me?"

Looking into his eyes, I nodded.

Reaching over, he grabbed my neck and pulled me across the console into his face. I gasped as I dangled across the car like a rag doll. I'd never been more turned on before in my existence except earlier today in his lap.

"He's not going to fuck with you. Not now. Not ever. Do you believe that I got you?"

Tucking my bottom lip in my mouth, I nodded.

Shio's eyes roamed my face and stopped at my lips. Using his thumb, he pressed down on my chin until my bottom lip was free. "Lesson number six... Real niggas do real shit. I got you, Solana. No matter where the fuck you are in the world, just know... I got you. This is the last time that nigga will ever put his fuckin' hands on you. Had I been one minute earlier, that shit wouldn't have happened, but I got there as quick as I could after Scarlett called."

He caressed my face with his thumb, making my body shudder. "I'm a disciplined man. But you're the candy store, and I'm the fucking kid, Solana."

Then, it happened. Shio pecked my lips once, then twice, then three times before sucking my tongue into his mouth. My eyes closed as I moaned into his mouth, nipples hardening, honey pot dripping, and body feeling as if it was floating.

"Sweet as fuck. Like candy. I know that pussy sweeter."

Pressure built in the pit of my stomach, my legs went stiff, and my panties flooded as he continued to wrestle with my tongue. My body felt like it had been relieved of something that I'd been holding for a long time as my kitty thudded rapidly until it released.

Ring ring riiiiing

Ring ring riiiiing

My phone interrupted the euphoria coursing through my body as I felt instantly relaxed from the release Shio gave me with his mouth on my mouth. He pulled back, and I slid back into my seat. There was a tap on his window, and then lights shone through the car while engines roared around us. His people had finally come out.

"Get the phone, Solana, baby."

Still stunned by the kiss, I couldn't move. Shio reached over me, pulled my seat belt on, grabbed my purse from the floor, and removed my phone.

It was my father again.

Shio slid his thumb across it to answer and handed me the phone. I took it, and at the same time, Shio pulled into traffic.

"H... Hola, Papa?"

"Solana. You have an appointment Monday, there in the

States. A driver will come to get you. Are you well?"

Looking over at Shio, who was weaving through traffic, I licked my lips and nodded as if my father could see me.

"Yes, Papa. I'm well. I'll be ready to go Monday. Gracias."

My father ended the call, and it was baffling to me that he hadn't mentioned sending my fiancé or my brother. That may have meant that my father didn't know they were in America. I was more confused than I had been when they had basically kidnapped me from my front door, thrown me on the plane, and dropped me at Shio's. I was starting to question everything and everybody except the man driving smoothly on the road as if he didn't just threaten people's lives over me.

My life was a mess, but with this man by my side, I was determined to thrive in the chaos, even if it meant facing the inevitable crash. But not everyone died when hit by a Mack truck. I just hoped whatever hit us when it did, we were prepared.

CHAPTER 21
SHIO CUPPACIO

The silence in the car was loud, but my thoughts were louder. It had only been half an hour since I'd shown up at the club and faced off with Vato 'nem. I wasn't surprised to see the Rodríguezes in Jagoda Bay. In fact, I would have been shocked if they hadn't shown up eventually.

When Scarlett hit my line, I hadn't even answered good before I was marching out of the Dungeon. My family, except for Vello, was right behind me. That nigga had been on a store run for some nipple cream that Discover had requested and never made it to Don's spot. Not knowing what they might walk into, everyone was still in their car, ready to roll. That's how it had been since before us Cuppacios got to Jagoda Bay. Now with the Rinaldi Mob, we had even more niggas ready to bust for the most minor problem. Don had even tagged along, which made sense since all the mob wives had all been together tonight. Metavello had made it to the club after getting word from Discover that something was going down. Our grapevine worked quickly, especially with the wives and all their fucking group chats.

I'd met up with the guys after showering Uriah off me. She'd pissed me off by trying to throw God up in my face, knowing damn well she was far from perfect. I was wrong for calling her Solana, but the theatrics were off. Uriah was never my lady; she'd always been a fuck, and she understood that when she agreed to be on-call for my needs. The sudden switch up was foreign to me, and although I wasn't no disrespectful-ass nigga, her trying to invade my personal life by asking questions was where I drew the line.

When I walked into the Dungeon, everyone took one look at me and knew I was going through it with Solana's fine ass occupying my space. I knew I'd crossed the line by being as close as we were tonight, which is why I thought I just needed to fuck something and nut my problems away. As much shit as I talked about my cousins, I was out here doing the same dumbass shit. I knew better, and I'd promised everyone around me that I was disciplined enough. That alone was telling me Solana was more than a house guest. She had me doing shit I'd never done and had me feeling shit I'd never felt. Solana stayed locked in her room when she wasn't working out with me, but even with the limited time we shared, I ended up feeling something for her ass.

She was pretty but lazy, stubborn yet obedient, and confident yet unaware of her impact on those around her. She didn't have any ambition to save my life or hers. She spent her days sleeping and out of sight. Still, I'd managed to see the parts of her that her father had kept under lock and key. She was eager to learn. In fact, discovering new things pushed her forward. She also didn't like to be defeated. No matter how much she hated working out, she didn't quit, even if she had to take a hundred breaks. Her beauty? Her beauty was unmatched.

Her body was sick as fuck. She had natural curves that were

defined over the last couple of weeks. Her eyes carried innocence that tugged at my chest every time I looked into them. When her father called tonight, it felt like a sign from God. I'd been silently praying for a sign, and I guess he'd delivered swiftly. I promised her father, Don, and my brothers that I wouldn't fall for her, and like a man on the edge of a cliff, I nearly slipped. I had no regrets about confronting her disrespectful fiancé at the club, but the kiss had crossed a line. The lap sitting earlier had crossed the line. Me promising to protect her always had crossed the line. I had fucking crossed every line created to keep us platonic.

Rubbing my lips together, I could still taste the liquor she had consumed from the kiss. Even though the sexual tension was thick enough to cut with a knife, I stayed on my side of the car as we made our way to my crib. As soon as we pulled up in the quiet cove of my home, she jetted out of the car, making her way through the garage before I could put it in park. Solana had been here just about three weeks and was walking in my shit like she was the queen of the fucking castle.

Grabbing her shoes and bag that she'd left behind, I dropped her purse on the counter and left her shoes in front of her closed door before heading to my own quarters. An hour later, I was showered and in bed on my back with my arm folded behind my head. I hated being in my head. When I was in my head, that was never a good thing for anyone.

Grabbing the remote from the nightstand, I powered on my TV, but before I could press the YOUTUBE button, I smelled her nearby.

"Solana."

The sound of her padded feet coming closer had me sitting up in my bed.

"Más temprano... (Earlier...)" she started but paused.

I waited because I wasn't going to coach her through what

she was trying to say. Solana's English was better than Ezio's, and his ass was born here. Sure, she sometimes mixed up words, but her comprehension of the English vocabulary was solid.

She huffed, frustrated just as I was. I wanted to fuck this girl so bad. "Earlier... you said to have fun. And I did, Shio. The American women in your *familia* (family) are amazing. But I want fun with you. I want to eat. I want to shop. I want to visit America with you."

I stared at the dark-skinned Mexican beauty, wanting to give her exactly what she was describing, but I had to figure the rest of this shit out first.

I may not have been willing to hand Solana over to her fake-ass fiancé tonight, but I wasn't sure how I would handle her father. I wanted Solana, but she was not mine, nor was she available for the taking. I was trying my hardest not to be ignorant like my cousins. All three of them niggas had a wild-ass story about how they'd secure their fiancés and wife.

Running my hand down my face, I licked my lips before throwing my legs over the side of the bed. "Solana... I meant everything I said tonight. But I'd be lying to you if I promised you any of what you just said. What you're describing is me courting you, baby... and ion think that's possible just yet." Giving it a moment for my words to sink in, I stood and walked over to her.

She'd stopped right at the entrance to my bedroom, and I appreciated the respect she'd shown. Had she come straight in, she'd have been in my bed by now with the pink silk pajama shirt and shorts on the floor. Standing face to face now, I could smell her scent mixed with the body wash and essential oils kept in the guest rooms. The shit had always smelled amazing on Solana, but tonight she smelled as if she wanted to be eaten. Closing my eyes for a second, I calmed my inner self. I had to fight my wants if I had any chance of straightening this shit out before it got even messier.

"Let's put this shit on ice for now. And I know I'm sending you mixed messages since I practically swallowed your face earlier, but I have to be a man of my word, baby. My word was that I wouldn't touch you, so I'll be keeping my hands to myself from now on. Do you understand?"

Her eyes said what her mouth hadn't. Solana wanted me, and I'd basically just rejected her. "I understand, Shio."

Before I could elaborate, she turned and walked away, taking her natural aroma and pretty face with her. I stood and watched her ass jiggle softly in the shorts. Kicking myself, I walked back to my bed and sat down. I needed to figure out why Solana was really here. I needed to figure out what hand Don had played in her being here. I needed to figure out how much bullshit was yet to come since I'd punked the Rodríguezes tonight. I needed to figure out if it was possible for Solana and me to be together without causing an all-out war.

It was too many questions to work out after the long day I'd had, so I grabbed the remote and got back under the covers on my bed. Going to my stepfather's channel, I scrolled down to a random sermon without even reading the title.

Pastor Washington appeared on the screen, this time in a royal blue suit, a tan shirt, and his favorite brown Gators. A new city, a new church, and a new congregation looked good on him. Much of the mob money had gone into his worship grounds, and he had voiced his gratitude any time he was in my presence.

Picking up the white towel, he dabbed his forehead.

"The word of the day is desire." My body went stiff as he spoke to me, as if this wasn't a pre-recording, and he had a peek into my life. "Can I get somebody to turn to Galatians 5:16-17?"

Reaching over, I grabbed my Bible from the nightstand and my reading glasses while sitting up in bed. Flipping to the instructed chapter, I read over the passage.

So I say walk by the Spirit, and you will not gratify the desires of the flesh. For the flesh desires what is contrary to the Spirit, and the Spirit what is contrary to the flesh. They are in conflict with each other, so that you are not to do whatever you want.

"So, you see my brothers and my sisters"

Not wanting to hear another word, I powered off the TV, removed my glasses, and placed my Bible back in its spot. I'd gotten the message loud and clear. Solana was off-limits. I wouldn't touch her anymore, but I meant what I said when I said that fuck nigga wouldn't touch her anymore either.

Feeling a sudden wave of exhaustion, I gave in to it until my lids grew heavy. I had to double down on my faith and remember that Solana wasn't here to be a nigga's fuck toy or a nigga's wife. I needed to disregard my wants and let God show me my needs. I just had to figure out how to do that while also fulfilling my duty to find a wife.

God first.
Make sure the family good.
Eye them Cuppacio boys, the little and the big ones.
Build a relationship with my brother.
Get my brother rich.
Health and wellness.
Stay on top of my mob shit.
Keep Hobo alive.
~~Get through the meeting with Ines Ledesma.~~
~~House a random.~~
Find the true reason Solana is here.
~~Figure out if Solana is supposed to be my wife.~~
Find a wife that isn't Solana.

CHAPTER 22
TUNAN "TUNE" PAYNE

T he sun burned the back of my neck as I stood on the doorstep of the neatly manicured lawn that the townhome sat on. Jagoda Bay heat was no fucking joke. The sun was setting, yet it was still blazing like it had just risen. Pulling my sweats up on my waist, I raised my fist to knock as I approached the front door.

Loud voices could be heard, causing me to sigh as I waited for my presence to be acknowledged. Beating on the door a second time, I heard the voices quiet down and the flapping of shoes. It had been a week and a day since she became my wife, a week since everyone found out we were married at the hospital, and six days since I'd seen her. After the hospital fiasco, I checked in on her on Mother's Day, meeting for breakfast. I was headed to Memphis to celebrate my mama, handle some business with my brothers, and see my nephew. I wanted to make sure Glow was aware I'd be in the M and that she had calmed down from the night before. She'd hardly said shit at breakfast, so I knew she was still fucked up about Glee. I was hoping today would show progression, but from the raised voices I'd heard when I first knocked, shit was anything but good.

I hadn't heard from Shio during the week besides him asking if I was in the Bay a couple of days ago. When I told him I wasn't, he told me to hit him when I touched back down. That was the plan, but I needed to visit my wife first.

The door flew open, and I was met with a mad, pretty, and fiery Glow. I didn't know what I expected when she opened the door, but a red face, tear-stained cheeks, and a puffed-up chest were the last things I expected.

"Now is NOT a good time!"

I towered over Glow, so I was able to see inside of her townhouse. It was neat, smelled good from the door, but that wasn't what had my attention. Seeing her little sister on the couch with her face in her hands while her shoulders vibrated had my chest tight.

"Glow, you gonna invite me in or do I gotta stand on this hot-ass porch all day?"

Sucking her teeth, she ran her hand through her hair that had been pulled back into a ponytail. She didn't have an ounce of makeup on and was in leggings and a tank, but she still looked beautiful as hell, even with her pissed off expression.

"How do you know where I live anyway?" she screamed.

Ignoring her yelling, I backed her into the house, closing the door behind me.

"Tunan!"

"Glow..." I reached into my pocket and pulled out a knot of money. "I brought the mortgage payment."

I meant to leave this with her before I went to the M, but I forgot to grab the bands, rushing to make sure I didn't miss my flight. Tulsaire was home, and there was no telling when his popular ass would disappear again.

Her brow rose as she looked at the bands of money I was

holding out to her. "That looks like more than two thousand dollars."

"It's twelve. Pay it up for six months."

I hadn't set up a bank account, nor did I have any credit cards, thanks to Stella fucking up my credit. I was a cash nigga for now, so anytime I had to break Glow off, it wouldn't be no Zelle or ApplePay.

"He... Hello." The voice behind us stuttered.

Glow turned on her heels, and when she realized her sister was on the phone, she damn near flew across the room and snatched it out of her hands. Glee jumped back and winced—probably still sore from childbirth.

"You think this shit is a fucking joke, Glee? Why are you answering the phone when I'm talking to you? Since you won't tell me who the fuck the father is, I should get this shit turned off!"

"I... I'm sorry, Glow! I didn't mean to get pregnant! If I would have known, I would have gotten rid of it!"

"You damn right, you would have! You don't need no fuckin' baby! If you were gonna have sex, you should have at least protected yourself! You are on a full scholarship! Mama is pissed, so she don't want y'all there! What the fuck are you going to do? Stop walking around like shit is all gravy!"

"I didn't know!" Glee covered her mouth and cried into her hands. "I'm sorrrryyyyy! Please stop being mad at me!"

"Fuck that! I'm beyond mad! I'm pissed! A motherfucker who can't tell a nigga to use a condom or at least get on birth control shouldn't be fuckin' nobody!" Glow screamed so loud her voice cracked.

Looking around the living room, the only signs of the baby were a pink carrier, a diaper bag, and a blanket. But I knew the baby had to have been here. Yet, they were in this bitch screaming' like they didn't have no sense.

"Aye, Glow."

"Nigga, what?" She snapped her head at me.

Licking my lips, I jutted my chin to the hallway. "Come holla at me in the back."

Glee was crying hysterically on the couch while Glow's chest was heaving.

"Now, Glow."

"UUUUGHHHH!"

Glee jumped as Glow stormed down the hallway. We walked past two doors; one was a bathroom, the other was closed, and the third had a pink blanket spread across the middle of the bed where a baby slept peacefully. I was surprised she hadn't woken up with all the damn ruckus they were making.

Entering Glow's bedroom, it looked exactly like I imagined it would. Creams, golds, and neutrals flowed throughout the space. The only thing out of place was the comforter on her queen-sized bed. It looked like she had gotten straight out of bed and got on good bullshit.

Closing the door behind us, I stood there with my arms folded as I watched this crazy-ass girl pace and talk shit. I let her get her shit off until she started raising her voice.

"You gonna wake up the baby, Glow."

Her head shot up at me with hate. "Fuck that baby! That baby shouldn't even be here right now."

This damn girl need a blunt or three.

"Aye..." Walking up in Glow's personal space, she stood frozen, chest heaving. "That's your niece at the end of the day, Glow. I know you mad and shit, but the baby here now. I'm sure she feels bad enough. Be dere for your sister, Glow."

I wish I'd been there for my sister when she was pregnant by that old dude, but I was too young and too happy to think logically. That old nigga was giving her money to buy us food, shoes, and other stuff, so I was cooling, unaware as fuck. My sister was the most important girl in the world to me. Just by seeing the regret on Glee's face, I could tell that she felt about her big sister the same way I felt about mine. I had enough money to get my own place, but I was still in the spare room at Tuscany's house. I loved my sister to death. I loved all of my siblings, but Tuscany, being the only girl, and knowing the sacrifices she made, had me holding her to a different standard.

"I... I...She's just a kid, Tunan! A fucking kid! What the fuck will she do with a baby?"

"The baby here, Glow. You can either keep dwelling on the fact that she fucked up, or you can help her figure this shit out."

"Nah!" Glow shook her head ferociously. "Nah, fuck that! I don't even have a baby of my own! What the fuck am I gonna do? I can't be rocking no baby! I got my own life to live!"

"It's *her* baby, Glow. Not yours. Help her... You ain't gotta step in as the mother. But you can be a big sister and auntie."

"She probably pregnant by a broke-ass college boy that doesn't want shit to do with the baby! She didn't answer my call for months! Monthsss! Still, I was putting money in her account and sending groceries. She was probably laying up with the nigga and letting him eat the groceries I paid for! Nobody showed up at the hospital for her. Nobody, Tunan! The only visitors she had were Pia's little sister, Pearla, and me! Her best friend isn't even here anymore, and I'm sure her ass was the fucking ringleader. My sister had her future mapped out! She was supposed to be a doctor! A fucking doctor! A future doctor let a broke-ass boy knock her up!"

"He ain't broke," I mumbled.

"What?"

"Nun, Glow. Just calm down. Everything gone be aite. I get

why you mad and shit... But you can't be mad forever."

Glow wasn't trying to hear shit I was saying, so I wasn't going to keep trying to reason with her. But Leader, if he was the father, wasn't broke by a long shot. The nigga was paid. He was behind bars, but his brother was still holding it down. It wasn't my place to tell Glow who her sister's baby father was or what he had. Shit, I didn't even know if he was the father. What I did know was that the girl Leader had mentioned was Glow's little sister for damn sure. There was only one Glow who did food vlogging. Who Glee made a baby with was her business to tell, and until I saw the baby, I wasn't saying shit to Leader either. I wasn't no gossiping-ass nigga, especially about some shit I wasn't sure about.

"You know what? She got me fucked up! The problem is, she has never had her ass beat before!" Glow nodded as she headed toward the door, but I grabbed her arm.

I pulled her back, but she swung on a nigga. I dodged her punch right in time, but she followed that shit up with another. Having no choice, I grabbed her in a bear hug, digging my chin in her shoulder.

"Tunan, get off me! Get the fuck off me!"

"I'm not 'bout to let you go fight that girl. She just had a baby, Glow. You just mad right now, and your heart is broken, but it's gone heal. The disappointment gone let up, and when it do, you gonna be mad as hell at yourself for how you been acting, bruh. Pipe the fuck down."

"I ain't fucking piping down! A loser-ass nigga knocked my sister up and made her a single mother! He probably don't even like her for real! Just wanted some ass! Glee so damn green and gullible!"

I closed my mouth like white people did when they passed a black person they didn't know. Glow was going to eat all her fucking words because Leader most definitely liked her little sister. That nigga loved that girl. He damn near regretted that he hadn't married her before they locked his ass up, even though she was way too young to be anyone's wife. He walked around like a lovesick puppy in our cell. The nigga wasn't even pissed that he was about to have a book thrown at him; he was mad that he wouldn't be out to see her be great. When he was sentenced in March, the nigga got ten years, and all he cared about was that his family took care of his girl. I didn't know who the chick was back then, but seeing her bawling on the couch now because her sister was basically telling her she wasn't shit because she'd had a baby, had my chest tight. If Glow found out Leader was not only a fucking kingpin but in jail for a decade, she would probably have a heart attack.

"Let me go! You fucking lied to me too! Fuck both y'all! Shio is your brother, and you didn't think to tell me that before we agreed to this fake-ass marriage, nigga? Do I look like a pass-around bitch to you? Y'all got me fucked up! I hate you!"

Glow kicked backward, getting me in the knee before I could stop her. With her arms still locked behind her back, I pushed her down on the bed and pulled her leggings down. I knew what would have her ass yelling a different tune.

"Tunan!" she gasped out, trying to wiggle from my hold.

Her glistening pussy wasn't the same type of mad that the rest of her body was. Using my free hand, I slipped my dick out of my sweats and sank into her. Glow was doing too fucking much. She was mad at her sister, but she was sexually frustrated too. I could tell at the hospital she needed a release, but she was too in her head about our arrangement and shit. I could bet every dollar in my pocket that she was madder about wanting to fuck me than she was about her sister being a young mom.

Her pussy was warm, wet, and snug as it pulled me deeper inside her walls. Her body squirmed beneath mine as I slid my dick out and rammed it back in. Glow fit perfectly around my dick, and the shit was too good to be true.

"Ohhhhh!" she moaned out, her walls pulsating as I roughly glided in and out of her.

I was straight fucking Glow today. She'd been on too much tough shit and needed to be reminded that her rules didn't supersede me being a man—her man, according to the state of Tennessee.

Grabbing her ponytail, still with her arms folded behind her back, I pulled her into my chest, creating a dangerous arch. My dick twitched at the shift, and it felt good as fuck.

"You hate me?"

Sliding out, I pushed my dick back in her gushiness. Our skin clapping sounded like there was a fucking lightning strike in the bedroom. She was soaking me, her juices spitting out, creating a sticky mess between us. Glow's mouth opened, but nothing came out but heavy gasps. Turning her head but not losing my grip or my stroke, I latched down on the skin of her neck.

"You hate me, baby?"

"Y... Y... YA-NOOOOO!"

I was fucking Glow so hard that my balls slapping against her thighs was creating a tingling feeling, and I knew I was going to blow soon. Her pussy juices were dripping down my legs, making a huge mess. Her essence was making it easy for me to stroke her tunnel as fast as I was. If the first time hadn't solidified it, this session had for sure. Glow had the fucking best of the best.

"Yeah... You can hate me. If this pussy gonna feel like this off hate, I want you to hate me forever, my baby."

Keeping her in that very position, I continued to fuck her like I didn't have any fucking sense. I'd never fucked a soul the way I was fucking Glow, and with the way her pussy was squirting, I knew she loved it just as much as I did. Her body had imprisoned mine in a web of arousal, and she bounced against me, feeling her ending coming as I felt mine.

"Tunannnnn! It's too muuuuch!"

"Shut the fuck up! I told you to stop all that screamin' for you wake up the baby."

"O... Ohhhkay!"

Turning her neck again so I could capture her lips this time, we engaged in a sloppy-ass kiss that would give porn stars a run for their damn money. Waves of ecstasy throbbed through me as our bodies melted against each other, and my stroke became erratic. She panted in sweet agony as I filled her up. Fuck pulling out. She wanted to fight? She could fight with Mother Nature.

Letting her hair go, I slid my throbbing dick out of her. Before I could stand up straight, she was covering her mouth and running to her bathroom. Pulling my pants up, I took off in the same direction as her to find her kneeling at the toilet, spilling out her insides.

"Damn, Glow."

Bwaaaa Bwaaaa

Holding her hair back while she let her food out inside the toilet, I grabbed a washcloth from the sink and wiped her mouth. Thankfully, my long arms allowed me to multitask.

"You're making yourself sick, my baby. You gotta calm down."

When she was done, she stood, eyes watery with the look of defeat. I wiped her face with a new washcloth and helped her back into the room. She got under the covers half naked and drove her back into the pillow as she looked up at the ceiling. The money I'd given her was on the floor, some of it scattered. I picked up most of it and placed it on the nightstand.

"We can't do this again, Tunan. We agreed that this

marriage was on paper only. It hasn't even been a week, and we broke one of the rules." She faced me. "Is he really your brother?"

Running my hand down my head, I sighed. "Yeah, man. Shio is my brother; we got the same dad."

She chuckled bitterly. "Yeah. We can't do this again."

"Why not, Glow? We married, and we've fucked before it was stamped in ink."

Instead of replying, she turned her back to me. I'd been constantly saying my focus was the money. Yet, I needed a wife to get to the money, and instead of going to Don and formally letting him know I'd done my part, I'd been avoiding the fact that I had a fake wife. Glow had claimed she was focused on getting in the circle, but the sixty-something messages flashing across her screen on the nightstand told me she hadn't even talked to the damn women since becoming my wife. We both had gotten into a marriage to get what we wanted and hadn't been pursuing the shit we wanted.

"Glow..."

Nudging her shoulder, soft snores could be heard, so I let her go. Reaching into my pocket, I pulled out the rest of the money I had on me and set it next to the other stacks. Backing out of the room, I closed the door, and just as I entered the hall, loud wails could be heard from the other room.

Walking into the living room, I saw Glee curled up on the couch, asleep with puffy eyes. The baby was crying, and the two who had been screaming were knocked out without a care in the world.

Going into the hall bathroom, I washed my hands and then went into the bedroom where the baby was. Picking her small body up, I grabbed the blanket and placed it over my chest. I knew all about babies from seeing my brothers raise their kids and being an uncle since before I could remember.

On the dresser, there was a four-pack of pre-made formula bottles that the hospital had given with unused nipples. I opened one while managing to quiet the baby. As soon as I got her to feed, the small cries stopped. Sitting on the edge of the bed, I pulled back the hat that had fallen over her eyes. Lowering my head, I couldn't believe my fucking eyes. This baby—this little girl was indeed Leader's child. I just didn't know what the fuck to do with the information yet.

After letting her drink as much as she wanted, I sat her on my knee, secured her chin, and rubbed her back until she burped. Babies were easy as hell at this age, and once Glow accepted their new reality, she would be able to enjoy this as much as I was right now. Deciding I would get up with Shio tomorrow since I'd already promised Athena I'd go to the mall for her today, I scooted back on the bed and got comfortable. I was going to rock the baby back to sleep, head to the mall, and then get myself a room for the night. I'd get up with Shio tomorrow to hash shit out, hit Don up with the news that I'd followed through with the task, although my deadline had come and gone, and then I was back on the road to the M.

I was more nervous about my talk with Don because I hadn't gotten married within his 13-day deadline than I was about telling Shio how Glow had ended up being my wife instead of his. Don hadn't said shit about me missing the deadline to get married, but I'd done the shit. There was no reason for that nigga not to let me in the organization. A Payne on your team was a certified win. He also should consider that I was hungry, and while I'd been sniffing behind Glow lately, the money was still the number one objective, especially now that she was on my payroll.

He had no choice, but I wasn't giving him one either.

Tunan Payne, member of the Rinaldi Mob, sounded good to me.

CHAPTER 23
SHIO CUPPACIO

Feeling warmth on my back, I turned onto my side so it could cool off in the chilly room. I kept the thermostat at sixty-seven degrees at night, but somehow, it felt more like a hundred degrees right now.

Damn.

I hoped that Solana hadn't touched the AC. She was always complaining about being cold and shit. As I shifted again, trying to get comfortable in my bed, I felt a loose, unstable, grain-like material against my skin. Knowing my alarm would go off at any moment, I sat up in the complete darkness and felt around the bed for my phone. Gripping the sheets, I clenched them and again felt looseness flow through my fingers. Grabbing another fistful, I lifted my hand, turned it over, and the substance brushed against my face with the flow of humid air. Slapping the bed, there was no bounce back. The four-thousand-dollar mattress I slept on wasn't what I'd been feeling around on. In fact, it felt like a bed of sand that I was in. The coarse fibers were hot and itchy as hell against my skin. In-haling and exhaling in the same huff and not being able to smell my home, I immediately knew what time it was.

"Aye, what the fuck!"

Ezio. Ezio was waking up too.

"Is this fuckin' sand?" he yelled out.

"On foe 'nem... I'm on Don's ass if he took me out of my bed and dumped me in one of Preston's sick-ass simulations."

Nel. He was here too.

"Shit, I'm supposed to be on leave! Why the fuck Ezio get some time off when Jisei had the babies, and I don't!"

Metavello's cranky, complaining ass.

"Shut y'all ass up! It's too fucking hot for you niggas to be bitching today," Matteo grumbled.

The gang was all here, which meant this was indeed one of Don's trainings. But why the fuck were we in the sand, and why in the fuck was it so damn hot?

Grrrrlllll Grrrrrlllll Grrrllllll

Short, low throaty moans were near, and judging by the pungent smell, it had to be an animal. They couldn't have been dangerous, though, because they hadn't attacked us, but then again, it was too dark for them to see unless they were nocturnal.

"Smells like an elephant's ass," Metavello complained.

"Aye, where Shio? Shiooo! Shio!"

"I'm here," I responded to Ezio, not in the mood for this shit.

Last night, I'd basically realized I was just as fucked up as the dick heads currently whining about shit they should've been used to. All in one day, I'd flirted past respectable boundaries with Solana, fucked my main fuck buddy and called her Solana's name, committed to protecting Solana from her fake-ass fiancé, sucked her whole face into my mouth, ready to fuck her in the Maybach to some Rick Ross, pulled back once I realized I'd be causing a war telling her we couldn't move forward but was still uncertain, to then deciding I was definitely not pursuing her after hearing my stepfather's random-ass sermon before passing out. My mind was too fucked up for Don and his games today. Everybody had better tread lightly because I would blow this shit up if pushed too far.

Touching my body, I felt a pair of pants on my lower half that seemed to be made from some type of material that could be wool. On my top half was the same, but there seemed to be a shawl there too. It was too damn hot for a shawl, but I wouldn't be removing it until the lights came on, and I could see the conditions of the climate we'd been dumped in.

Horns blared and tambourines played. The music around us sounded like something straight out of the movie *Aladdin*.

"Are we in India? Is this a fake-ass India, Twin?" Metavello asked his brother.

"Shit, ain't no fuckin' telling. Help me up."

I could hear the two help each other stand as I remained calm. There hadn't been a training that we hadn't conquered. I also knew that each one of us, except for Matteo, had taken the lead on a training except for me. I needed to focus and concentrate through my current mental state because knowing Don's pattern, this shit would be solely on me, and our survival would depend on it.

Feeling the pull from my family's hands, I let them help me rise from the scorching-ass sand. Ezio slapped my chest, and I knew it was him because I could smell his house on him.

"You ready?"

"'Bout as ready as I'm gone be," I answered, keeping my breathing labored.

"At least the nigga gave us shoes this time. They feel weird, but this hot-ass sand on bare feet would've been deadly."

"On foe 'nem." Nel backed up his brother.

The music grew louder and was starting to get annoying as

fuck. Still, I waited for what was next. Moving my feet because it felt like my weight was sinking into the sand, I felt a thump on my right ankle. Bending down, I ran my hand across a stick, so I picked it up and held it to my side. I didn't know what the fuck we would be facing when the lights came on, and I wanted to be prepared.

"Cuppacios!" Don's voice came over the music, making my muscles tense. "Welcome to ancient Egypt!"

"Egypt?" Ezio asked what we were all thinking.

"Yeah, Egypt, nigga. Cuz I know fasho one of you niggas questioning it."

"Welcome to ancient Egypt, niggas," Matteo said, reiterating what Don had just said.

"Today's mission is simple. You're going to walk your fellow Cuppacio through an obstacle course. If he survives the end, he will find the prize. And if he doesn't, then, well... you niggas are going to die of thirst." The music came back on, letting us know Don was finished after giving us those bland-ass instructions.

"Aye, where the fuck my bitch at?" Matteo asked another question that I'd been thinking.

Scarlett had always been the one to give us the directions before and during missions. At the very least, she told us about the climate, animal facts, and other important information we needed to survive, which was more than Don provided. His ass just didn't give a fuck.

"Hey, guys! Hi, baby! Y'all will do amazing, sweeties! I'm here!" Scarlett's voice came over the speaker.

"Aye, that belly dancing music is getting on my fucking nerves," I said out loud. "Shit feel like I'm getting put in a trance."

"Bro, facts," Metavello agreed.

"Hop on the camels, cousins. They are already lowered to

the ground and will rise up once you get on. They will take you where you need to go. They have been properly hydrated. Remember, camels can reserve water exceptionally well. They can go days without it, if need be, and they don't tire easily. As long as you stay on course, they can get you where you need to go without struggling. They can sustain speeds of up to forty miles an hour too!" Scarlett called out.

I still couldn't see, but I was storing all the information, just in case we needed it.

"I designed headpieces to shield you from the sun. They are in the front pockets of your pants. Put them on."

Reaching into the pocket I felt first, I pulled out what felt like a damn oversized cotton ball and tossed it over my head, shifting it until the hole of the nose and mouth was in front.

"Go ahead and get on the camels."

Listening to the grunts, I used my stick, holding it out in front of me until I hit a solid object. Using my palm, I placed it on what I assumed was the camel and ran my hands along the side. I'd never ridden a damn camel or any other fucking animal outside of a horse before, but it couldn't be too much different. Feeling for the middle, I put the stick under my armpit again and hoisted myself up. By the time I was on the camel, I felt way too damn high in the air, and the animal was still on the ground. This fucking camel smelled like it hadn't bathed ever. Still, I swung my leg around and took a seat, keeping my stick in place. Grabbing the reins, the camel lifted, throwing me all the way off, but I tightened my grip, making sure I didn't fall back into the scorching sand. I clicked my tongue to calm the one-humped animal, as it was beginning to move with the neighboring camels.

"Woaaah, Topsy. Calm yo' big ass down," Nel instructed.

Ezio grunted. "I damn near busted my balls tryna get on this muthafucka. Aite, we on them, pretty cousin. Turn the fuckin' lights on. I'm starting to see dots and shit."

I heard Matteo utter, but before he could curse Ezio out for calling Scarlett pretty, Don spoke over the speakers. "Remember, it's ancient Egypt, muthafuckas, Get active."

"About fucking time!" Metavello yelled as we all heard a clank above us.

"Shit! These camels tall as fuck. Damn! What don't Preston have?" That was Ezio; I could tell by the way he said *damn*.

Nel cursed under his breath. "Are we in the fucking desert for real, my nigga?"

"What the fuck we got on, Twin?" Vello asked, letting me know the lights had been activated since he could see his brother.

Everyone was shooting off questions while I remained calm and kept my balance. I still had the stick at my side, my institution telling me I'd need it eventually. Alarms were going off in my head, but I continued to balance myself on the mammal. The camel began to move forward faster, and hearing the rest of the men behind me told me they were moving as well. The sun was hot on my skin, damn near burning a nigga, and whatever clothing that had been draped over my body was needed because my skin would've probably dried out already without it.

I listened to the guys argue behind me, along with the music, for a good twenty minutes before my mouth grew parched and my curiosity piqued. "Aye... Can y'all see?"

My world was still dark. The rest of my senses were heightened since my eyes weren't working, but from the way they'd been describing the never-ending dunes of sand, someone had to be able to see.

"As a matter of fact, I can't," Ezio acknowledged.

"I can't see fuckin' shit outta this thing. It's these hot-ass masks!" Nel shouted.

Before the masks, I couldn't see shit. I don't think these niggas understood that I was blind as fuck riding this camel.

"Hol' up, lemme fix the hole." I heard a ripping sound, and Nel groaned. "I made the bullshit worse! Fuuuuck!"

"Who made this shit? Don got too much money to be giving us homemade KKK masks!" Metavello announced as if he wanted Don to hear him talking shit.

"Scarlett made this bullshit," Nel's shit-starting ass remarked.

Matteo kissed his teeth. "You niggas outta be glad my wife did anything for you ungrateful muthafuckas. Fuck y'all gone complain for? Do I see anybody else's bitch contributing to the cause?"

"I can't breathe in this shit, and I can't ride in this shit! I'm riding blind!" Nel screamed.

"Aye, it's hot as fuck, so they're protecting us from the sun. The bags were a good idea. Fall back off Scarlett. You niggas either wear 'em or you don't," Ezio expressed, hating when anyone had anything to say about his favorite cousin, Scarlett.

"Ion need you taking up for my bitch, junkie!" Matteo barked. "I keep tellin' you weird-ass niggas that she's a Rinaldi now. I'm 'bout sick of you incestual-ass niggas."

"Nigga, you only saying that incest shit because of me and Pia. Shit gettin' old. Everybody knows we ain't related!"

"Look, are we wearing the masks or not?"

Matteo sighed, ignoring my question. "Fuck all y'all. I be watching my wife get thrown into these bullshit-ass seminars to help you ungrateful sons of bitches, and all she get is criticized! I'll be so happy when y'all die! Hopefully, it's today."

"Aye, Django..." Ezio called out, causing all of us to laugh.

Matteo didn't respond, and that made the twins start up with nonstop jokes before Matteo threatened to shoot everybody's camel if they didn't shut the fuck up.

I'd already stopped laughing after the first two jokes because something was wrong.

"Yo', Matteo..." I uttered loud enough for them to hear me without yelling.

"Nigga, what?"

Licking my lips, I felt sweat drip down my back. "I can't see *with or without* the mask."

"Aye! Who the fuck is that up straight ahead? Is that another camel?" Vello asked before anyone could respond to what I'd just said. Hearing that someone else had been placed out here had my ears perking up.

"Is that Tunan?" Ezio asked.

Tunan.

My brother had been tossed in here too. I hadn't had the chance to explain the trainings and missions part of this with him in depth, but I did tell him that joining this shit was strenuous. We hadn't talked since he revealed he'd been married to Glow, and it wasn't because I was avoiding him, but so much was going on in my own house that I hadn't had the chance to chop it up about his new relationship status.

"Describe to me what y'all seeing," I yelled to whomever would answer.

"Take off the fuckin' mask, G," Metavello urged.

"I can't fuckin' see even without the mask. Did y'all muthafuckas hear me?"

I was getting tired of these niggas. This camel was uncomfortable as hell.

I heard trotting and then felt an object in front of my face. Ezio chuckled. "Shit, he deadass can't see."

"Ah, damn, cousin. Don done blinded ya ass." I could hear Nel smirking through his words.

Instead of responding to that nigga and getting him started back up, I skipped him and responded to Ezio. "No. I can't see.

Now, explain the surroundings. I know we on camels, and we in the desert."

"Yeah, that's pretty much it. We can only see sand, stretched for miles and on all sides," Ezio replied.

"And Tunan dressed like one of the Disciples, like the rest of us, standing next to his camel, looking confused as fuck. You ain't warn him about this shit?"

"Nel..." I exhaled.

I was hot and frustrated, and this nigga would not let up. You could tell he was probably bored as hell living in the Mansion of Dicks, as he called it. I wasn't in the mood for twenty-one questions right now. I'd rather be at the crib trying to find out as much as I could on the Rodríguezes. I'd been in the streets long enough to know that I'd not only embarrassed that nigga but wounded his ego. He'd be back to Jagoda Bay soon. My plan was to get at that nigga first, though. I wasn't trying to bring a war to my turf, where my people lived and thrived. And even though Don had gotten me into this shit, I still didn't want to bring a war to the mob. I was far from scared of any of them Mexican cartels. Ines feared the niggas; I didn't. I'd end the Rodríguezes and deal with the repercussions later.

"Aye, what the fuck is this, and why we gotta wear this mask? I can't see shit," Tunan groaned as our camels stopped.

Nel barked out a laugh. "Take that bullshit off. Ezio and Shio the only ones still got it on. Matteo not even wearing it."

"Where we at? How the fuck that nigga put us in Egypt? Is this shit really Egypt?" Tunan asked, but didn't wait for us to respond. "Last thing I remember is checking into the Westin, then I woke up halfway buried in the sand, and Don talking from the sky."

"We in Preston's sick-ass games. Don teams up with niggas that own whole-ass ecosystems and send us on fight-or-flight missions every now and again." I imagined Nel shrugging his shoulders after explaining.

"Hol' up... Who the fuck is Preston? And fight or flight? How the hell he expect me to do anything if he kidnapping niggas and dumping them with no preparation?" My brother sucked his teeth. "Never mind, never mind... Just tell me what the fuck I gotta do to get the fuck up outta this *ecosystem*."

"See... niggas be wanting to be down so bad and don't even know what the fuck they gotta do once they get in. You better be glad yo' ass even here because married or not, you missed the deadline, nigga. But I'm sure Don got something real sweet for yo' ass. You was better off playin' with them niggas on the prison yard. Welcome to hell, nigga."

Matteo taunted Tunan, but Tunan was more like me than he was like my cousins. I knew he wasn't going to respond. My brother didn't care about shit but money.

"*Sweet*...? Man, you said that shit too cute like, Django. You been hanging around Don Mecanio, ain't it?" Vello said before he, Nel, and Ezio were clowning again, followed by Matteo cursing them out.

"Aye," I spoke in the direction of Tunan. "Get on yo' camel. They gone lead us where we gotta go."

"Nigga, have you seen this shit? I can't ride no fuckin' camel! I got sand all in my fuckin' balls and shit!"

"You just asked what you gotta do to get outta here. Get on the fuckin' camel, Tunan, damn! The quicker we get through this shit, the quicker I can get from 'round you niggas." Matteo roared, causing the Three Stooges to laugh harder.

Don had to have put something else in their drugs or drink to transport their asses. These niggas had the fucking giggles out here as if we weren't waterless, foodless, and shelterless in the blazing artificial sun. I could hear Tunan try to get on the camel, and after a few attempts, I knew he'd done it because

Vello's dumb ass started clapping. I could hear Tunan yell as his camel stood and began walking. I would've yelled too if I could actually see.

"How the fuck this nigga get me out here?" Tunan asked.

"No telling. He got his ways. He probably drugged our food or laced our weed. I stopped tryna guess. Now, I just focus on getting through these dumb-ass lessons," Metavello grumbled. His mood had switched again that quickly, as if he were the one going through hormonal changes from pushing two babies out.

I hadn't figured out Don's methods either, and I wouldn't try to wreck my brain figuring it out. Don had been able to drag grown-ass men from their home's multiple times. If I did try to figure that shit out, it would force me to wonder who dressed us. More than likely, Don had gotten the ladies to do his bidding, but I was a single man. If this nigga had gotten the First Lady to dress me, I was on his ass the next time I saw him.

"It's so fuckin' hot out here, this shit don't make no sense," Tunan complained.

"On foe 'nem. Don so fuckin' dramatic. Why he leave you twenty minutes away?" Nel said.

Matteo snapped, sounding tired as hell. I knew his big ass was probably the sweatiest. "Don't fuckin' worry 'bout what the fuck my family did. You niggas just focus on completing the damn mission."

Ezio spoke up, sounding aggravated like me. "Aite, grumpy bitch."

The men all continued to bicker for the next thirty minutes, but by the time we reached nearly an hour of being on these camels, it wasn't shit funny anymore. Everyone was thirsty, soaked in sweat, and starting to see shit. Nel had hopped off his camel, thinking he'd seen a lake, and Ezio swore up and down he'd seen Jisei. I tried explaining to these niggas that it was a mirage, but they thought they knew every fucking thing.

"Aite, I know I'm not imaginin' this shit. Y'all see that building up ahead? Please tell me y'all do."

Since I still couldn't see, I stayed silent.

"Yeah, I see it..." Tunan croaked out, mouth probably dry as hell.

"Me too."

"I see it, Twin."

"What it look like?" I asked.

"Wait. You can't see it?" Tunan queered, and I damn near screamed.

"I can't see nuttin' but black, and it's not the mask." I was sick of these niggas, my brother included.

"It's a pyramid, Shio. Looks just like those ones we used to watch on the Discovery Channel. But it's bigger I'm talking colossal."

If this was a stimulation of ancient Egypt, it made sense for it to be a pyramid. Before I could ask Ezio if he saw a pathway to climb the pyramid, Don's voice blared over the music that had yet to stop playing. "Looks like you niggas made it."

"On the outside of the pyramid will be a screen where you all can see the inside. The one with only four senses is the only one who will go inside. The door will open for him *only*. He will rely on you dumb niggas to guide him through. When he reaches the end, or if he reaches the end, he will get the resource he needs to gain his lost sense back. Bye, bitch-ass niggas."

"Mane, what type of instructions is that?" Tunan grunted.

"Wait, you can't see for real, Shio? Like for real, for real? Like Stevie Wonder's vision?"

"Yeah, Metavello. Like Stevie... I can't see shit."

"You blind?" Tunan asked.

Realization set in that Don had really fucked with my

vision. I was temporarily blind—some shit I thought I'd never be.

"Damn, Bible man. We thought you was talkin' 'bout the masks." Nel said, sounding somewhat serious for the first time since we woke up in the desert.

"Fuuuuck. I know what this is..." Tunan gasped.

"What?" Metavello asked.

"Making a blind man see. It's in the bible."

"John 9," I responded.

"Okay. What happens in John 9, Bible freaks?"

"Jesus and his Disciples stumble across a blind man. They thought he was blind due to his or his parents' sin. He wasn't, though. He was born blind so that the works of God might be revealed to him and those around him. Then Jesus healed him."

"But y'all stumbled across me, so I was supposed to be the blind one."

Nel huffed before responding to Tunan. "Don just be doing shit. He didn't know no better."

I thought about the lesson in the scripture. I knew the blind man was healed with mud and told to go wash in the Pool of Siloam, and I knew the Pharisees didn't believe in the blind man's healing because Jesus did it on the Sabbath. Nel wasn't lying about how Don just be doing shit, but he'd gotten some of the details right since it was Sunday and I was surrounded by niggas who didn't believe in Jesus' power. But the blind man was healed in Jerusalem, and Don's non-reading ass had us in a fake Egypt. Ezio hadn't mentioned a pool, which I was thankful about because I refused to be swimming with sharks and shit like Nel had.

"Ooo weeeee! Glad I ain't gotta go in this bitch. You know, pyramids are zombie tombs, right?"

"Nel..." I warned.

The camels came to a stop and lowered to the ground. My whole body was stiff and drenched as I got off, catching myself from falling into the sand.

"So dey just gonna leave us?" my brother asked.

I could hear the grunts of the camel grow further away.

"How the fuck we gone get back?" Nel chimed in with his own question.

Ignoring both, I held my stick out until it connected with the pyramid.

"To the left a lil' bit, Shio," Ezio said.

Rock shifting could be heard as the sand underneath our feet vibrated. Holding my stick out, I could sense that a door was open.

"Look, a projector on the wall."

Everyone shuffled toward the projector screen, but I stayed in place, not wanting the door to close or the screen to disappear.

"It says, 'Shio, get yo' ass inside. You'll be able to hear us, and we will be able to see you.'"

Using the stick, I let it lead me inside. Mildew, dust, and stone particles filled my nostrils. The door slammed down hard behind me, giving me a little gust of wind. I couldn't see, but at least it was cool inside. If I was smelling mildew, that meant water was near.

Shit.

I didn't have an ounce of energy to be swimming after that long-ass camel ride to this bitch. I wouldn't be drinking from any water sources in here either. I wasn't putting anything in my mouth that I couldn't see.

"We can see you, Shio!" Ezio's voice blared a little too loudly.

I felt claustrophobic. Using the stick, I tried to stretch to the left of me; it hit a wall, then to the right, and it did the same.

"It's a tunnel. But it inclines... If you walk a few paces ahead, you gonna have to climb up. It looks like it goes for a few miles, but I didn't see nun' threatening," Tunan stated clearly.

Tucking the stick back under my armpit, I reached until I grabbed the beginning of the inclined floor.

"It's a rope if you stand straight up. You may have to crouch as you climb."

Standing, I reached above my head with my right hand and grabbed the rope. Using the rope, I pulled myself up the concrete hill. I could hear droplets of water and wind blowing in the distance. I was grateful I worked out faithfully because if I hadn't, my legs and arms would be on fire. I'd been walking for ten minutes and was still climbing.

A mile, my ass.

"You straight, Fav?"

"I'm good." I was grunting, tired as fuck, but determined to just do it.

"Okay, you're almost at the top. When you get there, don't move."

I nodded, continuing to keep a level head. I focused on my steps, listening to the water and wind as it sounded closer, while Vello and Nel tripped on how Ezio was always calling everyone his "fav" when we all knew his favorite cousin was Scarlett. I knew just the mention of Scarlett would have Matteo shouting any minute.

Tuning them niggas out, I thought about if Solana had gotten up and came looking for me to only find I wasn't there. I hoped she didn't think I'd left the house so early because of her. The thought of not being able to see her again had my chest tightening, causing me to pant even harder. I had only been blind for a little under two hours and was already praying that God healed the ones who suffered this shit daily. It was no fucking joke trying to navigate around without sight, but to live life not ever seeing someone as beautiful as Solana was a sin in itself. *Get it together, nigga.*

Just as my legs were starting to shake, I reached the top.

"Okay, stop! You at the top of a cliff. Let us zoom out to find a way down."

"Or he can jump," Vello added.

I nodded. "Yeah, I smell the water."

"Yeah, and you're 'bout thirty feet in the air, nigga. It's dark as fuck down dur, and we don't know what's in dem waters," Tunan chimed in, making a valid point, accent heavy as fuck ringing off the pyramid walls.

"Wait, you said you can zoom in? The screen that high-tech?"

"Yeah, Don got that pape. This shit touch screen, G." Metavello boasted.

A touch-screen projector on the side of a pyramid was some shit from a movie. Given how much energy Don put into these missions, I never understood why he didn't put that energy and his money into actually teaching us some shit. I'd learned nothing from these trainings except that he was a rich asshole who liked to fuck with people.

"So, to the right of you, if you walk and stay close to the wall cuz dur is a bend, it's a rope that you'll have to climb down."

Sighing, I got close to the wall and leaned on it, using my stick to guide me so that I didn't fall to my death.

"Good call, Tune. I didn't even see that fuckin' rope. Nigga would have had to jump fuckin' with me."

"On foe 'nem, Twin."

The pathway was slippery and wet, and the fucking sandals on my feet didn't have a good grip, so I had to be extra careful.

"Why the fuck we got these big-ass Jesus sandals on?" Nel asked what I'd been thinking.

"Shit, ask ya Don."

"Aite. Stop! Use dat walkin' stick and stretch it out in front of you."

I did as my brother instructed, and I felt the rope hit the stick.

"Pull the rope toward you, and den tug on it to see how secure it is. It looks like it runs to the top of the pyramid, but it's too dark for me to see up dur."

Jerking the rope, it felt sturdy enough. Pulling it toward me, I swung and nearly let go.

"Ahhhhhhh!"

Everyone screamed out, loud as hell, except for Matteo and me. Since they were on a loudspeaker, and my senses were heightened, my ears rang from the vibration and echo of their combined pitches. I hadn't fallen and was holding on, but them niggas must've thought I did die based on what they saw on that screen. I wasn't dying in any of these useless-ass trainings. If anyone knew what the fuck to do in these missions, it was me. Tunan was also proving to have some common fucking sense.

I waited until the rope steadied since I was still swinging in the air. I had the stick tucked under my arm tightly as my heart thumped from adrenaline.

"Okay, climb down slowly, nigga. Got us out here thinkin' you done died."

"Right, Tune. Nigga tryna be fuckin' Laura Croft."

"Who?" Tunan asked Nel.

"Tomb Raider, nigga. Fuck did you do during your childhood? Ours was shitty, but we know shit."

Tuning them out, I pulled the mask from my head and wrapped it around the rope. Tightening my legs, I then loosened them and let my body descend.

"This nigga here... shoulda went to the fucking Navy."

I could feel my clothes flipping and flapping around me as I zipped down the rope. I had climbed up and refused to climb down if there was an easier way. I needed to save my strength because I didn't know what was left for me to face ahead.

"Brace yaself... the rope doesn't"

Fighting the air, I ran out of rope and felt myself falling.

Seconds later, my back smacked the concrete with a thud. I instinctively rolled over, palming the floor and trying not to focus on my back that was on fire.

"Nigga, we tried to tell you the rope didn't reach the end. You're the one thinkin' you got wings and shit."

Taking a deep breath, I stood, putting my weight on the walking stick.

"You good, bro?"

"Yeah, Tune. What's next?"

My fucking head and back were pounding, but I had to push through this shit. I wasn't even the type of nigga that took baths, but I was going to need one after this shit.

"It's a boat, 'bout ten steps left. It's already halfway in the water, so all you gotta do is get in it and paddle."

"Yeah, and it's a door across the water, looks like..." Nel added to what Tunan described.

"Aite."

"Crazy how fuckin' big that damn pyramid is on the inside," Metavello prattled, and the guys muttered responses while I focused on getting the boat.

The stick reached the boat before I could, after I'd flapped it around for a minute. Tossing it inside, I carefully climbed in, and it was more of a fucking canoe than a boat only one person could fit inside. Using the paddle, I pushed the boat into the water and sat up straight to balance myself.

"Hi, Shio. This is a pre-recorded message," Scarlett's voice came over the speaker.

"Who is that?" Nel asked.

"Aye, shut up. It's Scarlett's voice."

Paddling, the water flow aided in carrying the boat.

"It has been said that pyramids were built as ancient tombs, but no one has ever found a mummy of any kind there. It is nearly impossible to understand how the pyramids were built by humans, due to the lack of their instruments and technology. This is not an original pyramid, but it was built to mimic one. The water you are rowing on is fresh. Always keep your body straight and your hands inside the boat at all times, cousin. I love you."

"Damn, Scarlett must be sick of this job. The facts are gettin' shorter and shorter with each mission."

Matteo scolded Metavello. "Nah, she's just sick of you niggas."

The boat jerked, so I stopped paddling and used the paddle to feel around in the water to make sure I didn't hit anything.

"Whatchu doin', bro?"

"I felt somethin' hit the boat."

"It's nothing in the water, Shio. Go head now," Vello alleged.

"You see how dark it is in there? You don't know what's in that muthafucka," Matteo said.

Since I couldn't see, I pulled the paddle in the boat and used the stick to poke in the water to check once more.

"Hold up! Zoom in, Tune! I think I see a tail!"

"A tail?" I probed.

The boat pushed forward with a jerk, and I nearly dropped the stick, trying to hold my balance.

"Nigga! That's three tails!"

"Shio! Stop fuckin' moving! It's some shit in the water!"

Tunan sounded in a panic.

Pausing, I held my breath while swiveling my head, trying to hear as much as I could.

"Awl, hell nawl! It's dinosaurs in that bitch! I see scales for sure."

"Alligators are *massive* semi-aquatic reptiles!" Scarlett disclosed, coming over the loudspeaker again.

"They are cold-blooded and found in freshwater habitats. They are carnivores, feeding on fish, small mammals, birds, and even sometimes deer."

"Nigga, if they can eat deer, they can eat a nigga. Awl nawl!" Nel panicked like he was the one in fucking boat.

"These alligators are unlike anything you've ever witnessed. They are all twelve feet in length, and their owner, Goal Navarro, keeps them on a special diet of... human flesh."

The boat jerked forward again, and Nel and Vello screamed over the loudspeaker.

"You need to get the fuck out of dur now, yo'! They are semi-aquatic, meaning they live in the water and on land." Tunan was now huffing into the speaker while Nel and Vello could be heard in the background, freaking out.

Using the paddle, I began rowing as fast as my arms would allow. The boat continued to jerk as the three reptiles pushed it with their noses from different directions as if they were playing volleyball. Still, I kept rowing.

"The bank is up ahead, but just as you can get outta the water, dey can too. It's shallow, too, Shio. You need a plan!"

Pulling the paddle back in the boat, I grabbed the stick I'd been using and put it against my mouth. Using my teeth, I bit into it, hurting the fuck out of my gums. Using my fingers to find the gnawed spot, I broke the stick there and grabbed the piece with the most rugged edge. Scrubbing the rugged edge up and down my arm, I winced at the burning sensation from my skin being rubbed raw. When I began to smell blood, I tore the bottom half of my shirt off, balling it up and pressing it against my self-inflicted wounds. I then tied the bloody shirt around the stick, slapped the water until I felt one nudge the side, and then tossed it behind me as far as it could go. I felt the water ripple and the slapping of tails. Wasting no time, I hopped from the boat. My feet hit the water, which came up to my knees.

"Go, nigga, go! One of them coming back!" Ezio hollered.

Nearly falling into the water from the gritty sand underneath my feet, I continued to push through until I was out of the freshwater, holding the canoe paddle in my hand.

"Jump over the gate! It's a gate in front of you!"

Using the paddle, I felt for the gate, and when I could see how tall it was, I jumped like my name was Jordan. I felt a nip on my back, ripping at my bare skin above my ass.

Fuck this!

Using the paddle, I swung it behind me, beating the reptile in the head.

"Yeaaaah! Beat his ass, Fav!"

The alligator roared, and then my body jerked onward. He'd pushed my ass forward.

"This pyramid will self-destruct in fifteen minutes," Scarlett's voice divulged.

"Okay, Shio, run. The alligators are back in the water, so you good. Just run straight ahead. Go straight through the door. We can hear the pyramid shifting from outside."

Don was the sickest nigga I knew. We had to be covered by the blood of Jesus, given how we had been able to constantly escape from these missions.

"Okay, I had a look in. You gonna run through the door, make a left, and then a quick right. It's gonna lead you to a room. So, straight, left, right..."

Following Tunan's directions, I was slipping and sliding since the wooden sandals were now saturated. Still, I kept moving. I was soaked and wet, blind, head hurting, back aching from my fall, and dehydrated. I was ready for this shit to be over.

"Okay, where I'm at?"

I was met with silence as I stood idle, waiting for more directions. I felt like I was in a smaller room, but I couldn't be too sure.

"Tune? Tell me sum'n!"

"Nigga, you in the room with a mummy."

"A what?"

"Pharaoh, Cleopatra, Ramses. Nigga, a mummy!" Nel imparted. That nigga loved to talk shit about my intelligence, but he was no fucking dummy either. He just chose to act like a clown.

"Your antidote should be inside the casket. It's gold and has a pharaoh painted on it, so I know it's heavy. You're at the foot, and you need to walk to the front."

Holding the paddle out, I used it to guide me to the front of the casket.

"Okay, you dur. Try and push it off. Liftin' it may be too hard."

"Please, Lord... Let this shit be the end. I'm so fuckin' hot out here," Nel begged.

Putting the paddle down, I pushed the top, and it was as heavy as steel. The shit wouldn't bulge. Planting my feet, I placed both hands on the casket top and pushed. It slightly moved with a grit.

"Yess! That's it!"

Sucking in more air, I continued to push until my ears popped. Just when I thought I was about to pass the fuck out, the top fell, shaking the whole damn room.

"Okay, there is a gold box sitting on the mummy's chest. Reach in and grab it."

Reaching inside the casket, I cringed, feeling that there was actually a mummy in this bitch. I felt his shoulders and then moved down to his chest area. Once my fingers grazed the cool box, I felt something grab my wrist.

"Ahhhhhhhhh! He's alive!"

"Oooohhhhh shhhhhiiiit!"

Them niggas were yelling, and for the first time today, I'd yelled out too.

Drawing my fist back, I punched the mummy on the head three times before grabbing the box, screaming for my life.

"Mission accomplished. You may leave the pyramid."

Following the warmth I felt, I ran through a door, and when my feet sank into sand, I knew I was outside.

"There he go!" I heard Ezio.

Clutching the box in my hands, I was trying to catch my breath, but it was difficult as it had seemed to get hotter out.

"Shio, you still blind?"

Whap!

My head snapped as my face stung.

"Aye, nigga! What the fuck?" It sounded like Tunan had pushed Nel. "Fuck you slap him for?"

"My bad. I was tryna see if he could see the lick comin'. He didn't, so that means he still blind."

"Nigga I'm blind, not numb! I can still feel!" I spat the words out, completely fed up.

"Aite, aite... Calm down. Open the box. I hear helicopters comin'."

Still pissed that I'd gotten bitch slapped, I carefully opened the box.

"What the fuck? Is that dirt?"

Someone reached their hand inside.

469

"Yeap. It's dirt and sand mixed, look like," Ezio confirmed.

Tunan snapped his fingers. "Okay, okay. In the Bible, Jesus used mud and spread it across the blind man's eyes and told him to go wash in the pool nearby to cure him."

Vello sucked his teeth. "But this is dirt..."

"And what happens when you get dirt wet, dumbass?" Matteo asked Vello.

The helicopter was now here, hovering over us, as the blades blew the hot ass air on us.

"Jesus wet the dirt and turned it into mud. Except"

"He used his spit. He used his fuckin' spit," I said, cutting off my brother. "You niggas got me fucked up. I'll just wait till I get to the crib. Ain't none of you muthafuckas putting y'all spit on my face. Just help me get in the helicopter."

Letting my ears lead me, I walked toward the copter with Ezio and Tunan on either side of me.

"That's gonna be your black ass, blind for life! How you know this shit don't have like a set time befo' you supposed to put the mud on, Shio? You may as well let me have all your old clothes. Ain't like you can see what you're puttin' on."

"Nel..." I said before leaning my head back, ready to get away from these niggas.

God first.
Make sure the family good.
Eye them Cuppacio boys, the little and the big ones.
Build a relationship with my brother.
Get my brother rich.
Health and wellness.
Stay on top of my mob shit.
Keep Hobo alive.
~~Get through the meeting with Ines Ledesma.~~

~~House a random.~~
Find the true reason Solana is here.
Figure out if Solana is supposed to be my wife, again.
~~Find a wife that isn't Solana.~~

CHAPTER 24

SOLANA DAMITA LEDESMA

ou can do it, Solana. You can do it, Solana. You can do it, Solana.

Repeating those five words over in my head had been the distraction I needed from the burn of my calf muscles. I'd been pacing for hours in this closet. I was sure that when I looked down, I'd see track marks from my feet being pushed into the wooden floorboards. I'd come in here a few hours ago after a much-needed cold shower and was triggered by what had been left on the closet island. I needed to get my shit together. I needed to get my head in the game. My fiancée had come into town, and now, Shio...

Shio.

We'd kissed. Shio and I had kissed last night, and it caught me off guard. I didn't know what to do besides sit there and let him take the lead. The way he sucked on my lips and then my tongue had ignited flames throughout my body. I'd never felt the way he made my body feel. If he could do all that just by kissing, I naturally wondered what he'd do with his other body parts. However, when I swallowed my fear and approached

Shio late last night, asking for a life with him, he had rejected me. I understood his reasoningI was a woman sired by my father and promised to another man. He was a member of an American mob where he had a Don to answer to.

Shio made it clear that his actions at the club were still true, along with his promise that Felipe would never touch me again, and I believed him. I didn't know what was more frightening: the fact that I believed Shio or facing my father's wrath once he learned of what had occurred. Ines had promised the Rodríguezes Cartel a daughter, and he would stop at nothing to make sure they got one. My father was unpredictable, and I'd seen what he'd done to the rest of our family for the sake of street politics. Nothing stood in the way of what he wanted, and I was no exception.

My eyes moved to the island that housed the last perfume I'd used, along with the earrings and the purse I wore to the club. Shio had given me so much in such a short time. The closet wasn't full since it was large in size, but for a stranger he didn't know that was supposed to be visiting temporarily, he ensured I had more than I needed. Shio was a man of class. Nothing in his home was cheap, and he made sure I wore nothing cheap while in his home.

He was a unique man. He was the man little girls dreamed of. He was a protector, a believer in God, family-oriented, wealthy, and *dominante* (dominant) in every way. He'd proven to be the ultimate alpha, a boss. Although he had the backing of the Rinaldi Mob and his family, he still commanded respect as his own person. That's why I had to do right.

Sé fuerte, Solana. (Be strong, Solana.)

I had to get my act together so I could stand beside him with a clear mind when things hit the fan with the Ledesma and Rodríguezes Cartels.

My mind was a mixture of hope and fear. Although Shio

had said we could not be intimate, I still had hope for my future now that I'd seen what was possible. But the newfound hope had doubled the normal fear that lived within me. Most of my life, I'd known I was expendable to my father. He held me closer to his heart than the rest of my siblings, but being the only girl meant I was the most valuable to him. I had no hope in Mexico. Hope was as foreign to me as America had been the past three weeks. I knew what my fate was and had come to terms with it before I'd stepped foot in Jagoda Bay, Tennessee.

Shio and the American mob wives had come along and given me hope. I'd never once felt like I could be freed from the arranged marriage until I was put in the presence of that man. I'd never felt like life could be lived carefree and luxuriously before meeting those gorgeous women who gave me the best night of my life yesterday. A real man had shown me so much in less than a month's time, and I would be forever grateful for him introducing me to his world.

So, even though I knew Shio would give it everything he had to protect me, even though he couldn't love me, that scared me. I didn't want my hope in what my life could be to get him killed. I'd surrender in a heartbeat before I let anyone harm him over me.

Looking at the closet island, I turned away, continuing my steps to prevent me from doing what I really wanted to do.

Clink. Clack.

Bang.

Boom.

Clank.

Gasping, I nearly leapt across the closet as the sound of something hitting the wall startled me. Icy fear twisted around my heart, and my stomach clenched tight. Shio wasn't here. I hadn't slept in today and went to find him, but when I noticed that the gym, his office, and bedroom were empty, I came back into the bedroom thinking he'd left to put some space between us. He always knocked on the door when he left and when he arrived back at the house, so I either had been dead asleep when he left, or he hadn't notified me. Whatever that noise was, it wasn't him. An intruder had entered his home, and I knew exactly who it was: Felipe.

Looking around the closet, I eyed my weapons of choice. There was nothing but heels, purses, jewelry, perfume, clothing, hangers, and evidence of last night's sins. Panic was rioting within me. I wasn't going down without a fight. If I were going to turn myself over to the Rodríguezes, it would be on my terms, and after I had my closure with the man who had come into my life like a drill sergeant but now felt like an angel.

"The gun."

Rushing from the closet, my bare feet slapping against the wood floors, I went to the dresser. It was the same dresser Shio had been getting pleasured near when I'd first arrived. I remembered he had pulled a gun from behind it and was hoping he'd put it back. Using the little strength I had, I pushed the dresser forward and saw a gun tucked in a holster attached to the back of the mirror. I didn't know how to use or hold a gun, but I wrapped my hand around it and pulled it to my chest. After opening the door, I stuck my head out to look down the hall and noticed one of the paintings was crooked.

Trying to remain as light on my feet as possible, my breath seemed to have solidified in my throat. I clenched the gun in my hands as my chest pounded so hard that it pained me.

Clank. Thump.

The sounds were coming from his office. Blinking, I nervously bit my lip as I approached the room. I pointed the gun at the room's doorway and pulled the trigger as soon as I stepped inside. The gun made a clicking sound, but nothing came out.

"Solana?"

The thrill of frightened anticipation touched my spine, but when I saw who it was in the room, I dropped the gun.

"Solana..."

My pulse beat erratically at the sound of his deep voice. Shio looked like he'd been through hell and back. His clothing —whatever the hell they were—had been torn and ripped. He had some hideous sandals on his feet, and I could see sand in his toes. He was leaning against his desk, and his eyes looked cloudy. It was like he was looking at me, but he wasn't. He tried sitting on the desk, making it shift, knocking the money counter and the worn leather notebook onto the floor. I'd been curious about that same notebook when he taught me to count money yesterday, but I wouldn't dare disrespect him by snooping. Looking from the floor back to him, I gasped as realization hit me.

Shio had clearly been hurt.

Rushing to his side, I grabbed his muscled arm to stop him from toppling over.

"*¿Shio? ¿Qué pasa? ¿Quién te hizo esto?* (Shio? What's the matter? Who did this to you?)"

He winced as I held on to him. Still, he looked so sexy even in the state of distress.

"Solana... English, baby. I can't fuckin' think right now."

"Okay." I sucked in air, trying to gather strength to steady him.

The muscles of his forearm hardened beneath the sleeve of his torn, cropped shirt. The thought of the Rodríguezes getting to him made my mind flutter with anxiety. The thought of what happened to the bottom half of his shirt and all the dried blood on his skin had me thinking the worst.

"Help me... Help me get to my bathroom. I came in here to

disable the alarm. I didn't mean to scare you."

A pulsing knot within me demanded more of an explanation than what he'd given me. I needed to know if he was in danger. I needed to know how this had happened. Instead of asking, I took his left arm and draped it around my shoulders since there was a gold box in his right hand. I swallowed underneath him but still pressed a hand to the side of his abs. He smelled of sweat, mildew, and heat. Still, a hint of his signature scent was lingering, and it was a delicious one.

Once we got to the door of the office, he paused. When his mouth lifted into a crooked smile as he looked down at me, my heart pounded. There was definitely something wrong with his eyes, and it made my chest feel as if it was about to burst. What had they done to him?

"I gotta teach you how to use a fuckin' gun, Solana. Lesson number six: take the fucking safety off before making your presence known. Aite?"

Batting away tears, I nodded. "*Si*. I mean... Yes."

Using his top teeth, he scraped his bottom lip before we continued our stroll to his bedroom. He hadn't put any of his weight on me. No matter how much I tried to get him to lean on me, he wouldn't. He wasn't even letting me guide him, moving from memory of his home by heart as he navigated us. Still, I remained at his side.

I poked my head into his bedroom this morning, but I didn't go inside. I'd seen how massive it was last night but had opted to remain outside the doorway then too. Now, as I walked through the space, a sense of tranquility washed over me. It smells like Shio, and the entire room felt like a comforting hug. The only thing out of place was one side of his Alaskan king-sized bed, where I could tell he'd been lying. The same brown, green, cream, and wood-grain theme from the rest of the house carried into his bedroom, and some classical music played somewhere in the distance. Floor-to-ceiling panels covered his windows, and since they were shut, I couldn't see outside. His room looked like something a mobster would live in. It was fitting for a boss. A king. A Shio. Letting my eyes wander around his space, trying to memorize every inch, we made it to his en suite bathroom.

The lights turned on automatically as soon as we stepped inside. Shio moved away from me and headed to the vanity, where his products sat neatly on one side while the other side was empty. There was a shower that could be entered from two sides, two closets existed that were separated by a large tub, and marble floors contrasting with the wood, like in the rest of the home, made up the walls and counters. All of his faucets and dials were gold, like the box he was still holding.

Not wasting any more time, I went to the tub, placed the stopper in, and turned the dials. Letting in more hot than cold but making sure I didn't make the water too hot, I picked up the bubble bath that had looked more like décor than something he actually used. It was the work of the housekeepers; I knew because they stocked my room the same way. Pumping a few squirts of bubble bath and bath oil in the water, I then picked up the jar of Epsom salt and dumped most of it in the tub. When bubbles began to form and the eucalyptus fumes permeated the air, I went back to Shio.

He had already begun to remove his tattered clothing. Pausing, I watched as he tossed it aside, gawking at the work of art that he was. His muscles were extremely defined in every part of the upper half of his body. I'd never seen a man more attractive than Shio Cuppacio, and I felt terrible for standing here admiring the beauty that he was when he needed my help.

Get it together, Solana.

He turned and reached for his toothbrush, then smeared

toothpaste on it. He'd done a sloppy job, which further proved that his eyes were damaged. Since he had it under control, I didn't interfere with him brushing his teeth. The motor on the electric toothbrush vibrated as he handled his oral hygiene. After about three minutes of brushing, he grabbed a floss pick from a clear jar and ran it between his teeth. Once that was done, he pointed to a bottle.

"Is this my face wash?"

Squinting my eyes, I read the bottle from where I was standing. "Yes... I think so."

He washed his hands first and then cleaned his face. I'd never seen a man put that much care into his appearance. My brothers—the older ones—barely brushed their teeth. When we were younger, they often had cavities during dental visits. Seeing Shio follow a full routine showed me why his teeth were so perfect and his skin so flawless. Even I had some pigmentation I needed to work on, but he was without a scar on his face.

When he lifted from the sink's edge, face glistening, he peered at me through the mirror.

"Come 'ere."

"Shio"

"Sshhh. Come 'ere, Solana."

I wanted to honor what he'd said last night. We had to have boundaries. It seemed Shio no longer cared about that from the way he was looking at me through the mirror with overcast eyes. I was sure he couldn't see me, but the aura coming from him told me he knew exactly who he was looking at. Desire was all over his face. Shio desired me.

I crept up behind him, pausing at the blood on his back. A long scar ran across his back above his butt, and it looked fresh. Lifting my finger, I pressed it against his wound, and he hardly flinched. Not caring about the fresh blood, my arms wrapped around his waist. My robe was ruined, but again, I didn't care. He felt so good against me. Whenever Shio was around, I felt something I hadn't in a long time, maybe something I never had. I felt safe. I felt so secure in his embrace. My ear was pressed into his scarred back, listening to his thudding heartbeat, letting it calm me.

He didn't remove my hands, but he did begin to remove his pants. I squeezed my eyes shut. Once they hit the ground, he moved toward the tub with me still clinging on to him like a damn koala bear.

Knowing he needed to soak, I let him go. The blood from his back remained on my chest, so I stepped backward to exit his space and go clean up and change. Keeping my eyes closed, I heard him lower into the tub and turn off the water as I started to turn around.

"Solana..." His voice vibrated through me, stopping me in my tracks.

Opening my eyes, his simple nod to come here had me walking the few paces to the tub. Reaching up, he grabbed my hand and guided me into the tub. My arms naturally wrapped around his neck as water splashed around us before settling. My legs were hanging out of the tub as the warm water relaxed my body. He grabbed my face and stuck his nose against my lips. Softly, his minty breath fanned my face while I stared into his disturbing eyes.

"You good?" He had the nerve to ask.

He was the one who appeared to have come from an ancient battle, but he was asking if I was good. I didn't understand the turn of feelings from last night. I'd spent the day altering my mind to respect his decision and to cast my feelings to the side so that we could at least unite against those who wished to force me to be someone I didn't want to be. Well, at least I didn't want to be that someone with Felipe. I definitely didn't mind the idea of being a wife.

Solana Damita Cuppacio-Ledesma.

"Shio," I gasped as he continued to nuzzle against my lips. "You said this could not happen? I'm not sure"

"Fuck all that, Solana. This what it is."

I inhaled sharply.

"This what it is."

Deciding not to badger him for more of an explanation, I answered his question truthfully. "I'm not good. Well... I wasn't. Until I met you, Shio. Now, I'm better. Not one hundred percent... But I'm better," I admitted.

With the way he was rubbing his nose against my lips, it had my body jolting. My breath wasn't as fresh as his, my hair was in a ball at the top of my head since I'd slept on it and didn't protect it in the shower, and I was unsure if I'd done a good job of wiping off my makeup, so last night's residue was still there. But he didn't seem to care. He was perfect even in his current state, yet I was a mess. Still, he looked at me with so much admiration, and I was certain he couldn't even see.

With his free hand, he reached under the water and placed each of my legs on the side of his. I was now straddling him, bloody, wet robe clinging to my body like a second skin. I could feel my nipples poking through the thin fabric.

"I don't need you at one hundred percent. I just need *you*. We can worry about the math later, baby."

His tongue traced the fullness of my lips. Then, his mouth covered mine hungrily. Matching his cadence, I sucked on his tongue as it explored my mouth. His kiss sent new spirals of ecstasy through me. I'd never experienced the kind of high Shio gave me, and I was already addicted after the second kiss. I could feel his monster of a dick growing beneath me, and it made me shake like a falling leaf. I caressed the string tendons in the back of his neck as he held me in place.

"I can't see shit. But I see you, Solana. So fucking beautiful. You know you fine as fuck. Right?"

I nodded.

"Good. Fuck all that shit I was spitting last night. You it. And today, when I felt like I was about to die, it solidified that shit. You gonna be mine, Solana."

I was now choking back tears.

"You know you can get whatever up out of me, right?"

I nodded, internally sobbing quietly.

"You know, when I get this pussy, I'm going against everybody for it. Your *papa* included. Right?"

The tears sprang free, hearing that as I nodded.

"Nah. You don't know. And that's why I'm not gon' touch you until you *do* know. You belong to another nigga. I want you to belong to me." He chuckled, a hint of arrogance in his tone. "He ain't letting up, and neither am I. When I'm the only nigga in the race, that's when you're gonna know I say what the fuck I mean and mean what the fuck I say. Aite?"

I didn't want to hear it because I needed to be touched. I needed to feel, but I knew Shio enough to know he was a man of his word.

I nodded, wiping the few tears that escaped. "How can... How can we fix your eyes?"

"Shit..." He grunted.

Letting me go, he reached over the side of the tub as I sat on his legs and waited. He held up the gold box with hieroglyphics written on it that resembled a jewelry box. Handing it to me, I opened the heavy box and frowned at the dirt staring back at me.

He cuffed water in his hand and drizzled it inside the box. "Mix it and cover my eyes for me."

Using my finger, I did as he asked, not stopping until the dirt was a paste-like mud. He sat back in the tub, hooking his arms around my waist, making my chest hit his front. My pebbled nipples brushed against his chest, and the friction felt heavenly.

He closed his eyes, and I smeared the paste on his eyelids. The mixture smelled more like ointment, even though it looked like mud. When his eyes were fully covered and there was no more paste, I placed the box on the side of the tub. His arms were stretched on the tub's sides, so I grabbed the loofah and began washing his chest. His head turned side to side as I washed his upper body.

"Solana."

"¿Si?"

"I got some shit with me, baby. I need a fuckin' queen. You gotta be willing to go against the world for me, cuz I'ma always do it for you."

"Is... Is that a lesson for me?'

Licking his lips, he scraped his bottom lip with his top teeth. "It's a fact. Some shit can't be taught, baby. It's gotta be in you."

"Is it in me?" I asked, sounding desperate but not caring. I wanted this man in every way.

"If it wasn't, I wouldn't be debating puttin' your pussy in my mouth, baby."

Father, God.

"Tomorrow. We going on a date. All that *fun* shit you listed last night, we gonna do all that and more. If we're gonna do this shit, we're doing it the right way."

"O... Okay. I have a doctor's appointment in the morning."

He paused. "It's cool. Go to your appointment. After, you with me."

Nodding, I dropped the loofah, wrapped my arms around his back, and lay on his chest. There was no place I'd rather be in the world. I just hoped it all worked out how I wanted it to.

"Solana. There will be some shit I have to keep from you, and that's only for your own good and safety..." His words vibrated my chest. "But you can't keep shit from me. What I said during your first workout stands. No secrets. Aite?"

Tensing, I nodded. "Sin secretos."

"English, baby. My head all fucked up."

"No secrets..."

"Good girl."

CHAPTER 25
SHIO CUPPACIO

Clamping my Jesus piece around my neck, it was the last thing I needed to do before leaving. I gave myself a once-over to check the fit. The hood of my leather jacket was pulled over my head, and a black Loewe shirt sat underneath. Leather pants covered my lower half, topped with Prada boots. My necklace was simple, but my wrists and fingers had some ice. I called and arranged for one of the newer steakhouses to be closed for the evening. It was Mexican-infused, and I knew she'd enjoy it. She had only been eating American food since she arrived here. We had about forty-five minutes before they expected us, so I was about to head down the hall and get Solana.

Last night, it took all my restraint not to take her pretty ass down. But there was too much shit in the way of us moving to the next level. That mission had put a lot in perspective, so I guess they weren't so useless as I'd always thought. Falling from that rope, I immediately thought of dying and leaving Solana vulnerable to her fuck ass daddy and those wack-ass Rodríguezes. I didn't give a fuck about restraint, discipline, or reason.

Solana was brought here so I could make her mine. That wasn't her daddy's doing. That wasn't the Don's doing. I felt strongly that it was God's doing. My stepfather's sermon wasn't about me giving in to temptation and lust to fuck the shit out of Solana, although I wanted to do that too. That sermon was about me consistently being a prisoner to my flesh, rather than being empowered by my spirit. Since I was a boy, I'd learned to be composed, disciplined, an apostle, but that was the flesh of me. My intuition had never steered me wrong because that was it was driven by God. For Solana, I was shedding the flesh, and solely trusting my spirit on this one, and it told me in that helicopter as Nel and Vello argued about whose kids were going to be cuter once Pia dropped, that Solana was to be my wife.

I spent the morning planning how this shit was going to go. My first task was to let her bitch-ass *papa* know what it was, and I had to be sure she even understood what being with me meant. Her father forced her into an arranged marriage, and essentially, her being mine would be the same. Either way, Solana would end up being a man's wife. I just needed to know which side she wanted to be on, and if the smell of her arousal anytime we were in close proximity could answer that, it was my side.

Chuckling, I ran my hand down my face because those Cuppacio boys had called it. I'd fallen for her pretty ass. I'd spent as little time around her as I could, being that she was living under my roof, and I still managed to fall for her. "The pretty little sinner," as my mama called her. She was right, Solana did have some issues with her. She was lazy, she slept all damn day, she was moody, she was spoiled, and she didn't know the first thing about routine or regulation. She was everything a man like me wouldn't go for in a wife, outside of the spoiled part, and yet, I'd fallen for her sexy ass.

On the other hand, there was no telling what she had experienced in her life. I had been through the worst and was still dealing with shit, but as a man, I process things differently. I wasn't forced to do anything outside of marrying someone, and even that was a choice. I'd extended Solana some grace because not only were there cultural differences and dissimilar upbringings, I could tell just in one encounter with her family that she really didn't have any allies outside of the smaller children. Partying had been her escape, and while I wanted her to do her, I also wanted her to enjoy other things outside of just dancing in the club and getting sloppy drunk. She was too pretty for that shit.

Last night, we fell asleep in the tub with her lying on my chest. By the time I woke up, the mud had restored my sight, and the water was ice-cold. Yet, she was sleeping peacefully on my chest. I didn't want to wake her until she sneezed, and her nose began to run. I had no choice but to get us out. She went to her room, changed, and came back with her phone and snacks. We stayed up the entire night, until it was time for her appointment, talking and vibing.

I didn't like the fact that her papa could send people to my house to escort her to her appointments. He shouldn't even care about her appointments unless she was really sick. That was another reason I wasn't touching Solana. It was a no-go until I knew I could dig her guts out without the possibility of her leaving my bed one day. I needed to figure out what the hell her papa had going on. I'd tried to take her to her appointment, but she declined, saying she had to go alone. This is my fucking house; he had no right to send a car to escort his grown daughter when I could handle it. If Solana were going to be mine, I wouldn't interfere with her and her father's relationship, but he was going to have to stand down or see me. I was cool with either one.

Snatching my keys from the dresser, I looked over my room to see if I was missing anything.

Just as I was about to walk out, her phone lit up on my nightstand. Walking over to it, I snatched it up, seeing a Mexico City number call it. Letting it ring to voicemail I tucked it in my pocket. I closed my bedroom door and made the walk down the hall. The glam team had left over an hour ago, getting her together, so I knew all she had to do was slip into the dress they had left for her. Those niggas cost a grip, but they were good at what the fuck they did. The four-figure bill wasn't shit to a nigga like me when it meant making Solana feel her best.

"Solana... Come on, baby. We gonna be late."

Her door was cracked, and I chuckled, thinking about how she used to be barricaded in this bitch. A Hispanic artist was singing loudly as I walked into her bedroom. The bed wasn't made, her dirty clothes were on the side of the bed, and two bottles of water that were half drunk sat on the nightstand. Scooping up her dirty clothes, I went to the hamper and tossed them in. The basket was nearly overflowing, but the house-keepers would handle it. Solana probably didn't know how to even operate a washing machine, and she wouldn't need to, but she was going to learn how to at least tidy up being with me.

Her phone vibrated back-to-back in my pocket, and when I pulled it out, I saw it was the same number. Looking up, she must have been in the closet because her bathroom was empty except for shit strewn all over the vanity. With the phone in hand, I went back into the hallway, deciding to answer. Swiping my thumb across the screen to accept the FaceTime call, I frowned when her brother's face appeared on the screen.

Esteban was a bitch like all of his brothers, but he earned a little respect from me when he didn't reveal that I was fluent in Spanish during the exchange at the club. I still didn't like his ass, but he'd at least proven he had some love for Solana and some respect for me. However, he got no cool points from me. There was no telling what he let his mother do to Solana while he and his brother stayed quiet.

"What?"

He looked to be in a makeshift warehouse. I could tell he wasn't expecting me to answer because he blinked instead of telling me what his ass wanted. She didn't even have his number saved, so that let me know she really didn't fuck with him.

"¿Está la perra en la línea? (Is the bitch on the line?)"

I bit down on my molars hearing Felipe's bitch ass call Solana out of her name.

"Uh... No... It-It's... Shio." Esteban's scary ass stumbled over his words.

"¡Perfecto!"

Esteban cleared his throat.

"He... He says since he received good news back from our father about her doctor's appointment, he wants to make a deal."

My frown deepened.

"Fuck outta here. And why y'all so worried about her health and shit?"

"It's not her health, friend. My father has been checking to see if..." Esteban looked off to translate whatever Felipe was telling me. "He's been checking to see if her virtue is still intact. Has been since she was a teen. Monthly visits."

He damn near knocked the air out of me with his revelation. What type of sick shit was that?

"Ion give a fuck what the doctor said to you. Solana is not up for tradin'. Does she look like she got four legs, a tail, and a branding on her ass? She ain't no fuckin' dairy cow, nigga."

Esteban swallowed. I knew Ines was fucking up, but having doctors stick their hands in his child's vagina monthly to check to see if she was a virgin was some sick-ass shit. She was grown as fuck. Knowing he would go to that extreme had me glad that I hadn't touched her until I looked further into these motherfuckers.

"Still, he wants to make a trade. *Una chica para una chica.* (A girl for a girl)"

I laughed in his face. I wasn't trading Solana. She was where the fuck she wanted to be. Even if I was up for trading, they didn't have shit I wanted. My mama was guarded like the president, and so were the rest of the women in my family, so I knew they didn't have anyone of value to me. If they had Uriah or any other girl I stuck dick in, and thought I'd trade Solana for a fuck, they didn't know me very well.

"Get the fuck off this phone. Me and Solana on our way out. Tell yo' bitch-ass daddy and Felipe that they can test that hymen tomorrow and watch they see that shit popped, broken, and that pussy stretched the fuck out. Fuck you mean!"

"Wait! Look!" Esteban flipped the screen around, and I could see his feet as he walked.

I didn't have time for this shit, but I stayed on the line because I'd vowed to trust my intuition more, and it was telling me to wait. When he flipped the screen around, I was taken aback like a motherfucker, but that was still a trade insult.

"Bahati... We have Bahati."

"I still don't give a fuck! That's pussy from years ago."

Bahati looked as good as she did when I spared her fucking life. I had every intention of killing her for playing with me, but I just choked her ass to sleep. I didn't like how I treated her, but I was a different nigga back then. I could tell she'd been roughed up, judging by her ripped shirt and the tears running down her face. Her hands were bound, and there was tape over her mouth, but other than that, she looked good. I still didn't fuck with her, and since I'd never been in love with her, snatching her from her world to get at me was pointless. They'd have better luck calling her daddy.

"I ain't fucked with Bahati in years. No deal."

"Wait... I wasn't done."

He pointed the camera at a mattress, and my entire body froze.

I could feel the yogurt I'd eaten trying to come back up, but I swallowed it down.

"He also has *her*. He says turn Solana loose and you can get them both."

The line disconnected.

I tried dialing it back, but I didn't know the damn password to Solana's phone.

With shaky hands, I burst back into her room and went straight into her closet because that's where she had to be. All kinds of thoughts were running through my head. What the fuck? How the fuck? My blood began to pound in my temples. There, on the mattress, was a body with skin the same as mine, curly hair wild, and arms taped to the front, with her mouth taped. I had only caught a brief glimpse and knew. They didn't have to say it because I knew.

"Solana! Unlock the ph"

My eyes were finally working, but Don must've messed with my 20/15 vision because the last two things I'd seen couldn't have been real. I couldn't have seen what I saw on the mattress. Nah, I was unwilling to believe it. I had been careful. I was always careful. *Weren't I?*

I thought I was just imagining what I'd seen, and if I was, then I had to be imagining this shit right in front of me. Baby hairs framed her pretty face, her makeup was perfectly applied, and the dress hugged every curve. She was so fucking beautiful. So fucking shapely and pretty. Nonetheless, the prettiest people do the ugliest things. That much I knew, and Solana was proving it.

I watched as she had a hundred-dollar bill rolled up and held to her nose, snorting a line of white powder. She was so into it that she didn't even notice me on her left side or hear me barge in, asking her to unlock her phone. In front of her was a floor-length mirror. I watched her reflection as her eyes rolled back, and she stood up straight and danced in front of the mirror. She tossed her head back in laughter, even though nothing was funny.

Pretty little fucking sinner.

She bent down to hit another line, and before she could sniff, I had her hair balled in my hands and her head lifted. Walking her to the mirror, I stared at her through it, and her eyes were bulging at the sight of me. It made so much fucking sense—the sleeping all day, the laziness, the throwing up during workouts, the barricading herself in the door. The excessive time spent in the bathroom and closet, where I didn't have a digital view like I did in the bedroom, to see her pretty face sliding across a hard surface as she sniffed the very drug the mob flooded the streets with.

"Solana..." I could hear the chill in my own voice.

She lifted her hands, palms facing the mirror. "Shio, I can explain..."

Her lipstick was smeared, and there was powder across her nose and hands.

There wasn't shit to explain.

"Shut the fuck up. Let's go."

Keeping her in my grip, I walked us out of the closet.

"What... Wh... Where are we going?"

Kissing her jaw, I pushed her forward. *"Para recuperar a mi maldita hija (To get my fucking daughter back.)"*

God first.
~~*Make sure the family good.*~~
~~*Eye them Cuppacio boys, the little and the big ones.*~~
~~*Build a relationship with my brother.*~~
~~*Get my brother rich.*~~
~~*Health and wellness.*~~
~~*Stay on top of my mob shit.*~~
~~*Keep Hobo alive.*~~
~~*Get through the meeting with Ines Ledesma.*~~
~~*House a random.*~~
~~*Find the true reason Solana is here.*~~
~~*Figure out if Solana is supposed to be my wife, again.*~~
~~*Find a wife that isn't Solana.*~~
Kill every breathing Rodríguez Cartel member
Fuck Bahati up
Get my fucking daughter

To be Continued....

ABOUT THE AUTHOR

Lisa Austin is an award-winning, National best-selling, independent Author who often creates tales about the grit and grind of the streets, but with a romantic twist. Born and raised in Memphis, TN, the on-the-rise Author has been penning stories her entire life.

Also by Lisa Austin

Yayo: The Beginning

Yayo:Riot's Revenge

Riot 3 (Yayo)

Death of a Nawf Memphis Trap King

Boostin' around the Christmas Tree

I choose you boo 1&2

Annihilate your love

You're My favorite Mistake 1&2

Peek it's boo 1-3

Bossed Up

Bayb

If Cupid was a Thug

Giving it a try with a street Guy: The Valentines

Forever Good in his Hood

Bound to a Bandit

Dreaming of Spring

Big Boss

Humbled by a Real n*gga 1-3

Humbled on Christmas Day- lani & Rut

Just like I taught you

Honey, I f*cked the Plug 1-3

Daddy's Lil Baby

Pregnant by a Muthaf*ckin Don 1&2

A Winter Crest Christmas: Pure & Luxe

A Winter Crest Valentine's: Snowy & Sphere

Wealth over riches & bad b*tches

Paradise Bay: Coastal & Bliss

Exhilarated 1-3

Put it on The Mob: Ezio and Jae

On The Mob: The Cuppacio Twins

Blake University: Leader and Calista

Hellcat Barbies: Saskia and Zodiac

Get your signed Paperback of Shio here. Features an autographed copy, bookmark, and stickers!

www.authorlisaaustin.com

Join my Facebook group and mailing list for exclusive sneak peeks, prizes, book gossip, and never-before-released short stories! Also, follow my Amazon Author page for first dibs on new drops!